A DOUBLE SHOT OF HARDCASES AND HUSSIES FOR ONE LOW PRICE!

SHOWDOWN AT HELLS CANYON

''Paw—look out!'' Davy screamed as the .44 American Smith and Wesson cavalry issue revolver slid out of the holster.

Time seemed to freeze then, and Davy watched the next motions of the men with a painful and intense clarity. Suddenly the horror thawed in a series of roars and bright flashes that came from the mouth of the Smith and Wesson's long barrel.

''Paw!'' Davy cried as the slugs tore into his father's body at close range. Davy sprang to his feet and ran to his father's side. But by the time he knelt beside him, John Jacob Watson was already dead.

ACROSS THE HIGH SIERRA

''Judas Priest!'' the young Kansan exclaimed when he learned that Faith, Hope and Charity Mudree had been spirited off by Harvey Yancey ''You see any tracks?''

Soaring Hawk nodded. ''Seven horses. Plenty tracks.''

''Which way they headin'?''

''South and west.''

Davy grimaced as he recalled Yancey's words about selling the Mudree sisters to brothel keepers in California. ''Sweet Jesus,'' he muttered. ''We gotta find them girls!''

THE KANSAN

SHOWDOWN AT HELLS CANYON/ ACROSS THE HIGH SIERRA
ROBERT E. MILLS

LEISURE BOOKS ⬛ NEW YORK CITY

This book is affectionately dedicated to
Kaye Hood Warner and Hondo.

A LEISURE BOOK®

October 1992

Published by

Dorchester Publishing Co., Inc.
276 Fifth Avenue
New York, NY 10001

THE KANSAN

SHOWDOWN AT HELLS CANYON/

Chapter 1

Blam! Blam! Blam!
Three shots rang out in the frosty autumn air of Kansas.
They were immediately followed by the shrill alarm of
shattering glass, as Davy Watson's last shot blew an
empty whiskey bottle to smithereens. It was a bottle of
Old Overholt, and had stood on top of a fence post
thirty feet away from the shooter, silhouetted against
the setting sun. When the bullet shattered the bottle, it
sent forth a rain of glass that caught the red glow of the
sun and danced in the air like sparks from a cutler's
wheel. And as the whiskey bottle was transformed into
corruscating bits that shot up into the air and then fell to
the prairie grass in long, graceful arcs, Davy Watson
grinned from ear to ear.

He was a tall and husky lad with tousled hair the color
of winter wheat, whose curls framed a face made
squarish by high cheekbones and a prominent jaw. His
eyes were the blue of a late afternoon sky, set deep in his
head and far from the bridge of a nose that brought to
mind the beak of a hawk. Broad shoulders, big feet, and
big knobby hands, along with the hard-muscled body of
a young farmhand, completed the picture of David Lee
Watson on the eve of his seventeenth birthday.

Behind him, smiling a restrained smile of pride, was
his father, a lanky, rawboned man whose face and
hands were tanned like leather from long years of
exposure to the strong, harsh sun that shone down on
the Kansas prairie. John Jacob Watson's forbears were
of the American pioneer stock, men and women who

had settled in the Ohio River country in the days when Indian and French were the only tongues spoken in the forests and on the plains and along the river banks. They were the people who had opened up Illinois, Indiana, and Iowa, traveling the long, hard and dangerous distances in their canvas-covered wagons armed with muskets and an unshakable faith in Almighty God.

John Jacob was the continuation of their line, having come to Kansas when its prairies were still virgin land. Few white men had settled there at the time; the plains shook to the thunder of the great buffalo herds and the clear air rang with the cries of the Osage, Kaw, and Pawnee.

Having led his people into Kansas, John Jacob Watson halted one evening by the rich lands on both sides of Pottawatomie Creek. The setting sun had turned the creek into a ribbon of molten gold, and the prairie grass looked as dark and green as a memory of the Ohio Valley.

"It's here we'll stop," John Jacob had told the others in his band, "for I think we're not likely to do better."

So they halted and arranged their wagons in a circle, the women building campfires in preparation for the evening's meal and the men posting scouts and dressing the game shot by the hunters. The laughter of the children and the wailing of infants warmed the cool evening air; the sweet sopranos of women singing at their chores and the deeper grunts and chuckles of the men setting up camp; the creak of leather and the flap of canvas, the jingle of harness and the clanking of metal: these were the sounds made by the pioneers, sounds never before heard over the open sea of grass that was the Kansas prairie.

Before the company ate, they offered up a prayer of thanksgiving. Led by John Jacob, they swore to cherish the land and hand it down to generations yet unborn. As God had entered into his covenant with Father Abraham, giving him the sweet land of Israel, so would the settlers revere their new land and always acknowledge their debt to Him. Here they would sink their roots.

They prospered in that new land, and in time John Jacob had a fine, grand farm, one whose yield was the glory of the region. The first winter was long and hard, but Watson and his wife, the former Annabel Mullenax of Franklin, Indiana, worked together lovingly. And it was in January, in the very heart of that bleak and endless winter, that their first-born, David Lee was conceived.

"Got it, Pa," Davy said as he turned to face his father, the grin on his face returning the older man to the present. "Dead center on my last shot," he went on, waggling the hand that held his Colt Walter revolver, causing the barrel of the four-pound sixshooter to rotate as it pointed up at the sky.

"'Bout time, I say," his father replied, after knocking a grasshopper off a blade of grass with a gob of tobacco juice. "I was beginnin' to think you was either cock-eyed or near-sighted."

"I betcha it was jus' luck," piped up Davy's kid brother, Lucius Erasmus, a pudgy and pimply-faced thirteen year old. "He ain't never been able to hit a barn door nor a buffalo's ass."

"Aw, crawl back in yer hole, ya fat little prairie dog," Davy growled at Lucius Erasmus. "Set up another bottle, an' I'll show ya what shootin's all about."

"Save yer bullets for another day, Dead-eye," John Jacob told his son, smiling the wry, tight smile of a man embarrassed by overt displays of affection. "You 'n me is goin' into town."

"Kin I come too, Paw?" Lucius Erasmus asked, his voice suddenly cracking into the soprano register.

For an instant, the thin line of John Jacob Watson's smile curved into an arc that registered his affection for the boy. "Uh-uh," he grunted, shaking his head. "You're a mite too young to be a-headin' into town of a Saturday night, son."

"Well, sir, Davy ain't never gone before," Lucius protested, sniffling back his dismay.

"That's right, boy," his father responded. "But it's David Lee's birthday, an' today he's a man."

Davy grinned knowingly at his kid brother, feeling a surge of excitement rise in his gut like a covey of quail flushed from the brush.

"You'll get your turn soon enough, Lucius Erasmus," said John Jacob Watson. "But it's time you got back to the house. Your mother an' sister need your help in puttin' up preserves for the winter."

"Aw, that's woman's work," the youngster objected as he turned and stalked off toward the Watson house.

"Ain't no such thing as woman's work," the pioneer called out after his son. "Your mother fought Indians beside me, an' I shelled peas beside her."

Davy watched as his brother stopped short to listen to his father's words.

"Only thing I can do that your mother can't," John Jacob went on, "is heave a anvil onto the back of a wagon. An' birthin' young 'uns is about the onliest thing she can do that I can't. What we done out here, we done together. Fifty-fifty. Now, you go on back to the house, Lucius Erasmus, an' don't you never let nobody try to tell you that puttin' up preserves is unmanly."

"Yessir," the boy whispered before he left.

"What're we goin' to do, Paw?" Davy asked, trying to hide the excitement that he felt.

"That's a surprise, son," John Jacob told him. "All I'll say is that it's your birthday, an' I'm a-gonna be gettin' you a present in town. Now, finish your chores, an' then get yourself cleaned up."

"Yessir," Davy said, holstering the Walker Colt and then taking off the gunbelt.

Three quarters of an hour later, he and his father were sitting in a buckboard, with Davy holding the reins of the team that drew it along Pottawatomie Creek. He was puzzled by his father's secretiveness on this occasion. He had no idea of just what might be in store for him that night. But trusting his father as he did, he was sure he would enjoy it. Why, here he was, all duded-up, with his boots polished and his hair slicked back, on his way to the town of Hawkins Fork. And to a lad who worked on a farm from sun-up to sun-down, the prospect of a night in town smacked of high adventure.

John Jacob Watson smiled his narrow smile as he looked over the prairie. The flat expanse was washed in the colors of sunset.

"I like this country, boy," he told Davy. "The air's sweet as a baby's breath, an' the soil's as rich as a Beacon Hill widder."

Davy nodded contentedly. He had heard this refrain many times before. It was his father's declaration of love, and as close to poetry as the man ever came.

"Y'know," John Jacob went on, "when I stand on top of the ridge that overlooks the creek, sometimes the wind comes up through the grass there an' sings to me with the voice of a woman." He nodded his head and squinted into the setting sun. "It's like the earth was a woman, an' it's her voice I hear, a-singin' an' a-whisperin' to me up on that ridge. An' each time I hear her voice, she seems to be tellin' me that if I treat her right, an' remain faithful to her, she'll always do right by me. Do you know what I mean, son?" he asked, casting a sidelong glance at Davy.

"Kind of, sir," Davy replied, pulling the reins to the left as he saw a gopher hole up ahead of the team. What his father had just said reminded him of the poetry of that English fella he'd read in one of his uncle Ethan's poetry books. That man sure had the feel of the earth, knowing the way it cushioned a man's tread, and how it felt between his fingers. Davy knew this, but he was still too young and inexperienced to be touched by love for the land.

The sun had been down for some time when the Watsons rode into town. Overhead, the stars shone in the sky like diamonds gleaming on a swatch of black velvet. The autumn moon was full, and the objects that

9

its light fell upon took the look of things freshly bronzed.

The town of Hawkins Fork was a rough-hewn jumble of log and wood frame buildings, stretching out for two hundred yards on both sides of a quarter-mile-long Main Street that turned to muck with each heavy rainfall. At one end of town stood the Calvary Baptist Church; at the other, the Red Dog Saloon. These two buildings represented the poles of western life. In between them, in varying states of maintenance or decrepitude, the visitor to Hawkins Fork could find the Overland Coach depot, the combined barbershop and dentist's office, the town jail and adjoining sheriff's quarters, the Silver Spur Saloon, Doc Kincaid's office, John Minter's smithy, Josh Cable's Livery Stable, Hertis Smithy's funeral parlor, and right across the street from it, the bawdy house run by Mrs. Lucretia Eaton.

As the buckboard made its way toward the far end of Main Street, the honkytonk sounds of a pianoforte could be heard issuing from within the Red Dog Saloon. Davy's jaw hung open as his father pointed to the place and told him to stop there.

The Red Dog had always been a place that had aroused Davy's curiosity, a place where grown men congregated at the end of the day to celebrate the mysteries of their kind. And now, Davy realized, his heart beating like a tom-tom at a war dance, he was going to be one of them. Hot damn! It *was* going to be an exciting night.

Seen from the outside, the saloon was unimposing, having the look of many of the other two-story buildings in Hawkins Fork. But on the inside, it differed from all the other buildings as does day from night. An inch of sawdust carpeted the floor, and overhead a number of kerosene lamps with cut-glass shades and sputtering wicks bathed the large, open room in their yellowish, flickering light. The Red Dog's chairs and gambling tables were crudely made, and three of the four walls were unadorned; but beyond all this, one came to the heart of the honkytonk—the bar.

Where the rest of a saloon might be plain, or even ugly, the bar was its centerpiece, an oasis of baroque elegance in a sea of sawdust and drabness. Davy gaped in wonder as he took in the elaborately carved fluting and scrollwork on the gleaming, hand-rubbed, hardwood bar. To the rough men of the West, the bar was an institution, a reminder and standard of quality and richness, the emblem of their aspirations.

When Davy looked up from the bar, past its cut-glass mirrors and rows of colorfully labeled bottles, his jaw hung open on its hinges when he saw the huge painting mounted just above eye level.

There, enclosed within a carved and gilt frame, was a life-sized oil-painting of a beautiful and amply endowed young woman who smiled demurely as she reclined on a sofa, naked as a jaybird.

"Well, that's what they look like, son . . . more or less," John Jacob said flatly, when he saw where Davy had rivetted his glance.

As he continued to stare ahead, mesmerized by the revelation in oils before him, Davy felt his ears go hot. Waves of excitement rose and broke in the pit of his stomach, and animal vitality throbbed in his groin.

"Shut your mouth, boy," his father cautioned, "the place is full of flies." And saying this, he dragged Davy over to the long and ornate bar.

"Howdy, John," said the bartender, a gaunt, stoop-shouldered man with a kneecap skull and the pallor of a corpse on the third day of a wake.

"Howdy, Fred," John Jacob replied. "Brung you a new customer." He turned to his son. "Say hello to the man, David Lee."

Blushing to the color of a radish, Davy lowered his eyes from the goddess above the bar and automatically extended his right hand. "Pleased to meet ya, sir," he mumbled.

"By God, he's a big 'un, John," the bartender said.

11

"I ain't seen 'im since Grandmaw Beldon's funeral."
He took Davy's hand in his own damp bartender's
hand, and shook it heartily. "Got his mother's looks,
I'd say," he went on. "And a lucky thing."

Proud and embarrassed at the same time, John Jacob
Watson smiled his narrow smile.

"Well, what'll it be?" the bartender asked.

"A bottle of your best," John Jacob muttered,
struggling to compose himself. "It's my boy's seventeenth birthday."

"Then the first drink is on me, John," the bartender
replied warmly, reaching under the bar and coming up
with two shot glasses, which hit the bar with sharp and
simultaneous thumps. Then he pivotted and took a
bottle from a shelf, turned back, and set it down with a
bass thud. Two light chinking sounds, each followed by
a brief gurgle, announced that the drinks had been
poured.

"David Lee would like to buy you a drink, Fred,"
John Jacob said, nudging Davy with one of his sharp
elbows.

"Uh—yessir, I would," Davy grunted, snapping to
attention and pulling a five-dollar gold piece out of his
pocket and slapping it down on the bar.

"Why, thank you, son," the bartender replied,
impressed with the Watsons' display of cordiality. "I
s'pose I could allow myself to partake of a wee dram
with you-all." Fred's people were Scots out of Glasgow,
and every so often the expressions of their native land
would crop up in his speech.

"Let's hoist this one in honor of your birthday, Mr.
Watson," the bartender said, having poured himself a
drink. He raised his glass and clinked it against Davy's.
"Many happy returns," he said, as John Jacob clinked
glasses with his son. Then they all drank.

Seeing the two men down their whisky at a gulp, Davy
did the same.

"Whoof!" Fred the bartender exclaimed, puffing
after he had swallowed his whiskey. "That's a bonny

drink."

"Tear the balls off a bobcat," John Jacob seconded, sniffling as he put down his glass.

Davy's contribution to this appreciation was the gasp of a man expiring, followed by a series of coughs that caused the gamblers at the other end of the room to look up from their cards.

"Steady, lad," John Jacob said, thumping his son on the back repeatedly. He smiled at Fred. "Right strong stuff."

The bartender nodded. "Well, if it didn't buckle a young fella's legs, I'd think it was undercooked." He proceeded to pour another round for the Watsons.

"Hoo-wee," Davy said, reaching for his second drink a shade more reluctantly than he had the first. "I wasn't ready for that." He gripped the edge of the bar with his left hand as he raised the glass in his right.

"Comes as a shock," the bartender told him, putting down the bottle. "It's like the first fart after swallowin' a percussion cap. But it gets easier with practice."

"I surely do hope it does," Davy muttered before knocking back his second drink.

"That wasn't so bad," the bartender observed as Davy slammed his glass down on the bar.

"No, sir," he croaked, wiping his eyes. In the background he could hear the sharp plunking of the pianoforte, and the cracked, whiskey-tenor of the piano player rising above it as he sang the words of a sentimental tune.

> "Captain, Captain, stop this ship,
> I see my sweetheart there.
> O let me go to him and die,
> Me and my orphan child."

As the bartender poured the third drink, Davy felt a surge of confidence within him, and he looked up deliberately at the huge nude above the bar. He ran his eyes over the vast landscape of her body: over the rises and slopes of her shoulders, hips and calves; down the cascades of golden hair that spilled over her shoulders; through the ravine that led between her full breasts; and down at last to the hillock and grasslands that peeped out above her compressed and swelling thighs.

"She looks right nice, Paw," he mumbled shyly, once he had recovered from his third whiskey.

John Jacob Watson stole a sidelong glance at his son before he looked up at the painting. "Yup," he agreed. "You could say that."

The bartender smiled knowingly as he turned and walked down the bar.

After several more whiskies, John Jacob led his son out into the cool autumn air.

"That was a nice surprise," Davy slurred. "Thanks, Paw."

"It ain't over yet," the laconic man replied, putting an arm around his boy's shoulder and leading him across the street.

"Where we goin' now?" Davy asked.

"Right over there," his father told him, pointing a long, crooked finger in the direction of Mrs. Lucretia Eaton's bawdy house.

Davy gulped, and then caught his breath. The bawdy house was even more mysterious than the Red Dog Saloon to Davy and all the boys in the area. Many were the stories they told each other about the goings-on in that particular establishment, tales of prodigious bouts of venery and exaggerated amorous feats. And now he was on his way to the house of mystery, to that temple of Venus—as his uncle Ethan called it. Now the veil would be lifted. It would be not only a night of adventure, but a night of initiation as well. Davy felt eager and excited . . . and not a little scared.

"You let your mother get wind of this," his father remarked solemnly, "an' we'll both spend the winter in the barn."

Unable to speak, Davy nodded in acknowledgment of his father's warning. They were up on the porch of the house now, and John Jacob pulled the bell cord next to the front door. Davy took a deep breath and wiped his clammy palms on his pants as he made ready to enter the temple of Venus.

"Evenin' Miz Eaton," his father said when the door swung open, revealing the high priestess.

"Good evening, Mr. Watson," Lucretia Eaton replied, with a smile that reminded Davy of his aunt Hester. The madam was a big woman who looked about to overflow the low-cut maroon dress she wore, like a river at floodtide threatening to overrun its banks.

Her breasts were set high, their bared upper portion reminding Davy of watermelon halves. Her waist was cinched in tight as a young girl's, and below it her hips swelled out like a hill at the base of a tree. Rings glittered on Mrs. Eaton's fingers as she beckoned the Watsons inside, and her black hair was piled atop her head as high as a haystack after a haying.

"It's the boy's birthday, ma'am," the elder Watson said to the mistress of the bawdy house. "So I brung him over for a birthday present, if you take my meanin'."

"I do indeed," Mr. Watson," Lucretia Eaton replied in a breathy contralto, as Davy's father gave her some money. "I shall see to it that the young man is properly entertained."

"Thank you, ma'am," John Jacob replied, clapping his hat squarely down on the crown of his head. "Boy, I got me some business to tend to," he said, taking a last look at his son before he went out the door. "I'll meet you back at the Red Dog later on."

"Yes, sir," gulped Davy, wide-eyed and shallow-breathed as his father turned and left the bawdy house.

"Well, well," cooed Mrs. Eaton. "What is your name, my dear?"

"Uh, David Lee, ma'am," he mumbled, carefully inspecting the tops of his shoes. "Watson," he added.

"Well, David Lee," Lucretia Eaton said warmly, "if you will be so good as to accompany me into the parlor,

I shall introduce you to my bevy of young goddesses."

"Yes, ma'am," he grunted as the procuress hooked her arm into his and swept him into the parlor.

Then, in that big room furnished with chintz curtains, overstuffed armchairs, horsehair sofas, cut-glass lamps, a thick Persian rug and a brilliantly polished pianoforte, Mrs. Eaton introduced Davy Watson to her charges.

"This young lady," she began, still holding the blushing young man in an armlock as she edged him toward a tall, consumptive-looking woman with dirty blonde hair, "is Sarah, a graceful lily of the Ohio valley. This young man is Mr. David Lee Watson, who is calling upon us for the very first time."

Sarah looked up from where she sat and smiled like a marionette.

"And over here," Mrs. Eaton warbled, steering Davy in the direction of a plush red armchair, where a beefy woman with jet-black hair and dark, oily skin sprawled, "is Conchita, a swarthy enchantress from far-off Mexico."

"*Bienvenido, chico,*" Conchita whispered, licking her thick red lips and smiling lasciviously.

"Ma'am," Davy mumbled, going even redder in the face as he watched the woman's breasts swell as she took an artfully deep breath. His eyes widened as he caught sight of the dark semicircles that peeped out above her low neckline.

"And this is Ginger," Lucretia Eaton purred as she whipped Davy over to the opposite side of the parlor, where a redhead with a pinched face sat up in her chair, straight as a ramrod. "She is one of Boston's fairest daughters."

Davy mumbled another greeting. The woman turned her face to him and squinted as she gave him a brittle smile. His stomach soared and dipped like a hawk on the hunt. He was nervous and confused—and soon he would have to choose.

"And last, but *certainly* not least," the procuress

16

announced proudly, "we come to this prairie flower over here."

Davy caught his breath. For once, Lucretia Eaton's florid description was not belied by the reality which attended it. There before him, sitting demurely upon a tasseled horsehair sofa, hands folded in her lap, sat a girl no older than Davy himself.

She had hair that fell to the small of her back in ribbons of spun gold, it seemed to Davy, and the face of an angel. Her eyes were as blue as the columbine that grows wild on the prairie; below them was a fine, straight nose with slightly flaring nostrils; and lower still, were lips whose pout and swell hinted at a sensuality somewhat less than angelic. The girl's skin was like alabaster, and tinged with just the faintest hint of rose.

"This is the fair Deanna," Lucretia Eaton cooed in a voice that reminded Davy of a squab at mating time. "She is a nymph of the Golden West, a native of this great land, and a newcomer, as well."

Davy felt the whiskey course through his veins as a hot flush spread over his body. He took a deep breath and, with an effort of will, looked into the eyes of the vision of gold, rose and alabaster before him. And as his eyes traveled over her form, he noticed that the blue of her dress and the single ribbon around her neck provided the sole adornment to her beauty. Both echoed the unsettling blue of her eyes.

As Davy looked at her face, the girl's eyes met his. She held his glance for an instant and smiled like the sun breaking through a bank of clouds. Then, as she lowered her eyes, she murmured, "Pleased to meet you, David Lee."

"Pleased to meet *you*, Miss Deanna," Davy gulped, feeling his ears burn.

"And now, David Lee," Lucretia Eaton said in her squab's voice, "you must choose from among these fair maidens. Which one will you pick to initiate you into the sacred mysteries of Venus Aphrodite?"

17

Beyond asking him to choose, Davy didn't know what the hell Lucretia Eaton was yammering about. But as he cleared his throat and studied his shoes, the young man raised his hand and pointed to the young Deanna.

"Oh, isn't that sweet," the madam cooed. "Youth initiating youth. Ah, just like Daphnis and Chloe—but with none of the problems." Mrs. Eaton possessed a great fund of classical knowledge, with which she continually regaled her guests.

"Let me offer you both a cordial," she said, bustling over to the sideboard at the far end of the room, where she proceeded to pour two drinks into graceful, long-stemmed glasses.

She bustled back over to the other side of the room, thrusting her intimidating bulk so close to Davy that he fell back onto the horsehair sofa, beside the quiet and lovely Deanna.

"Here, my children," the procuress said with maternal sweetness, "drink this liqueur before you journey into the garden of earthly delights." She sighed wistfully as her eyes traveled up the inseam of Davy's trousers.

Davy took the proferred glass and sniffed curiously at the dark green liquid within it. Then he sipped it. He was surprised and pleased to discover that it tasted like peppermint candy.

"Umm, that's right good, Miz Eaton," he told the hovering madam. "What d'you call the stuff?"

"Chartreuse, David Lee," she replied, drumrolling the second "r" in the liqueur's name. "It is made by an order of monks in France."

"Here's lookin' at you, Miss Deanna," Davy whispered shyly, raising his glass aloft as he looked everywhere but at the young beauty. Then, after he heard her glass clink against his, Davy looked over his glass as he drank.

"And now," Lucretia Eaton warbled authoritatively, snatching the glasses out of their hands, "you must be off to your bower of love."

18

Deanna rose from the sofa. Davy gulped and followed suit. Then she turned and walked out of the room, with a red-faced Davy Watson shuffling off behind her.

"Farewell, Daphnis! Farewell, Chloe!" Mrs. Eaton declaimed theatrically. "Take your time, my little love-birds," she called out as Deanna and Davy went up the carpeted stairs that led to the second floor of the house.

Deanna turned left at the head of the stairs and walked down the long, carpeted landing to a door at its far end. She opened the door and stood at the threshold, beckoning Davy inside.

Breathing like a spent percheron and shaking like a hound dog picking up its first scent of possum, Davy followed her into the bedroom, his innards consumed in a raging blaze that was fueled by an equal admixture of eagerness and dread.

"How, uh, long you been in this line of work, Miss Deanna?" he asked awkwardly as she lit a kerosene lamp on her dresser and then banked its flame to a low and almost evenly flickering glow.

"Couple of months, now," she whispered, unlacing the bodice of her blue satin dress as Davy closed the door. "An' you can call me Deanna . . . David Lee."

He cleared his throat. "Thank you, Deanna," Davy croaked. "An' I'd be obliged if you was to call me Davy."

"Davy." Her voice was light and clear, and he wondered what her singing voice would sound like.

'I, uh, ain't got much experience in a establishment of this nature, Deanna," he told her, intending to be matter-of-fact, but perceiving that he sounded pathetic, just like a dumb farmboy on his first jaunt into town. Yet he felt like a man as he watched Deanna step out of her dress in the lamplight. His manhood ran up his trousers like Old Glory going up a flagpole on the Fourth of July.

"Will you undo the ribbon round my neck, Davy?" she asked, coming up and turning her back to him.

19

As his palsied fingers fumbled to undo the bow, Davy marveled at the whiteness of her shoulders. She stood before him in her white underwear, its cotton and lace expanse dotted with frills, bows, and other parts whose name and function were as foreign to him as the implements of the farm would have been to an Eskimo.

"There you go," he grunted as the ribbon came open, the scent of her body reminding him of spring on the prairie.

"And now," she whispered, "could you please open me up in the back?"

As he unlaced her underthings, the fire in him rose in a blaze of animal longing, all fear having since been consumed. He opened the last laces, and Deanna began to shimmy out of her underclothes. Then, as they hit the floor, she stepped out of them delicately, and stood poised like a doe at a water hole.

Her perfect, unblemished back ran down to her incredibly tiny waist, below which Davy saw pert buttocks that seemed made to be caressed. Her legs were trim at the ankle, and as finely modeled as any Kentucky thoroughbred's. Davy flexed his fingers, as he felt an almost irresistible urge to run his hands over Deanna's beautiful body.

She took a sudden backward step and pressed her naked body flush up against Davy's clothed front. "Hold me," she told him in a voice thick with desire. Then she pressed her firm buttocks up against his groin, centering on his engorged shaft, and began to move her hips in a slow, churning motion that took Davy's breath away.

Slowly, tentatively, he reached his big hands over her rounded shoulders, marveling all the time at the whiteness of her skin. Then his hands went down a gentle slope, as they made contact with her firm breasts. Davy began to rub the pink nipples between his fingers; and as they came erect under his touch, he felt Deanna's body quiver. After that, he caressed her perfect breasts, running his fingers over them lightly and then cupping

20

them in his hands.

"Oooh," Deanna murmured, sighing like the wind on the prairie as he continued to massage her breasts. She turned her head and looked up at Davy, parting her red lips as she did. Their lips met, and she darted her tongue into his mouth with the flickering motion of a lizard entering a buffalo skull.

His heart stopped when Deanna took his right hand from her breast and began to guide it down over the range of her supple body. Down it went, over her ribcage, into the dip of her waist, past the light rise of her belly, and down into the blonde, furry patch between her firm young thighs, coming to rest upon her pouting nether lips, which were swollen and warmed by her passion.

Davy nuzzled her neck while Deanna deftly moved his hand over her sex. Once, as she moved it down, parting her outer lips, Davy hooked his middle finger in and entered her. There was a soft, squishing sound, and he felt her inner warmth and the wetness of her juices.

"Oh, oh, oh," she gasped, suddenly whipping her head from side to side, lashing him gently with her golden hair. Deanna was squirming vigorously now, and moving her hips in sharp, hooking motions, bringing her pelvic bone into contact with the base of his palm.

They continued in this fashion for some time, with Davy standing behind her while Deanna churned her hips, pressing the cleft of her buttocks against his throbbing rod, dancing a dance as old as the human race itself.

"I don't reckon I can handle a whole lot more of this," Davy gasped in Deanna's ear while she moaned and growled like a catamount in heat. And, as if punctuating that sentence, he groaned loudly. Then his body began to heave convulsively, as he fired off a load of jism into his long johns.

"Too late," Deanna said with a chuckle.

"Oooh," groaned Davy, looking both baffled and

21

buffaloed at the same time. "Does that mean we're finished?" he asked plaintively when he had stopped shaking.

"No, silly," his young, blonde angel told him, turning to unhook his belt buckle and help him out of his trousers. A few moments later, he was undressed and standing beside her bed. She had bent over him with a washrag, and was wiping away the last traces of jism. "We've just begun," she said with a hot, eager smile.

"I'm right glad of that," he sighed, while she dabbed at the insides of the long johns in her hand. "'Cause I'm mighty proud to be in your company, Deanna.''

"Why, thank you, David Lee," she replied sweetly, flattered by this. Davy was blushing furiously now, red as a raspberry. "It's not often I get such nice company," she confided, hanging his underwear on her bedpost to dry. "Most of the time I get rough, drunken cowboys or fat, sweaty little men from the town. Or cold-handed, cold-hearted drummers an' card sharpers. Or sod-busters an' sheepmen who all smell wuss'n a pigsty, men who wouldn't take themselves a bath at gunpoint."

"Well, I done took me a bath before I come to town, tonight," Davy told her proudly as she cupped his testicles in her hand.

"I can smell that, sweetie," Deanna told him gaily as her fingers closed around his flaccid member. And, being a virile young man, his member did him proud, standing up like a buck private coming to attention in the presence of a drill sergeant.

"Oh," Deanna said in mock-alarm as she ran her small cupped hand up the underside of his swollen shaft, "you're so hard!"

Davy opened his arms, reached out, and drew her close to him, obeying the promptings of an instinct much older than the laws of Moses or the teachings of Calvin or Wesley. Deanna snuggled up to him, feeling like a part of his body that had been suddenly restored after an unnatural amputation years earlier. He ran his

22

trembling hands down her supple back, and then encircled her squirming warmth within his arms.

Davy brought her down onto the bed, his shadow falling over her face and accenting her half-lidded eyes and bared white teeth. They kissed as she squirmed beneath him. When he had taken his lips from hers, he kissed the warm, ivory column of her neck. And he kept on kissing her, his mouth traveling down into the hollow above her breastbone, and then over the firm swell of her breast, where he kissed and nuzzled, tongued and suckled until the trim body beneath his own was all a-quiver.

"I want you inside me," Deanna whispered, panting like a Union Pacific steam engine taking a steep grade. Davy caught his breath as he felt her fingers encircle his shaft and draw him toward her. He had no breath left when he entered the tight encircling warmth of her sheath. And then he slid into her as surely as Leviathan of the Bible plumbed the depths.

She gasped as he entered her, and thrust her pelvis toward his. At Deanna's urging Davy stroked slow and he stroked fast, his instincts and American ingenuity combining to extend the number of ways to increase his and Deanna's pleasure.

She seemed to prefer it when their pelvises made contact, so Davy hooked his groin in to her and rubbed himself against her, as well. Deanna cried out as if she were being assaulted, although she forbade him to stop. And Davy felt a molten, mind-sapping glow travel up his spine and suffuse the space behind his eyes with its golden radiance.

He moaned like Lazarus coming back from the dead, and beneath him, the hot, squirming body suddenly stiffened. Just then, he surrendered his consciousness to a blackness that was pierced intermittently by bullets of light.

They came together, his soul-wrenched moans mingling with Deanna's high, urgent cries. What they had done, Davy Watson realized as his soul fluttered back into his body, was something strange and terrible and indescribably beautiful.

He raised himself upon his elbows and looked down at Deanna, noting the flush that had spread over her pale cheeks, and feeling as she raised her head to kiss him, the coldness that follows the "little death."

"Lord, that was like bein' born again," he whispered huskily as he sat up on the side of the bed minutes later. "It was real nice, Deanna."

She smiled up at him, his angel of passion. Her fine golden hair streamed over the pillow, its highlights reflecting the flickering glow of the lamp on the dresser.

"I liked it too, Davy," she whispered back. "I don't usually get to go with . . ." She paused and lowered her eyes. ". . . someone I like."

"How'd you get into this business?" he asked, curious to learn what had set her on such a path.

"My folks was killed by the Osage," Deanna told him in a quiet, solemn voice. "Man name of John Hartung found me in the ruins of our cabin, an' brung me into town. He told me that Miz Eaton was a good friend of his, an' that she'd take me in, seein' that I was an orphan, an' had no one to look after me."

"She give you this . . . job?" Davy asked.

Deanna nodded and then sat up beside him, running her cool, small hands over his hard-muscled back. "Miz Eaton's been right kind to me. She divvies up my earnin's, takin' her cut an' bankin' mine. She says it's for my dowry."

Davy looked down at Deanna, and saw that she was blushing. "You're gonna clear out of here someday?" he asked.

She nodded. "When I'm square with Miz Eaton."

"Square with Miz Eaton!" he interjected angrily. "Why, it's you done her the big favor!" It was his turn to blush. "An' anyway, what's it like—makin' love to all them fellas?"

"Mostly I don't feel much," she told him after a moment's reflection. "But I pretend I do. That way, it's

24

over quicker." She reached over and squeezed his hand. "It was real nice with you, Davy. I felt everything."

"Well, maybe," he said huskily, "I'll come back here someday soon an' take you outta here."

"I'd like that," she whispered, snuggling up close to him. "An' I'll be waiting."

"Well, I guess I gotta be goin'," he said, turning to look at her face once more, turning to look into those eyes as blue as prairie flowers.

"Not yet," Deanna whispered, her hand running over his thigh and coming to rest upon his sex, which began to throb and engorge the moment her cool fingers touched it. "Your paw gave Miz Eaton a gold piece," she told him, stroking his swelling member. "We got us a whole heap of time left, Davy."

"Praise the Lord," he murmured as they went back down onto the bed.

"Happy birthday, David Lee," Deanna murmured back as he nuzzled her neck and became drunk with the heady scents of arousal that perfumed her lithe young body.

Chapter 2

Two hours later, Davy Watson left the bawdy house of Mrs. Lucretia Eaton, realizing that, while he had entered the place a boy, he was leaving it a man. He had been initiated into the mysteries of carnal love in the grandest fashion imaginable, he believed, by someone who actually *cared* about him and had given herself to him freely and completely.

Deanna had touched his heart as well, and Davy vowed to return and take her away one day. And she had whispered back, while secure in his arms, that she would go with him.

There was even more spring in his step than usual, as he crossed the dusty street, on his way back to the Red Dog Saloon. "Deanna MacPartland," he whispered over and over to himself, repeating her name as if it were something holy, as if he were a medicine man chanting an invocation. And, like a medicine man or shaman, he felt himself filled with a strange and powerful spirit, his life suddenly transfigured by some great and healing magic.

He had become a man and known a man's love for a woman all at the same time. It was surely the most wonderful day of his life. He felt himself to be something more than a man. Davy was sure that nothing could mar the happiness that he felt today.

> *"I'm ridin' out on the windswept plain,*
> *Where only the buffalo goes,*
> *And men will never see me again,*
> *'Til I find my prairie rose . . . ."*

Even the song sung by the pianoforte player made Davy Watson think of Deanna as he entered the honky-tonk. And when he strode confidently up to the bar, this time he stared up at the canvas nude with a knowing smile.

"Well, young fella," Fred the bartender said by way of greeting, "you got the look of a body who'd jus' had a load took off'n his mind, so to speak."

"I'd like a shot of your finest," Davy told the bartender, plunking down a silver dollar on the bar.

"Comin' up," Fred said, turning to the shelf of bottles behind him.

"My paw been back yet?" Davy asked as the man began to pour.

"Not yet," the bartender replied.

"Y'know, Fred," Davy confided, "Miz Eaton gimme this here French likker to drink. Green stuff, name of, uh, Charters or Shurtrues, or somethin' like that. Ever hear of it?"

The bartender frowned. "Sounds more like somethin' ol' Dic Kincaid oughtta be handin' out. What's it taste like?"

Davy licked his lips as he recalled the taste of Chartreuse. "Kinda like a peppermint candy stick, I spose. An' it's thick an' green an' sticky. They say it's a high-class drink from France."

The bartender scratched his head. "Now, I don't get the point," he muttered. "It sounds like some syrup you'd give a young 'un, when he's down with the croup or the hoopin' cough. Were it strong?"

"Not as you'd say," Davy told him.

"Well, then," the bartender retorted, slapping down a palm on the bar with a wet thud, "what's the damn stuff good for?" He leaned across the bar and looked the young man right in the eye. "Don't you know what a real drink is supposed to do to a man? You think drinkin' is sposed to be fun—like ladies sippin' lemonade at a church social? Huh, do ya?"

"Uh, well . . . I, uh," Davy blustered.

27

"A good shot of whiskey goin' down should feel like steel runnin' out of a smelter," the bartender interrupted, passionate now. "An' when it settles in your gut, it should sneak up on ya an' open your eyes, like someone a-thumpin' ya on the back of the head with a two-by-four."

Davy stared at the bartender over his shot glass as he swigged his drink.

"An' lemme tell ya what corn likker—real corn likker —should do to a man."

Davy belched and emitted a boozy gust. His forehead was dotted with beads of sweat.

"Good corn likker," the bartender pontificated, "that is to say, white lightnin', should have the smell of gangrene startin' in a mildewed silo. An' when you guzzle it, the stuff oughta taste like the wrath to come, an' after that, a body should feel all the sensations of havin' swallowed a kerosene lamp. Why, a sudden, violent jolt of the stuff has been known to stop a man's watch, snap his suspenders, an' crack his glass eye right across."

"Gol-lee," Davy whispered.

"That's what good likker can do," Fred went on, smiling broadly now, as he poured Davy a second shot.

"Hey, fart-bender!" a man called out from the other end of the bar. "How 'bout breakin' away from that lad an' moseyin' on down here with that bottle. I'm dry as dust."

"I was jus' educatin' this young fella about good whiskey," Fred replied, straightening up and putting down his bar rag.

"There's enough bullshit out in the pasture, Fred," the man said tartly. "Just stick to dispensin' spiritous liquors." The men around him laughed.

"Humph," Fred grunted, picking up the bottle and starting down the bar. "You ain't no con-no-sewer your own self, Bob. Why, many's the time I coulda peed in your glass, an' you'd have never knowed the

28

difference." The men all laughed again.

"Well, if it come from you, Fred," the tart man observed, "chances are it'd still be a hundred proof." This set everyone at the bar to laughing, Davy included.

Leaning back against the bar with his elbows behind him, Davy looked around before reaching for his second drink. And as he did, the honkytonk's swinging doors flew open, and a man shot through them to skid spreadeagled across the sawdust. When the man came to rest, Davy saw that he was an Indian, and not much older than himself.

An instant later, Davy saw the author of the force that had propelled the Indian through the swinging doors of the Red Dog Saloon. He was a tall, gaunt man with black hair and sideburns that ran the length of his jaw, the left one intersected by a livid scar that ran across his cheek to end under his eyes. The man's eyes were gray, and cold as ice in a mountain pass; and the nose beneath them was long and thin. Vaulting eyebrows, as well as the long face with its pointed and dark-stubbled chin, gave him a baleful and satanic look, which was accentuated by the cruel, perpetual sneer he wore. His spurs jingled as he walked into the honkytonk, and his gun was worn low and tied to his leg with a thong of rawhide. Behind him came six other men, evil-looking hombres all.

"Redskin wants a drink," the satanic-looking man called out to the bartender as the dazed young Indian wiped a trickle of blood from his chin and rose unsteadily to his feet.

"Now, Ace," the bartender whined as he scuttled down the bar to where the gaunt man stood, "you know I can't serve no likker to Injuns. That's the law." He winced as the cold gray eyes fell upon him.

"Put a bottle an' two glasses down here on the bar, Fred," the man said in a voice no warmer than the winter wind. His smile made Davy think of death's heads carved on tombstones. The bartender sighed and did as he was told.

"Who is that there fella?" Davy asked the man beside him.

"That's Ace Landry," the man whispered, ducking behind Davy. "Meanest man in these parts. Been said he's behind most of the robbin' an' rustlin' that goes on around here. But ain't nobody ever caught him, nor been fool enough to call him out about it."

The young Indian was on his feet, and shaking his head as he tottered over to the bar. And just as he managed to look up at the grim man called Ace Landry, one of the desperadoes stepped forward suddenly. The Indian's grunt could be heard in the street outside as the bully-boy's fist slammed into his gut, driving him against the bar and doubling him up.

The man leaned over and wrenched the gagging and gasping Indian's arms behind his back, and pinioned them against his own chest with one arm. Following that, he grabbed the Indian's lustrous black hair and yanked his head back brutally.

Davy Watson looked around the honkytonk as the Indian moaned in pain. No one, it seemed, was about to stand up for the man. He wished that his father were there; *he* would have spoken up—and Davy knew that he should do the same.

"Ah think he's 'bout ready t'have that l'il drink with y'all, Ace," the man who held the struggling brave called out.

"Why, so he is," Landry acknowledged cheerfully in his winter voice, proceeding to knock back one of the two shots that stood before him on the bar.

Davy wiped his palms on his trousers and looked up and down the bar once more.

"I told you to get off'n the sidewalk when a white man passes," Ace Landry told the Indian. "But you was jus' too muleheaded to move, wasn't you, buck? Well then, let's drink to your pride an' stubbornness." He put down the empty glass and raised the full one.

"Here's to redskin impertinence an' stupidity," Landry

said, as a second man roughly yanked the Indian's jaws apart. After that, Landry dashed the whiskey into the young brave's mouth.

"Hit 'em again, Fred," Ace Landry told the bartender as the Indian sputtered and coughed.

"But, Ace," the bartender pleaded, "if I get—"

"Careful, Fred," Landry interrupted, shooting the bartender a rattlesnake look.

"Anything you say, Ace," Fred muttered, white in the face as he refilled the two shotglasses with a trembling hand.

"I drink to the noble redskin," Landry jeered, an instant before he knocked back his drink.

The second man to grab the Indian pried the brave's jaws open once more as Ace Landry put his empty glass down on the bar.

"Now, hold on a minute," Davy Watson called out, fighting to master the quaver in his voice.

Everyone looked his way: the crowd at the bar, the desperadoes, Ace Landry, even the Indian, who stopped struggling after Davy had called out.

"Aw, shoot," the burly man who held open the Indian's jaws rumbled disappointedly. "It's only some dumb kid. It ain't gonna be much fun bustin' him up."

Davy's ears burned, and he could feel his knees wobble as he walked up to the man

"Whyn't you let him go, mister?" he asked in a hoarse voice, realizing that his throat had suddenly gone dry.

"*Haw! Haw! Haw!*" brayed the burly man, tightening his grip on the jaws of the struggling Indian. His coarse, flat-nosed face reddened as he continued his jackass laugh. "You must be drunk, boy," he said finally, after catching his breath. "This here's only a Injun. It ain't even human, like you an' me."

"You done had your fun, now," Davy persisted. "So whyn't you let up on him?" He felt a chill as his eyes darted over to the bar, where Ace Landry gave him a smile as sharp as a skinner's knife.

"An' what if I wasn't to let up on this here red trash, boy?" the flat-nosed man asked. "What would ya do?"

Davy wiped his sweaty palms on his trousers and took a deep breath. "I'd, uh . . . be obliged to make you let up on him, mister," he croaked.

Considering this reply impertinent, the man cleared his throat, hawking up a mouthful of phlegm, which he promptly spat smack onto the breast of Davy Watson's new jacket.

Davy's fear suddenly left him as the desperadoes broke out into laughter while he contemplated the mess on his chest. He flushed red with anger when he saw the contemptuous smile on Ace Landry's angular face.

"*Haw! Haw! Haw!*" guffawed the bully-boy who had spat upon Davy's coat, his ugly face now as red as the young sodbuster's.

At that precise instant, Davy decided what he must do. He pivoted on his left foot and came around with an overhand right, throwing behind it the full force of his one hundred and eighty pounds, and smashed his fist into the red, braying face before him.

"*Hu-u-uk!*" was all that the man said as Davy's fist drove his already flattened nose deeper into the mask of his face. The force of the blow caused him to let go of the Indian and lurch backwards out of control, to fall on top of a gambling table, which promptly collapsed under his weight and sent him crashing to the floor.

Shaking his stinging fist, Davy watched with satisfaction as the man crashed to the floor in a shower of playing cards and poker chips. Then, cocking his right arm back and wheeling around, he turned to the man who held the young Indian's arms behind his back.

The man had already let go of the Indian, and was about to lunge at Davy. But as he did, his former victim leaned over and rammed an elbow into the bully-boy's groin. With a piercing scream, the man doubled up and pitched head-first to the sawdust of the Red Dog Saloon.

Suddenly, someone hit Davy on the side of the head,

and he fell to the floor. As he rolled over on his back, Davy saw the four other desperadoes advancing on him. And through the legs of the foremost, he saw the young brave rise to his feet—only to sink back down onto the sawdust, as the man called Ace Landry smashed a whiskey bottle over his head.

As Davy was struggling to his feet, the foremost man kicked him in the chest, sending him backward into the arms of the two hardcases behind him. They caught him and pinioned his arms. Then the man who had kicked him stepped forward and planted a fist in Davy's gut.

Groaning and gasping for breath, Davy fought to straighten up, still held fast by the two desperadoes. He gritted his teeth and tried vainly to break loose, as the man before him raised a ham-like fist and came at him. Turning his head away, but still watching the ruffian out of the corner of his eye, Davy winced in expectation of the blow to come.

But the blow never came. Davy saw the man's eyes widen, as the latter pulled back his hand and stepped backward suddenly. An instant later, behind him, Davy heard a rush of air, followed by a sharp thwacking sound. Suddenly he felt the pressure on his right arm relax. When Davy darted a look to that side, he saw the man who had been holding him crumple to the sawdust.

He ducked instinctively as the man on his left suddenly released his grip and began to back off. Another whoosh and an attendant thwack were heard, followed by a groan of pain, as Davy spun around. And there behind him, gripping a stout new axhandle in both hands, was John Jacob Watson!

Davy's father had finished his shopping at Ransom's General Store, and had returned to collect his son. The moment John Jacob had perceived what was going on, he went into action—putting his new axhandle to good use.

Before the second bully-boy hit the floor, John Jacob had singled out another, and was already advancing on him, brandishing the axhandle as he came. Davy launched himself at the fourth desperado, slamming into the man's midriff as he tackled him. And as they went down to the floor, Ace Landry leaned back on the bar and smiled his cruel, wintry smile.

The bully-boy held his arms up before his face and squealed like a stuck pig as John Jacob Watson advanced relentlessly. He stopped short as his back made contact with the edge of the bar. The axhandle whistled through the air, accompanied by its wielder's grunt. The man howled as the blow snapped his left forearm with an audible crack. He brought his arms down and cradled them at his stomach. John Jacob's second blow dropped him like a poled ox.

Davy was still rolling on the floor with his adversary; the man was strong, and he was so far unable to break the iron grip on his windpipe. Above him, he saw the first man he'd hit stagger to his feet, wiping away the blood that gushed from his nose like water from a tap. And as Davy heaved the man choking him onto his side, he saw that the desperado whom the Indian had elbowed was still curled up on the floor.

His face went from red to purple as Davy fought desperately to break free with the last of his remaining strength. His vision began to go black as he managed to climb on top of the man. Then, still held fast by the throat, he put his palms on the man's broad chest and thrust himself away, bringing his knees up into the air.

When he brought them down again, Davy planted his knees square in the pit of the strangler's groin. The man screamed like a tortured bobcat and released his grip on Davy's windpipe. Just as he rolled off the man, Davy saw his father bring down the flat-nosed man. Then he lay back on the sawdust, gasping for breath as he fought to retain consciousness.

As the bloody-nosed man hit the floor of the saloon with a loud thump, John Jacob Watson lowered the axhandle and stood panting as he surveyed the results of his handiwork.

Of the group that had been fighting with Davy and

the young Indian, only the dark man with the mean smile was still on his feet. He leaned back against the bar and flexed the fingers of both hands as he smiled and looked John Jacob Watson up and down.

"That's my boy, mister," Watson told the gaunt, sneering man, breathing hard as he pointed to his son.

The man nodded. "He's a game lad, but he's got to learn not to stick his nose in places where it don't belong."

"He done what nobody else had the stomach to do, mister. You had no right to pick on that there Injun the way you done. All the people on the street outside was a-talkin' 'bout how you 'n your boys done run him in here."

"Injun like that don't mean nothin' to your boy," Landry said, his curiosity aroused now. "Why'd he have to open his big mouth an' git in my way? It's only an Injun."

"Maybe it's cause I done taught the boy that an Injun's a man jus' like anybody else, an' that we're all equal in the sight of Almighty God."

Landry shook his head. "So you think your boy oughta risk his life in a barroom brawl for some stupid, greasy Injun?"

"It's the duty of the strong to protect the weak and the unfortunate," John Jacob told the man with the cruel smile. "That's what our people believe." He looked down at Davy, who had just heaved himself up to a sitting position on the floor. "I'm proud of the boy, for what he done," his father affirmed.

"I see where he gets his foolishness from," Landry said, smiling as he flexed his fingers once more.

"Standin' up to bullies an' scum like you'n your lot ain't foolish," John Jacob told the man. "This here'd be a right peaceful country if more folks'd take a stand like my boy did."

"You're a real brave hombre, ain't you, mister?"

"Watson's my name. John Jacob Watson. An' what's yours, mister?"

"Ace Landry's my handle," the man told him, still smiling.

Davy sat on the floor, not moving a muscle as he watched the confrontation.

"I think you owe my boy an apology," John Jacob Watson said quietly, hefting the axhandle in his right hand.

Suddenly the smile left Ace Landry's face. "Watson, I don't think you know who you're talkin' to," he said in a voice both quiet and cold.

John Jacob Watson looked around the Red Dog Saloon. "It's just you'n me now, Mr. Landry," he replied calmly. "So what's it gonna be?"

The cold smile lit on Ace Landry's lips once more. "I guess I'm gonna have to pay you for your trouble, Mr. Watson," he said, his fingers going still. "By sendin' you to hell."

Then, as John Jacob raised the axhandle over his head and advanced on him, Ace Landry's right hand dropped to the gun at his side.

"Paw—look out!" Davy screamed as the .44 American Smith and Wesson cavalry issue revolver slid out of the scarred and weathered leather holster.

Time seemed to freeze then, as it does in nightmares, and Davy watched the next motions of the men with a painful and intense clarity. He saw the veins stand out on his father's neck as he raised the axhandle high in the air, and he saw Ace Landry's cruel smile harden on his face as the Smith and Wesson came up in his hand.

Suddenly the horror thawed in a series of roars and bright flashes that came from the mouth of the Smith and Wesson's long barrel.

"*Paw!*" Davy cried as the slugs tore into his father's body at close range, throwing him backward violently, like a scarecrow torn loose by a twister. By the time that John Jacob Watson hit the sawdust, he had been flung back more than halfway from the bar to the swinging doors.

Davy sprang to his feet and ran to his father's side.

But by the time he knelt beside him, John Jacob Watson was already dead.

Ace Landry! The name flared and smouldered in his brain, as if it had just been branded there. Quivering with rage, Davy got to his feet and charged at the man who had just gunned down his father.

One more shot rang out in the Red Dog Saloon that day, as Ace Landry gunned down the son, as well as the father.

Chapter 3

The slug entered Davy Watson's body and spun him around, sending him down to the floor and rolling him over in the sawdust. And as soon as the body hit the floor, Ace Landry holstered his smoking revolver and turned back to the bar, where he proceeded to pour himself a drink.

When he did this, people all over the Red Dog began to edge toward the door. Landry knocked back his drink and then pointed to a group of men who looked at him furtively as they sidled away from the bar.

"You fellas," he told them quietly. "I want you to tend to my boys there." He pointed to the floor. "Get 'em up an' about."

"Fred," he said to the hovering bartender. "throw these gents a couple of bar rags."

The bartender complied, and the men spent the next ten minutes reviving the fallen bully-boys. During this time, Ace Landry poured himself another two shots of whiskey. Then, as the last man was helped to his feet, the desperado tossed a gold piece onto the bar.

"It's time we were leavin' this town, boys," he told his men.

"Mr. Landry! Mr. Landry!" a small boy squealed as he burst into the bar. "Word's out about the shootin', an' there's talk of formin' a posse. Folks is already talkin' about a lynchin'. There's a whole passel of 'em a-gatherin' in front of Sheriff Reynolds' office."

Landry nodded and reached into his vest pocket. He came out with a silver dollar, which he tossed to the boy, who caught it and ducked under the swinging doors.

"Time to hit the trail," he said, his spurs jingling as he walked away from the bar. The ruffians began to file out after him, and as they left the Red Dog Saloon, all seven of them stepped over the dead body of John Jacob Watson.

Hours later, when Davy Watson came to, he found himself in his own bed, back on the Watson farm at Pottawatomie Creek. His sister Amy was at his side, applying a cold washrag to his forehead. As he attempted to sit up, a stab of pain tore through his shoulder. Amy shook her head and gently pushed him back down onto the pillow.

"Don't move," she whispered. "Doc Kincaid said you wasn't to fuss about for a while."

"How did I . . . get here?" he croaked.

"Doc brought you back in the buckboard. There was this Indian with him."

Davy recalled the brave who had been tormented by the desperadoes. Then he thought of his father.

"Paw's dead, Amy," he said hollowly, looking up at his fifteen-year-old sister.

"I know, David Lee," she said, sniffling.

He noticed that her eyes were red-rimmed. "Where's Maw?" he asked.

"Out back," Amy told him. "Preparin' Paw's body for the wake."

"How is she, Amy?"

"You know Maw. She's a strong woman. But I seen the look on her face when she first seen the body. It was jus' for an instant, but she looked as if her heart was like to break."

He hung his head. "It was my fault, Amy," he said miserably. "If it wasn't for me, Paw would still be alive."

"Now, you hush up," Amy told him, putting a finger on his lips and staring at him with brown, compassionate eyes. "Doc told us the story. Paw was proud of what you done. You done right. Sometimes a man has to take risks—that's what Paw always told us."

A knock sounded at the door. Amy got up and went over to open the door.

"This gentleman would like to see you, David Lee," she announced as the young Indian entered the room. Then Amy left, closing the door behind her.

"Come in," Davy said to the Indian, who stood hesitantly by the door. He noticed that the young man wore a large white bandage wrapped around his head.

Davy held out his right hand. "I want to thank you," he said, looking into the Indian's grave eyes, "for gettin' the doc an' bringin' my father's body back home."

The Indian took Davy's hand in his own. He had broad cheekbones, a prominent nose, deep-set eyes and lustrous black hair that fell to his shoulders. His grip was firm and his eyes were clear; Davy's instincts told him that here was a man who could be trusted.

"I thank you," the Indian said in a strong, clear voice. "You stand up for Soaring Hawk when no others help him. You save my honor as a man."

"Soaring Hawk," Davy Watson repeated. "That your name?"

The Indian nodded. "I am Pawnee. My people hunt the buffalo on the plains to the west."

Davy grinned as he remembered the way that Soaring Hawk had jammed his elbow into the groin of the bully-boy in the Red Dog Saloon. "You took good care of that fella with your elbow."

There was just the hint of a smile on the Indian's face. "And you hit hard," he said, holding up his fist and shaking it in the air, "in the way of your people."

"That felt good," Davy whispered as he recollected smashing his fist into the red, grinning face of the ruffian who had spat upon his new coat.

"Your father was a brave man," the Indian said, staring at Davy with grave eyes.

Davy looked away, suddenly devastated as he felt the loss of his father. "Best an' bravest man I ever knew in my whole life," he muttered.

40

"Tonight I will build a fire and dance to the Great Spirit," Soaring Hawk told Davy. "I will dance to honor a fallen warrior. I will ask the Great Spirit to receive the spirit of your father, to take him to the place where honored men dwell. Tell me his name."

"His name is John Jacob Watson," Davy said in a voice that cracked. A single tear made its way down his cheek.

The Indian repeated the name several times. "And what is name of brave warrior's son?" he asked finally.

"David Lee Watson," Davy told him, sniffling as he did. "My friends call me Davy."

The young Pawnee looked at him as Davy held out his hand once more. "We will be friends—forever," he said, taking Davy's hand.

"When I get better, I aim to go after the man who shot my Paw."

The Indian nodded. "Then I ride with you. I wish to kill him, as well. He made sport of my honor."

"That man's name was Ace Landry," David Watson told him.

"Ace Landry," Soaring Hawk repeated.

"Ace Landry," Davy said with finality as he looked up into the Pawnee's dark eyes. "I swear on the grave of my father not to rest until Ace Landry is dead."

"And I swear to ride at your side until this thing is done," Soaring Hawk added.

"Do you know where that sidewinder went to?" Davy asked.

The Indian shook his head. "But I will find out. When Landry and his gang rode off, the men of Hawkins Fork made a posse. Many were angry when they heard of the murder of your father."

"He will be avenged," Davy said in a small, cold voice. "I pledge my life on it."

"He will be avenged," echoed the Pawnee.

Thirty miles south of the town of Hawkins Fork, the man who had gunned down John Jacob Watson sat on

41

his blanket roll, drinking black coffee as he gazed into the flames of his campfire.

Ace Landry had led his gang to Buffalo Gulch, as was his custom whenever things got too hot in the area. There the desperadoes made camp and unrolled their blankets. It was a long, hard ride, Landry knew, but at the end of it he always found security. His reputation was too awesome for anyone to light out after him for anything so inconsequential as a barroom shooting, the outlaw thought. But he had not reckoned with the love and esteem in which the townspeople and those in the surrounding area had held John Jacob Watson.

On the second night after the shooting, Landry and his band sat around the campfire in Buffalo Gulch, drinking bitter coffee after a meal of hardtack, bacon and pinto beans. The outlaw took great pleasure in administering pain, and then observing its effects; his laughter was summoned forth only by the humiliation and discomfiture of his fellow human beings. The subject of his mirth tonight was the beating that the Watsons, father and son, had administered to his hardcases.

"That was really somethin' to see," he said through a smile of contempt, "how you boys came up lookin' so bad against a boy an' some ol' red-neck farmer."

The desperadoes stared sullenly into their coffee.

"Though I must admit," Landry went on teasingly, "that young 'un sure did pack a wallop. Didn't he, Riker?" He turned to face the flat-nosed man.

"Aw, the little bastard hit me when I wasn't expectin' it," he mumbled, the flush of embarrassment on his face visible by the light of the campfire.

"An' you, Taggart," the outlaw chief continued. "You was 'bout de-molished by that ol' cracker with the axhandle."

A balding, bearded man shot Landry a dark look, but said nothing.

"An' you, Carmody," Landry said lightly. "That

greasy redskin near rammed your balls up'n your throat.''

The chunky, thick-lipped man whom Landry had addressed spat contemptuously into the fire and then studied the toes of his boots.

"What a bunch o' pussies," Ace Landry told his band of ruffians, looking around the campfire with a sneer on his lips. "I'd've done better with six boys from the Hawkins Fork Sunday School to back me up. Who'd a thought that a bunch as ornery-lookin' as yourselves wouldn't be able to hold your own against a farmboy an' some ol' cracker.''

No one replied. The bully-boys all glowered into their coffee or down at the toes of their boots.

"If this keeps up, boys," Landry said in a voice whose tones of sarcasm were thick as molasses in winter, "I might as well get me a pack of six ol' grannies, an' start ridin' with them. 'Cause it seems to me that most of them ol' pioneer women could take your measure.''

He looked around the campfire again, his cruel eyes glittering with its light. "Ain't nobody got nothin' to say? Nothin' at all?''

The desperadoes were as silent as the grave.

"I'm waitin' for an answer," Ace Landry whispered through a smile that was all ice and contempt. If any of the outlaws had the courage to look him in the eye at that moment, they would have seen that he was having a high old time.

There was dead silence in the camp as Landry waited for a response. All that could be heard was the crackling of the fire and the distant, occasional hooting of an owl. But suddenly, Ace Landry heard a sound that made his hackles rise: the whinnying of a horse. And it did not come from where the gang's mounts were tethered. It came from somewhere out in the night. Someone was after them!

Landry stood up and whipped out his Smith and

Wesson, turning in the direction of the sound and stepping back, away from the revealing light of the campfire. The other men, conditioned by their lives as outlaws, immediately followed suit, none of them so much as uttering a word.

The last man to rise was the chunky, thick-lipped man whom Landry had called Carmody. He flung his coffee cup away and reached for the sixshooter that was holstered on his left side as he began to step backward into the shadows. But before he left the campfire's glow, several points of light flared in the darkness across from him, and the sound of gunshots rang out in the night. Clutching at his chest, Carmody emitted a gurgling cry and fell to the ground.

"Git over to the horses," Landry told his men, just before he fired off two shots at the spot where he had seen the flares of light. He smiled with grim satisfaction as a man cried out in the darkness. Then he went into a crouch and started toward the place where the horses were tethered.

The next volley of shots that came from across the campfire increased threefold in number, as the members of the Hawkins Fork posse gathered together and began to blast away at the band of outlaws. But their mistake was in concentrating their forces, and the now-scattered desperadoes were able to return the posse's fire and create havoc in their ranks.

"Scatter, boys!" Ace Landry heard someone cry out in the distance, after the cries of the dying and wounded had reached him across the campfire. He bent down to untether his horse and then, still crouching, began to lead it away. As he heard his men near the horses, he fired off another two shots in the general direction of the scattering posse. Their answering fire was high and wide, indicating to Landry that his pursuers were rattled.

"What about Carmody's horse?" he heard Taggart call out.

"Take it with you," the outlaw boss ordered. "No

44

sense in leavin' it for these sons o' bitches."

Shots rang out intermittently in the darkness. Fortunately for the Landry gang, the moon had gone behind a bank of clouds, and the posse had nothing to aim at but the occasional flash of an outlaw's gun.

"Scatter, boys," Ace Landry whispered into the surrounding blackness. "We'll meet at Hilliard's Grove."

The desperado swung himself into the saddle, fired off a last brace of shots from his Smith and Wesson Cavalry issue revolver, put spurs to his horse, and rode off into the night. With a jingling of spurs and a creaking of leather, followed by a volley of shots, the other outlaws all did the same.

John Jacob Watson's funeral was one of the biggest ever held in Kansas. Men and women came from miles around in all directions to pay their law respects to the man who had settled the country around Pottawatomie Creek and Hawkins Fork. Also in attendance at the service was one of the state's U.S. Senators, and several members of the House of Representatives.

At his own request, Davy Watson was borne into town in a wagon, and then propped up on a cot by the graveside. His wound had been a clean one; Ace Landry's bullet had entered the upper left side of his chest at a slight angle, and came out of his back just below the shoulder bone. Doc Kincaid had pronounced Davy well enough to attend the funeral, provided he did not move about on his own, and told him that all the tissue torn by the slug would heal in the course of time.

"Be merciful unto me, O God! for man would swallow me up; he fighting daily oppresseth me," the Reverend Hosea Michaels intoned in a deep, resonant voice.

Next to Davy's cot stood his mother, sister and brother. Amy and Lucius Erasmus were weeping as the minister spoke, but Annabel Watson was dry-eyed, and looking just as proud of her dead husband as ever she had while he lived. She bit her lip and held Davy's hand in a firm grip, her eyes raised to the heavens.

"Mine enemies would daily swallow me up; for they be many that fight against me, O thou most high."

Looking around him, Davy was amazed to see the number of people at the burial, most of them folks whose lives had been touched by the strength and goodness of John Jacob Watson, that shy, quiet man whom he had loved and respected with all his heart.

"What time I am afraid, I will trust in thee."

Soon he would be well, Davy Watson told himself, fighting back his tears as he watched the townspeople lower his father's coffin into the ground, into the dark, rich earth that John Jacob had loved so deeply and tended so well.

"In God, I will praise his word," Reverend Michaels said as he threw a spadeful of earth down onto the pine coffin. "In God I have put my trust; I will not fear what flesh can do unto me."

Those words echoed and re-echoed in Davy's mind. They strengthened his resolve, and he swore to track down Ace Landry—to the very ends of the earth, if necessary—and avenge the murder of his father.

I will not fear what flesh can do unto me.

The reverend went on as the gravediggers began to shovel earth over the coffin. Davy's mind was a blur, an indistinct patchwork of sounds and impressions, as he realized with numbing horror that he would never again in this life see his beloved father.

"My soul is among lions: and I lie even among them that are set on fire, even the sons of men, whose teeth are spears and arrows, and their tongue a sharp sword."

Davy would spend the time it took his wound to heal in preparation for the day when he would ride out after Ace Landry. He would put the affairs of the farm to rights for his mother, and hire hands for the autumn harvest and spring planting.

"The righteous shall rejoice when he seeth the vengeance: he shall wash his feet in the blood of the wicked."

And in the long hours of waiting that lay ahead, he would go out into the pasture with the Colt Walker and perfect his aim. He would be ready for Ace Landry, by the time that they met again.

"So that a man shall say, verily there is a reward for the righteous: verily he is a God that judgeth in the earth."

On the day after his father's burial, Davy had a visitor, the last one he expected to see on the Watson farm. A rig drew up before the house, and Davy, sitting up in bed, caught a glimpse of a man in its driver's seat. And then, just for a split second, as the rig rolled by, he saw a figure in a pale blue satin dress.

Several moments later, the door to his room creaked open, and his mother looked in on him.

"You've got a visitor, son," she told him. "Are you feelin' up to receivin' one?"

Davy's eyes went wide. "Who is it, Maw?" he grunted, raising himself up on his pillow.

"Young lady name of Deanna MacPartland," his mother told him, causing his ears to go red as a beet. "Care to see her?" she asked, studying her son's expression.

"Yes'm," Davy mumbled. "I reckon I would."

Annabel Watson nodded and stepped back out of the room. A moment later, Davy caught his breath as the lissome blonde beauty in the pale blue satin dress entered his room, radiant as an angel in a vision.

"Hello, David Lee," Deanna said as she approached the side of his bed.

Davy gulped. "Hello, Deanna," he whispered. Then he reached out involuntarily—or so it seemed to him— and took her hand in his.

"I was worried about you," she murmured shyly, lowering her eyes. "I heard that you'd been shot."

He squeezed her hand. "I'm all right. I jus' got

winged. No big thing.''

She raised her eyes and gave him a sad look. "I'm right sorry about your paw, Davy," she whispered. "He'll be missed by a passel of folks, according to everything I heard.''

He nodded his head. "I made a vow to go after the man who killed Paw, once I'm well again.''

Deanna gave him a look of alarm. "You can't do that," she whispered. "Ace Landry's an awful man. He's killed a lot of folks.''

Davy looked down at his blanket. "I've got to, Deanna," he muttered. "'Cause if I don't, I'll never be half the man Paw wanted me to be.''

"But, Davy—''

"Don't say nothin' more about it," he interrupted. "A man's got to do what he's got to do.''

It was Deanna's turn to look away.

"But when I come back," he said, squeezing her hand, causing her to look into his eyes, "all right, if I come back, I want to take you out of Miz Eaton's. Understand?" He was blushing now.

"*If* you come back," she repeated sadly.

"*When* I come back, Miss Deanna MacPartland, I'm acomin' for you.''

She leaned over the bed and kissed him. "First, come back," she whispered in his ear.

"I expect you'll be talkin' to Maw on your way out," Davy said uncomfortably, causing her to give him a wondering look. "I, uh, wish that when you do you, uh, won't mention nothin' concernin' your. . . profession.''

By way of answer, Deanna smiled and then kissed him again.

It was a day for visitors. Less than one half hour after Deanna had driven off in Mrs. Eaton's rig, Soaring Hawk rode up on his pony.

He told Davy all about the posse's unfortunate brush with the Landry Gang at Buffalo Gulch. One of the

48

desperadoes had been killed; the posse lost two men, with three more wounded.

"Where'd they go after that?" Davy asked.

"To the west, in the direction of the land of my people." Soaring Hawk nodded. "We will be able to pick up their trail."

"I'll be ready soon," Davy told his friend. "And then we'll ride after Ace Landry."

"I have danced the dance of the departed warriors in honor of John Jacob Watson," the Pawnee said.

"Thanks for your kindness," Davy muttered.

"And now there is one thing more," the Indian told him, suddenly drawing a long knife from its sheath on his fringed belt.

Davy shot him an inquiring look.

"We are pledged to the same journey, and our lives are now woven together," Soaring Hawk said. "We must become blood brothers."

"Suits me jus' fine," Davy whispered, holding out his right arm.

"It shall be so," the Indian replied, making a slash on the inside of his own wrist with the scalping knife. Then, as blood began to flow from the cut, Soaring Hawk did the same to Davy.

After that, he joined their wrists. "Now, your blood and mine flow together," the Pawnee told him. "Now, we are brothers."

"Amen to that," said David Lee Watson.

Chapter 4

Things do not always go the way that men wish them to, and Davy Watson's patience was sorely tried over the winter of 1867-68. His wound had been more severe than he cared to admit, and had taken a long time to heal. But Davy laid his plans with determination and made himself do exercises every day, progressive exercises prescribed by Doc Kincaid that would gradually restore the use of his left arm.

Over and above this, the winter turned out to be one of the worst in the new state's history, with blizzards raging until the middle of March. With his father gone, there was much to do around the farm; and as he worked, Davy did his best to impart to Lucius Erasmus the skills that he had learned from John Jacob. For his little brother would soon be the man of the house, once Davy had ridden off.

Soaring Hawk was also a prisoner of the weather, and consequently spent much of the long, hard season as a guest of the Watsons. The Indian's skills were many, and he proved an asset to his blood brother over the winter.

Many of the skills they practiced were not of the household variety. The Pawnee shared his extensive knowledge of the plains with Davy, and after the spring thaw they rode out to put these lessons to the test. And during the spells when they were snowbound, Davy learned to throw a knife with almost uncanny accuracy, and to stalk a man or beast practically as noiselessly as an Indian.

They would practice in the big Watson barn, chunking knives into a target drawn on a rough-hewn beam, and stalking each other in the darkness. And Davy had, upon the Pawnee's request, taught Soaring Hawk to use his fists like a white man. The Indian had been much impressed with Davy's right hand, and had dubbed him "Hammer Hand" in the language of his tribe.

Having been snowbound all winter, Davy had not been able to hire hands to help with the spring planting. So he, Amy, Lucius Erasmus, his mother and Soaring Hawk all attended to it themselves. And when it was finished, he rode into Hawkins Fork and found two good men who would work for his mother.

He was chafing to set out on his quest for vengeance, but his responsibility to his family came first. The patience that he acquired in that season of discipline and commitment would serve him well when he finally rode west after Ace Landry. And Davy was consoled by the knowledge that a man like Landry would always leave a trail of misdeeds and victims, no matter how far he ran. They would meet again.

God grant me the serenity to accept the things I cannot change, the courage to change the things I can, and the wisdom to know the difference.

That was what Davy prayed each night before he went to sleep. And with each day, he gained patience; his resolve was never shaken, even though his mother would continually attempt to dissuade him from his mission of vengeance.

" 'Vengeance is mine, saith the Lord,' " Annabel Watson sternly reminded her son. "You know that, David Lee. You learned it at my knee. The Lord will attend to that man. Your place is here with your family."

But Davy would not be dissuaded. "Well, Maw," he told her softly, "I'm prayin' to be the instrument of the Lord's vengeance. I intend to seek Ace Landry out, an' pay him back in kind."

"This is madness," his mother told him, tears coming to her eyes.

51

"I swore a vow, Maw," he whispered, taking his mother's hands in his own. "An' I'll never have a moment's peace inside o' me until this matter's settled."

When spring came, after the planting had been done and the new hands hired, Davy was able to pay several visits to Mrs. Eaton's and spend an occasional hour in the arms of Deanna MacPartland.

She, too, did her best to lead Davy off the path of vengeance, but he would not be moved.

"Trust in me," he whispered in her ear, as they lay side by side on the bed, naked in the flickering light. "Your faith in me is part of my strength. You've got to believe I'm comin' back to you, girl—because I am."

"I pray God you will come back," she said. And as Deanna drew him down to kiss her, Davy saw that there were tears in her eyes.

After the skirmish with the posse from Hawkins Fork, Ace Landry led his band of desperadoes into Abilene. But his stay there was a short one, as was his subsequent sojourn in the town of Hoxie. A wave of outrage had swept through the state of Kansas, once word of John Jacob Watson's cold-blooded murder had spread, and Landry felt he had no choice but to ride west, into the Colorado Territory.

He rode out of Kansas on the trail that ran west from Saint Francis, and crossed the Arikaree fork of the Republican River in eastern Colorado. The outlaw band made their way over that trail, heading through cow towns such as Akron, Brush and Fort Morgan, until they came to Greeley. The winter had come in right behind them, and so the Landry Gang settled in.

They stayed in Greeley as the guests of a man named Cliff Hagen. He was a former associate of Ace Landry's, and they had made big money years ago rustling cattle. When they parted company, Hagen rode on into Greeley and proceeded to open a grand establishment—a combination saloon, gambling house and bordello. As Colorado was just opening up in those days, Hagen prospered greatly.

Landry, however, was unable to hold onto his share of the rustling profits, for his passion for gambling strongly asserted itself at the time. A losing streak that ran a full week put the desperado right back where he had been before he entered into partnership with Cliff Hagen. But since it was he who had brought Hagen into that partnership, Ace Landry always considered the other man to be in his debt.

So when things in Kansas got too hot for the outlaw, Landry hightailed it into Colorado, where he had decided to lay low as the guest of Cliff Hagen, who was now one of Greeley's most prosperous and prominent citizens, a man beloved by all who knew him. Less than pleased to see his former associate, Hagen was careful not to show it; Ace Landry had a nasty habit of taking offense easily, and of paying back any slight— real or imagined—with hot lead. Hagen's only condition was that Ace and his boys behave themselves while in Greeley, and remain as inconspicuous as possible.

The winter was even more ferocious in Colorado than in Kansas, and the Landry Gang was bottled up in Greeley. The outlaws grew restless, and tempers flared, but Ace Landry maintained order among them. He ruled with an iron hand, and none of his bully-boys ever found the nerve to go up against him. Landry's calculated cruelty and rattlesnake instincts caused his men to fear him, and the outlaw preferred it that way.

"You can turn your back on a man who's afraid of you," he was fond of saying, "an' even if that sum'bitch is holdin' a horse pistol, he won't dare plug ya, for fear of what you'll do to him if he don't kill you. You rule his mind.

"But in the same situation, a man who says he respects you would just as soon blow you away as look at you, if he felt that you'd rubbed him wrong. He'd kill you out of hurt pride. A proud man can be fickle, an' tetchy, but a man you make afraid stays afraid."

One particular winter's night, Ace Landry was feeling especially well. He'd had a three-day winning streak at the poker table, and had been drinking heavily to celebrate his good fortune. A flush of desire singed his skin as he stared at the Mexican girl by the faro table.

Landry swept a bottle of bourbon off the bar and sauntered over to the faro table. Then, grinning broadly as he passed, a cigar clenched between his teeth, he nodded to the Mexican. After that he went upstairs, to his room in Cliff Hagen's emporium. And right behind him, waggling her behind saucily for the benefit of the men at the bottom of the stairs and smiling a hot smile of anticipation, came the woman known as Pacquita.

Ace Landry was breathing heavily as he began to undress the Mexican beauty. She was nearly as tall as he, with long, raven hair and dark eyes. Her skin was a rich, olive color, firm and smooth to the touch. Her breasts were full, with dark aureolas and taut nipples. She moaned as Landry ran his hand over the swell of her belly, down into the jet-black shock of hair below.

He felt the warmth of her pouting nether lips, and then her interior wetness. He cupped her breast with his other hand. Pacquita squirmed in his arms as Ace Landry kissed her neck and caressed her womanhood.

"Oh, Ace," she moaned, looking up at him through heavy-lidded eyes. "I wait so long for you to take me up here."

Landry looked down at the open-mouthed, wet-lipped Pacquita and smiled a straight razor smile.

"I going to work hard to please you," she whispered into Landry's ear as she began to unbutton his shirt. "I going to make love to you all night, like you never been love before."

A moment later, they were both undressed. Pacquita pushed Landry down onto the bed. She stood above him, smiling hotly as she caressed her beautiful body, exciting herself before his eyes, and inflaming the outlaw thereby as much as herself.

When she stopped touching her body the raven-haired beauty was wide-eyed and gasping, shivering from head to toe and barely able to contain herself. She leaned over Ace Landry and kissed him, thrusting her tongue into his mouth. And as she did this, her hand ran down over his hairy chest and belly, to his hard and standing sex.

She stroked him with her hot hand, all the while licking his face and neck like a she-cougar washing its young. Next, Pacquita leaned over and thrust her full, firm breasts against Landry's chest. She bore him down to the bed, wriggling over him and placing her hand in the space between their groins. Then, as she drew back to smile at him lasciviously, he felt her fingers encircle his throbbing rod and guide him into her warm, wet sex.

He took a deep breath as she moved over him, sliding up and down, taking him progressively deeper within her. Landry was about to say something when she sat up and began to ride him with all the ardor of a mare in heat.

In and out, up and down, side to side and circling around: her lips churned and her belly quivered as Pacquita called the stroke and ground herself down upon the groin of Ace Landry. And in a short while, the outlaw was puffing like a locomotive as he fought to contain the geyser of pleasure that welled up irresistibly inside of him.

Seeing this, Pacquita began to move even more fiercely, determined to rip his pleasure from him in a gut-wrenching spasm, determined to please Ace Landry. At the same time, the desperado arched his back and thrust himself even more deeply between her gleaming, sweat-streaked thighs. Then, unable to contain himself any longer, he came with a death rattle gasp.

When he was still, Pacquita stopped bucking and sank down onto Ace Landry's chest with a sigh. The outlaw lay still as a corpse, eyes closed and his breathing shallow, his face turned to the wall. They lay there in silence for a long time.

Finally, when Ace Landry opened his eyes, Pacquita snuggled closer to him. "*Querido*," she murmured lovingly. "*Mi amor*."

"Sit up," he told her gently.

Not understanding what he wanted, Pacquita obeyed her lover all the same.

Landry squirmed under her until he felt his flaccid member slide out of her dripping sheath. Then he raised himself up on his elbows.

"Don't you know that's where the man's supposed to ride?" he whispered through clenched teeth, smiling at her grimly. "The man should always be on top. Understand?"

Saying this, he backhanded her across the face, knocking Pacquita off the bed. She uttered a shrill cry as she hit the floor. Raising her hand to her mouth, she stared at the outlaw with hurt, accusing eyes.

When she took her hand away from her mouth, Ace Landry saw a trickle of blood running down over her chin. Then he smiled at her warmly.

If good things are said to come in little packages, then Davy Watson was prepared to believe that misfortune arrived in Conestoga wagons. Not only had the winter been severe, delaying his setting things to right at the farm, but less than two weeks into spring the barn had caught fire.

It had been a sudden and unexplained blaze, which Davy attributed to spontaneous combustion in a hay stack. He had seen it in time to save all the animals in the barn, but the damage to the structure itself had been extensive.

The folks from the neighboring farms, already deeply moved by the untimely death of John Jacob Watson, rallied to the aid of his son. They came from near and far, donating their skills and labor on Sundays and after their own chores. Within six weeks' time, the Watson barn had been rebuilt. Davy was constantly moved by the great love and respect in which the neighbors held his father's memory.

The worst was yet to come, however. Less than two days before Davy and Soaring Hawk were ready to ride out in search of Ace Landry and his desperadoes, his mother took sick. A diptheria epidemic had spread across the country, and Annabel Watson contracted the disease as she nursed its victims.

For several weeks, she hovered between life and death. Coming out of her room one afternoon, Doc Kincaid informed Davy, Amy and Lucius Erasmus that medicine had done all it could; now was the time for prayer.

The prospect of losing a second parent frightened the Watson children. During all the weeks wherein Annabel Watson fought for her life, at least one of her offspring was always by her side. The fever broke one morning in late May, and Davy led his siblings in a prayer of thanksgiving to Almighty God.

He had no wish to upset his mother, and therefore resolved to postpone his departure until her convalescence had been completed. There would be time enough to get Ace Landry, he told himself. Men like that could always be traced; if not by the law, then by their own kind.

So Davy contained his furious impatience as spring ripened into summer, and he managed to visit Hawkins Fork once or twice a week, where Deanna waited for him. But he never let the flame of his desire for revenge die out; he kept it alive, smouldering like a bed of coals, ready to be fanned into a conflagration at a moment's notice. He vowed that he would not rest until he had taken the life of Ace Landry.

Soaring Hawk, who understood the virtue of patience, consoled his blood brother and told him that he had already alerted the Pawnee tribes to the west; if Ace Landry were still in Kansas, his people would know of it. And even if he were not, they would have some idea of where the outlaw had been headed.

"Oh, we'll find him, all right," Davy said in a cold, low voice. "You can damn well bet on that."

Finally, two weeks after the Fourth of July, they rode out. Annabel Watson had recovered her health, and now had two trusty hands to help her with the work of the farm. Davy had done his duty by his family and was now ready to set out on his manhunt, ready to ride after the man he hated more than anyone or anything in the whole, wide world.

He vowed that only one of them would ever ride back alive—either he or Ace Landry: there would be no compromise, no half-way measures. Davy Watson was out for blood.

Chapter 5

So they rode west at last, across Pottawatomie Creek, the Republican and Salmon Rivers, into towns like Tipton, Natoma, Wakeeney and Grainfield; through Riley, Lincoln, Ellis and Trego Counties, heading west for revenge, in search of Ace Landry and his desperadoes.

Finally, in late August, they met their first Indians. The blood brothers were out on the sweeping plains of western Kansas, when Soaring Hawk suddenly reined-in his mount and told Davy to do the same.

As he did, Davy saw that the Pawnee was squinting into the distance before them. Taking his cue from Soaring Hawk, Davy did the same, shading his eyes with his hand as he peered into the shimmering air of the August prairie. There before him, no bigger than ants on the far end of a dining room table, were six figures.

"Injuns?" he asked Soaring Hawk, unable to make out any details of the riders' appearance.

The Pawnee nodded.

"Friendly or otherwise?" Davy followed up, leaning forward in his saddle with a creak of leather as he unloosened his rifle in its boot.

"Too far to say," Soaring Hawk replied. "But we know soon enough."

"I don't like the look on your face, Soaring Hawk," Davy muttered as he saw the Indian frown. Nor did he like the potential odds: they were outnumbered three-to-one.

"Kaw," Soaring Hawk told him, tersely naming the oncoming riders.

Davy groaned as his blood brother hefted his rifle, a breech-loading Sharps carbine, of the sort used—when chambered for the heaviest calibers—by the buffalo hunters. This formidable single shot rifle had become famous when the Kansas aid committee, headed by the abolitionist Reverend Henry Ward Beecher had shipped a number of them to John Brown. The Sharps rifles were then used by Brown during his historic attack on the U.S. Arsenal at Harper's Ferry. After that the weapons caught the popular imagination, and became known as "Beecher's Bibles."

Davy's own rifle was an M1860 Henry, a lever-action repeating rifle. The Henry had been made famous by the marksmen of the Kentucky Volunteers in the Civil War, and was renowned for its superior firepower. At the time of the Henry's first issuance, the factory boasted that "a resolute man, on horseback, armed with one of these rifles, positively cannot be captured." As the six Kaws drew nearer, Davy prayed that this boast would not be in vain.

"Hell, they must still be a mile off," Davy objected as Soaring Hawk shouldered his heavy-calibered weapon and took aim at the distant horsemen. In addition to that, he thought that the Pawnee was aiming too high. The Sharps fired with a resounding crack, and Soaring Hawk sat back on his horse while the slow-moving slug traveled through the air in a wide, leisurely arc.

About two seconds later, by Davy's calculation, one of the Kaws in the center of the six-man line pitched headfirst off his horse.

"Hot damn!" Davy cried out, as Soaring Hawk let loose a bloodcurdling shriek of jubilation. "You got that sum'bitch!" Davy yelled. "I don't believe it, but you got 'im!"

Suddenly, the Kaws reined in their horses. The two riders who had flanked Soaring Hawk's distant victim dismounted and went to the aid of their fallen comrade. After having slung him across the back of his own pony, the two Indians mounted once more.

Then, just as Soaring Hawk and Davy were about to

put spurs to their horses and charge full-tilt at the hereditary enemies of the Pawnees, the Kaws did something that totally surprised the white man. They reined in their horses and wheeled around, bearing the wounded man away as they retreated.

"Hoo-wee! Hoo-wee!" Davy Watson whooped, rearing his horse as he watched the Kaws depart. "You done scared 'em shitless, brother!" he roared. "That's what you done!"

Soaring Hawk sheathed his rifle and smiled modestly, secretly sharing his blood brother's relief at seeing the backs of the Kaws.

They made camp early that night, and spent the evening regaling each other with tall tales from two cultures. Early the next morning they set out across the plains once more, always heading in a westerly direction.

"Buffalo not so far off," Soaring Hawk told Davy that evening, as he studied the trail before him that was studded with buffalo chips. "Maybe one day. Maybe two."

"These is almost too fresh to burn," Davy remarked after having dismounted to collect a pile of buffalo chips for the night's campfire. He thrilled at the prospect of seeing one of the great buffalo herds that were rapidly being whittled down by men like Bill Tilghman, Tom Nixon and Bill Cody.

That night, as he began to doze by the campfire, Davy saw his Indian companion sit up and reach for his rifle.

"What's up?" he muttered softly, sitting up himself and groping for his Henry. The Pawnee silenced him with a gesture, and listened to the sounds of the night with deep concentration.

All Davy could make out over the intermittent crackling of the fire was the hooting of an owl.

"It's jus' some ol' owl," he whispered.

"Not owl," Soaring Hawk replied as he got to his feet. "Indian."

Davy bit his lip and rose to a standing position as

61

quietly as he was able. Soaring Hawk motioned him away from the light of the campfire, and then signaled for him to move behind a clump of nearby scrub bushes.

All of a sudden, the Indian wheeled around and went into a crouch as an owl hooted behind him, taking aim with his Sharps as he did. Behind him, Davy squinted along the sight line of the Indian's gun barrel, over to a cluster of boulders to the east of the camp.

He watched Soaring Hawk listen intently as the creature that he had taken for an owl hooted again, and was immediately answered by one of its own kind. Davy gulped when he realized that the answering cry came from the brush to the west of the camp, meaning that they were surrounded.

Just then, his eyes bulged in his head as Davy watched Soaring Hawk cup his hands over his mouth and begin to hoot like an owl. The Pawnee did this several times.

A moment later, a series of owl hoots came back from both the east and the west. Then Soaring Hawk cupped his hands over his mouth once more and gave a call that Davy was unable to identify. A moment later, two identical calls sounded in the darkness.

"It is well," Soaring Hawk told him, standing up and lowering his rifle. "Pawnee."

Davy sighed as he got to his feet. A moment later he saw a number of figures appear in the moonlight, approaching the camp from both the east and the west. Soaring Hawk went to greet the Indians.

The young white man hunkered down on his haunches as he waited patiently for the Indians to finish greeting each other. After several minutes of animated conversation, the Pawnees grew silent as Soaring Hawk led them over to meet Davy Watson.

From the look of the visitors, as they tramped through the prairie grass, Davy could tell that the four men behind Soaring Hawk were presently employed as scouts for the U.S. Cavalry.

He knew all about Captain Frank North, the former trading store clerk who had recruited a band of Pawnee scouts for Major General Samuel R. Curtis' 1864 campaign against the Sioux and Cheyenne. The man had such success leading the Pawnees that he did the same thing in Major General Patrick Connor's Power River Campaign of the following year. And for the last three years, Captain North could be found in the field with two to four companies of Pawnee scouts.

The Pawnees greatly admired and respected Captain North, who taught them to hold their own against the usually dominant Cheyenne and Sioux. It was obvious to Davy, after seeing the insignia on their dark blue shirts, that these Indians were serving under Frank North.

"These are brave warriors of my tribe," Soaring Hawk told Davy, indicating the scouts with a wave of his hand. "Spotted Eagle, Bobtail Horse, Red-Armed Panther, and Wolf Voice."

Davy held up his open hand, palm-forward, as he had been shown earlier. "Pleased to meet you gentlemen," he said, nodding at the scouts, who merely stared at him impassively.

"This one is my blood-brother, who fought to save my honor," Soaring Hawk told the other Indians. "I have named him Hammer Hand." Then he went on to describe Davy's Sunday punch in the saloon.

"And now," Soaring Hawk concluded, "we ride to find and kill our common enemy. Make him welcome."

Hearing this, the scouts broke out into broad grins. "You are good man," one of them told him. "You are Pawnee, now. Welcome."

Davy blushed as the four Pawnees all shook his hand, one after another. "Nice to make your acquaintance," he mumbled as the scouts pumped his hand.

"In the morning," Soaring Hawk later informed his white brother, "we will all ride to the camp of my people."

"Did you tell these here fellas how you done shot that Kaw from near a mile off?" Davy asked.

The Indian nodded, smiling proudly as he rolled himself up in his blanket. "And tomorrow, they will tell everyone in camp. I will be a big man."

"For my money, you are already," Davy said as he lowered his head onto the saddle that served as his pillow.

The Pawnee hunting camp had a peaceful look when seen from a distance, what with its twenty-odd tepees gleaming warmly in the sunlight, the smoke from their fires spiraling up in thin white wisps to the blue, cloudless sky. But once within the precincts of the camp, Davy found himself immersed in the sounds of Indian life.

Babies squalled and metal pots clanked against pans or stones; dogs yapped and barked, horses whinnied; women called out to each other, and men called out to Soaring Hawk and the four scouts in deeper voices. Two old men began to sing and shuffle back and forth on bent legs as a third beat a small tom-tom. And over it all rang the laughter of young girls and boys, rising into the air like birds taking flight.

The party was received by the chief, and ate their dinner outdoors, in the bosom of the tribe. Soaring Hawk's exploit had made him a big man indeed, and his Sharps rifle was passed from hand to hand around an admiring circle of warriors.

After dinner the chief, old Running Buffalo, made a speech to the assembled tribe, wherein he told them of Davy's intervention in Soaring Hawk's behalf. By the grave expressions on the faces of the tribe, Davy could see that they were much impressed by the fact that a white man had stood up for an Indian. And then the tribe offered their collective condolences on the death of his father. Davy was deeply moved by the dignity and quiet humanity of the Indians.

Later that night there was a celebration. It turned out to be a threefold celebration, Davy's deed being one of the causes, along with the return of the scouts and Soaring Hawk's wondrous rifle shot and subsequent dispatch of the Kaw braves.

First the warriors danced, beginning with measured tread and solemn cadences, and ending up with flying feet and cries of fierce exultation.

After the men came the young women of the Pawnee tribe, dancing with light, graceful steps, pantomiming the daily tasks of the women and expressing each woman's longing for a brave and worthy husband.

As the young women danced by, Davy became aware that one of them kept staring at him. She was tall and lissome; her eyes were like a doe's, and she was as graceful as a squirrel. The color of her skin was a deep bronze and her hair was long, black and lustrous. Her nose was aquiline and her lips were full. And Davy realized, as he flushed and returned her stare, that she was a handsome woman.

"Why's she keep ganderin' me that-a-way?" he whispered to Soaring Hawk over the sound made by the little brass bells on the ankles of the young women.

"She think you are much brave warrior," the Indian told him. "Bright Water not like many brave. She is daughter of Dull Knife, brother of Running Buffalo. It is great honor that she show her favor to you."

Davy watched the breasts of the beautiful Indian move freely beneath her shirt as she danced. "What's her name?" he asked.

"Bright Water."

"What d'you mean, show her favor to me?"

"She wish to take you to her tent tonight."

"But we're ridin' out early tomorrow."

"We have time."

"Oh."

"Do you want Bright Water's favor?" Soaring Hawk asked.

"But she's the chief's niece," Davy protested. "I can't mess around with her."

"It is great honor for her to have such a brave warrior to share her blanket."

"Gol-dang it, I ain't no brave warrior!"

The Indian permitted himself a slight smile of amusement. "You are. I told her all about the bravery of Hammer Hand."

"Oh, Lord," Davy groaned. "You're still impressed by that lucky punch."

Soaring Hawk shook his head. "That not luck. That take strength and skill. With one blow you make Ugly Face let me go and fall to the ground like wounded buffalo. And you were brave enough to face that bad man, Landry, as well as other big men."

"Yeah, but—" Davy protested once more.

"You are brave warrior," Soaring Hawk told him matter-of-factly. "It is great honor for Bright Water to have you share her blanket."

"You really mean it?" Davy whispered, impressed by this reassurance, and suddenly becoming aroused as his eyes met those of Bright Water.

"Pawnee never lies," Soaring Hawk told him solemnly, looking away as he fought to suppress a smile.

"Well, now that you put it that-a-way," said Davy, "I s'pose I should have some respect for this here honor she's a-wantin' to bestow on me. Ain't that right?"

Soaring Hawk nodded, still unable to face Davy. "It is well," he snickered, covering his mouth with his hand. "I will sleep in tepee of Pretty Nose, who is friend of Bright Water."

Davy looked impressed. "Well, 'when in Rome,' as Uncle Ethan always says," he murmured, turning back to the circle of dancers. And this time, when his eyes met those of the handsome, dancing young woman, Davy Watson was smiling warmly.

An hour later, escorted by Soaring Hawk, Davy took his blanket roll and saddle over to the tepee where Bright Water lived with her family.

"You *sure* this is all right?" he whispered nervously as they neared the tepee.

Soaring Hawk nodded. "You are Pawnee by blood,

now." He lifted the tent flap that hung over the entrance. "Go in."

"But what about her family?" Davy squawked, thinking of his mother despite himself.

"Go in, Hammer Hand," said the Indian, grinning in the darkness.

Davy nodded resignedly. "G'night, my brother," he whispered as he drew aside the flap at the entrance to the tepee.

"Sleep long and well, my brother," the Pawnee replied, chuckling softly as he went off to the tepee of Pretty Nose.

There was a small fire burning inside when Davy entered, and he saw Bright Water standing behind it, waiting for him.

"Uh, howdy, ma'am," he said awkwardly, doffing his hat. He looked around. "Where's your folks, Miss Bright Water?" he asked.

She smiled at him from across the fire and shook her head.

"Judas Priest," Davy muttered to himself. "She don't speak a lick of English—an I ain't got enough Pawnee to carry on a civilized conversation. But at least her folks is gone for the night."

He looked up at the handsome young woman, and saw that she watched his every move with ardent, admiring eyes. She murmured something to him, and then lowered her eyes modestly.

Davy was fairly new at the game, but he recognized her play: she wanted him to come over to her.

"Well, it ain't polite to keep a lady waitin'," Davy said as he smiled and began to walk around the campfire.

When he reached her, Bright Water smiled nervously and murmured something just before she glanced at him, only to lower her eyes again an instant later. Davy didn't catch most of what she'd said, but he did make out the Pawnee words for his warrior's name, Hammer Hand. She must be welcoming him.

"Thank you, Bright Water," he whispered, reaching out to caress her high-planed cheek. He repeated her name in Pawnee, causing her to look up at him and smile shyly. Then, as she repeated his Pawnee name, he said it in English, followed by his real name.

"Day-vee Was-son," she repeated, struggling with the pronunciation. "Davee Wasson."

He nodded, drawing her close to him. As their bodies came together, he hugged her tightly. Bright Water's arms went around him, her hands caressing his back as she murmured Pawnee words in his ear.

Leaning over slightly, he began to nuzzle her long, graceful neck. It pleased her, he could tell that by the way she began to murmur excitedly. Bright Water ran her long fingers through his blond hair, which had earlier fascinated all the Pawnee girls, Davy recalled. He drew her even closer to him, aroused by the scent of musk on her.

They don't go in much for lip-kissin', he reminded himself as he reached up and gently explored one of the young woman's firm, high breasts. Her nipple grew long and hard between his fingers. Davy's other hand traveled down her trim back, to caress her full hips and firm buttocks.

The Pawnee girl pressed her groin against Davy's, making contact with his throbbing rod, rubbing herself against him vigorously.

"Hot damn," Davy croaked, gently thrusting her back. "We'd do a lot better if we was to get out of our clothes." He let go of her and began to unbuckle his gunbelt.

She looked on, her face alight with eager anticipation as the young white man proceeded to undress, his pale skin almost glowing in the light of the fire.

"Lemme give you a hand there, honey," he whispered hoarsely, stepping over to her side once he was naked. As he did, Davy loosed her beaded shawl, which slid to the ground with a series of light, chinking sounds.

Once again he kissed her neck, as he undid her flannel shirt. And when the shirt was open, he thrust his hand inside it and ran it over her sleek body, until he enclosed the warm swell of her breast in his hand. Bright Water gave a little gasp as she felt Davy's gentle hand on her breast.

Next, he took the shirt off, and followed it with her buckskin skirt. And after that, he removed the cloth drawers that she wore over her private parts. Her bronze body gleamed in the firelight, and the deep black of her tresses was echoed by the small black patch between her quivering thighs.

Bright Water murmured something in Pawnee while she looked away and took Davy's erect sex in her hands, cupping and stroking it gently.

"Oh, I like that," Davy whispered. His skin broke out in goose pimples as the young Pawnee woman ran her hands over his pulsating erection and raked his thighs lightly with her fingernails.

Reaching down with his right hand, he stroked the fine, black hair on her mound of Venus, and gently cupped her warm sex in his hand. When he removed his fingers, they were slick with the juices of her arousal.

Bright Water's blanket was behind her, and Davy took her down upon it. He sighed contentedly as his mouth went to her breast; he began to knead her long nipple between his lips and tongue. The young woman began to gasp loudly. As he did this, Davy put his hand on her warm, musky pussy once more and stroked with gentle persistence.

Soon her juices were flowing copiously, he discovered as he penetrated her with his fingers, and this excited him immensely. She began to buck under his hands and utter sounds that reminded him of birds and animals, cooing and yipping in his ear. Her lithe, bronze body glistened with sweat, and Bright Water looked up at Davy with glazed eyes and motioned for him to come inside her.

This he did willingly, gliding into her sopping sheath

easily. Once inside her, Davy was amazed at how snugly she gripped him. He began moving with long, slow strokes, and could hear a slurping sound each time he went toward her. Breathlessly, she urged him to quicken his stroke, bucking against him urgently.

Bright Water's trim belly heaved as she thrust her groin up at Davy's. Her legs locked around the small of his back, and she clung to him like moss to the underside of a stone.

Faster he stroked, and faster—until his soul shot out of his body along with his jism. The Pawnee gasped and cried out; Davy sighed like a man expiring. And when she was still beneath him, he sank down upon her musky, sweat-streaked body, resting his head on her breast. And in that instant, he wished that he could spend the rest of his days frozen in that sweet aftermath of pleasure.

A little while later, Davy opened his eyes as he felt Bright Water stroking his thigh. Not understanding her words, he listened to the tone of her voice, which told him that it was going to be a long and memorable night . . . .

The following morning, the chief invited Davy and Soaring Hawk into his tent. Seated beside Running Buffalo were his son, Plenty Bird, and the tribe's medicine man, White Wolf.

After a breakfast of berries, goat's milk and buffalo meat, the chief took out his long pipe and stuffed its bowl with a mixture of tobacco and sweet-smelling dried grass. He lit it and took several puffs, inhaling each one. Then he passed it to Davy, making a solemn pronouncement as he did.

"What's he sayin'?" Davy asked Soaring Hawk once he had stopped coughing.

"Running Buffalo says he will work medicine for you," his blood brother explained. "Medicine that will help you to find and kill the man who insulted me and killed your father."

"That's just the kind of medicine I'm lookin' for,"

70

Davy muttered as he nodded to the old chief and handed the pipe to Soaring Hawk.

They smoked in silence, Soaring Hawk passing the pipe to Plenty Bird, who passed it in turn to White Wolf. Then, having put down the pipe, the medicine man brought forth a buffalo skull that had been hollowed out. As he began to mumble an incantation, he reached into the canvas bag at his side once more and came out with a small straw figure. While White Wolf deposited the figure inside the buffalo skull, on a small bed of dried grass, Davy saw that it had no limbs.

"What's that thing for?" he whispered to Soaring Hawk.

"That is medicine Pawnee use to kill enemy."

"So I should think of that there li'l mannikin as Ace Landry, huh?"

"It is so."

Davy nodded his head. "I surely do hope so," he said as the pipe came around once more.

The medicine man sang loudly, in a quavering, mournful voice. He reached down into the bag and brought forth a handful of black powder, which he sprinkled liberally over the little limbless doll bedded within the buffalo skull. Following that, White Wolf leaned over and took a burning brand from the fire. Keening the same words over and over, the medicine man thrust the brand into the buffalo skull.

Pwooof! A bright flash leapt from the skull, followed by a great cloud of smoke. And when it cleared, Davy saw that the straw figure had been consumed.

The medicine man sat back and nodded his head, smiling complacently at Davy and Soaring Hawk. After the smoke had cleared, he lectured the two at length in Pawnee, with Running Buffalo and Plenty Bird grunting periodic affirmations in the manner of congregants at a tent meeting.

"White Wolf says," Davy's blood brother summarized, "that his medicine heap good, heap strong. It will work until our enemy is dead. It will work on the

71

desert, on the plains, and in the mountains. Landry will not escape."

Davy bowed to his Indian hosts. When he straightened up, he turned around and reached for his saddle. Opening his left saddlebag, he drew out a number of objects and handed them to the Pawnee. Soaring Hawk had often spoken of this visit to his people over the long winter, and Davy had been sure to bring along an ample supply of gifts for the Indians.

To Chief Running Buffalo, Davy gave a belt of hand-tooled leather and a big brass buckle. Obviously pleased with his gift, the old man nodded and commented upon the high quality of the leather. White Wolf received a Missouri Meerschaum pipe, upon whose bowl the head of an Indian had been carved. And to Plenty Bird, Davy presented a shiny new Bowie Knife.

Each man was extremely pleased with his gift, and Soaring Hawk's chest swelled with pride at the good manners and generosity of his blood brother. From that time on, he knew, both he and Davy Watson would be respected men among his people.

Davy had one more gift to bestow among the Pawnees. He found Bright Water washing her family's laundry in the stream that ran behind their tepee. She rose when he came into view and approached him with downcast eye, although there was a slight, shy smile on her lips. He took her hand and squeezed it.

Bright Water looked up and smiled at him, taking his breath away with the sight of her dark, doe's eyes and dazzling white teeth. She squeezed his hand in reply and then drew close to him, looking down at the ground by their feet.

"I, uh, brung ya a little farewell present," Davy whispered, flushing as he suddenly became aware that all of the women at the stream were watching them intently. He reached into his pocket and came up with a necklace of amber beads.

Bright Water spoke in hushed Pawnee as she took the necklace in her hands and put it on. The other women looked on admiringly, making occasional comments among themselves.

"That's for you, honey," he whispered just before he leaned forward and kissed her lips. "Thanks for all your lovin' last night." After he had kissed her, Bright Water raised her fingers to her lips and gave him a look of surprise.

When Davy stepped back, ready to take his leave of her, that look changed to one of sadness. "Goo'bye, Davee Wasson," she murmured, a sad little smile on her lips and a wistful look in her dark, Indian eyes.

Just before Davy and Soaring Hawk were ready to leave the Pawnee camp, Plenty Bird escorted them to a spot where the braves had gathered. The warriors were all in high spirits, laughing and joking among themselves as the three approached.

"Well, so long, fellas," Davy said heartily, thrusting out his hand. "It was a great pleasure to make your acquaintance."

One by one, the braves approached, gripped the proffered hand, and shook it vigorously. The scouts were last, having gathered behind the others.

"Well, uh, Wolf Voice, Spotted Eagle, Bobtail Horse, uh, Red-Armed Panther," Davy said, not knowing which was which, as he shook one hand after the other.

The last scout approached. Davy smiled and reached out for the hand that the Pawnee proffered from under the striped blanket that he wore.

"*Yi-i-iii*!" Davy yelled, horrified as the scout's hand came off the man's arm. He stepped back, thunderstruck, staring wide-eyed at the cold, severed hand gripped in his own. And as he looked up from the grisly thing, the Pawnee scouts burst into raucous laughter.

Soaring Hawk was laughing too, as he explained the presence of the hand to Davy. "Early this morning, they come upon two Cheyenne. That Cheyenne hand."

"Odd sense of humor you folks have," Davy observed, grimacing as he handed the ghastly trophy back to its owner.

Chapter 6

"I still say that's a helluva thing to make a joke about," grumbled Davy, still buffaloed by the grisly humor of the Pawnee scouts. He and Soaring Hawk had ridden for almost two days, and were at the westernmost part of the state of Kansas.

They had gone through Oakley, Monument, Wallace, and Sharon Springs as their search for Ace Landry continued. Mount Sunflower, the highest point in all Kansas, loomed before them as the two men headed northwest, into Colorado.

Although Landry's trail was relatively cold by now, rumors had filtered into Kansas of the outlaw's doings in the Colorado Territory. Word had spread of how the desperado had fallen out with his host and former partner, Cliff Hagen, in the town of Greeley. It appeared that Hagen had caught Landry cheating at cards, and ordered him out of his sanctuary. But Hagen had wound up on the losing end of that play, as the outlaw had turned on his benefactor and shot him dead. That was the latest news of Ace Landry that his stalkers had obtained, although Davy and Soaring Hawk never learned Cliff Hagen's name.

Crossing the north fork of the Smoky Hill River, the blood brothers entered Colorado, Soaring Hawk on his Indian pony and Davy on the gray mustang that had been John Jacob Watson's pride and joy.

Colorado's eastern prairie was part of the arid lands of the Great Plains: while an occasional butte or sandhill broke the brown and parched landscape, the country remained as level as the tidal flat it had been ages ago.

74

Less than four hours' ride from the Smoky Hill River, Davy and Soaring Hawk heard a rumbling in the distance. Looking back they were dismayed by the size of the cloud of dust they saw, a cloud that betokened a great force of advancing horsemen.

"Judas Priest!" Davy exclaimed, shielding his eyes as he squinted into the sun and attempted to distinguish the ant-like figures within the ever-growing cloud of dust. "I wonder who they are—friend or foe?"

Once again, it was the keen-eyed Pawnee who was the first to identify a band of distant riders.

"White men," Soaring Hawk told Davy, after a long, hard look at the source of their concern. "Forty, mebbe fifty. War party. Many rifles."

"What d'you suppose they're after?" Davy asked, tilting back his hat in order to scratch his forehead.

"Mebbe rustler, mebbe Indian," Soaring Hawk replied. "Not soldiers. But that many white men with rifle mean heap trouble for somebody."

Davy grew suddenly anxious as the drumming thunder of horses' hooves grew louder. "Say, you don't suppose these fellas is out after Ace Landry, do ya?" He felt threatened somehow, as if the riders might deprive him of the chance to gun the outlaw down.

"Good for us, if they are," the Pawnee answered calmly. "We jus' join up with white men. Then, when we find Landry, we all shoot 'im down like dog—like General Culpepper shoot down heap many Sioux with Gatling gun."

"Well," Davy admitted grudgingly, "I guess it wouldn't hurt none to have a passel of guns on our side when we go up against the Landry Gang."

As the band of horsemen drew near, Davy saw that two of the men at their head wore the blue uniform of the United States Army. But the rest were all civilians, most of them bearing the unmistakable look of the individualist that stamped so many of the intrepid men who roamed the open West.

They were armed to the teeth, he realized when he saw

the number of Colts holstered at their sides and the many rifles they held, seven-shot Spencer Repeaters most prominent among them. And to a man, the riders looked as if they could hold their own in a fight.

Studying the horsemen as they drew near, Davy noted the composition of the band. Quite a few of them appeared to be plainsmen, men who would be well versed in the ways of Indians, friendly or hostile; by their dress he saw that there were trappers, buffalo hunters and traders among them, as well as government scouts. And mixed in with these hard-bitten Westerners were men who had the look of having come from elsewhere in the recent past. He reckoned that they were both young drifters and veterans of the great war between the Union and the Confederacy.

"Well, let's mosey on up an' talk to that gentleman in the blue suit," Davy told Soaring Hawk, flicking his reins and beginning to walk his horse in the direction of the oncoming riders, who were themselves reining in their mounts by this time.

The officer at the head of the armed band wore the insignia of a major in the cavalry, and a gunbelt over the yellow sash that was tied around his waist. He was a youngish man—hardly thirty, Davy guessed—whose tawny hair had its complement in a full and drooping mustache of the same color. Although presently holding the rank of major, his men called him "Colonel,' which Davy later found out had been the man's brevet rank in the Union Army during the last years of the Civil War.

"Greetings to you, sir," Davy said amiably, nodding his head as Soaring Hawk held up both hands in the palm-outward peace sign. He noticed how the expressions on the faces of the plainsmen softened when they recognized his blood brother as a friendly Pawnee. "Might I be so forward as to inquire to the purpose of your party?" he went on.

The young officer had a fair complexion and an unlined face; he stared back at the two men out of warm brown eyes. "I am Major George A. Forsyth, at your service, gentlemen," he told them in a firm, clear voice. "I have recruited this punitive expedition," he continued, indicating the party behind him with a sweeping gesture, "on the express order of General Philip H. Sheridan, Commanding Officer of the Department of the Missouri. We are out to take reprisal for a recent series of murderous Indian raids."

Davy listened open-mouthed, and Soaring Hawk watched Major Forsyth through narrowed eyes.

"Last month," the officer went on, "a combined force of Cheyenne, Arapaho and Sioux from the north began a series of incursions in violation of the Medicine Lodge Treaty of 1867. This war party raided along the Saline and Solomon Rivers, as well as the Smoky Hill road, killing more than one hundred settlers."

"Sweet Jesus," Davy murmured.

"The marauders have seized perhaps twelve women and children, and burnt to the ground a score of ranches."

"We jus' come across the Smoky Hill River," Davy said in a small voice.

"Then you were fortunate indeed in not having encountered the raiders," Major Forsyth told him.

"Yessir," Davy replied, gulping as he thought of fire and scalping knives.

"Since there is a scarcity of military personnel in this particular area," Forsyth said, "I have recruited these gentlemen—all of them civilian volunteers—to track down and engage the hostiles, with the ultimate object of heading them back into Indian territory."

The major appeared to be—and was, in fact—an upright and decent man; but what he had neglected to tell Davy was the reason that the Indians had taken to the warpath.

In October 1867, several thousand Kiowas, Cheyennes, Comanches and Arapahoes had met in conference with a United States peace commission at Medicine Lodge Creek, in the south of Kansas. As a result of the treaty that came out of the meeting, the

Indians had been herded into reservations to the south of the state. But although they were to reside in that area, the tribes were allowed to roam north if their hunting required such an action.

The Congress of the United States, however, acting with its usual lethargy and lack of concern where the needs of Indians were at issue, did not ratify the treaty until July of the following year. This indifference to the requirements of the various tribes deprived them of vitally needed food, clothing and other supplies, which were the prime inducements to sign the treaty in the first place. Therefore, feeling neglected and cheated by the white men, and with a certain amount of right on their side, the Indians went on the warpath.

"Since there are great numbers of hostiles roaming this region," Major Forsyth told Davy and Soaring Hawk, "I submit that it is in your interest to ride with my group."

"That's right kind of you, sir," Davy replied. "My friend 'n me is headin' up Greeley way."

"I, too, am traveling in that general direction for a time," the major told them. "And you are most welcome to join us."

Davy turned to Soaring Hawk. The Indian nodded. "Thank you, sir," he told Forsyth.

Feeling secure in such formidable company, Davy rode northwest with Major Forsyth's band. In the days that followed, he made the acquaintance of a number of scouts, buffalo hunters and Civil War veterans, foremost among them such old hands as John Hurst, Eli Zigler, Louis McLoughlin, and Sigman Schlesinger.

But the man he liked best was a scout by the name of Jack Poole. The man was a burly, broad-shouldered fellow with brown hair, square jaw and a nose like a baked potato. Poole had a wry wit, and his comments upon a great variety of subjects were constantly amusing. Paradoxically, the scout was both easy-going and opinionated at the same time.

He had taken to Davy and Soaring Hawk on the first

day into the Colorado Territory, and had made a place for them at the campfire that night. Shunning cigarettes as bad for a man's health, the paradoxical Jack was never without a quid of "chawin' tobaccy" in his mouth.

"If the good Lord had intended for man to smoke," Jack commented that night, sending a jet of tobacco juice into the campfire, "he'd have created him with a chimney comin' out of his skull."

"Whyn't you finish off these beans, Jack?" Davy said, offering the scout the remainder of his supper.

"God Almighty," Poole exclaimed, snatching the plate out of Davy's hand, "if I eat any more beans tonight, I'll be fartin' like a Missouri mule. As it is, this bunch passin' wind at night makes more noise than all the musketry at the Battle of Gettysburg."

"Then why you eat more bean?" asked Soaring Hawk.

"Well, why the hell not?" Jack Poole asked in return. "Couple o' more pops ain't gonna make a dent in the general fusillade."

Davy grinned, fascinated by the scout's extravagant speech.

"An' besides," Poole added, "I like beans, even if they don't like me."

"You got to take the snappers out of 'em before you cook 'em, Jack," Eli Zigler advised.

Once he had finished the beans, Poole got to his feet and went to urinate in a clump of scrub brush fifteen feet beyond the campfire.

"Watch out it don't git bit by a rattlesnake, Jack," Eli Zigler called out.

"That don't bother me none," Poole replied casually, looking over his shoulder as he unbuttoned his fly. "Damn thing's half rattlesnake already."

The men gathered around the fire began to laugh and hoot, all of them showing a keep appreciation for the scout's wit. In the hard life of the frontier, a sense of humor was a highly prized attribute.

"Most hombres have to gun down their opponents," observed John Hurst from across the campfire. "But ol' Jack, he jus' buries 'em in bullshit."

The men laughed heartily at this.

"Now, John," Poole replied, buttoning himself up as he returned to the fire, "you ain't no slouch at bullshittin', your own self. Why, I reckon you done spread more manure in your day than most of the sodbusters in Kansas."

"*Haw! Haw! Haw!*" the men brayed.

"You tell 'im, Jack boy!" a man named Culver called out. "Hoo-wee!"

"Well," Jack Poole told the company, after discharging his mouthful of tobacco into the campfire and washing his mouth out with the last of his strong, bitter coffee, "I'm goin' to unroll my blanket an' get me some shut-eye, before you-all get to blastin' away at each other in the dark."

"Watch out fer Injuns, boy!" an old trapper called out.

"Ain't no Injuns 'bout to attack this camp," Poole told them as he walked over to his blanket roll. "Leastways, not if they're downwind of it."

Reaching out involuntarily for his rifle, Davy Watson hoped that the scout was right.

On the morning of September 16, 1868, Major Forsyth's expedition picked up the trail of the hostiles, which they had lost the day before due to the Indians' habit of scattering when pursued. It ran up the bank of the Republican River, and they followed it for the entire day.

The next morning, the trail revealed something new: the marks of lodge poles. This indicated that the Indians were now traveling with their families. And that undoubtedly meant that they were trailing the main force of the hostiles.

"Well, Mr. Poole," Major Forsyth called out as the

burly scout rode back to rejoin the armed band, "what is your estimate of the situation?"

Jack Poole paused to splatter the petals of a prairie flower with a gob of tobacco juice. "Way I see it, Colonel," he replied, using the scouts' habitual form of address to their chief, "there's bound to be more Injuns up ahead than a mangy dog's got fleas. I make out from them pole marks that there must be four, mebbe five hundred lodges—an' that means near 'bout a full thousand braves."

"Jee-ho-sa-phat!" exclaimed Eli Zigler, reining in his horse by Major Forsyth's side. The commander of the expedition now wore a grave and thoughtful expression on his face.

"I'm fer hightailin' it outta here," volunteered a trader named Big Jim Moreland.

"Them's heavy odds," Jack Poole admitted.

"Mebbe we oughtta head back to Kansas," another man said hopefully.

"Gentlemen," the major said suddenly, breaking his pensive silence, "it is my opinion that the hostiles are concentrating in order to attempt a mass raid on the settlements in the vicinity."

A number of the plainsmen nodded in agreement with this.

"Therefore it is my intention," Forsyth went on, "to interpose our expedition between the hostiles and the settlements in the hope of crippling their force or turning them away from their objective. At the very least, we will be buying time for the settlers, who will hopefully be alerted by our exertions in their behalf.'

A thousand to fifty: 20 to 1! thought Davy, reaching down to pat the butt of his Henry. He didn't much care for the odds.

"Well," Jack Poole sighed, "that's what we're gettin' paid for, I reckon." Murmurs of assent rose from the band of horsemen behind him.

George A. Forsyth smiled warmly at his colorful followers. "My thanks for your confidence, gentlemen," he told them. Then he turned to Davy and Soaring Hawk. "I would be curious to know whether or not you gentlemen intend to continue on in our company," the courteous major said.

"What say?" Davy asked his Pawnee blood brother.

"Better to meet enemy with fifty-two rifles than with two," the Indian replied with characteristic conciseness.

"Yup. That's my thinkin'," Davy agreed. He turned back to Major Forsyth. "Seems like good sense to us if we continue to partake of your hospitality, sir," he told the leader of the expedition. But as he looked around, the band of fifty men no longer seemed so formidable as it had earlier.

"Then we are agreed," Forsyth said, nodding contentedly. "Keep your weapons at the ready gentlemen," he called out to his riders. "I have the feeling that you will soon be called upon to use them."

Jack Poole drew his horse up beside Davy's. "Pretty soon, we'll be doin' more than jus' puffin' farts, lad," he observed. "Ever seen action against the plains Injuns?"

"Nope," Davy replied, wiping his clammy palms on his trousers.

"They come a-sweepin' down at ya," Poole informed him, "whoopin' an' hollerin' like the devil with a toothache. They's painted up like bogies from a nightmare, an' the feathers trailin' from their war bonnets an' lances gives 'em the look of a flock of avengin' angels."

Davy looked impressed.

"They can ride better with no hands than most white men can with two," Jack Poole continued. "An' they's a damn sight more accurate on horseback with their rifle fire than anyone this side of Bill Cody."

"Looks like it should prove interestin'," Davy said gamely.

"It should, indeed," the scout agreed, sending a gob of tobacco juice whizzing between the ears of his mount. "How 'bout you, Soaring Hawk?" he asked.

"Ever mixed it up with the Cheyenne, Sioux or Arapaho?"

The Pawnee pointed to the scalps that hung from his belt. "Two Cheyenne," was his terse reply.

"Cheyenne, huh?" Poole reflected, looking at the belt with great interest. "What's them others?"

"Osage and Kaw."

Jack Poole nodded. "You gonna be all right, that's for sure," he told Soaring Hawk. "Jus' stick with ol' Davy here."

"I reckon I can take care of myself," Davy protested, feeling his ears burn.

"I wasn't sayin' nothin' with regard to your courage, David," Poole told him softly. "It's jus' a question of savvy. You ain't never skirmished with the plains Injuns before. That's all. See what I mean?"

"I s'pose I do," Davy mumbled, embarrassed now by his unwarranted outburst.

"I'm sure you're a man what can hold his own in a fight," Jack Poole told him warmly.

"Davy good with fist," Soaring Hawk informed the scout. "Hit like hammer."

"Well, if I'm lucky," Poole reflected, "I'll get to see him unload it on somebody, one of these days. Not on yours truly, of course." He winked at Soaring Hawk.

Major Forsyth's band followed the trail of the hostiles all day, and when they camped late that afternoon, they were at Arikaree Creek, which they mistook for the south fork of the Republican River. The riders dismounted at a spot where the grazing was good, on the north side of the dry creek, opposite a small island. And it was fortunate that they did, because the entire force of hostile Indians lay in wait for them less than a mile ahead, intending to ambush their pursuers.

At the very same time that Davy, Soaring Hawk and their companions were heading toward a deadly encounter with the massed Cheyenne, Arapaho and

Sioux, a smaller band of horsemen rode west to avoid pursuit.

Once again, Ace Landry had gunned down a man with many friends. And once again, as in the shooting of John Jacob Watson, this meant that a large posse had been formed, and dispatched after the killer and his pack of desperadoes.

The six outlaws made their way across the northern part of Colorado, crossing the Mummy Range, riding down to Michigan Creek and heading south there to skirt the Continental Divide. Through Rabbit Ears Pass the band made its way down to the Yampa River, which they followed through Steamboat Springs, Hayden, Craig, and Maybell.

At that point, guided by a member of the gang who had formerly prospected in western Colorado and adjoining Utah, the outlaws rode to the northwest. Over Vermillion Creek and into Vermillion Bluffs they rode, on their way to the Utah Territory, where they stopped at last at Dutch John, a town to the north of the Uinta Mountains.

Feeling certain that the Greeley posse would not extend its pursuit into the Utah Territory, Ace Landry was finally able to slacken his pace. The outlaw had been much moved by the beauty of the land as he rode into northeastern Utah, having been partial to the high country ever since he was a boy.

It seemed to Landry that he was crossing the wall of mountains as a pilgrim; he had the conviction that on the other side of that high and wild barrier there would be a place where he would find rest and peace.

Even murderers have their beautiful and cherished dreams, and even a man as mean and hardened as Ace Landry was no exception. Perhaps the territory was invested with the spirit of the Mormons, who had come there in the 1840s, led by the resolute Brigham Young. But whatever it was, the leader of the dreaded Landry Gang felt as happy and excited as a ten-year-old boy waking up on a sunny summer's morning and suddenly realizing that it was his birthday.

> "Down in the valley, valley so low,
> Hang your head over,
> Hear the wind blow . . . ."

Ace Landry sang the mournful song in a husky bass voice, smiling sweetly as he rode at the head of his bully-boys.

Behind him, the ruffians exchanged looks of disbelief and amazement. If anyone had been taking bets at that moment, it would have been odds-on that the desperadoes would have been less surprised if they had suddenly come upon a rattlesnake singing a lovesong to a jackrabbit.

> "Write me a letter;
> Send it by mail;
> And back it in care of
> The Barbourville jail . . . ."

Chapter 7

"Did I ever tell you the story about Little Bat Tessier?" Jack Poole asked Davy as they picketed their unsaddled horses out to graze near the bank of Arikaree Creek.

The new camp site was alive with activity, as the company tended to their mounts, made fires and began to rustle up their suppers. Major Forsyth, uneasy at the thought of being so close to the huge Indian force, had doubled the guard, so that a goodly number of keen-eyed plainsmen and Civil War veterans hefted their rifles and paced back and forth at the perimeter of the camp.

"Little who?" Davy said, turning to face the burly scout and look directly into his mischievous eyes.

"Fella name of Baptiste Tessier." Poole pronounced the name Ba-teeste, as the French would. "He was a mountain man, a trapper who been to places on this continent that most white men ain't even dreamed of. He was a short, stocky l'il fella, an' they called him Little Bat."

"Have the sentries all been posted, Mr. Zigler?" George A. Forsyth called out from the far end of the camp.

"Yes sir, Colonel!" Eli Zigler called out from a spot on the camp's perimeter not far from Davy and Jack Poole. "They's doubled an' ready for b'ar!"

"Thank you, Mr. Zigler."

"Well, as I was sayin'," resumed Jack Poole, "this here Little Bat Tessier was just about the toughest little devil you ever did see. Once't in a barroom brawl in Saint Louis, he bit the ear off'n some big dockwalloper who had the misfortune to pick a fight with him."

The scout paused for effect.

"Don't ever fool with them mountain men, lad," Poole went on. "'Cause there ain't nobody tougher. Why, if you was to lock one of 'em in a back room with a grizzly bear, I'd lay you three-to-one that when you moseyed back an hour later an' looked inside that room, you'd find the grizzly dead an' the mountain man wearin' a fur coat."

"Now, *that's* tough," Davy muttered.

"You best believe it," Jack Poole told him solemnly. "Now, in case you're wonderin', there's a point to my story. Y'see, Little Bat prob'ly come up against more unfriendly Injuns than any white man you ever met—an' so I figger there's somethin' we could learn from him. 'Specially since we'll prob'ly be engagin' in a bit of disputation with the red men our own selves—an' right soon."

As the scout paused, Davy nodded, not yet comprehending what point Poole was trying to make.

"Well, to continue, I got this first-hand from an ol' buddy of Little Bat's, fella name of Charlie Bindhammer, who used to pal around with him in the days when he spent some time in the lowlands 'round Nebraska an' along the Missouri."

Davy fidgeted impatiently.

"Y'see, Little Bat was courtin' a gal name of Evelyn Fairwether, whose daddy was a trader at a post somewhere along the River Platte. That's a whole story in itself." The scout chuckled at the recollection. "Little Bat was the tobacco chawinest man east of the Great Divide. Folks 'spected that he even chawed in his sleep."

Davy scratched himself and swayed back and forth restlessly.

"But," Poole continued, "Little Bat was so took with Evelyn Fairwether that out of consideration for her sensibilities, he always took a dog along with him—a shaggy, snuff-colored dog—jus' in case there weren't no spitoons around."

"Jack, I'm beginnin' to wonder if there really *is* a

point to this story," Davy said, looking up as he fretted with the rawhide thongs that were tied to his belt.

"Well, sure there's a point," the scout answered, his storyteller's pride stung by Davy's impatience. "Now, Little Bat's suit was rejected by Evelyn Fairwether, y'see. So, bein' down in the mouth an' all broken-hearted, he rode out in search of adventure. D'you follow me?"

"Lord, I guess so," Davy moaned.

"So what Little Bat up and done, in view of bein' rejected by the light of his life, was to join the local militia in their campaign against the Indians thereabouts —I forget which tribe—who was runnin' wild."

"Uh-huh," Davy grunted, resigning himself to the fact that Jack Poole was not about to be hurried.

"Besides bein' a inveterate tobacco chawer," Poole resumed, "that l'il devil would eat anything when he was hungry. I figger that, one time or another, Little Bat done took him a bite out of just about every creature that slithered around, walked upon, or flew over God's green earth."

He paused to scratch the stubble on his chin, making a sound like a brush fire crackling in the distance. "He tol' Charlie Bindhammer that alligators was edible, an' that buzzard was not. Now here's the point, lad. So listen up good."

"Yessir," Davy mumbled, rousing himself to complete attention.

"After one of them skirmishes, the militiamen come upon a bunch of wild hogs that had been feedin' upon the dead Injuns. And ol' Baptiste Tessier, he was hungry. So he shoots him one of the hogs, butchers the thing, an' proceeds to eat him some pigmeat."

"Cripes," Davy said, an expression of distaste on his face.

"Well, Little Bat's got hisself plunked down on a rock, gobblin' up this here big pork chop, when who walks by but the commandin' officer of the militia company. An' when he takes a gander at what Little

Bat is eatin', why that ol' officer is like to puke.''

Once again, Poole paused for dramatic effect. "So," he resumed, "ol' Little Bat looks up at the man, his chin all drippin' with hog fat, an' smiles.

" 'By Gar, Cull-o-nell,' " Poole said, mimicking the trapper's French accent, " 'I know why you not eat de pork. Because he eat Indian. But I jus' as soon eat Indian if he well fried.' "

Jack Poole fell silent, a wry smile on his lips.

"You finished, Jack?" Davy asked after a long silence.

"Yup."

"Well, what's the point?"

"Think about it."

Another silence ensued.

"I thought about it," Davy told the scout. "But I still don't get the point."

"The point is," Poole said as he turned and began to walk away, "that how you feel about Injuns is just a matter of taste."

"Huh?" Davy grunted, flabbergasted by his friend's reply. Then, shaking his head as he reflected upon what Poole had just said, Davy made his way back to the campfire. Suddenly he saw a light rise in the air, to the south of the camp. A few moments later, another went up, immediately followed by several more, all coming from different directions.

"What the Sam Hill was that?" Davy asked Jack Poole when he reached the campfire.

"Flamin' arrows," the scout told him. "That means we're gonna get a heap more for breakfast than we done had for supper."

It was not yet morning when Davy Watson awoke. The sun had not come up, and the sky was lit only by the faint, pale glow that precedes the dawn. A sudden whoop had caused Davy to open his eyes. But he groggily passed it off as the sound of a wild goose, and rolled over in his blanket.

But the sounds of rifle fire, followed by more whoops, persuaded Davy that what he had heard was not geese, but Indians.

Jack Poole was already on his feet, working the lever of his Winchester "yellow boy" carbine, as he put a bullet in its chamber. "I reckon we got us some company," he informed Davy, who looked past him and saw flashes in the gloom. The guards were firing—the Indians had attacked!

"Saddle up, gentlemen! Saddle up!" Major Forsyth called out behind Davy.

Jack Poole and Davy were among the first to saddle their horses, and Forsythe dispatched them, along with several other men, to drive off a number of Indians who had hidden themselves behind some rocks on a hill to the north of the camp.

Whooping and yelling as they put spurs to their mounts, the riders charged up the hill, sending a volley of hot lead ahead of them. The Indians scattered and scrambled down over the far side of the hill, leaving a number of dead and wounded behind.

Holstering his Walker Colt, Davy felt exalted, all fear gone now, as he watched the Indians flee. But when he looked past them, his jaw dropped.

There in the distance, coming up hard to the relief of their scouts, was the main body of hostile Indians. And there were hundreds and hundreds of them, Davy realized as he watched in awe—all mounted on horses, all fiercely painted and in war costume, feathers flying in the breeze, whooping like fiends from hell as they brandished their lances and rifles.

"Jesus God!" Jack Poole muttered at Davy's side. "Did you ever see so many Injuns?"

"Cheyenne, Sioux, Arapaho," Soaring Hawk commented, reining in beside them. "Heap many."

"Heap too many for my taste," sniffed Jack Poole. "How many do ya reckon, Sigman?" he asked the scout beside him.

"Plumb near a thousand, Jack," Sigman Schlesinger told him. "More'n I ever seed in one place."

"To the island!" Major Forsyth cried out, realizing that his expeditionary force was no match for the Indian horde on open ground. "To the island!"

The nineteen-year-old scout, Jack Stillwell, rode by. "To the island, boys," he urged in passing.

"Sounds like a good idee," Jack Donovan, another scout, agreed. He split off and led a group of men over onto the island's east end, while young Jack Stillwell and his party occupied the west end.

The island was no more than 40 feet wide and 150 feet long. Barely a vantage point, it rose a mere three feet above the sandy bank of Arikaree Creek, whose dry channel extended roughly 70 feet on both sides of the island. Tall blue stem grass and small cottonwood trees covered the west end of the island; at the east end, a slope facing north—the direction from which the Indians were coming—offered protection for the men who had ridden there.

Davy had barely tethered his horse and dug a small pit in the sand, as he had seen a number of Forsyth's men do, when an Indian was upon him. Screaming wildly, a fierce, painted warrior rode straight for him! He would surely have been trampled, but for the fact that the Indian's pony shied at the last moment.

Opening his eyes as horse and rider streaked past, Davy raised his Walker Colt and spun around. Steadying the big pistol with his left hand, he fired off a shot. An instant later, he whooped with delight as he watched the warrior pitch off his horse. But there was no time for self-congratulation; the thunder of hooves in back of him caused Davy to wheel around and level his weapon, readying himself for further onslaughts.

Bewildered by a concentrated firepower that seemed to come from all over the island, and seeing a great number of men and ponies go down, the Indians broke off their charge.

Soaring Hawk had been with the horses as the first

wave of hostiles broke over the island, and now he made his way back to Davy's side. Crawling through the high grass, the Pawnee was startled by a sudden rustling up ahead. He paused, squinted into the blades before him, and lay flat and still on the ground, thrusting his rifle into the blue stem grass. An instant later, his Sharps discharged with a thunderous roar. Ten feet ahead, a dead Sioux rolled over onto his back. When the Pawnee reached the corpse, he swore as he hacked off the little that remained of his enemy's scalp.

"Get those horses out of there!" someone roared as the Indians charged again. Jack Poole and Eli Zigler began to snake their way over to a small patch of brush near the spot where the horses were tied. The animals reared and whinnied in terror as the bullets of the onrushing hostiles tore into them.

Several horses had fallen by the time the scouts were able to untie the rest and lead them over the slope.

"You can come with me," George A. Forsyth called out, pointing at Eli Zigler, once the latter had led the horses over the slope. "I want you around that side with me."

"Yessir, Colonel," Zigler replied.

A volley of shots rang out and lead whizzed through the air, buzzing around George A. Forsyth like a swarm of angry hornets.

Jack Poole heard the unmistakable sound of a slug punching its way into human flesh. "I'm shot," Major Forsyth called out, reaching down to put a hand on his thigh. Then the scout saw him fall to the ground and roll over several times. "I am shot again," George Forsyth cried, struggling vainly to rise. Firing back heavily at the Indians, Poole and Zigler scrambled out from their respective positions and dragged the major to the relative safety of the island's south-central section.

"Helluva way to start the day," Eli Zigler grumbled as he hunkered down to reload his sixshooter. "Not even a cup of coffee for breakfast."

"Well, from the looks of it, Eli," Jack Poole opined

as he, too, reloaded, "the onliest thing we're gonna get for lunch is a couple of pounds of lead."

Major George A. Forsyth had been wounded both in the left calf and the right thigh during the second charge; and later in the day he was wounded yet again, as a bullet grazed his forehead. He was not aware of it at the time, but the slug had fractured his skull. But the major's wounds never prevented that worthy man from exercising diligent command of his expedition and maintaining his continual concern for the welfare of his men.

Despite the fact that the situation looked hopeless, what with Forsyth's band trapped and surrounded on the small island in Arikaree Creek by the better part of a thousand hostile Sioux, Arapaho and Cheyenne, the issue had not yet been decided.

On the first day the Indians had made a number of fierce and determined charges, but the concentrated firepower of the white men effectively prevented them from taking the island. Yet the Indians seemed intent upon wiping out the little band, and so they ringed the island and the far bank of the creek, where a number of Forsyth's men remained, and kept sniping away at the expedition for the rest of the day.

"I'm shot in the arm, and I would like to have someone tie this handkerchief around it to stop the blood," someone called out on the morning of the second day of the encounter.

Davy rolled over in the sand pit he presently occupied with Soaring Hawk, Jack Poole and Eli Zigler. "Who's that?" he asked.

"Henry Tucker, I expect," Zigler told him, raising his head cautiously to peer out of the pit, while arrows and bullets whizzed overhead.

"Can you see him, Eli?" asked Jack Poole.

"Yup. An' someone's goin' to help him—John Haley, it is. He's almost—damn! Haley just got shot, an' he's rollin' away from him."

Lying next to Davy, Soaring Hawk raised his head.

An instant after he did, a flying arrow clipped off one of the feathers in his hair.

"Goddamn!" the Pawnee swore, ducking his head back down. "Never see so many arrow. Like flight of wild goose when head south."

"Henry," Eli Zigler called out suddenly. "Henry, can you hear me? It's Eli."

"I hear you, Eli."

"Well, we're sorta pinned down, Henry. But if you can find your way over here, I'll tie that handkerchief for you."

For a moment it seemed that the barrage of bullets and arrows increased in its intensity. And then, at the height of the storm, Henry Tucker dove over the lip of the sand pit and landed right on top of Jack Poole.

"Ooof!" grunted Poole, throwing Tucker off his back and rolling over to train his pistol on the new arrival.

"Easy, Jack—easy!" cautioned Eli Zigler. "It's only Henry."

"Now, don't shoot, Jack," Henry Tucker said as he lay on his back, grimacing as he held a dirty handkerchief to the bloody wound in his upper left arm.

"Judas Priest, Henry," Jack Poole growled. "I ain't no doormat."

Eli Zigler scurried over to Tucker's side and began to bind his wound.

"Ouch!" Tucker called out suddenly, jerking away from Zigler and causing him to lose his grip on the handkerchief. Tucker looked down at his right thigh.

"There's an arrow in my leg, Eli," he calmly informed his fellow-scout.

Zigler nodded. "So there is, Henry. It brushed my side on the way in." He studied the wound for a moment. "Head's gone clean through."

"Pull it out, Eli."

"All right, Henry."

Davy looked on as Zigler tugged at the arrow in Tucker's thigh, causing the latter to scream in pain.

"Hold on, Eli," Tucker grunted. "That's too much for me."

Zigler nodded. "Lemme try somethin' else, Henry," he said. Then, as the others looked on while Henry Tucker took a deep breath and closed his eyes, Eli Zigler grabbed hold of the arrow just above its head. With the heel of his other hand he hit the base of the feathered end of the shaft, tugging on the front end as he did. Tucker screamed and rolled over as the arrow came out of his thigh.

Before Zigler had finished bandaging up Tucker's original wound, another figure dove into the already crowded sand pit.

"Don't shoot! Don't shoot!" it yelled. "It's me—Jack Donovan!"

They welcomed the scout, who then proceeded to inform them about the heavy fighting that had gone on by the creek's north bank.

"And so," Donovan concluded, "after we done stopped their last charge, them divils got the idea to start creepin' up on us. But Louis Farley, who bruk his leg an' was stranded on the north bank, got a gander of 'em as they come along a sand ridge. Well, sir—"

"Shit!" Jack Poole roared, as a bullet tore his hat off his head. "Somebody grab that Stetson!" he ordered. "I paid good money for that hat."

Wincing, Davy lunged at the passing hat.

"Good lad!" Poole cried out as Davy returned the battered Stetson. "Go on, Jack," he told Donovan.

"Well, as I was sayin' " Donovan resumed, "them Injuns come along that sand ridge in full sight of Louis Farley, who up an' plugged two of 'em in the head. That kinda made the rest of 'em think twice't about that little bit of business."

"That's good to hear," Eli Zigler said.

"You boys got anything to eat?" Donovan asked. "My belly's been makin' more noise than the Injuns."

Jack Poole shot him a sour look. "There's plenty of horsemeat around. An' you can chaw on a bullet to keep from gettin' thirsty."

"Ain't much of a menu," Donovan grumbled.

"Well, there's always Injun," Poole told him, meriting a dirty look from Soaring Hawk.

There was general consternation in the Indian camp. Roman Nose, the war chief of the Cheyenne, had not yet entered into the fray, and the hostiles were greatly upset by this. In fact, they attributed their general lack of success to the fact of the chief's reluctance to do battle, and were as anxious to get Roman Nose back on the warpath as were the Greeks to persuade Achilles to don his armor again during the siege of Troy.

Of all the warriors in the confederation that had Major Forsyth's band currently under attack, Roman Nose was by far the most fearless in battle. And the reason for his extraordinary bravery was that the chief was protected by a great medicine. But this potent magic could be neutralized, so Roman Nose believed, by the act of touching his cooked food with iron.

Just before the battle at Beecher Island (as the encounter became known, due to the presence in Forsyth's band of Lt. Frederick H. Beecher, nephew of Henry Ward Beecher), Roman Nose had eaten dinner in the lodge of a Sioux chieftain. To his horror, he later discovered that the Sioux's squaw had served his food with an iron fork. Consequently, Roman Nose had become convinced that his magic was gone, and that he would surely die if he entered the battle.

It was not until noon of the second day that the war chief was persuaded to take his place at the head of the Indian host. And as the sun was high overhead, Roman Nose led a massed charge of nearly 800 braves on horseback. The hostiles were greatly encouraged by the presence of the heretofore invincible chief, and all were confident that the Forsyth expedition would be wiped out to the last man.

"Jee-hosaphat!" Henry Tucker exclaimed to his

comrades in the sand pit, as he watched the Indians forming their ranks upstream. "This is gonna be one helluva charge!"

Davy Watson nodded. "Looks like they mean business this time," he said gamely, turning to Soaring Hawk, who nodded back at him.

"They got ol' Roman Nose with 'em," Jack Poole observed.

"Who's he?" Davy asked.

"Craziest sum'bitch in these parts," Henry Tucker informed him. "They say bullets can't touch him."

"Well, now," Poole told his fellow-scout, hefting his "yellow boy" Winchester as he did, "I aim to disprove that, right soon."

"You got your chance, Jack," Eli Zigler piped up. "'Cause here they come!"

Davy leveled his Henry and squinted along its barrel as Roman Nose led the Indians toward the island. Whooping and screaming like a legion of demons pouring out of the gates of hell, they made their way down the dry creek bed.

"Hold your fire until they are almost upon us!" Major Forsyth called out. "Make every shot count!"

"I couldn't agree more," Jack Poole muttered as he drew a bead on Roman Nose.

By the time they reached the upper end of the island, the hostiles were met by a withering hail of gunfire, one that was as telling as it was concentrated. The scouts were all crack shots, and they poured their fire into the ranks of the oncoming Cheyenne, Sioux and Arapaho with deadly accuracy.

No sooner had his horse put hoof to the sand of Beecher's Island than the war chief pitched backwards out of his saddle, mortally wounded. A great cry of dismay went up from the ranks of the Indians as Roman Nose was dragged off.

"*I got 'im! I got 'im!*" Davy screamed ecstatically.

"The hell you did," Jack Poole informed him. "It was my shot what unhorsed him."

"Bull-dickey!" growled Henry Tucker. "'Twas my bullet cut him down."

"No, you're all full of beans," corrected Jack Donovan. "I am the man who plugged ol' Roman Nose."

Soaring Hawk nudged Davy. "Now, every man here shoot Roman Nose." He shook his head. "Just like white man."

"Well, I hope to God you fellas will quit squabblin' soon," Eli Zigler told them between rifle shots, "an' help me out with them other 800 Injuns."

The hostiles kept coming after Roman Nose had fallen, but the killing fire of the defenders was just too much for them. And when the charge had finally been broken off, the Indians left scores of their dead on the sands. Dry Arikaree Creek ran red with their blood.

"Well," Jack Poole said, lowering his rifle, "I'm goin' to make me a horsemeat sandwich. Anyone comin' with me? How 'bout you, Davy?"

Davy Watson made a face. "I'll think I'll pass on that one, Jack."

"Those Injuns don't show any sign of leavin' yet," Poole remarked as he surveyed the area beyond the north bank. "So I reckon you'll develop a taste for horsemeat, soon enough."

And he was right. The Indians had no intention of riding off. Although the charge had seen the shooting of Roman Nose and been a disaster, the hostiles continued to surround the island and ring it with arrows and rifle fire.

That night, Davy Watson had his first taste of horsemeat. Hunger had changed his mind; and the meat, roasted over a small fire, was far tastier than he'd expected.

Major Forsyth, feverish now and in great discomfort due to his several wounds, dispatched two volunteers—trapper Pierre Trudeau and young Jack Stillwell—to take a dispatch to Fort Wallace. Covering their feet with rags and disguising themselves as Indians, taking enough roast horsemeat to last them four days, the two left the camp under cover of darkness.

On their way through the Indian lines, Stillwell and Trudeau found themselves face to face with a rattlesnake. The scouts were in a wallow when the rattler emerged from a buffalo skull and began to slither down toward them. To fire their guns—or even utter a sound—would bring the nearby Cheyennes down upon them.

Young Jack Stillwell looked from the advancing rattler to Pierre Trudeau. The older man returned his glance as he chewed reflectively on a quid of tobacco. Suddenly Trudeau's eyes lit up, and he gave Stillwell a "watch this one" nod.

Jack Stillwell watched anxiously as the rattler continued to advance, almost within striking range now. Masticating furiously, Trudeau watched the snake carefully. The mountain man's cheeks began to puff out, and a trickle of brown juice ran down his chin.

Closer and closer the rattlesnake came; faster and faster chewed Trudeau. Then, as the snake reared to strike, Trudeau let fly with an enormous gob of tobacco juice.

Splat! The jet of tobacco juice broke over the side of the rattler's head, going right into its eye. Suddenly, with a sharp hiss, the snake retreated and promptly quit the wallow.

Pierre Trudeau wiped his chin and winked at young Jack Stillwell. A second later, the two were on their way to Fort Wallace.

By the third day of the siege, Davy Watson had become a connoisseur of horsemeat. Still sharing a sand pit with Soaring Hawk and Jack Poole, he was in the process of roasting a piece of meat when a volley of shots came from behind a tree stump on the south channel of the creek.

"Oh, shit," murmured Jack Poole. "The bastard's got me."

Dropping the horsemeat into the fire, Davy picked up

his Walker Colt and sighted on the tree stump, after which he rose beyond the rim of the pit and fired off three shots in rapid succession.

"Goddamn! Got him!" exulted Soaring Hawk, clapping his blood brother on the shoulder. Then they went over to Jack Poole, whose scalp had been creased by one of the sniper's bullets.

"You all right, Jack?" Davy asked.

"I suppose," the burly scout growled. "But my hat is shot to shit."

"It's only a hat."

"Only a hat, my butt!" Poole grumbled. "I plunked down twenty bucks for that Stetson!"

"Better to lose hat than head," Soaring Hawk commented stoically.

At the end of the second day, the Indians charged once more.

"Hold your fire till they get close," George A. Forsyth ordered. "But don't let them ride over us."

Although furious, the charge was successfully repelled. That had done it: the second day was the most crucial, and the Indians, skirmishers that they were, never again attacked with comparable intensity.

On the third morning, a smaller part of hostiles charged the island, but were again thrown back. Once more Major Forsyth dispatched two scouts to Fort Wallace. This time Jack Donovan went, accompanied by a man named A. J. Pliley.

"Godspeed, gentlemen," George Forsyth whispered as the scouts left under cover of darkness.

The major was in great pain, and by the fourth day of the siege, he took a straight razor and cut out the slug that had lodged in his thigh.

"Gol-lee," said Davy Watson, wincing as he cut a piece of meat from the carcass of a long dead horse. "This stuff is sure beginnin' to stink."

"Smells worse'n Eli's feet," Jack Poole added.

"Look at the bright side, fellas," Eli Zigler, an optimist at heart, told them. "Every day it sits there, it gets tenderer.''

By the fifth day, the horsemeat was even more tender —and more fragrant.

"Pee-yuu!" Davy said, wrinkling up his face and pinching his nostrils together. "Either we move that damn carcass, or I'm findin' me another place to squat.''

But his complaint was premature: they were forced to rely on the decaying horsemeat until the night of the eighth day.

"Boys, we've got to the end of our rope, now," Major Forsyth told his assembled men. He pointed to the low hills beyond the creek. "Over there the Indian wolves are waiting for us. But we needn't all be sacrificed . . . . To stay here means you know what.'' He nodded tiredly.

"Now, the man who can go, must leave us to what's coming. I feel sure now that you can get through together, somehow, for the tribes are scattering. It is only the remnant left over there to burn us out at last. There is no reason why you should stay here and die. Make your dash for escape tonight.''

"It's no use asking us, Colonel," one of the scouts rumbled. "We have fought together, and by heaven, we'll die together.''

"That's right, Colonel," Sigman Schlesinger seconded.

"For damn sure," Eli Zigler agreed.

"I wasn't goin' nowhere in particular, Colonel," Jack Poole told George Forsyth.

The major looked at Davy and Soaring Hawk. "And what of you gentlemen?" he asked.

"We couldn't see our way to runnin' out on all these here friends of our'n, Colonel," Davy told Forsyth, using his brevet rank just as the scouts had done. Soaring Hawk nodded his assent.

"It is a great honor to be with such men as yourselves," George Forsyth whispered, deeply moved by the vote of confidence.

On the ninth day, while Davy Watson squatted before his fire, holding his nose as he began to roast a piece of horsemeat, a shot rang out in the air.

Men rushed back to the camp from all points of the compass, readying their weapons and digging in for another onslaught.

"There is something moving out there," Eli Zigler announced, lowering the rifle that had fired the warning shot.

"I think it is the relief," Major Forsyth told him. "But get the men all in, and we will be ready for anything."

"By God," Eli Zigler exclaimed a few moments later, as a man rode toward the camp at breakneck speed, "that's my old pal, Jack Peate!"

Davy cheered as loudly as any man present when the rider presented himself to Major Forsyth, and he cheered even louder at the news that the man had brought. Jack Donovan was on his way back—accompanied by Colonel Carpenter and a company of the 10th U.S. Cavalry!

Stillwell and Trudeau had gotten through, it turned out, to Fort Wallace, whose commanding officer promptly contacted Colonel Carpenter at Cheyenne Wells and dispatched him to Forsyth's aid. Donovan and Pliley, who both reached Fort Wallace later, accidentally made contact with Carpenter's cavalry while leading a band of scouts back to the relief of the band at Arikaree Creek.

"Hot damn, we're saved!" Davy yelled, thwacking Soaring Hawk on the back. "We're saved!"

"Hey, Eli," Jack Poole said dryly, "you can have the rest of my horsemeat."

But Zigler did not hear him. He was too busy whirling Jack Peate around in the air.

Colonel Carpenter rode into camp holding a handkerchief to his nose as he surveyed the dead and wounded who lay amidst the carcasses of the horses. After exchanging salutes with Major Forsyth, the colonel lowered his handkerchief.

"What are your losses, Major?" he asked Forsyth.

"Five dead, and eighteen wounded, sir," George A. Forsyth replied, supported on both sides by Sigman Schlesinger and Eli Zigler.

"And the enemy's?"

"I estimate between two and three hundred, Colonel."

Colonel Carpenter looked down from his horse and smiled. "You have done well, Major Forsyth."

Davy nudged Soaring Hawk as they approached his favorite scout. "Shake them slugs outta your Stetson," he told Jack Poole. "We're movin' out."

"You ain't never tol' me where you two was headin'," the scout remarked.

"Me 'n Soaring Hawk is goin' over Greeley way, to look someone up."

"Well, well," Jack Poole said, smiling as he dusted off his battered black Stetson. "I jus' might mosey along with ya, since the Army's after them Injuns now. I know a great sportin' house in Greeley."

He winked at Davy. "It's run by a close pal of mine. Fella name of Cliff Hagen."

Chapter 8

Jack Poole was in the bathtub when Davy returned to the hotel room, soaping the breasts of a fleshy woman with curly black hair and a hearty laugh. A bottle of rye whiskey stood on the floor beside the tub, flanked by two half-empty glasses. The scout wore a contented smile as he puffed on a cigar, which he only smoked on special occasions, and continued to lather the impressive mammaries of his tubmate. The tub itself was filled with suds, and the reek of cheap perfume hung heavy in the air, competing with the reek of Poole's cheroot.

Once the 10th Cavalry had come to the rescue of Major Forsyth's embattled expedition, Jack Poole had asked for, and been granted, a leave of absence from his duties as a scout. Forsyth and his superior, Colonel Carpenter, had both become convinced that using civilian volunteers was not the most efficient way of dealing with hostile Indians; military operations would be required. So Jack was free to accompany Davy Watson and Soaring Hawk to Greeley, in the Colorado Territory.

Davy had not revealed the reason why he was going to Greeley, and Poole had not asked him about it; men tended to mind their own business in the West. But he and Soaring Hawk were glad to have the capable and entertaining scout as their companion. And as soon as they had entered Greeley, Poole took them straight to the Wheel of Fortune, the huge establishment that Cliff Hagen had built. There the scout made them plunk down their share of the money for a suite of rooms upstairs, and told them that he was heading for a hot bath and a thick beefsteak. After that, he promised his companions, he would look up his old pal.

"I'll, uh, come back later, Jack," Davy mumbled, averting his eyes from the amazing sight of the black-haired woman's stupendous bosom and turning to go.

"Hold on there, lad," Poole called out from the steaming tub. "I want you to meet my lady friend."

Clearing his throat, Davy turned toward the tub.

"This here's Frenchy," Poole announced, puffing away on his cheroot. "That there's my good friend, Mister Davy Watson."

"'Ow do you do, Meestair Watson," the woman purred.

"Ma'am," Davy said, blushing as he tipped his hat.

"Now, you go on into your room, lad. I done ordered dinner for you."

"Well, thanks, Jack," Davy said, impressed by his friend's consideration.

"An' I do hope you enjoy the dee-sert," the scout added mischievously.

When Davy entered the adjoining room and looked at the table in it, he was pleased to see a huge and steaming slab of beefsteak on a giant platter, smothered in onions and surrounded by fried potatoes. And he was even more pleased when he caught sight of what Jack Poole had referred to as "dee-sert."

Just behind the table, seated on the edge of a big brass bed, was a woman. The first thing Davy noticed about her was the fact that she was clothed only in the welcoming smile she wore upon her full, red lips. Her long hair was chestnut brown—reminding him of the darker shade of his Uncle Ethan's roan stallion—and her eyes were two shades darker. She was lean as a coon dog, and her breasts were twin cones that jutted saucily into the air. From between her trim thighs peeped a patch of dark brown hair that was as full and thick as the back of a hedgehog.

"My name is Marcy Jean Gebhardt," she cheerfully informed him. "Mr. Poole sent me to look after you."

"Right nice of you, ma'am," Davy mumbled while his ears burnt.

"I drew your bath," the lean, winsome brunette said, pointing to the tub at the far end of the room.

Blush as he might, Davy admitted to himself that he was not sorry to see this young woman. A moment later, he was soaking in a hot tub. Marcy Jean fed him with one hand and stroked his erect maleness with the other, as it jutted out of the water like a rock on a coastline. The beefsteak was washed down with hookers of rye, and less than a half hour later, Davy was stretched out on top of the big brass bed, enjoying his dessert.

Every nerve in his body was tingling as Marcy Jean's long, tapering fingers traveled the length and breadth of his body. From head to toe, from front to back, she stroked him, alternating a feather-light massage with long, grazing runs of her nails.

He lay on his stomach, sighing contentedly as the bright-eyed Marcy Jean played him like a pianoforte. Fingertips, nails, pressure from her palms: running down his back, circling his buttocks, delicately grazing his perineum and testicles. His body trembled with a delicious anticipation, and his penis was stiff as a gun barrel.

"Now, roll over," Marcy Jean Gebhardt ordered.

Davy did as he was bid, and closed his eyes as her deft, artful touch set the front of him to quivering.

"You just relax, Mr. Watson," she whispered. "For I'm about to do somethin' nice—somethin' that Frenchy taught me."

His body stiffened involuntarily as her expert fingers closed around his burning rod. Stroking, massaging, and lightly running her nails down the underside of it, Marcy Jean leaned over Davy's midsection, a look of intense concentration on her pretty face.

Already breathing heavily, Davy gasped as he felt her tongue on his cock, darting and nimble as a minnow beneath a sunken log. Licking, tripping, running and circling, her tongue was like a small animal, and its attentions inflamed his senses.

Finally, when she took him in her mouth, and her full

wet lips encircled the head of his cock, to gently pull and suck and tease, Davy lost control. Moaning and jerking spasmodically as Marcy Jean Gebhardt employed her oral artifice to its full extent, Davy Watson shot his wad, gave up the ghost, and died the little death that culminates the act of love.

"Damn!" Jack Poole exclaimed later, when Davy reentered his room. "From the sound of things in there, I thought you was done for."

Davy shook his head. "That l'il ol' gal was like to stop my heart, Jack," he told the scout, while the latter turned back to the wall mirror and continued to shave.

"Where's Soaring Hawk?" Davy asked.

"Over to the livery stable," Poole told him.

Davy knew that his Pawnee blood brother considered the white man's carousels beneath his dignity, and would have nothing to do with them.

"Well, every man to his own tastes, I always say," Jack Poole informed Davy philosophically.

But when they went downstairs, seeking Cliff Hagen, and the scout learned that his old range buddy had been gunned down, he lost his philosophical detachment.

"Who done it?" he asked angrily, causing the bartender who had delivered the news to step back from him involuntarily. "What dirty dog murdered Cliff Hagen?"

"Fella name of Ace Landry," was the bartender's reply.

Davy gasped. "Jack, that's the man who gunned down my paw—when he wasn't even wearin' a gun. That's the man me'n Soaring Hawk come to Greeley for to kill!"

"He ain't in Greeley no more," the bartender told them. "Posse done chased him clear across to the Utah Territory."

Jack Poole's face was livid. His eyes were hard as lead, and his jaw muscles stood out in ridges as they twitched. "Well, you jus' got you one more gun for the showdown," the scout told Davy Watson in a low, even voice.

The insignificant little town of Corinne, Utah had suddenly taken on the imposing and venal aspects of Babylon, as the Union Pacific Railroad laid its track there. Led by the Casement brothers, Dan and Jack, the railroad crews brought with them a swarm of attendant camp followers.

Gamblers and gunslingers, pimps and peddlers, teamsters and prostitutes all peopled the tent-city and shanty town that kept pace with the ingenious track-laying train devised by the Casement brothers. Hell on wheels was the name given to that assemblage by the men who worked on the Union Pacific. The Casement train and its supply system were so efficient that they had already set a record of laying one mile of track in a day, which was in the process of being pushed to two and three and even more, as the railroad raced to beat the Central Pacific to Promontory, Utah, where the golden spike would be driven into the ground, commemorating the completion of the 1,775 miles of track between Omaha and San Francisco. And now, this mighty operation and its men, this traveling Babylon, had come to Corinne.

A rail-bearing flatcar headed the train, preceded by grading crews who leveled the roadbed and dropped the ties onto it. The iron—a 500-700-pound rail—was pulled from the flatcar by Jack Casement's "iron men," whenever the track foreman gave the command, "Away she goes!"

Then, as the foreman barked "Down!" the rail was placed on the ties with great precision, waiting to be fastened in place by an oncoming crew of spikers and fasteners.

The flatcar was an almost self-sufficient unit, containing steel bars, cable, rope, switchstands, iron rods, and a complete blacksmith's shop in its rear section. Behind it were sleeping cars and eating cars; a kitchen, counting room and telegrapher's car, all in one; private cars, a general store, supply and water cars.

Jack Casement's crews were composed of mustered-out Confederate soldiers, freed slaves, brawny Irish immigrants and toughs from the cities of the East. They were more than a match for the Indians who occasionally attacked the train, and the iron men were the roughest of the lot.

It was at Corinne, Utah that the Union Pacific Railroad and Ace Landry crossed paths. The desperado was in his element as he went through the tent-city and quickly got the lay of the land. He found a number of old acquaintances amongst the assembled pimps, sharpers and bully-boys, and made a score of new ones.

The Landry Gang attached itself to the railroad, and Ace himself initiated a winning streak at the poker table—by dealing skillfully from the bottom of the deck. And while he exercised this lucrative talent, his bully-boys were busy in their own fashion: rolling drunks, picking pockets and extorting money at knifepoint. It appeared that the gang stood upon the threshold of a new era of prosperity.

"Three queens," the brawny track-layer boomed as he spread his cards out on the table, watching Ace Landry like a hawk.

"Nice try," the desperado told him softly. "But I've got three aces."

The big man gave him a hard look. "You'd only have two," he said, "if you didn't deal the last one off the bottom."

Landry's eyes narrowed, and he smiled his icicle smile. "Now don't be a sore loser, friend," he whispered, reaching for a pot which amounted to over three hundred dollars.

"Touch that money, an' I'll crack your skull like an egg," the big man growled.

Landry drew back his hands.

"I been watchin' you, Landry," the track-layer went on. "An I'll stake my life that you been dealin' from the bottom ever since we started to play poker." He held out a big calloused hand. "Lemme see them cards."

Ace Landry nodded. "You done staked your life all right," he told the man. "By callin' me." Suddenly, he sprang out of his seat with cat-like speed and agility.

Someone cried out then, and the other three men at the table overturned their chairs as they dove to the floor. Before the iron man was out of his seat, Landry had drawn his gun. And by the time that the man was on his feet, he found himself staring into the big, black maw of the outlaw's pistol.

"Landry," the man said firmly, despite the fact that his face had suddenly been drained of all its color, "you'd better back down. Or else Jack Casement an' the boys'll settle your hash for good."

"Is that a threat?" Landry sneered.

The iron man shook his head. "That ain't no threat. It's a promise. Jack Casement loves to throttle snakes like you with one hand. Why, he'd wring your scrawny pipestem until your eyes pop out."

Ace Landry's only reply was a bullet that tore off the top of the track-layer's head.

As the huge body hit the ground, the desperado looked around the tent, sweeping his venomous glance over the men there. "Gentlemen, I assume that this ends the dispute," he whispered coldly. "Are there any further questions?"

There were none.

"Good," said Ace Landry, holstering his gun. "Now, get that heap of trash out of here, an' let's play us some high-stakes poker."

As far as Landry was concerned, the case was closed. But Jack Casement didn't see it that way at all. Good track-layers didn't grow on trees, and so the track boss decided it was time to clean house once more. He had already done so twice before, at Cheyenne and Laramie, and knew exactly what had to be done.

He armed a group of iron men with rifles and led them through the town the next night, starting at one end of the place. By the time his band had reached

110

Corinne's opposite end, things were peaceful once more.

"Are the gamblers quiet and behaving, Jack?" asked General Dodge, the railroad's chief engineer.

"You bet they are, General," the track boss replied. "They're out there in the graveyard."

Indeed, many of the tent-city's former occupants now dwelt beneath six feet of earth, but the corpse of Ace Landry was not numbered among them. Always one to keep a finger on the pulse of things that concerned him, the outlaw had been warned by one of his many paid informants, well in advance of Casement's clean-up.

Having taken the measure of the Casements and their iron men, Landry decided that discretion was certainly the better part of valor in this instance. So he rounded up his ruffians and rode west once more. And when the gang left Corinne, it was joined by nine more riders, the elite of the tent-city's bully-boys and cutthroats.

Davy Watson, Soaring Hawk and Jack Poole had picked up Landry's trail earlier, and arrived in Corinne the day after Jack Casement's house cleaning. To their disappointment, they discovered that the outlaw was not there; but they were cheered by the fact that he was still alive, and they were not that far behind him.

Landry had gotten word of the men who were trailing him. A man named Charlie Huckemeyer rode into Corinne from Greeley, having been at the bar at the exact moment when Jack Poole had learned of the death of Cliff Hagen. As was his custom, the desperado rewarded Huckemeyer lavishly, and rode out of Corinne that same night.

Riding west once more, Landry was amused by the thought of Davy Watson and Soaring Hawk coming after him. The young pups had grit, all right, the outlaw told himself, and he intended to see that they were properly rewarded for their pains. He had no idea who the man called Jack Poole was, but in coming after him, the fool had drawn up his own death warrant. He would attend to them all at his convenience, Landry decided,

111

but his first move was to get out of the Utah Territory, beyond the reach of Jack Casement and the powerful railroad interests.

Westward the outlaw band, now a full fifteen strong, rode, heading north at Salt Lake City, where the Mormons had made it abundantly clear that they were not welcome. Onward they went, past Roy and Ogden, beyond Brigham City and Thornton, until, at Portage, they rode out of the Utah Territory.

Landry reflected upon the curious coincidences that were the foundation of his continual flight. He wryly acknowledged that he'd had the misfortune to gun down the wrong men in his last three killings, men with influence or connections, or both. Reluctantly, the desperado admitted to himself that he would have to be a little slower on the trigger in the future. But even as he made this decision, Ace Landry smiled when he recollected the killings, for the godlike feeling that came from gunning a man down was one of the greatest joys of his existence.

Entering the Idaho Territory almost in the center of its southern edge, the Landry Gang headed north through the sagebrush plains and arid prairies to Malad City, McCammon, and Pocatello, until they came to the banks of the Snake River. There, on that major tributary of the Columbia, they headed west once more, following the course of southern Idaho's lifeline.

Looking westward along the irrigated farmlands that bordered the Snake River, Ace Landry surveyed the country before him with a smile on his gaunt face. Then, as he stretched in his saddle and took a deep breath, he felt a stirring in his loins and a tickle of lust that spread throughout his groin like a brush fire with a strong wind behind it.

Ace Landry smiled wistfully as he recognized the urge. The outlaw had a strong desire to be with a woman.

Riding through the great open spaces of the Colorado, Utah, and Idaho Territories, Davy Watson had begun to form an impression of the true majesty and vastness of the American West. How full of life and color it was; how rich in teeming life and hidden treasure. What a vast new frontier to be settled in the years to come; what a bonanza for the young nation.

"West sure is a big place," Davy said casually, as he rode between Soaring Hawk and Jack Poole.

The Pawnee remained impassive, making no comment. It was his considered opinion that all whites talked too much. He understood what the paleface meant by "bullshit."

"I hear tell they been strikin' gold all over the place, up Boise way," Jack Poole said.

Hearing that, Davy was reminded of a speech he'd read, made by Daniel Webster to the Congress in 1852: *"What do we want with this worthless area—this region of savages and wild beasts, of shifting sands and whirlwinds, of dust and cactus and prairie dogs?"* the great statesman had asked. *"To what use could we ever hope to put these great deserts and these endless mountain ranges?"*

And now, less than sixteen years later, the man was proved wrong daily. The West was already being developed and exploited for its riches in many areas. Ol' Daniel had surely been talking through his hat that time.

"Now, there's a sight for sore eyes," Jack Poole said as they came in sight of the Union Pacific gangs laying track in the distance before them. They had been riding for several days in the open country, and the sight of human activity was a reassuring thing to the three men.

"That's a right big operation, sure enough," Davy remarked, his glance traveling from west to east as it went from the track-laying iron men to Hell on Wheels with its many attendant cars to the tent-city still forming at its rear, as the sun began to go down beyond the Great Salt Desert.

"They's comin' from Californee with tracks, too,"

Poole told his companions, "laid by gangs of Chinamen, who is tough little devils, as I hear tell. They does their work right enough, an' minds their own business after work, readin', prayin', gambling' amongst themselves an' smokin' opium. They never get drunk an' rowdy like the other track gangs."

"What is Chinaman?" Soaring Hawk asked, never in his life having seen one.

"Fellas who come from halfway across't the world, on the other side of the big water off the coast of Californee," the scout told him. "They's a passel of 'em livin' in that there Spanish town—San Francisco, I believe it is. These here Chinamen's a mite smaller than most folks, with hair as black as Injuns' an' eyes that sorta goes up a little in the corners, like this." Here Poole put his fingers to the outer corners of his eyes and pulled them upward.

"Not sound like white man," was Soaring Hawk's comment.

"Some folks calls 'em yellow men," Jack Poole informed him.

The Indian nodded tiredly. "White man call Indian red man," he said. "But that just bullshit."

Both Poole and Davy burst into peals of laughter.

"White man big bullshitter," Soaring Hawk allowed."Talk like old squaw at meeting of tribes."

"Well, different folks has different customs," Poole explained. "My folks was Irish, an' their people set great store on fancy talkin'. They take poets an' singers of ballads an' speechifiers to be their heroes."

"Ain't there somethin' about kissin' this here rock?" Davy asked.

"That's the Blarney Stone," Poole told him. "When a Irishman kisses it, he gets the gift of gab."

"What 'gab' mean?"

"Good talkin'."

"Like bullshit," the Pawnee opined. "All whites have gift of gab."

"You ain't met too many Irishmen, me lad," Poole

told him. "But o' course, to an Injun, anything more 'n a sentence is blabber."

Soaring Hawk looked puzzled. "Why these Iris-men kiss stone?" he asked.

"'Cause it's got a kind of magic," the scout replied.

The Pawnee stared at him. "Iris-man do that here," he said, indicating the countryside with a sweep of his hand, "lizard jump out and bite his nose."

Davy and Poole laughed again.

"You're a funnier fella than I done give you credit for," Poole told Soaring Hawk.

"Davy no think Pawnee so funny," the Indian said, a wry smile on his lips.

Davy told Poole the story about his shaking the severed hand of the dead Cheyenne.

"Well," commented the scout after the story was over, "things of that sort are like to tickle the funny-bone of an Injun."

Davy sighed as he nodded in agreement.

"For instance," Jack Poole went on, as they drew near to the railroad encampment, "lemme pass on to you-all what some miners up Cheyenne way told me once't." He paused to doff his Stetson and fan himself with it.

"It seemed," he went on, "that these here prospectors workin' some claim around Crandall Creek, up by the headwaters of the Yellowstone River, wound up on the losin' end of a fracas with a band of young Crow bucks. An' when the bodies of them prospectors was found, they was minus the heads. An' each of them corpses was a-holdin' a spoon in his hand."

Davy made a face as he heard this. Soaring Hawk listened impassively, leaning forward on his pony.

"The heads turned up near the site of the prospectors' campfire," Poole told them, "a-settin' on the points of two pickaxes that had been drove into the ground. An' right in front of each head stood a cup full of coffee."

"Gol-lee," Davy whispered, as Soaring Hawk began to nod his head knowingly.

115

"Later on," the scout continued, "someone asked the old Crow chief, Plenty Coups, about it. 'Young men make joke,' the old fella said. 'Put spoon in hand so men can stir coffee'."

Davy Watson sighed and shook his head.

"Heap good joke," Soaring Hawk told Jack Poole.

"I figgered you'd like it," the scout told the Indian.

Chapter 9

"D'you know what all this means?" Jack Poole asked his companions, indicating the railroad tracks, Hell on Wheels, and the tent-city that traveled with the Union Pacific Railroad.

Davy looked at him blankly, Soaring Hawk impassively, as they walked their horses through the tent-city.

"It means," the scout told them, "the end of the West."

"That ain't gonna be the end of the West, Jack," Davy responded, "jus' 'cause folks can get about a mite easier an' faster."

The scout shook his head. "Oh, yes it is. When the last of that track is laid between Omaha an' San Francisco, it's gonna open up the West."

"What's so bad about that?" Davy asked, reminded once more of Daniel Webster's incredible underestimation of the area west of the Missouri. "There's a world of riches out this-a-way, a world of resources that can be exploited for the benefit of the people of the United States."

Jack Poole shot him a sour look. "What you say is true, lad. But you're only seein' the half of it. Them riches ain't gonna wind up in the pockets of the Common Man, any more'n you can find tits on a boar. No, sir. They's jus' gonna become the property of some ol' cartel or other."

Davy looked puzzled. "What in the Sam Hill is a cartel?"

"It's when a bunch of hombres in the same business gets together an' sorta locks things up, puttin' a strangle-hold on competition, so's they can call the tune as to how much they's gonna stick you for, an' jus' how much of it they's gonna 'low you."

"Kinda like a Cattlemen's Association?" Davy asked.

The scout reflected on this. "Kinda," he agreed. "Only it's like they also controlled the price of cattle once't it was slaughtered an' sold for beef in the big cities back East."

"Oh," Davy said, nodding slowly.

"Iron horse come," Soaring Hawk commented, "bring heap more white men."

"That's for shit-sure," Jack Poole agreed. "Only they ain't gonna be white men the likes of any you ever seed before."

"Soaring Hawk not understand."

"Why, you're gonna see a whole new breed of folks, Soaring Hawk," the scout explained. "Folks who never had the nerve to head West when things was wild an' unsettled. You're gonna see a heap of timid little pencil-pushers an' store clerks; low-down lawyers worse'n claim-jumpers; pious, mealy-mouthed politicans who'll steal from folks better'n if they was bank robbers. These ain't the best people, in my opinion."

The scout shook his head. "These jaspers is comin' in after all the hard work's been done. Why, the West was settled by brave an' hardy folk; the cowards never started, an' the weak ones fell by the wayside." Poole sighed. "But now, it don't take much of a man to plunk his butt down in a plush railway car an' zip along the plains at thirty miles an hour. The only consolation, as I see it, is that there'll be a bunch more women comin' out this way."

"Women come, papoose follow," Soaring Hawk observed.

"Oh, they'll be papoosin' right an' left when they come out here," Poole agreed. "They'll be papoosin' all over the prairies, valleys an' mountains—from Saint Louis to the Pacific Ocean. An' them papooses'll build them a passel of big towns, an' start fencin' everythin' in. So you can jus' say goodbye to the West, boys. Look around an' catch her before they cover her naked beauty with the garments of ci-vi-li-za-tion.''

"You sure paint a dark picture, Jack.''

"Dark, hell,'' the scout retorted. "Jus' look what they done to the buffalo already. Them hunters is a-slaughterin' them without so much as a thought to replenishin' the herds. I been all over the Great Plains for the better part of thirty years, man an' boy, an' I'm here to tell you that them herds ain't but a fraction of what they used to be.''

"That's kinda sad,'' Davy muttered.

"*Sad*?'' Poole said angrily. "*Sad*?'' Wait'll you see the carloads of ginks, milksops an' pencil-neck geeks that'll soon be comin' out here in their numbers. Mama's boys, tenderfeet, soapbox orators an' tax collectors,'' he said in a voice thick with disgust. "You boys don't know what sad is.''

"Buffalo gone—bad for Indian.''

"Well, my friend,'' Poole told Soaring Hawk, "don't look for things to get no better. Them buzzards in Washington is pretty good at finessin' the Injuns outta their holdin's by now.''

"Pawnee friend of white man. Great White Father not do that to Pawnee.''

"I hope to Christ that you're right, ol' buddy. But jus' watch your ass when the Injun Affairs people comes around with their lawyers, an' asks you to sign some papers.'' The Scout shook his head. "Lawyers is worse'n rustlers. You can't trust them varmints no further than you can tote a bull buffalo on your back.''

"Yup,'' Davy seconded. "Always read the fine print on what they're askin' you to sign.''

"An' get yourself someone who can translate all that lee-gal gobbledygook,'' Poole admonished. "'Cause it ain't real talk. It's more like some secret code that only lawyers can de-cipher.''

Poole fell quiet, and the others joined him in that somber silence, each suddenly depressed by his own reflections on the future of the West.

In marked contrast to the silence of the three riders,

the vast canvas encampment around them was a-buzz with the sounds of its daily life. Fires crackled and hissed as drops of fat splattered over their embers; pack mules and jackasses brayed, while tethered horses heralded the sunset with whinnies and snorts; cutler's wheels screamed and whined, and the *tap-tap-tap* of cobblers' hammers sounded throughout the tent-city in an occupational telegraphy. The plaintive voices of harmonicas wailed over the plunking twang of banjos and guitars; empty whiskey bottles shattered against stones with high-pitched tinkles; and even in the few moments of relative quiet in the camp, a keen ear could make out the riffle of shuffled playing cards and the *chuk-a-chuk* rattle of dice.

"Jack Poole, you ol' saddletramp!" a voice called out from among the tents on the left-hand side of the three riders.

Hearing this, the scout looked in the direction of the sound. And there, standing before a campfire with a dented coffee pot in one hand and a scored and pitted tin cup in the other, was a stumpy little man with a head as smooth as a cueball and a beard as long and white as the fleece of a lamb.

"Why, if it ain't George Amos," Poole called out, dismounting to lead his horse over to the campfire. Davy and Soaring Hawk followed suit.

"Jine me fer supper, boy," the old-timer said to Poole. "Yer friends is welcome, too."

"That's right nice of you, George," Poole replied as the companions tethered their mounts.

Poole went up to George Amos and threw his arms around him, thumping the old man vigorously on the back. "Why, you're still alive an' kickin', you ol' goat," he said.

The old man began to thump the scout on the back, causing the trail dust to issue from his buckskin jacket in billowing clouds.

"Son, you're more full of dust than the Abilene trail," George Amos told Jack Poole.

"We been doin' our share of ridin', George. I won't deny that. What're you doin' workin' for the railroad?"

"Jus' rustlin' me up enough money fer a grubstake," the old-timer replied. "I hear tell they been a-strikin' gold up north, so, I figger to mosey on up there an' have a look-see, one of these days real soon."

"George here's a prospector," Poole told Davy and Soaring Hawk. "The ol' billy goat's done panned an' dug an' tapped his way from the Missouri to the Pacific several times over."

"An' all I got to show fer my pains is big muscles an' a set of calluses thicker'n a Gideon Bible." He held out his hands for them to see.

"But he don't never get dirty," Poole told his friends. "That ol' knee-length soup strainer of his covers him better'n a tarpaulin. An' at night the ol' geezer jus' wraps hisself up in it an' lays him down to sleep. He don't never need no blanket."

Davy and Soaring Hawk smiled as George Amos chuckled and nudged Jack Poole with an elbow. Then Poole introduced them to the old man.

"Damnation, boy," the prospector told the scout after the introductions had all been made, "you ain't changed none since I last seen you." He motioned for them to sit down by the campfire. "Make yerselves t'home, boys. Any friends of Jack Poole is friends of mine."

They seated themselves around the fire as the prospector poured them strong black coffee and then proceeded to rustle up supper. Davy was impressed by the old-timer's friendliness and generosity, which were, he realized, characteristic of the men and women who had shared the hardships of life in the West.

And that West would soon recede into history, Davy reminded himself. When the golden spike was driven into the ground, emblematic of the linkage of West with East, it would at the same time be driven deep into the heart of the old West.

Sourdough biscuits, salt pork, beans and dried fruit

were the fare at George Amos' campsite. To Davy, fed up with the hardtack and jerky he'd been subsisting on for days, it was a repast fit for Ulysses Simpson Grant himself. And that illustrious gentlemen would not have been displeased by the presence of the jug of "corn likker" that the old-timer passed around after the meal, for U.S. Grant had been known to take a nip or two in his time.

"George, the Sultan of Turkey couldn't be no more lavish with his hospitality than you are," Jack Poole said after dinner. "You always was a hospitable sort."

"Shucks," the old man mumbled, his face reddening as he scraped the leavings on his plate into the fire. "Man don't need a mansion to entertain his friends."

Then, as they all stretched out before the campfire, George Amos pulled out a sack of Bull Durham and proceeded to roll himself a cigarette. And while he did, Davy Watson shot Jack Poole an urgent look. Absently fingering the bullet holes in his dusty Stetson, the scout nodded to Davy and turned to face the old prospector.

"Reason we-all come up this-a-way," Poole began, "is 'cause we's trackin' down a man."

George Amos looked up at the scout and tugged with his right hand at the tobacco sack, whose drawstring he held clenched between his teeth.

"All of us here, George," Poole went on, "got a special score to settle with this hombre. He done spit on Soaring Hawk's honor, gunned down Davy's paw, an' shot one of my closest friends."

The old man nodded solemnly. "What be the varmint's name?" he asked.

"Ace Landry is his name," Davy answered, hatred suddenly blazing up inside of him.

"Oh, him," the old-timer said, as the others all leaned toward him expectantly. "He an' his bunch was doin' business here fer a while, a-cheatin' folks at cards, an' robbin' 'em outright, as well. But one day Landry got caught cheatin' by one of Jack Casement's iron men . . . ."

"You mean he's dead?" Davy interrupted anxiously, fearing that he had suddenly been deprived of the object of his vengeance.

"No sich luck," George Amos told him. "What happened was that Landry got the drop on the iron man, an' blew the top of his head clear off. They was brains splattered all over that tent."

"Got him a heavy caliber shootin' iron, I s'pose," Jack Poole opined.

"You ain't jus' whistlin' Dixie," the old man replied. "He totes a big Smith an' Wesson, one o' them heavy-frame .44 Americans that the Cavalry uses. Damn thing's got a barrel 'bout as long as a broomstick."

Davy nodded. "Yup. That's the gun. Sum'bitch shot me with it from across't the room. The damn thing blew me off my feet, an' tore a piece as big as a dinner gong out'n my shoulder." He rubbed his wound involuntarily, as it suddenly began to ache.

"What happened then?" Jack Poole asked George Amos.

"Well, the next day, ol' Jack Casement armed his iron men an' sent 'em around to clean up things," Amos continued. "But that dirty dog, Landry, had been warned somehow, an' he an' his bunch had lit out the night afore. Took 'bout eight or ten more badasses with 'em."

Davy sighed with relief. *He still had a chance to kill Ace Landry.* "Got any idea of where they was headin', Mr. Amos?" he asked.

"Trail led north," the old-timer replied. "An' I'm plumb sure Landry ain't fer stayin' in the Utah Territory, not after Jack Casement put the word out on 'im. So that prob'ly means he's a-headin' up where I'll be goin' one of these days."

"Where might that be, sir?" Davy asked, struggling to mask his anxiety.

"Up Idyho way. They done been strikin' gold all over the place, from the Boise Basin in the south to places all over the north of the territory."

"By God, that's a wild place," exclaimed Jack Poole. "Got territorial status only five years back."

"South ain't so bad," George Amos informed Poole. "Mormons been settled down there since 1860." The old-timer chuckled. "Thought they was still in Utah."

"So if you was Ace Landry, George," Jack Poole said, "where in Idaho would you head?"

"Wherever they's easy money," the old man replied tartly. "An' that's wherever they's a-minin' gold. Look fer that buzzard there—work yer way north from the Boise Basin." He winked at Poole, Davy and Soaring Hawk. "An' if you *do* bed that skunk down beneath six feet of earth, you'll be doin' a big favor fer them what comes after ya . . . sich as your truly."

"Well, George, you ol' billy goat," Poole told his friend, "we'll surely do our best on that score. I give you my word on it."

Davy Watson and Soaring Hawk nodded their heads in solemn agreement with the scout's sentiments.

As he stared into the fire, Davy felt a surge of excitement fanning through his guts with the intensity of a wind-driven forest fire. He loosened his Walker Colt in its holster and smiled at Soaring Hawk, who nodded contentedly.

"You boys watch yer butts, now," old George Amos cautioned. "That snake is travelin' with a small army."

"That's okay," Davy told him. "He's gonna need 'em."

> "When I was a bachelor, I lived by myself
> And I worked at the weaver's trade;
> The only, only thing that I ever did wrong
> Was to woo a fair young maid.
> I wooed her in the winter time,
> And in the summer, too;
> And the only, only thing that I ever did wrong
> Was to keep her from the foggy, foggy dew."

Ace Landry was singing again. The shooting of Jack Casement's iron man had gone far to raise the outlaw's spirits, but what had really elevated them was the great amount of gold he had lifted from the miners of the Boise Basin. The pickings had been exceptionally good, and the desperado and his bully-boys were now worth a great deal more than they had been when they first entered the Idaho Territory.

While the profit of his labors had been great and easily realized, the methods used to obtain it were less than gentle. Once he had the lay of the land, the outlaw led his band—now fifteen strong—in a series of lightning raids throughout the goldfields of the basin. Many miners on small claims were intimidated by the large group of masked horsemen, and surrendered their earnings in return for their lives. Those who resisted were gunned down. Claims with five or more armed men working them were assiduously avoided.

Working in that fashion, the Landry Gang had gathered a small fortune by the time its leader had given the signal to quit the area. And in the northwestern part of the territory, the outlaw chief told himself as he gloated over the prospect of future acquisition, there would be even more gold.

First the Landry Gang headed due west, following the course of the Boise River, riding along its banks, until they reached the spot where the river's waters merged with those of the Snake.

At this point the going proved rough, as the outlaws rode into the southern portion of some of the wildest and most remote country on the face of the North American continent. Escarpments and ravines, rock formations and gorges made up much of the terrain along both sides of the Snake River, and the Landry Gang, with its burdened horses and pack animals, found their progress slowing down to a crawl.

Having reached a point where the river banks were studded with rocks and boulders in a manner that rendered the way passable only to salamanders and mountain sheep, Ace Landry led his band over the bluffs that towered above the east bank of the Snake. And there, in a clearing within a grove of blue spruce trees, stood a log cabin.

Smoke from the cabin's chimney rose into the brisk autumn air, its streamers dissipating into wispy tendrils that were absorbed into the fabric of the bold blue sky. Unsure of the welcome that fifteen armed men on horseback would receive, Landry motioned them back into the trees.

"Keep out of sight until I give the signal to come ahead," the desperado told his bully-boys. "When it's all right to come on, I'll wave my hat in the air. But first, I want to find out who's there to greet us."

Saying this, the outlaw began to walk his horse in the direction of the log cabin. When he was about twenty yards away from his objective, the door to the cabin opened and a woman appeared in the doorway.

Ace Landry smiled and took off his ten-gallon hat with a flourish when he saw the woman. She was an Indian, probably a Nez Percé, he thought, and not a bad-looking little piece either, standing so proud and handsome in that doorway.

The only thing that Landry found objectionable about the Indian woman's appearance was the carbine she held in her hands. Further adding to the effect of this one jarring note, was the fact that the weapon was pointed right at him.

"You stop now," she told Landry, when he was no more than fifteen feet from the cabin.

"Yes'm," the outlaw said in a gentle voice, smiling shyly as he reined in his horse.

"What you want?" the woman asked, her finger on the carbine's trigger as she eyed Ace Landry suspiciously.

Still smiling, boyishly, the outlaw leaned forward with a creak of leather that was audible in the expectant silence of the clearing.

"I'm headin' north, ma'am," he told the Indian woman. "Up to Coeur d'Alene Lake. I'm goin' up there to join my cousin, Tom Carver. We're members of the Church of the Latter Day Saints. A bunch of my people have gone up there to settle. My name is Howard Landry."

"You Mormon?" the woman asked, still eyeing Landry suspiciously.

The outlaw nodded. "Our people is out of Ogden, Utah, ma'am. But Tom Carver an' me figger it's gettin' just a mite too crowded for a body to breathe free down that-a-way. So by the grace of God Almighty, we intend to settle in the Idaho Territory—if it be His will."

"You alone?" the woman asked.

"Yes'm," Landry said quietly, noticing her finger slide off the carbine's trigger and come to rest on its guard. "I had to tend to some special business for the elders of our church. That's why I'm comin' up behind my people."

But the woman was still not totally convinced by Landry's story. "Praise the Lord with heart and voice," she said suddenly, narrowing her eyes as she gazed at him.

"Let all men on earth rejoice," the outlaw replied, causing the woman to smile as he supplied the second half of the phrase used by the Mormons.

"The glory of God is intelligence," he added, quoting a favorite Mormon aphorism.

Smiling broadly now, the Indian woman lowered the carbine. "Mormon good people," she said. "You are welcome in my house."

"Thank you, ma'am," the desperado said humbly, just before he dismounted and tied up his horse at the hitching post in front of the door to the cabin.

"Come in," she told him, the carbine now at her side.

"God bless you, ma'am," Landry said as he entered the log cabin. "God bless this house, an' all who live in it."

Inside, she seated him at a rough-hewn table and

served the outlaw a glass of cool spring water. Across the room, sitting in a rocker beside a stone fireplace, where a small fire warmed the room against the chill of approaching winter, sat another Indian woman. Her face was webbed with the wrinkles of age, and her hair was as white as the snow that falls on the peaks of the mountains to the north.

"Afternoon, ma'am," Landry said in a soft voice, smiling gently and half-bowing to the old woman.

The younger woman said something in an Indian tongue, and the old woman smiled back and nodded at Landry.

Looking around the snug and homey place, the outlaw praised its appearance. The younger woman responded with a slight smile and a nod.

"Will your husband be home soon, ma'am?" he asked. "I don't know my way around hereabouts, an' perhaps he could tell me the best route to Coeur d'Alene Lake."

"My husband not here now," she replied.

"Oh, isn't that a pity," the humble visitor said quietly.

"But I tell you," the woman said. "My people Nez Percé. They live up north. I make trip to Coeur d'Alene Lake many times."

"God bless you, ma'am."

"My name is Natona," she told him. "And that my mother, Taiga."

"When will your husband be back, Miz Natona?" Ace Landry asked with a sweet smile.

"Not for two, three day," she told him, a puzzled look coming onto her face. "Why you ask?"

"Because," he said, suddenly flashing the handsome woman a cold, wintry smile, "I reckon it's about time we got to know each other better."

There was no mistaking the look in Ace Landry's eyes as he came at her. "You not Mormon!" she said accusingly as she backed away from the desperado.

"I was once," he told her. "A long time ago." Then

he reached out and tugged at the front of her buckskin shirt. The old woman cried out at this, and tottered over to Landry, her hands held out and curled into claws.

The outlaw laughed and backhanded the old Nez Percé woman, sending her flying across the room, to land in a heap on the floor, unconscious the moment she made contact with it. Tearing loose from Landry's grip, the younger woman ducked beneath his arms and dove for the rough-hewn table, where a carving knife lay beside a platter of venison. But the desperado was on her before she could turn to face him, and he wrenched her arm behind her back.

Ace Landry smiled warmly as the Nez Percé woman grunted in pain. And when the carving knife clattered onto the floor, he spun her around and buried his face in her half-exposed bosom.

"We got to become better acquainted," he muttered, biting the firm flesh above her small, dark aureola and nipple. Then he pinned both her arms behind her back with one of his and leaned forward upon her until she half-lay across the table. His free hand tugged at her buckskin skirt. And as it slid down her thighs to the floor, Ace Landry's hand was already groping for her private parts.

"An' after we get to know each other," the outlaw whispered hoarsely as his fingers browsed the sparse, dark thatch above her vulva, "I want you to meet some friends of mine . . . ."

Chapter 10

Westward they rode through the Utah Territory, through Promontory and around the northern tip of the Great Salt Lake, across Grouse Creek, and then to the north. Davy, Soaring Hawk and Jack Poole entered Idaho somewhere near the point where Utah and Nevada join to run perpendicular to the straight line that is the southern edge of the territory.

Threading their way among the foothills of the Sublett Range, the riders made their way down to the Snake River Plain. And there they began to follow the river, past Shoshone and Twin Falls, through Hagerman and Glens Ferry, past Hammett and Swan Falls, where they headed due north, on their way to Boise.

As they entered the Boise Basin, the companions had little difficulty in picking up the trail of Ace Landry. Reports of robberies and bushwhackings abounded in the area, some of them only a few days old. The desperadoes had fattened themselves upon the fruits of the goldminers' labors, and they would still have been there, had it not been for the recent formation of a Vigilance Committee. And Ace Landry, glutton for punishment at the gambling tables that he was, knew when to quit as far as vigilantes were concerned.

"It won't be long now, boys," Jack Poole told his friends as they covered the last miles to Boise. "The day of reckoning with that damn snake, Landry, will soon be at hand."

Soaring Hawk nodded solemnly.

Davy Watson flushed as he thought about the imminent encounter. It had been many months since the day his father had been gunned down. He had waited a long time to avenge the death of John Jacob Watson.

A long silence followed Jack Poole's last remarks, and the men rode into Boise town as the sun went down on their left hand, into the ocean beyond the coast of California.

"Does it ever bother you boys that we're goin' up against twelve or fifteen men?" the scout asked suddenly, breaking the heavy silence in which the riders had been steeped.

"After Beecher's Island, that don't seem like such bad odds, does it?" Davy replied, answering Poole's question with a question of his own.

The burly scout smiled and scratched the three-days' growth of beard on his chin. "Not when you put it that way, lad," he said. "Shows you're an optimist by nature, I reckon."

"No need to have shoot-out in street," Soaring Hawk advised. "We stalk 'em like Pawnee, an' kill heap many before they even find out who come."

Poole nodded. "Yup," he said. "Them's my thoughts. If we start pickin' off the hindmost, an' laying the occasional ambuscade, I'll bet'cha we could whittle 'em down to size in no time."

"All I care about is gunnin' Ace Landry down," Davy said bitterly.

"I know what you mean, lad," the scout told him. "But we're surely gonna have to get past all them other owlhoots before we get a crack at Landry hisself."

"Okay," Davy replied, "then we'll jus' do what we have to do."

"Uh-huh," Jack Poole agreed, launching a great gob of tobacco juice an instant later. It traveled through the air in a wide arc, and splattered dead-center upon a small, smooth stone at the side of the trail.

"I got to get me some more chawin' tobaccy," Poole reflected. "What I got in my mouth's the last of my supply."

"So I take it that the general store's gonna be our destination, rather than some place which dispenses food an' drink," Davy remarked dryly.

131

Raising his eyebrows as he caught this, Jack Poole said, "Well I get kinda tetchy when I ain't got me no tobaccy to chaw. You boys don't want me to go off the deep end an' start tearin' up this nice little town, do ya?"

Davy shook his head in mock indignation. "That's wuss'n bein' a opium addict," he told the scout. "It must be a terrible thing to be the prisoner of your cravin's."

"Lad, everybody's addicted to somethin'," the scout told him. "Don't you know that? Some fellas is hooked on smokin', some on drinkin'. Others is hooked on thievin' or gamblin'. Some folks is even hooked on work—or religion, for that matter. So what's a quid or two of chawin' tobaccy in the great scheme of things, anyway?"

"I ain't addicted to nothin'," Davy challenged.

"Oh, yes you are," the scout rejoined.

Davy narrowed his eyes and frowned as he stared at Jack Poole. "Oh, yeah? What's that?" he asked.

"Revenge, lad. You're as hooked as any addict I ever did see."

Soaring Hawk shot the scout a look of disgust. "You talk heap big bullshit." This caused Davy to burst out into a series of hearty guffaws.

Red in the face, Jack Poole turned to the Indian and waggled a thick index finger under his nose. "Now, jus' because you're 'bout as lively as a dummy in a store window," he scolded, "that don't mean you're no angel your own self."

Soaring Hawk just looked straight ahead, into the distance, his face unmarked by any trace of emotion.

Frustrated, Jack Poole shook his head. "Well, I'll say this much," he added. "If you Injun boys was to take up the game of poker, we'd be in big trouble."

"If you're expectin' to get a rise out of him," Davy told the scout, "you're gonna be at it till hell freezes over."

"Here general store," the Pawnee told Jack Poole,

reining in and pointing to his right. "Get tobacco. Then put in mouth, so no more bullshit come out."

Davy burst out laughing once again.

"Aw, teach yer granny to suck eggs," Jack Poole muttered as he dismounted and stormed off to the general store.

After Jack had purchased his chewing tobacco, the trio led their horses down the muddy street to a honky-tonk known as the Three Deuces.

As he shuffled through the sawdust that covered the floor, and heard the plangent tinkle of the pianoforte, Davy Watson broke out into a cold sweat as he began to relive the murder of his father.

"Lad, are you all right?" Jack Poole asked with concern in his voice as they reached the ornate, polished bar.

"You sweat and shake like man with dog fever," Soaring Hawk told his blood brother, grabbing him by the arm.

"I'm all right," Davy told his friends. "It's nothin'."

"What'll it be, gents?" the barkeep asked as he came up to Jack Poole. Suddenly he frowned as he recognized Soaring Hawk for an Indian. "I can't serve no spirits to the red man," he told them.

Davy shot an anxious glance at his blood brother. Having become a Pawnee, he had begun to alter his feelings regarding the quality of the relations between whites and Indians.

"Give my friend here a sassparilla," Jack Poole told the barkeep. "He ain't here for to drink. He come to play poker."

Feeling better now, Davy laughed at Poole's dry wit. After that, he looked up above the bar's cut-glass mirror and saw the ever-present painting of a reclining nude. As was its counterpart in the Red Dog Saloon, this canvas was also enclosed within an ornate, gilt frame. The young Venus depicted in the painting was fat and glossy, just like her sister, Davy realized; the only difference was that this one was a brunette, whereas the reigning beauty of the Red Dog was a blonde.

> *"Flow gently, sweet Afton, among thy green braes,*
> *Flow gently, I'll sing thee a song in thy praise;*
> *My Mary's asleep by thy murmuring stream,*
> *Flow gently, sweet Afton, disturb not her dream."*

The pianoforte player sang in a high, nasal whine, with a vibrato wide enough to drive a Conestoga wagon through. A cigar burned on top of the instrument, its ash threatening to fall onto the keyboard. Beside it stood a half-empty glass of beer. An old prospector hovered behind the pianist, wiping tears from his eyes as he mumbled the words of the song.

In the background, the riffle of cards and the hollow *chink* of poker chips came floating through the smoky air. Images seemed to shift in space, as the honkytonk's many bright kerosene lamps bathed the place in their asynchronously flickering glow. The poker players at the side of the room were directly beneath two of those lamps, and the cigarette smoke that went up from their table combined with the glaring light to give them the look of otherworldly beings surrounded by some great, glowing nimbus. It seemed to Davy as if they were wagering their very souls in some demonic contest.

"By Gar, I catch you sheat me dis time!" an angry bass voice called out suddenly from the tables, bringing the music of the pianoforte to a jangling, discordant halt. Davy and his companions wheeled about, as did everyone else at the bar, to see what was going on.

"Someone's in a heap of trouble," Jack Poole informed his friends. "'Cause by the sound of it, he's fuckin' with a mountain man."

The bar was crowded with miners, lumberjacks and cowboys, and every one of them watched the scene at the poker table with great interest.

A slickly dressed man with ruffle cuffs and pomaded, thinning brown hair that was plastered down on his skull had been yanked out of his seat by a huge bearded man in buckskins. Aside from the latter's evident bulk, Davy realized that the mountain man had the biggest nose he had ever seen in his life. It was a fine French nose, Davy observed, only much more so.

Flowing down from a high bridge, the lines of that great organ widened prodigiously as they went, culminating in a pair of flaring nostrils that made Davy think of elephant ears.

"Thunderation!" squeeked the old-timer next to Jack Poole as the rest of the men at the poker table scattered. "This ought to be a dilly!"

"I'm a stranger here myself, pop," the scout informed the old man, never taking his eyes from the scene at the poker table. "Could you tell me who's who over there?"

"The tinhorn goes by the name of Larry McDaniel," the old man replied in a breathy voice. "He's a big card sharper hereabouts."

"Who's the mountain man?" Poole asked.

"He's a trapper from up north, name of Big Nose Vachon."

Poole nodded as the mountain man raised the gambler's hand into the air. "He's well named," he told the oldster, "for that's the biggest honker I ever seen on a human critter."

The old man chuckled. "But you dast not say it to his face, boy. Or he'll tear off your head, an' shit in the hole."

"Them mountain men is 'bout the toughest things in all God's creation," Poole opined.

"Dere de card he want to deal," the mountain man called out for all to hear, manipulating the gambler's body as if he were a puppet, holding up a clawed hand that still held an ace in its palm.

Then he moved the gambler's hand from left to right, for all to see. "See what he done," the trapper said in his deep, booming voice. "See 'ow dis *cochon* win all de money. Dat 'ow 'e win—on account 'e deal from de

135

bottom an' palm card.''

''He's breakin' my bones,'' the gambler squealed in pain. ''Help me, boys. There's fifty dollars in gold to the man what gets 'im!''

''The man has friends,'' Jack Poole observed as eight men sprang up and came forward from a collection of diverse spots within the honkytonk.

''Pack o' curs,'' the old man growled. ''Hired bullies that he keeps around to cover his traces, the black-guard!''

''Let him go, you big-nosed bastard,'' a thickset man ordered, stepping in front of Jack Poole and drawing a bead on the mountain man, ''or I'll blow that horn right off'n yer ugly puss!''

Moving with the speed of a striking copperhead, Jack Poole reached around the man's body with his left hand and took hold of the bully-boy's wrist. Then, as the man turned in surprise, the scout wrenched him around and dropped him as he brought the butt of his revolver down upon the base of the ruffian's skull.

''Don't worry about him, *mon ami*,'' Poole called out to Big Nose Vachon as the gunman crumpled to the floor. ''The lad appears to have fallen asleep.''

The gambler yipped in pain as the mountain man squeezed his hand once more.

''*Merci mille fois, monsieur*,'' the trapper called out, thanking Poole as two of the tinhorn's hired ruffians closed in on him.

''*Pas de quoi*,'' Jack Poole replied off-handedly.

''I didn't know you spoke French,'' Davy remarked, impressed by his friend's reply.

''Picked it up from the Canucks,'' Poole said, while Big Nose Vachon lifted the gambler up as easily as if he had been a child and threw him smack at the two oncoming bully-boys. McDaniel uttered a shrill scream as he hit the two men, who went down to the sawdust under the impact of his body.

Another ruffian had made his way to the top of an adjoining poker table, where he then proceeded to launch himself through the air at the mountain men. But Vachon had seen the man out of the corner of his eye, and—quick as a cougar—he spun around and hit the ruffian a backhand slap that stopped him dead in mid-air and nearly tore his head off.

"Judas Priest!" Davy exclaimed. "I'll bet they heard that slap in Kansas!"

"By God, the man's got a hand as big as a Lacrosse racquet!" Jack Poole said in awed tones.

The four remaining bully-boys gathered together and made a concerted rush at Big Nose Vachon. But the mountain man broke a chair over the back of the first, and sent the second to the sawdust with a hard, clonking butt of his head. That took care of the men in the center, leaving Vachon flanked by the last of McDaniel's standing ruffians.

He disabled one with a lightning *savatte* kick to the solar plexus, and, thrusting himself back with the help of the resistance of his victim's body, the behemoth in buckskins launched himself at his remaining adversary.

A bonecrushing thud resounded throughout the otherwise silent honkytonk as Big Nose Vachon, after raising the bully-boy aloft with both hands, suddenly dashed that unfortunate to the floor.

After that, the huge mountain man just stood where he was, panting like a bull as he looked around the room. But what he could not see, because it had occurred directly behind him, was the sudden appearance of yet another opponent.

This one was an older man, portly, well-dressed, and as distinguished-looking as a judge. During the fracas, he had emerged from a rear office and stood outside its door, taking aim at the trapper's great head with a Smith and Wesson .22, a tiny revolver with a blue barrel and a silvered brass frame.

The delicate-appearing seven-shooter was favored by gamblers and honkytonk girls. The story goes that a tenderfoot pulled a .22 Smith and Wesson on a fron-tiersman one day. "Boy, don't you shoot me with that

137

thing," the old-timer exclaimed. "Because I might get awful angry, if I ever find out about it." All in all, while the little pistol may have looked laughable enough, a .22 slug or two in the head at close range could certainly prove fatal. And even a scratch from the slug carried with it the risk of tetanus, whose spores were ever-present, residing as they did in the horse dung and overall filth of frontier towns.

Seeing the look of alarm on the faces of the men at the bar, Vachon whirled around. But he froze into sudden immobility when he saw the tiny Smith and Wesson pointing at a spot right between his eyes.

"*Nom du chien*," the trapper swore in consternation. "Crookston! Where did you come from?"

Squinting along the barrel of the miniscule weapon, the portly and distinguished-looking man said nothing as his finger tightened on its trigger.

Men held their breath all over the honkytonk during the fraction of a second that remained before the man fired off his pistol into the face of Big Nose Vachon. Davy's breath rattled in his throat in that frozen, night-mare instant, and he saw John Jacob Watson standing before him where the mountain man had been. Only a fraction of a second would elapse before the portly man pulled the trigger, and there was not enough time for Vachon to regain his composure and save himself.

Everyone in the Three Deuces waited to hear the first sharp pop of the Smith and Wesson. It seemed a sure bet that the trapper had been dealt his final hand in life's poker game. It appeared to be all over for Big Nose Vachon . . . .

Suddenly, a brief whooshing sound cut through the fabric of the funereal silence that had enshrouded the Three Deuces. The portly man cried out in surprise and pain, and Davy's eyes widened as he saw him drop the pistol and clutch at his arm.

"You done saved ol' Big Nose's life!" he said to his blood brother, after he had recognized the latter's knife protruding from the would-be assassin's forearm.

"Good shot, old son!" Jack Poole exclaimed, clapping Soaring Hawk on the shoulder.

The Pawnee looked away modestly, and fought unsuccessfully to suppress a smile of pride and triumph.

"You don't get dat chance no two time!" the enraged Vachon roared as he charged the portly man, who backed off, white-faced and gasping with fright.

In another instant, the trapper was upon him. Vachon grabbed the man by the collar and spun him around. Davy winced as, a second later, the trapper broke the portly man's back over a knee the size of a skillet.

"Knows how to settle a score, don't he, pop?" Jack Poole said to the old-timer beside him. "Who was the lucky fella?"

"That was McDaniel's partner," the old man told him. "He owned this j'int."

Flanked by Soaring Hawk and Jack Poole, Davy turned back to the bar, where the bartender, making his way down the line at a clip, poured them drinks.

"Set dem up again for dese fine man," Big Nose Vachon boomed as he walked over to the bar. As Davy turned to face the trapper, he saw two men dragging the body of the portly man across the sawdust.

Jack Poole handed Vachon a glass of whiskey. The huge, bearded man with the huge nose clinked his glass against Soaring Hawk's sarsaparilla.

"Son of a bitch," Big Nose Vachon said with a smile, "I almost get killed wit' dat pop-gun. You save my life, *mon ami. Salut!*" The trapper tossed down his whiskey. Then he looked over to Jack Poole.

"You, too, come to my 'elp when dat *salot*," he pointed to the man whom Poole had cold-cocked, "go to shoot me down." He kicked the unconscious man in the belly. Then he clapped Jack Poole on the back vigorously, causing the scout to cough up his drink.

"More wheeskey for my frens," the trapper called out to the bartender. "Leave wit' me dat bottle."

"Hey, Mister Vachon," a man said respectfully, coming up behind the mountain man. "McDaniel is

139

comin' to. What'll we do with 'im?"

"T'row dat skunk out," Vachon replied. "An' tell 'im dat 'e better be out from Idaho Territory in two day."

He turn back to the others. "My name is Emile Vachon," he said, holding out a hand as big as a Smithfield Ham. "It is a great pleasure to meet such fine man as you t'ree."

"Jack Poole's my handle," the scout told him, his own big hand positively lost in Vachon's gigantic mitt. "These here's my good pals, Soaring Hawk an' David Watson."

"'Allo, Dah-veed," Vachon said, applying his bone-crushing grip to Davy.

"An' dis fine gentleman, he is Pawnee, *n'est-ce pas*?" the trapper asked, causing Soaring Hawk to nod and smile as they shook hands. "You t'row de knif wit' great skill."

The bartender poured them all another round of drinks.

"I am in your debt, gentlemen," Big Nose Vachon went on. "Tell me what I can do to 'elp you."

"Well, Mr. Vachon," Jack Poole said hesitantly, "we could use a favor."

"Anyt'ing," the trapper told them. "No fay-vor is too great."

"To come to the point," Poole went on, "we-all's trackin' down a man name of Ace Landry, who's got hisself this here big gang. He killed Davy's paw, gunned down my friend, an' made light of Soaring Hawk's honor. We aim to kill him."

Vachon scratched his enormous nose as he listened intently.

"Landry an' his boys stirred up a passel of trouble in the Boise Basin, an' then lit out for parts unknown. He was headed north, last we heard, prob'ly for the goldfields up that-a-way. D'you know the country north of here, Mr. Vachon?"

"Like de back of my 'and, Meestair Jacques Poole,"

the mountain man replied with a smile.

"Well then," the scout told him. "This here Landry an' his bunch rode outta here only a day or three ago. If you could put us on his trail, we'd sure consider that one heap of a favor."

"Dat is pair-fec', *mon ami*," Big Nose Vachon said, clapping Jack Poole on the back. "I live up dat way. I 'ave jus' sell my furs, an' now I go 'ome. If dis Lan'ry ride out dat soon, I tell you now we find 'im before 'e get to 'Ells Canyon."

"Ells Canyon?" Davy repeated.

"Hell," said a miner at his elbow.

"Beg pardon?" Davy said, turning to the man.

"Hells Canyon," the miner told him. "It's mebbe the deepest ol' gorge on this whole continent. Near to 8,000 feet deep. An' it ain't a bit like the Grand Canyon. Damn thing's got trees growin' all over it.

"Wild place, huh?" Davy asked.

"You bet your butt, sonny," the man told him. "It's the place where the Snake River joins the Salmon, which be the wildest damn river I ever did see."

"Well, I hope we get our men before we have to ride into Hells Canyon," Davy told him.

"You ain't just a-whistlin' Dixie, boy," the grizzled miner agreed. "For once't you've rode into Hells Canyon, it's every man for hisself, an' the devil take the hindmost."

"When're you up to leavin' Boise?" Jack Poole asked Emile Vachon.

"In de mornin'," came the bass reply. "Tonight, you be my guest. We 'ave suppair, an' den we get shit-faced, *alors*!"

"Don't that mean Ace Landry'll gain at least half a day more on us, Mister Vachon?" Davy asked anxiously.

The trapper shook his head. "Not when you goes wit' me. I see you catch up wit' dem outlaw before dey get to any goldfield, by Gar!"

"Sounds fair enough," Davy told Vachon, feeling

confident that the huge man's words were nothing less than the gospel truth.

"Now you come wit' me," Vachon told them, starting across the sawdust and motioning to a big table before him. "An' we eat steak an' venison, an' den get drunk, *hein*?"

As Vachon crossed the floor, one of the ruffians he had earlier laid out began to stir. Dazedly the man got to his hands and knees, and then began to shake his head in an attempt to clear it. Vachon calmly walked up to the man and gave him a swift kick in the jaw, sending him rolling under a table, where he came to rest against its base, unconscious.

"Not the boy to cross, is he?" Jack Poole muttered to Davy as Vachon continued on his way to the table he had indicated earlier and sat down.

"Not if'n you value your hide, I reckon," Davy agreed.

Soaring Hawk muttered something in Pawnee, causing Jack Poole to laugh out loud.

Davy turned to his blood brother. "What'd you say?" he asked.

"I give him Pawnee name," Soaring Hawk replied.

"Well, what is it?"

"Heap long name."

"Okay, tell me."

"Too hard to say in white man talk," the Indian replied. "Ask Jack Poole."

Davy turned to the scout. "Say, Jack," he muttered, looking across the room to where Vachon sat. "What's the name he give Mr. Vachon come out to in plain English?"

Poole thought for a moment, casting a surreptitious glance of his own over to the Goliath at the table. "'Tain't easy to render," he told Davy. "It's a whole mouthful of Pawnee, an' even more in English."

"Well?" Davy asked impatiently.

"Okay," Jack sighed. "It goes somethin' like this: 'Man-big-as-mountain-with-nose-like fallen-tree'."

Davy laughed. "I guess that's a pretty apt moniker."

"Well, jus' don't let ol' Vachon get wind of it," Jack Poole warned in a whisper. "'Cause I hear tell he's downright tetchy 'bout that honker of his."

"Well, sir," Poole said loudly as the three companions sat down at the table. "I'm so hungry, I could eat me a bear—claws, asshole an' all. What's good here, Mr. Vachon?"

"Call me Emile, *je vous prie*," Vachon told them. "Best is de venison. I know, 'cause my friend, Denis Maisonneuve, 'e shot it 'imself, only dis morning."

"Sounds fine by me," Poole said. Davy and Soaring Hawk seconded his choice.

"*Ah, bon!*" the trapper said contentedly. "I will order for ever'one."

In the background, as the bartender brought a bottle of rye whiskey and a bottle of sarsaparilla over to the table, someone played the pianoforte and began to sing a sentimental song.

> "*Oh, if I had the wings of an angel,*
> *Over these prison walls I would fly.*
> *I'd fly to the arms of my true love,*
> *And there I would stay 'til I die.*"

They caroused for hours at the Three Deuces, gobbling up venison and beefsteak, and swilling down rye whiskey. As was his custom, Soaring Hawk retired to attend to the horses and then get some rest. But Davy, Jack Poole, and Big Nose Vachon stayed at their table all night, telling jokes, smoking cigars and swapping tall tales.

The three men were all flushed with drink and sweating profusely as they sat enshrouded in a mantle of cigar smoke. Jack Poole explained that he only smoked cigars on the rarest of occasions. But what else could their unusual meeting with Emile Vachon be called? he asked Davy and the mountain man.

"Dat's right," the trapper agreed. "You don't see

ever' day what we done here today." He thumped the scout on his shoulder, nearly dislodging him from his seat. "An' you boys are my true frens. You are like brother to me."

"You're a fine fella, your own self," Jack Poole said, waxing sentimental with drink. "Why, you're one hell of a man, an' a real shitkicker, if I ever did see one." The trapper was glowing with pride as Poole concluded his testimony. "I'm right proud to call you my pal, Big Nose."

Big Nose.

Davy didn't believe his ears. He saw the mountain man's eyes go wide as saucers, and a silence as heavy as a blacksmith's anvil sat on the table. Davy caught his breath when he heard Jack Poole call Vachon Big Nose. In his expansive mood, the scout had apparently forgotten the old-timer's admonition: To call Emile Vachon Big Nose was tantamount to committing suicide.

Davy looked at Jack Poole, and noticed that his face was as white as a sheet on a washline. His mouth hung open, wide as a beartrap, and his forehead was creased like a crumpled coattail.

When he stole a glance at the huge figure beside him, Davy saw that Vachon was trembling all over, causing the fringes on his buckskins to sway like a Kansas wheatfield in a high wind. And where Jack Poole had gone chalky-white, the trapper was livid, his face now as dark as a day-old bruise. He stared at the scout from behind his enormous nose, his eyes suddenly narrowing to a pair of menacing gimlet holes.

"What was dat you say?" he rumbled in a quavering basso profundo.

"Well, I uh . . ." Jack Poole stopped to clear his throat.

Davy's eyes darted from the livid mountain man to the pallid scout. He began to pray silently. Judging from what Poole had told him about the ways of mountain men, and from what they had already seen of the incredibly formidable Emile Vachon, things were going to get pretty awful in the next few minutes.

"What you call me?" Vachon rumbled once more, his beady, angry eyes burning holes in Jack Poole's consciousness.

"I said, uh . . ." Another fit of throat clearing interrupted the scout's reply.

Oh Lord, Davy Watson prayed, *don't let Mr. Vachon kill Jack!*

The table groaned suddenly, as Vachon rested his forearms on it and leaned forward, bringing his enormous nose close to the scout's in an intimidating manner.

"Did you call me Big Nose?" the man-mountain whispered in a rumble that reminded Davy of rocks falling down into a chasm.

Having held his breath until he could hold it no longer, Davy exhaled in a rattling sigh as he saw Jack Poole's trembling hand move almost imperceptibly down to his side.

"Well, did you?"

Jack Poole gulped and swallowed as if he had a horseshoe lodged in his throat. He puffed out his cheeks and expelled air between his compressed lips in a tight, hissing stream. Davy saw that his broad, high forehead was studded with beads of sweat.

"I say, did you call me Big Nose?"

Poole had to clear his throat several times more before he could regain the power of speech. And when he finally spoke, Davy heard him answer in the harsh, croaking voice of an old man.

"Yup, Emile," Poole rasped. "I kinda reckon I did."

Vachon's wide-open mouth looked like a cave in the dark field of his thick beard, and when he leaned back, the shadow cast from the overhead kerosene lamp gave it the look of a gopher hole in prairie grass. Cold and hard, his eyes looked like the balls that were fired from horse pistols, and his flaring nostrils reminded Davy of an enraged bull.

"You 'ave de nerve to tell me dis to my own face?" Vachon went on incredulously, in a whisper that was like the blast of a brazen trumpet. "Jacques Poole, you tell me dis t'ing?"

Davy saw that Poole's hand was now on the butt of his pistol.

"That's, uh, right . . . Emile," the scout said in that weird, eighty-year-old voice.

Deliver us, O Lord, prayed Davy Watson, realizing that the moment of truth was at hand.

Slowly, deliberately, the mountain man reached across the table with his tree trunk arms and Smithfield Ham hands. With equal slowness and deliberation, Jack Poole leaned back and began to ease his gun out of its holster. Davy watched it all with a painful clarity, and an anticipation that caused his stomach to buck like an unbroken horse.

By the time that Vachon had put his two meaty mitts on the scout's shoulders, Davy saw that his friend's six-shooter had cleared its holster. In one more second, he realized with terrible finality as he leaned back in his seat, one or both of the men beside him would be dead.

Vachon gripped Jack Poole by the shoulders and shook him once, causing the scout's finger to tighten on the trigger of his weapon.

"You know somet'ing?" he began in his earthquake rumble. "You right."

Davy was sure he'd misheard him. Jack Poole just sat still, with his finger on the trigger and a stupefied smile on his face, looking as if he had been carved out of ice.

"You know what I mean?" Vachon went on, his hand still resting upon the scout's shoulder.

Jack Poole blinked his eyes rapidly and cleared his throat. "I don't . . . get yer drift, Emile," he croaked finally.

"Well," said the huge, terrible man, shaking Poole one mighty shake for emphasis, "I say dat you right—I got one big nose."

As his pistol slid back into its holster, Jack Poole

began to slide under the table. If Big Nose Vachon had not been gripping his shoulders, Davy was certain that the scout would have disappeared from sight.

Amen, and thank you, Lord, Davy Watson thought, sighing inwardly.

"I t'ink I got maybe de most big nose I ever see," Emile Vachon rumbled on, clapping Jack Poole on the shoulders one last time before he lowered his arms and leaned back in his seat with a smile.

"Well," Jack Poole admitted with a weak smile of his own as the color began to return to his cheeks, "it ain't the littlest honker I ever seed."

"No, by Gar," Vachon roared in a voice that could have stampeded cattle. "It's de mos' biggest!"

Davy and Jack exchanged puzzled looks, wondering if the trapper had gone off the deep end.

"Uh, well . . . if you say so, Emile," Poole agreed quietly.

"But," the mountain man bellowed suddenly, causing men all over the length and breadth of the honky-tonk to look his way, "it is also de mos' beautiful."

"I'll drink to that," Jack Poole said with a smile as he lifted his glass in a toast. "*Au nez le plus beau du monde*," he said in French. "Ain't that right, Emile?"

"What'd you say?" whispered Davy, nudging the scout.

"Here's to the handsomest honker in the world," Poole told him.

"You know," Vachon said, "I got no reason to be 'shame of my nose. Hell, she's de biggest an' de finest— like Cyrano de Bergerac. To my nose—*salut*!"

"To your nose, Mr. Vachon," Davy Watson toasted.

They all drank then, and Vachon immediately refilled their glasses.

"And 'ere's to my great friend, Jacques Poole," he toasted. "A man 'oo 'ave de courage to tell me truth. *Salut, ami bien aimé*!"

They drank again . . . and again and again. Poole

147

and Vachon were still toasting each other in English and French (and various combinations of both) when Davy took his leave of them, and tottered off in the direction of the upstairs room he had rented for the night.

"Hey, cowboy," a breathy voice called out behind him as he went up the stairs. "want some company?"

Davy turned and saw a tall blonde woman at the foot of the stairs. Inside himself, he felt a pang of longing and a stab of regret as he thought about Deanna Mac-Partland and realized that he might never see her again in this life.

Feeling suddenly glum, Davy gave the blonde a sad smile and a shake of his head. Then he reflected upon what lay ahead: in a few days, at most, he would have his long-awaited showdown with Ace Landry; the odds were not at all in his favor, and chances were that he would never return to Kansas and see his loved ones again, nor ride back into the town of Hawkins Fork and call at the bawdy house of Mrs. Lucretia Eaton, where he would claim Deanna MacPartland as his own.

"Ma'am, I've done changed my mind," he called out as the blonde began to walk off. "An' I'd be right pleased if'n you was to accompany me to my quarters."

The woman turned and walked up the stairs, smiling her honkytonk smile. But once they were naked together in bed, she soon became tender as a lover. There was something about Davy—his innocence or his openness, perhaps, that touched the women of the honkytonks deeply.

Her fingers explored his body as if she were blind and learning all about him through braille. Her full lips grazed his, and the darting of her tongue into his mouth stirred his groin. The blonde woman rubbed her firm, full breasts against his chest, and he could feel her stiff, pink nipples trace their way across his flesh.

She slid over Davy, her body and hair teasing him with their soft, silky delights. Then, halting suddenly and drawing herself up on her haunches, the woman took his rod in her cool hand and guided him into her sheath.

As he entered her, Davy Watson gasped with the intensity of the pleasure that he felt. And as she began to call the stroke, churning her wide hips and descending upon his swollen maleness in slow, gliding motions, he thrust himself deep inside her and moaned in happy anticipation of the surging release to come.

He grabbed her buttocks and pulled her to him, feeling the sudden warmth of her breasts upon his chest as she leaned over to kiss him and her upper body made contact with his. Now calling the stroke himself, Davy listened excitedly to the small, squishing sounds his rod made as it churned into her warm and welcoming womanhood. The smell of her perfume blended with the musk of her arousal, and he took it in as if it were Rocky Mountain air. And then, shortly thereafter, he came with a wrenching groan and a plaintive sigh.

In the very instant before he surrendered himself to the dark inner pulse that overbore his consciousness, Davy Watson realized that this might be the last time he would ever make love.

Chapter 11

Ace Landry stepped out of the log cabin and breathed deeply of the frosty autumn air. Then he exhaled with a sigh of contentment. Overhead, the sun shone in a sky of blue; the weather was clear and near-perfect, except for the slightest hint of a chill in the air and a vague promise of snow.

Taking the Indian woman had done the outlaw a world of good; her resistance and suffering had excited him intensely. Pain was always the spur to Landry's pleasure, and the admixture of it with sexual contact thrilled the desperado beyond words.

When he made love to the Nez Percé, it had been a soul-shattering experience for him. All his poisonous fantasies were unleashed by the act of violation, and Ace Landry pumped out his jism to the vivid accompaniment of his mind's cruel imagery.

Whips and spurs, knives and prods, cuts and scars: these were the adornment of his fantasies—fantasies of punishment and violation, of rape and desecration. Such were the dark passions that welled up inside the twisted soul of Ace Landry.

The woman had resisted with all her strength, causing Landry great exertions to subdue her. This excited him infinitely more than willing compliance, and he violated the Nez Percé several times. He had bound the older woman, in order that she would not be in his way while he took his pleasure.

After that, when he was spent and satiated, he gave the woman to his fourteen bully-boys.

Still breathing deeply of the fresh Idaho air, Landry strolled around the clearing before the cabin, where a number of his men sat cleaning their guns and rifles, sharpening their knives and feeding or tending to their horses.

"Nice day, ain't it, boys?" he said pleasantly, passing among his men.

"Shore is, Ace," one of them agreed.

"Only thing," another told Landry, "is that we-all better get our butts up to them gold fields before the snow falls in the passes up north. It's gonna snow any time now, sure as shit."

"Couldn't be much of a snowfall," Landry reassured the man. "It's a mite too early."

"Yeah, but it's a touch colder'n it got a right to be this time of y'ar," piped up an old-timer called Bart McKecknie.

"Think so?" Landry asked, respecting the old man's opinion in matters pertaining to the Idaho Territory.

The old-timer gave him a "could be" look in answer to his question.

"Say, Ace," a big southerner drawled, "y'all think them dudes is still trailin' us?" he asked, referring to Davy Watson and his companions.

"Shit," Landry said with a cynical smirk, "I hope not—for their sake." He recalled with a certain warmth the shooting of John Jacob Watson and his son. "I done shot that fool kid once't already. He's really askin' for it if he comes 'round again."

"I ever tell you about Bullet-Proof Jerry Grayson?" old Bart McKecknie asked the outlaw chief, straightening up with a wheeze as he finished inspecting his horse's shoes.

"Who?" Landry asked, turning to face the old desperado who had served as his look-out and inside man for years.

"Bullet-Proof Jerry Grayson," McKecknie repeated. "He was the sheriff of a town in western Kansas, called Pecalia, or Piculia, or somethin' like that. It ain't important." He dismissed the name with a wave of his hand.

"What's important," the old-timer went on, "was the sheriff of that there town, the name of which I never could recollect proper, who went an' got hisself im-

151

broiled in a sort of feud with some big cattleman, name of Fred Crenshaw, I believe. Ol' Jerry Grayson accused Crenshaw of changin' the brands on other folks cattle, an' then swallowin' them in that great big damn remuda of his.''

The old man paused to scratch the white stubble on his chin. In the background there could be heard the anquished moans of the younger Nez Percé woman and the keening wail of the elder.

"So?" Landry urged.

"Well, sir," McKecknie continued, "Fred Crenshaw got a mite aggrieved at Jerry Grayson for sayin' what he done. An' you can add to that the fact of Grayson's constant snoopin' around Fred's herds. So he figgered it was time to put that ol' sheriff in his place once't an' for all.''

"Who's next?" a man called out from the doorway of the cabin.

"I am," a consumptive-looking man with fair hair and mutton chop whiskers replied, holstering the Colt he had been oiling. "She still up to it?" he asked the man in the doorway, who stood buttoning up the front of his red union suit.

"You bet'cha, Todd," the man answered. "She's a reg'lar little hellion, that one." He raised his hand to his cheek and gingerly touched the scratches on it. "Got a lot of fight left in 'er. You'll have to slap her about a bit afore you can get down to business.''

The consumptive-looking man nodded. "Well, I reckon I can quiet the filly down," he said, walking over to the doorway of the log cabin.

"You was sayin'?" Landry prompted the old-timer.

"Where was I?" McKecknie muttered. "Oh yeah. Fred Crenshaw had got it into his head to settle Jerry Grayson's hash. Determined to end his snoopin', he was. So what he done was to send his foreman, fella name of Ledoux, an' a couple of his boys after ol' Jerry.''

"Sent 'em out to bushwhack the sheriff, huh?"

growled a balding man with a cauliflower ear.

McKecknie shook his head. "No sich thing," he told the man. "Fred Crenshaw had 'bout as much power in them parts as ol' Jeff Davis had in the heart of the Confederacy in 1861. Them boys didn't bushwhack Jerry Grayson. Shit, no. They was bold as brass. They up an' shot the man down right in his own office. Now, what d'ya think of that?"

The man with the cauliflower ear nodded. "Anybody what does that must have the balls of a brass monkey," he agreed.

"Yup," continued McKecknie. "They jus' up an' gunned ol' Jerry down in his office. Didn't even give him time to get out of his chair, much less draw his gun. Blew 'im out of his seat an' had him rollin' across't the floor like a tin can."

"That don't sound too bullet-proof to me, Bart," Ace Landry told the old-timer.

"Shit, Ace," the old man growled. "I ain't come to that yet. I mean, it's bullet-proof enough if you gets plugged eight times an' lives to do somethin' about it. Ol' Jerry lived through the whole thing, got hisself recovered in jig-time, an' went on to bury Ledoux an' the two cowpokes what shot 'im."

"What about that Crenshaw fella?" someone asked.

"Well," Bart McKecknie told him, "when he heard what Grayson done to his boys, he lit out for parts unknown, an' was never heard of again. An' for his pains, Jerry Grayson assumed ownership of Crenshaw's herds an' property. Warn't no one who contested it, either."

He turned to Landry. "That bullet-proof enough for ya?"

The desperado nodded. "That sum'bitch got him one hell of a resistance to lead poisoning. He still around, these days?"

"That's the funniest dang thing," the old-timer told Ace Landry. "One day, he was at home—a-hangin' up a picture in his own parlor, when he loses his balance

153

an' falls backwards off'n the chair he was a-standin' on. Fractured his skull an' was unconscious for weeks. Then one day, he up an' died." The old man shrugged. "Ain't that a pisser."

"Shore 'nuf is," Landry agreed. "You never know, do ya?"

The other outlaws were in accord with this sentiment.

"Well, boys," Landry told them, "git your gear in order, for we'll be saddlin' up afore long. How many's left who hasn't been with the Injun?"

Three men raised their hands.

"Okay," Landry told them. "But make it quick. I'm jus' 'bout ready to move out."

The men nodded.

"Well," the outlaw chief said pleasantly, "who's got the jug? I could use me a l'il drink."

By the time that Ace Landry was handed the jug of "corn likker," Davy and his companions, led by Big Nose Vachon, had been on the trail and heading north for several hours.

They were more impressed by the country with each mile that they traveled, marvelling at the beauty and purity of the landscape. The northern part of Idaho was a land of verdant forests and many rivers; the sides of the mountains were covered with abundant stands of cedar, spruce and hemlock, larch, fir and pine. It was a free, open country, as big and rich as the continent that harbored it. And the men who rode through it were continually moved by its wild beauty.

"Sure picked yourself a sweet piece of territory, Emile," Jack Poole told the trapper, determined never to call him Big Nose again.

Vachon nodded. "Dis place so good dat a man never need not'ing else in his 'ole life."

"What Indian live here?" Soaring Hawk asked the trapper.

"Up 'ere?" Vachon said, turning to Soaring Hawk.

154

"In dis 'ere country, you got Nez Percé—dat mean Pierced Nose in French. An' up nort', Kootenai an' Flathead. In de sout', you got Blackfoots an' Shoshone."

The Pawnee nodded.

"French trapper come 'ere an' give many name to dis country," Vachon went on. "Dat's why you got name like Nez Percé, Pend Oreille an' Coeur d'Alene. Even Boise. Dat *les bois* in French, mean de woods."

Vachon paused to scratch his big nose. "Up nort', dis country she get very wild. When Lewis an' Clark first come to explore dis place, dey have to cross back over Continental Divide into Montana for to get to far north of Idaho, 'cause she's so wild in de middle."

"Dey meet Indian 'oo never see white man before. Was virgin country—de pure nature as God made 'er. An' when dey get to center of Idaho, wilderness was too much for dem. No one able to pass canyons of Salmon River—what de Indian call 'River of No Return.' So dey 'ave to go back into Montana, for to cross panhandle up nort'."

"Hunting good here?" Soaring Hawk asked the trapper.

Vachon smiled and nodded his head emphatically. "Like you 'ave never see in your 'ole life, *mon cher ami*. Plains Indian like you never believe 'ow much game run up dis way. An' so many fish dat all you got to do is reach you 'and in stream an' catch 'ow many as you like."

"Bein' that you're a trapper, Emile," Davy Watson speculated, "this here must be right good country for fur-bearin' animals."

"Oh, la la," the huge mountain man replied, waggling his head and gesturing expressively. "You 'ave never see so much animal in any place. Beaver was so many 'ere," he reflected, a note of regret in his voice, "dat *beaucoup* trapper come in de 1820s and 30s, an' take all de beaver skin dey could carry."

He shifted in his saddle, leaning forward to scan the

trail ahead. "Well, first de Indian kill 'undred an' 'undred of trapper, an' many more die in blizzard an' freezing weather, but dey take *beaucoup* beaver skin from 'ere—from de Snake River Valley. Why, in one season, I 'ear dey take as much as eighty t'ousand beaver pelt."

"Why trapper need kill so many beaver?" Soaring Hawk asked Big Nose Vachon.

"'Cause in dem days, ever'body back East, he wear de beaver 'at."

The Pawnee frowned and shook his head. "Not smart kill so many beaver. Soon be no more."

"Our friend here don't understand about the dictates of fashion, do he?" Jack Poole said, a wry smile on his lips.

"Indian smarter den us in many way," was Vachon's reply. "Indian understan' 'ow to live wit' nature."

"I guess it was the Oregon Trail runnin' along the valley of the Snake that first brought lots of folks into Idaho," Jack Poole told the others. "Before the wagons rolled through, there was only trappers an' missionaries."

"Ah, but now," Vachon said with a sigh, "since dey find gold up nort' an' down by Boise, I t'ink many folks dey keep comin' now."

"I'm afraid you're right, Emile," Poole agreed, a mournful expression on his face. "But it's happenin' all over the place now. That's jus' the fate of the West, I spose, as well as the northwest."

"Well," the trapper told him, "if you ever gets too closed in, you go up by the Salmon River, in de center of Idaho, an' nobody never find you, by Gar!"

"I'll jus' keep that in mind, Emile," Poole replied. "For the railroad's comin', an' the slickers are movin' in right after it, quicker'n you can bat an eye."

"Dis talk, she make me sad," the big trapper admitted. "What's de point in gettin' worried before anyt'ing 'appen? Jus' look aroun' an' be glad for what we got today. *N'est-ce pas?*"

"He's right," Davy told his companions. "It makes a whole lot of sense to live for today. I mean, yesterday's past, an' tomorrow ain't here yet."

The others nodded in agreement with this.

"An' this is surely," Jack Poole said admiringly, "some of the mos' beautiful country this side of heaven."

"Like I say," Big Nose Vachon told them, "when I die, I don' want to go to 'eaven. I want to go 'ere."

"I can see your point," Poole said. "But if'n you don't go up to heaven, Emile, ain't you gonna miss seein' all them angels wheelin' overhead like eagles on a mountain top?"

The trapper shook his head. "I don' got to go to 'eaven for dat," he told his companions. "On account I got an angel right 'ere on eart'."

Poole gave him a knowing look. "Sounds to me like a man in love," he said.

"*Vous avez raison, cher ami,*" Big Nose Vachon replied with a smile. "You are absolutely right, Jacques Poole. I 'ave de sweetest little wife you ever see."

"What's her name?" Davy asked.

"You going to meet 'er real soon," Vachon told hs new friends. "For we stop at my place on de way. You see my wife real soon."

"I didn't catch her name," prompted Jack Poole.

"She is Indian," Big Nose Vachon said, nudging Soaring Hawk with his elbow. "Nez Percé. 'Er name is Natona."

> *"He said, 'Get you down, Romy,*
> *While I tell you my mind.*
> *Now, my mind is to drown you,*
> *And to leave you behind.'*
>
> *Well, he kicked her an' cuffed her,*
> *To the worst, understand.*
> *Threw her in the deep water*
> *That flows through the land."*

Ace Landry sang a ballad of love and death, a song that told how George Lewis drowned little Romy, his pregnant lover. And as he sang the chilling song, he smiled a happy smile and thought about the gold fields up north.

The outlaws were back on the Snake again, leading their pack animals over the steep and rocky banks that bordered its turbulent waters. Hells Canyon was still twenty miles distant, but the going had already proved rough, as the Salmon River Mountains began to crowd in upon the Snake with every passing mile.

Riding single file along both banks of the river, and often finding it necessary to dismount in order to lead their mounts over particularly rough stretches of terrain, the members of the Landry Gang swore and grumbled as they made their way northward with ever-increasing difficulty. And the fact that their chief was singing merrily at their head, oblivious to their discomfort and hardship, did little to raise the spirits of the desperadoes.

"I swear he's losin' his gol-durn mind," Hary Armstrong, one of the cutthroats who had joined the gang at Corinne, said in a low voice to the man who followed behind him on the east bank of the Snake.

Walter Baker, one of the original members of the Landry Gang, sighed and shook his head. "He's a strange hombre," Baker told Armstrong, speaking none too loudly as he glanced up to the head of the file of horsemen. "Seems like the more dirty the deed, the more happy he gets. I never done figgered out what makes him tick."

"He never smiles but when somethin' dirty's been done to someone," Armstrong added. "Like what we all done to the Injun wench."

Baker nodded. "Seems like rape is one of his favorite pastimes. Makes 'im happier'n a pig in shit."

"The way he been singin' all the way up from the cabin gives me the willies," Armstrong confided.

"You ain't alone in feelin' that, brother," Baker told

him. "For Ace Landry's got hisself the power to give a rattlesnake the shivers. Why, I heerd tell that one even bit him years ago." He paused for effect.

"Well, what happened?" Armstrong asked impatiently.

"They found the damn thing 'bout two hundred yards up the road," Baker went on. "Deader'n a doornail. An' ol' Ace Landry, why he recovered lickety-split, without hardly feelin' a thing."

"You tryin' to tell me he poisoned the rattler?" Armstrong asked incredulously.

"Well now, I ain't exactly sayin' that," Baker told him. "But look who done come out second best."

Near the end of the file that traveled along the east bank, old Bart McKecknie swore at his pack mule.

"Git along, you lop-eared, cock-eyed, spavined son of a bitch," the old-timer growled. "Git along, I say! Judas Priest, you're a contrary critter." He tugged at the mule's reins. "Mover yer dad-blamed butt, ya cantankerous bag o' bones!"

As McKecknie tugged again, the mule brayed in protest.

"Now, don't you go gittin' raboshus with me, you fugitive from a skinner's knife!" the old man roared. "By Gad, if I had me a length of bullwhip, I'd flay the livin' hide off'n ya—ya damn rebellious critter! Git along afore I whip out my sixshooter an' turn ya into a gelding!"

"Hey, Bart," whispered Herbert Briscoe, another of the Corinne contingent, dropping back to where the old-timer stood. "You don't have to shoot that ornery mule. Jus' get ol' Ace to come on back here an' sing to the critter. That'll *scare* the balls off'n it."

"You heard the man," Bart McKecknie whispered menacingly to the pack mule as he began to tug on its reins again. "If'n you don't move now, you big-eared, bucktoothed son of a bitch, you'll answer to Ace Landry!"

Briscoe nodded approvingly. "That'll get him movin'

surer than a stick of dynamite wedged up his ass."

Orrin Tweed and Marcus Lavellee struggled on at the head of the file on the west bank. After casting a surreptitious glance across the Snake, Tweed turned to Lavallee.

"What d'you make of that?" he asked, rolling his eyes in the direction of the singing outlaw chief. "It ain't natural fer a body to be happy in a sit-chee-ation the likes of this 'un."

Lavellee, a scar-faced, bearded giant, nodded thoughtfully. "Man like that," he replied, "would be likely to ask for Tabasco sauce in hell."

"I don't believe they'd have him down there," commented Tweed in a hoarse whisper. "'Cause the devil'd be goin' 'round lookin' over his shoulder all the time. He'd be afeered that Ace might bushwhack 'im."

"Well, if anybody could," Lavellee growled, "he'd be the boy."

"Even the devil was once a angel," Tweed told him. "Landry got hisself nowheres to go but up."

Behind the man in question, third and fourth respectively in his file, were Robert Smylie and Benjamin Klinger. They, too, had become unnerved by the desperado's ghoulish cheerfulness.

"What's he got to chirp about?" Klinger whispered to Smylie. "I swear, that man could sing whilst he danced barefoot on a bed of nails."

"The more I get to know him," Smylie whispered back, "the less I think he's human. He don't do nothin' like normal folks. He's hard as iron, an' colder'n a cake of ice. His father was a copperhead an' his mother was a polecat. An' there ain't nothin' meaner than him on the face of the earth."

"Then why do you ride with him?" Klinger whispered, after glancing up to the head of the file.

"He got us out of Corinne ahead of Jack Casement's boys, didn't he?" was Smylie's reply. "An' we's all laden down with gold, ain't we?"

"Well, that's true," Klinger admitted.

160

"An' he did see to it that we-all got us a little poon-tang a while back, didn't he?" Smylie went on.

"That he did," Klinger agreed, smiling as he recollected his turn with the Indian woman. "She was a right smart little vixen."

"Well, add all them things up," Smylie told him, "an' you'll see why we ride with ol' Ace. He ain't nice, but he sure is one hell of a provider."

"I guess you got a point there," Klinger said. "But I jus' wish he'd stop singin' for a spell, 'cause it's downright spooky, if you ask me."

> "*Then up spoke her mother,*
> *And her voice was the sting:*
> *'Well, only George Lewis*
> *Could have done such a thing.*
>
> *Well, a debt to the devil,*
> *George Lewis must pay,*
> *For killin' little Romy,*
> *And for runnin' away'.*"

Ace Landry finished the murder ballad, and then began to chuckle. George Lewis might pay a little debt to the devil, he reflected with amusement, but no one else ever laid hands on him in this world. Only a dumb shit would hang around the scene of a crime.

Tugging at the collar of his sheepskin jacket, Landry realized that it was getting colder. He sighed with relief at the thought that it would not snow, after all. His boys were having trouble enough without the weather against them. And then, as he began to hum the melody of *Barbara Allen*, the desperado wondered whether the Watson kid and the Pawnee brave were still on his trail.

Landry had to laugh out loud, spooking his men even further, as he recalled what the Watson boy and his father had done to his bully-boys in Hawkins Fork. It would be fun if the kid ever got lucky enough to catch up with him, he told himself. But Ace Landry realized that no one could ever catch up with him in such wild country . . . .

"We go off de river, now," Big Nose Vachon informed his companions. "An' soon we come to my place, where you get to meet my woman an' 'er mother."

Jack Poole winced as he turned to Vachon. "You didn't tell us you had your mother-in-law livin' up here with you."

The mountain man nodded. "Yeah, she live wit' me. She very old squaw. But she still 'elp aroun' cabin, an' cook damn good food, too."

"As long as she's quiet," the scout reflected. "I guess if'n you got to have a mother-in-law, a body could do a lot worse'n havin' one who's a Injun."

"Indian woman heap different than white woman," Soaring Hawk told them. "Not chatter all day like blackbird."

"An' I'll bet they spends a lot less wampum too, ol' hoss," added Jack Poole.

"You ever been hitched, Jack?" Davy asked the scout.

"Me?" Poole asked, shifting in his saddle as the horses made their way up the bluffs that towered over the Snake River. "Nope. Never had the inclination strong enough. Done came close once't, though. When I was younger. But I never tied the knot."

"Who almost roped ya?" asked Davy Watson.

"Oh, some gal from Denver, whose daddy run a general store there," Poole told him, a wistful smile on his rugged face. "I was right sweet on her. Still am, I reckon."

"So why you not marry 'er?" asked Big Nose Vachon.

"Almost ddid," Poole replied. "But she didn't cotton to my workin' as a scout. She wanted me to settle down."

"Hard for scout to settle down," was Soaring Hawk's comment.

Poole nodded. "Damn right it is. Scouts is a restless breed. Why, I'm 'bout as settled as the stomach of a man with a hangover ridin' shotgun on the Overland Coach."

"So that was it, huh?" Davy asked.

"'Fraid so," Poole replied. "Neither of us was willin' to compromise. She told me she didn't want to spend her nights sittin' around waitin' for some saddletramp to mosey on home whenever it suited his fancy. An' I told her that I couldn't sit still long enough to take root anywheres." He sighed. "Not for love nor money."

"*Ah, mon pauvre ami*," Vachon said, clapping Poole sympathetically on the back. "You should marry Indian woman. Dey understan' a man 'oo like to move about."

"Yeah, I reckon you're right there, Emile," the scout agreed, sighing once more.

"*Alors*, don't you worry, Jacques Poole," the trapper reassured his friend. "Over dat rise, we see my cabin. An' when we get dere, I ask my wife to find you nice Nez Percé girl to keep you warm at night."

"It's never too late, Jack," Davy told Poole. Then he smiled wistfully, as he thought of Deanna MacPartland.

Big Nose Vachon was in high spirits as they rode into the clearing in the grove of blue spruce trees and drew near to the cabin.

"Dat's my place," he told the others proudly. "Where you meet my wife, an' eat some of the best damn venison stew you ever eat in your 'ole goddam life."

But the trapper's ebullience suddenly disappeared as they walked their horses the last forty feet to the cabin's door.

"She always come to door to meet me," he said, puzzlement creeping into his voice. "Mebbe she no feel so good. *Mon Dieu*. I 'ope not."

Vachon dismounted, looped his reins over the hitching post and rushed inside the cabin. Davy, Soaring

Hawk, and Jack Poole all exchanged wondering looks.

By the time that the companions had dismounted and followed the trapper inside the cabin, they were greeted by the sight of Vachon kneeling by the side of an old Indian woman who sat cross-legged on the floor, in the cold ashes before the fire, rocking back and forth with bowed head and wailing in a shrill and desolate voice.

Davy looked on with concern as the huge mountain man spoke gently to the pathetic old squaw.

"Taiga, it's me, Emile," Vachon said in Nez Percé, gently shaking the old woman and cutting short her lament.

"Emile," she croaked sadly, still not looking up at Vachon.

"What's wrong, Taiga? Where is Natona?"

"Out back," the old woman whispered. "In the woods."

"Outside where?" the trapper persisted.

"In the trees behind the house," was all the old squaw said. Then she resumed her keening.

An expression of horror suddenly came to his face, and Emile Vachon slowly rose to his feet.

"Emile, what's wrong?" Jack Poole asked as the mountain man staggered over to the cabin door.

But Big Nose Vachon did not answer, and Davy stepped aside as the trapper stumbled blindly through the doorway.

"You don't think—" Davy began, turning to face his friends.

Soaring Hawk looked from Davy to the old Nez Percé woman. "Something bad happen," he told his blood brother.

"Well," Jack Poole said with a heavy sigh, "I s'pose we better haul our butts outside an' look after Emile."

They found the mountain man about forty feet behind the cabin, at the blue spruce trees by the end of the clearing. He stood stock-still, seemingly rooted to the spot as firmly as the trees, staring up at the body of a young Indian woman, as it swayed in the wind. She had hanged herself by the neck.

"Oh, my God!" Jack Poole muttered as they drew up beside Emile Vachon.

Davy saw that tears were streaming down the mountain man's cheeks, flowing past his great nose and running into the forest of his bristling beard.

"Mister Vachon," Davy whispered, feeling the muscles of his throat constrict as his emotions began to overwhelm him. "Are you . . . all right?"

"Leave me alone," the trapper rumbled in a voice that broke. "Go back inside."

Davy was about to say something when Soaring Hawk pulled him away from the trapper. And then, nodding solemnly, the Pawnee led Davy and the scout back into the log cabin, where the old woman sat on the floor and continued to mourn for her daughter.

Outside, among the blue spruce trees, Emile Vachon cut his wife down and cradled her corpse in his massive arms as tenderly as if she were a newborn infant. Then he went into the cabin and laid the body of Natona down on a bed.

Whispering the old Nez Percé woman's name, the mountain man knelt beside her once more. Prompting her gently and exercising great patience, he proceeded to elicit from her the story of Ace Landry's visit and the subsequent mass-rape of the woman he loved.

"An' so," Vachon concluded, having told his companions the dreadful story later, his bass voice cracking as it had throughout his terrible narrative, "Natona did not want me to see de shame in 'er eyes when I come back." He paused to wipe his eyes. "So she take 'er life. Indians very proud people."

Soaring Hawk began to chant softly in Pawnee. Vachon looked up at him from where he sat on the bed, his wife's cold hand in his.

"He's prayin' for her soul," Poole told him.

Vachon nodded as he looked from Jack to Davy. "You know 'oo do dis t'ing?" he asked them softly.

Both Davy Watson and the scout nodded

immediately.

"It's the same man we're after," Davy whispered. "Ace Landry."

Vachon sniffled as he nodded, bending over to kiss the small, pale hand of his dead wife.

"Now I make sure you find dis man," he told them. "An' all de men wit' 'im. I go wit' you. We catch dem in one day, mebbe two. When dey deep into 'Ells Canyon."

Davy Watson and Jack Poole nodded again.

"An' when we catch 'em," Big Nose Vachon went on, a grim smile coming to his lips, "we make dem pay."

Chapter 12

"Christ, he finally stopped singin'," muttered a burly, red-bearded man named Ed Niles as the Landry Gang came in sight of the great gorge that is Hells Canyon.

"Ain't gonna be much to sing about from here on out," replied Phil Nelan, a short, dark-haired man.

Another member of the gang, Frank Logan by name, led his horse and pack mule up to the spot where the two men were standing.

"Ol' Ace really got hisself somethin' to worry about now, don't he?" Logan commented sourly.

They stood on the eastern bank of the Snake, Landry and seven of his desperadoes. Seven of their companions were on the opposite bank. And indeed, Landry was silent now, as he reined in his horse at the head of his band of ruffians, while the others all contemplated the vastness and raw power of Hells Canyon in open-mouthed awe.

"Sweet Jesus!" Nelan exclaimed, his voice barely audible above the sound of rushing waters that came from the mouth of the gorge, now only several hundred yards distant. "Do we have to make our way through that God-awful place?"

There was a look of resignation on Ed Niles' face when he spoke. "You heard Ace, Phil," he told Nelan. "The country along both sides of the Snake is jus' too damn wild to travel in. But when we get to the far side of the canyon, there'll be gold a-plenty for all."

As Phil Nelan shook his head, Frank Logan said, "Ain't that the damnedest thing you ever did see." He looked up at the steep canyon walls, whose wooded benches andd sharp crags loomed above the river.

167

"It sure is somethin'," Niles admitted.

Indeed, Hells Canyon was an unforgettable sight. Flowing through it, coming down from the north, were the icy waters of a number of mountain tributaries, foremost among them America's wildest river, the Salmon. Gargantuan walls towered more than a mile above the Snake—hard, unyielding rock faces of andesite and rhyolite, green stone and basalt, with wooded stretches interspersed among the cliffs. At some points, the depth of the canyon measured nearly 8,000 feet.

The gorge was broad, and bore little resemblance to the barren and narrow slit that was the Grand Canyon. Heavily wooded with pine, cedar and spruce trees that rose in series of levels, with the wild river pulsing below it, was an awesome spectacle. The traveler to Hells Canyon had the eerie feeling of standing in the very heart of untamed nature. The rock walls towered imposingly over the crashing, dangerous waters that swirled and churned furiously by, barely contained by the rocks and soil of the riverbanks. It was a place where man realized his relative insignificance in the great scheme of things, and was humbled by that overwhelming display of the raw, elemental power of nature.

Even Ace Landry, a man whose satanic pride rarely allowed him to acknowledge few things greater than himself, was humbled. He had stopped singing when the power of it all immediately overwhelmed his senses. And even this man, who thought nothing of desecrating places of worship or gunning down men of God, was awed.

"By Gad, I've never seen the like of that, man or boy, in all my born days," the desperado said aloud, unaware that his bully-boys had come up behind him. "This is surely the wonder of all creation."

The ruffians looked from one to another, their own awe deepening as they realized the depth of their leader's wonder. Ordinarily quick to reflect his moods, the desperadoes were deeply impressed by Landry's unusually humble reaction to the spectacle of Hells Canyon.

"That river'd give a man a thrashing he'd never forgit, if he ever had the bad luck to fall into it," old Bart McKecknie remarked as he came up beside his chief.

Landry nodded. "Why, it roars, rushes an' sputters like an' angry bear. An' those walls just sneer down at a man, as if they was remindin' him of what a pitiful l'il thing he is."

"Ain't there no easier way to get up north, Ace?" McKecknie asked.

"Not as I know, Bart," the desperado replied, still staring into the mouth of Hells Canyon. "Less'n you got a couple of weeks to spare while we double back into Montana. We're surrounded by the Salmon River Mountains—here an' on the other side of the river, in the Oregon Territory. Goin' this way may not be easy, but it's the surest route."

Ace Landry sat up in his saddle and gave the signal to move on. And so the gang entered the fearsome chasm known as Hells Canyon. And every man among them, with the possible exception of Ace Landry himself, did so with a troubled heart and a mind full of vague, ominous misgivings.

The four horsemen rode like the wind, as if the devil himself were at their heels, traveling through the wild Idaho country along paths and byways that were virtually unknown to white men and inaccessible to all but the craftiest of Indian woodsmen.

Riding at their head was Emile Vachon, his face as dark as a thundercloud, his features as hard and unyielding as the walls of Hells Canyon. In addition to his Colt and the Winchester carbine that hung in a sheath from his saddle, the mountain man carried a long, sharp knife in his belt.

Behind him, riding single file through the dense woods, were Jack Poole, Davy Watson and Soaring Hawk. Each had his guns well-oiled and his knife honed to a razor sharpness; each had his features set in a grim reflection of his inner resolve and determination. They were on their way at last, headed for the final showdown with Ace Landry.

None of the four horsemen uttered a sound as they sped along the path to vengeance. Each was steeped in his own thoughts; each in his own way prepared himself for the long-awaited vendetta.

Emile Vachon's mind was like ice, amidst the fires of rage that threatened to consume his soul. He needed a clear head, the trapper told himself, to find Ace Landry and then tear him to pieces. He would need all his cunning and skill for the task at hand. Later, if he survived, there would be plenty of time to mourn his beloved Natona.

Jack Poole gritted his teeth as he thought about the impending encounter with the man who had gunned down his buddy, Cliff Hagen. There was going to be a great deal of killing to do in a short while, and the scout felt more than ready to do his share of it.

Soaring Hawk's eyes narrowed, reflecting the Pawnee's inner satisfaction, now that he was launched upon the warpath. He smiled a smile as sharp as the scalping knife in his belt whenever the figure of Ace Landry appeared in his mind's eye. Many times over the past year had he fantasized taking the desperado's life, shooting him down and cutting off his scalp while he still lived. Soon he would have his chance.

His father was about to be avenged, Davy Watson realized exultantly as he spurred his horse on. The time had come to repay Ace Landry for his misdeeds, to settle the score forever. And then, no matter what the outcome, the terrible weight of hatred and vengeance would be lifted from his soul. He would know peace of mind once more . . . or at least the quiet of the grave.

He realized wistfully that he might never see his

mother again, or Amy, or Lucius Erasmus. A stab of longing made him gasp for breath, and he wondered how they were faring in his absence. But he was suddenly cheered by the thought that even if he did not see the living again, he would then be reunited with the dead. John Jacob Watson stood ready to receive him, on the far and sunlit shore that lay on the other side of the river of life.

Sadness flooded his being as Davy Watson thought lovingly of the farm by Pottawatomie Creek, and of the way that the wind on the ridge had sung its song of promise to his father in the dulcet voice of a woman. And he recalled how the wheatfields dancing in the wind looked like rippling carpets of gold spread out over the brown floor of the Watson farm. The night stars shining like diamonds on black velvet came back to him with sudden, heartbreaking clarity, and he felt the presence of the big, dinner gong moon that sat above the prairie as if it were shining on him at that very moment.

But it was only mid-day, and the autumn sun was high over Idaho. And far from the peaceful wheatfields of Kansas the horsemen rode, through the wild forests and foothills of the Salmon River Mountains.

Longing pierced his heart and desire scorched his loins, as Davy thought about Deanna MacPartland. He ached to hold her blonde loveliness in his arms again, to inhale deeply of the musky perfume of her arousal, to touch her lithe body of ivory and rose with hand and mouth and mind.

Suddenly pain stabbed through his left shoulder, as if the wound inflicted upon him by Ace Landry were crying out to its author in the raw accents and gutturals of violation and outrage. And the pain drew Davy's thoughts away from tender things, causing him to harden his heart and steel himself for the killing to come.

Up ahead, Emile Vachon reined in his lathered mount and drew to a halt on top of a bluff. Davy and the others joined him, and looked down to where he

171

pointed, into the depths of Hells Canyon.

"So that's Hells Canyon," Davy said in a hushed voice.

"By God, it's a mighty sight!" Jack Poole exclaimed.

"Place where Great Spirit walk on earth," Soaring Hawk said, moved by the power and magnificence of what he saw before him.

"Lan'ry is down dere," Vachon rumbled in his bass voice. "Now, we get dat *sale cochon*."

"You think he's in the canyon, Mr. Vachon?" Davy asked.

"Look 'ard," the mountain man told his companions. "Way over to nort'east. Up ahead on river, very far down. You can see dem."

"I see," Soaring Hawk, the most keen-eyed among them, was the first to say.

"Where?" Davy asked, casting a beseeching look at his blood brother.

"Yup. I see it," Jack Poole remarked, while Davy peered over Soaring Hawk's pointing finger, into the far distance.

"Oh, yeah," he said, finally spotting the dark files of men, horses and pack animals that threaded their way, insect-like, along both banks of the Snake River.

Emile Vachon scowled darkly as he rubbed his enormous nose. "It don't be long time now," he told his companions, "before we catch up wit' dis Ace Lan'ry."

Each of the three men who heard him looked the trapper in the eye and nodded in solemn agreement.

"Grab hold of them reins, gol-durn it!" old Bart McKecknie swore as his pack mule slipped off the rocky bank and fell, braying with fear, into the icy, rushing waters of the Snake.

"Shit—missed 'em!" grunted Ed Niles, after a dive that sent him sprawling onto the side of the gritty riverbank.

Twice before disaster had threatened, with horses and pack mules losing their footing as the banks crumbled beneath their feet, nearly precipitating them into the turbulent river. And weighed down with gold as they were, some of the unfortunate animals would surely have gone into the water and drowned, had it not been for the swift and concerted action of the desperadoes. Ace Landry had no intention of losing an ounce of gold, not if he could help it.

But they were all tiring now; the passage through Hells Canyon, while still less than half completed, had been a hard and grueling task. No one had foreseen how difficult the route along the craggy shores of the raging Snake would be. And even Ace Landry had begun to entertain second thoughts.

"Git that fucker afore the current takes his butt clear to Mexico!" McKecknie cried as the current began to take hold of his struggling mule.

The flat-nosed man whom Davy Watson had punched almost a year ago, in the Red Dog Saloon, leaned over and made a wide swipe for the mule's trailing reins. But he overreached himself, and pitched out of his saddle, diving headfirst into the chill, rushing waters.

Bellowing and spluttering, the flat-nosed man splashed frantically as he scrambled back onto the shore. The mule was now in the center of the Snake, bobbing up and down and braying shrilly in panic, as the waters swept it downstream.

"Ace," old Bart McKecknie, panicked himself, called out imploringly to his chief. "What happens if we lose the mule?"

Keeping his eyes on the mule, as it bobbed downstream and was about to disappear, Ace Landry smiled a smile as cold as the waters of the Snake.

"Why, that's your share of the loot an' more, ain't it, Bart?" he asked in mock-innocence. "If it goes under, I reckon you an' a few of the boys is goin' to be in for a big fi-nancial loss."

"Save my mule!" the old man cried out, waving to

the men downstream. "A thousand in gold to the man that saves my mule!"

"A thousand an' you're on!" whooped Charley Ivy, the youngest of all the desperadoes. He wheeled his horse around and went galloping downstream, the shoes of his mount striking sparks on the rocks by the river-bank. A moment later, he rounded the bend in the river and was lost to sight.

"You're lucky we got that wild young 'un with us, Bart," Landry told the old-timer. "Elsewise, you'd be up Shit's Creek without a paddle."

"Praise the lord," the old man muttered, wiping the sweat from his forehead.

"*Hoo-haw! Hoo-haw!*" whooped young Charley Ivy, filled with thoughts of gold and the spirit of the chase. The current was extremely swift in that stretch of the Snake, and the mule was still at least a hundred feet ahead of him. "*Hee-yaw!*" the seventeen-year-old desperado shrieked, putting spurs to his horse just as the mule disappeared around yet another bend.

Young Charley Ivy was screeching like a plains Indian as he took his mount around that bend. But a moment later, after he had disappeared behind the jutting can-yon wall, his cries were suddenly cut short. And on the far side of that bend, had any of the Landry Gang been there to see, they would have been shocked by what had happened to the youngest of their band.

No sooner had Charlie Ivy, his eye on the mule and riding hell-bent for leather, rounded the bend, than a huge figure hurtled at him from a rock ledge that over-hung the riverbank. The impact of that massive form tore the youth out of his saddle, and he had neither time to shout nor resist before he was dead.

Rising slowly, a grim smile of satisfaction on his lips, Emile Vachon looked down at the body of seventeen-year-old Charley Ivy. The long knife in the trapper's right hand was covered with blood from the tip of its blade to the hilt.

Then the trapper bent over, while Charley Ivy looked

up from the pool of blood wherein he lay, and stared with glassy eyes, his throat cut from ear to ear. Vachon wiped the blade of the knife, and two red streaks scumbled the front of the dead youth's checkered blue-and-yellow flannel shirt. The trapper looked downstream to where his companions waited. They acclaimed his savage deed with slow nods of their heads.

"Now," he told them when he had reached their side, "we tether de 'orses. For we goin' to climb up dere," he said, pointing to the canyon walls above them. "An' make big surprise for de rest of Lan'ry's bunch."

When Charley Ivy failed to return the Landry Gang began to worry.

"Jee-hosaphat!" old Bart McKecknie swore, turning to his chief. "Now, you don't s'pose the young 'un run off with my mule, do ya, Ace?"

"There ain't much point in that, Bart," Landry told him. "For Ivy left his own mule behind."

"Well, what in tarnation's keepin' him?"

Not the man to indulge in idle speculation, Landry cautiously dispatched four of his bully-boys—two on each bank of the Snake—to ride downstream and find out what was keeping young Charley Ivy.

When the bully-boys rode back with Ivy's carcass and dumped it onto the ground before him, Ace Landry scowled and shifted uneasily in his saddle.

"Looks like we got company," he told his men. "So keep your wits about you, an' let's make 'em welcome."

"We goin' on, or we goin' back, Ace?" Ed Niles asked, standing up in his saddle as he looked downstream.

"Well, the one thing we know 'bout our new friends," Landry told his ruffians, "is that they's comin' up behind us. So we might as well move ahead a piece, until we come to a spot where we can lay for 'em. That's my thinkin'."

So ahead the Landry bunch rode, into a stretch of

Hells Canyon where the cliff walls gave way in many places at the lower levels to cuts and benches covered with trees on both sides of the river that roared and churned wildly downstream. And at the same time, the riverbanks grew even more inhospitable, and several riders, horses and pack mules went sliding into the Snake.

Suddenly a great roar split the air, and echoed and re-echoed through Hells Canyon like the sound of a giant hammerblow. At the head of the file of riders on the west bank, a man known as Bud Eustis threw up his arms and flew backward off his horse.

Ace Landry's gun was out of its holster before the body hit the ground, and he scanned the heavily-wooded benches above both banks of the river.

"Back against the walls!" he called out to his bully-boys. "Up there!" he yelled, gesturing up and ahead with the barrel of his Cavalry issue Smith and Wesson. Eustis had fallen backward off the west side of his saddle, so Landry deduced that the shot had come from the benches of trees somewhere above and to the front of the east bank.

And indeed, in a heavily-wooded stand of pine trees, lying on the ground alongside of Emile Vachon, Soaring Hawk wore a grim smile on his face as he lowered his smoking Sharps rifle.

"Bravo," Big Nose Vachon whispered in his rumbling bass. "Two is dead. Now we got only thirteen more to butcher."

Across the Snake, in a wooded tier higher than the one that sheltered Vachon and the Pawnee, Davy Watson and Jack Poole crouched among the trees and undergrowth. Their trousers were still damp from the hips down, having been wet nearly a half hour earlier during their crossing of the river.

"Here lad," Poole said, thrusting his Winchester "yellow boy" at Davy. "Now, pass me your Henry. It's a more trustworthy piece for sharpshootin'."

Davy handed the rifle to Poole, who proceeded to

brace his left arm on a rock, and line up one of the bully-boys behind Ace Landry in his sights.

"Which one you gonna shoot?" Davy asked the scout in a whisper.

"You'll see soon enough," Poole told him, as his finger began to tighten on the trigger of the Henry.

The rifle discharged with a loud crack. Again the gunshot echoed through Hells Canyon. In the center of Ace Landry's file, a man fell forward over the neck of his horse, and then slid to the ground in a rag doll sprawl.

"Damn it—now they're behind us!" Ace Landry cried out angrily. "Who got hit this time?" he asked as he wheeled his mount around.

"Walter's been hit, Ace," Bart McKecknie called out from the rear.

"My back," moaned the man who had just been shot. "I think my back is broke."

To a man, Landry's bully-boys were jumpy now, and they repeatedly looked up and down, ahead and behind, squinting as they peered into the wooded benches above and across from them. Within the last sixty seconds, two of their number had been shot, to say nothing of the recently butchered Charley Ivy.

"What'll we do, Ace?" the flat-nosed man called Riker asked his chief in a quavering voice. "We're sittin' ducks here."

Landry looked over to his men across the river, and then back to those directly behind him. He began to heft his pistol in his hand and straighten up in his saddle. Then, just as he opened his mouth and was about to address his men, one more rifle shot resounded throughout Hells Canyon.

Whinnying pitifully, Landry's horse suddenly reared into the air and threw itself backward—into the raging waters of the Snake. But a split second before it did, Ace Landry hurtled to the ground, clawing at the sand and rocks of the riverbank like a spider skidding down a length of wet drainpipe. And as the horse hit the water

177

with a shrill whinny and a loud smack, sending jets of water up into the air on all sides, Landry managed to obtain a handhold before he slid into the icy waters. But the horse, whinnying horribly all the while, was soon swept out of sight by the fierce current.

"Lan'ry! Ace Lan'ry!" a bass voice boomed out from somewhere above the east bank, echoing loudly against the canyon walls.

Ace Landry wiped the barrel of his Smith and Wesson against his trouser leg and peered at the wooded tiers above, a puzzled expression on his face as he caught Emile Vachon's accent.

"Dat was my wife you an' your pigs dishonor back dere!" Vachon called out loudly. "She take 'er life on account what you done. Now I make you pay!"

Two gunshots rang out and traveled along the canyon in a diminishing series of echoes, as Ace Landry fired in the direction of the disembodied voice.

"I jus' aim for your horse, Lan'ry," the deep voice boomed once more, chilling the blood of the bully-boys with its sound and its ominous message. "I save you for last. First, I take care of your boys!"

Several more shots rang out, as the jittery outlaws pegged a random volley after their fearsome and unseen enemy.

Across the river, Davy Watson waved to Jack Poole from the cover of a cluster of rocks. Thirty feet below him, the scout waved back, wobbling as he stood on a somewhat less steady footing than his friend had obtained.

After the sniping, and Vachon's subsequent warning to Landry, the next item in the mountain man's strategy was for the four companions to roll a number of rocks and boulders down upon the members of the Landry Gang, with the intention of catching the desperadoes before they had time to scatter and run for cover. But just as Jack Poole was about to send down the first boulder, the scout lost his footing.

Leaning back, about to thrust both legs forward and

dislodge a big stone, Poole's left hand suddenly began to skid along the ground, and he lost his balance. Above him, Davy Watson watched in horror as the scout's body slid down the escarpment above which he had formerly been situated.

By the time that Jack Poole had clawed his way to a halt, Ace Landry was up on his feet and pointing across the river to the spot where the scout hung.

"There's one, by Jesus!" he roared to his bully-boys. "Blast the sum'bitch off that rock!" Saying this, he aimed his gun at Jack Poole, who was now inching his way back up to the safety of the ledge he had just quit. The outlaw fired his Smith and Wesson until its chambers were empty.

Bam! Bam! Ba-blam!

The guns of the outlaws barked in staccato bursts, and the sound of their shots reverberated along the walls of Hells Canyon with the menacing sound of some gigantic, demented blacksmith hammering away at his anvil in a fit of insane fury.

Bullets spanged around Jack Poole as they richocheted off the rock surface to which he clung. Davy cried out to his friend, in an effort to spur him to greater exertions as he fought his way back up to the rim of the ledge above.

Finally, Poole's hands made contact with the rim, and he proceeded to pull himself up to it with a chinning motion. Davy Watson began to cheer, but halted abruptly as two bullets hit the scout almost simultaneously, just as he had risen to his knees on the ledge's rim. Davy gasped as he saw Jack Poole sway back and forth, a hail of bullets striking all about him, and the odds in favor of his pitching off the ledge. Then Davy gave a little moan of relief as Poole fell forward, and rolled to safety behind the rocks.

If Jack Poole's move had misfired, the moment that Emile Vachon was waiting for had arrived. Seeing the Landry Gang all standing up by both banks of the Snake, firing away at the scout for all they were worth, the mountain man promptly signaled to Davy and Soaring Hawk, who would follow his lead in sending a number of rocks and boulders crashing down upon the heads of the desperadoes.

With the sounds of the first rush of stone coming down behind them drowned out by the echoing blasts of their volleys of gunshots, the desperadoes on Ace Landry's side of the river never became aware of what was happening until the rocks actually tore into them.

The earth beneath their feet shook to the rolling thunder of the boulders in the instant before the great stones that Vachon had loosed smashed into men, mules and horses alike, breaking bones and rending flesh, sending broken bodies into the swirling, icy waters and spattering the riverbank with bright red blood.

The rocks sent down by Vachon and Soaring Hawk hit in the center of Landry's file. Herbert Briscoe and Benjamin Klinger, along with their mounts, were pitched into the Snake with the awful sounds of meat and bone smashing beneath unyielding stone.

Briscoe was never seen again, and Klinger splashed frantically in the water, as he fought his way ashore.

One pack mule lay on its side, its head nearly torn off, gold dust spilling out of its saddlebags. Old Bart McKecknie's horse had bolted, making its way downstream, past the body of young Charlie Ivy. McKecknie himself lay flat on his back, clutching at his chest while he jerked spasmodically and moaned in an eerie and feeble voice.

"*The gold! The gold!*" Ace Landry cried out, oblivious to the sufferings of his men, as another pack animal skidded into the rushing waters.

It was at this time that Davy Watson sent down his share of rocks, which then wrought havoc with the desperadoes on the west bank, while they stood watching the ghastly spectacle on the other shore with pop-eyes and gaping mouths.

Four boulders rolled down upon the outlaws in rapid

succession, one after another. The first that hit bowled over a horse and rider, while the second knocked a pack mule smack into the Snake. The third went wide, and hit the water with a great, resounding splash. But the fourth tore the flat-nosed Riker out of his saddle. Davy nodded grimly whem he saw that the man's head had been crushed like an empty tin can beneath a boot heel.

Down below, big Lavallee fished his friend Tweed out of the icy waters. Then he swore like a trooper as his braying, crippled mule began to go under.

By this time, Ace Landry had recovered from the shock of the two-pronged attack and collected his wits about him. "Take cover up there!" he cried, pointing to the wooded tiers that went up in steps above both banks of the Snake.

"You all know where that jasper we winged is lyin', right, boys?" he went on hoarsely. "So it stands to reason that his pals is somewhere in the vicinity, and in a like spot on the other bank. Let's get up there an' flush the bastards out!"

Then, as Soaring Hawk and Emile Vachon sent down a fusillade of rifle fire, Landry's bully-boys ran for cover and began to scramble up the face of Hells Canyon.

At the same time, Davy Watson made his way, Indian-style over to where Jack Poole lay. He found the scout on his back, attempting to raise himself to a sitting position. But a fit of coughing interrupted Poole's efforts, and he slid back down the rock he had been leaning upon, blood seeping out of his mouth and running down onto his chest.

"Best you lay there a piece, Jack," Davy cautioned his friend. "You jus' rest a spell afore you think of sittin' up again."

The scout answered Davy in sputtery, gurgling tones, speaking to him through a mouth full of blood. "Don't make no plans fer me, *amigo*. I'm a goner." He paused to spit up copious quantities of blood. "I've run my course," he said weakly.

Davy fought back the tears and shook his head violently. "Bullcorn!" he said in a voice that cracked. "You're jus' gonna have to set still for a spell, ol' hoss."

Poole coughed up more blood and then looked up at Davy, his eyes crossing as he began to lose the power of focus. "Nope,"he muttered. "I can hear my chips bein' cashed in already. But maybe if I'm lucky, I can stay here, instead of goin' to heaven."

Davy looked away and wiped his eyes. By the time he looked down again, the scout was dead.

"*Lan'ry*!" the voice of Big Nose Vachon boomed throughout that embattled stretch of Hells Canyon. "Come on up! I meet you 'alf-way! I come shake you 'and . . . an' cut out you liver!"

Davy mumbled a quick prayer over the mortal remains of Jack Poole, picked up his Henry, and then rose to his feet.

"Now is only nine of you, Lan'ry," jeered Emile Vachon. "L'il while ago, was fifteen. Pretty soon, be only you. An' you don' even know how many we be."

Whoever that sum'bitch is, Ace Landry told himself, he knows Hells Canyon like the back of his hand. Despite the havoc wrought in his ranks by the man's ambuscades, the desperado grudgingly conceded the brilliance of his foe. But judging from the earlier gunshots, and the way the rocks came down upon his men, Landry didn't think that there were more than two or three men above him. And only two on the tiers above the opposite side of the Snake, including the man whom the gang's fire had surely put out of action.

There were three men remaining with Landry on the east bank, facing two or three foes, while it was probably four-to-one in his favor on the west bank. Therefore, he concluded, all he had to do was to stall for time and hang on until his boys got their man and then came across the river to reinforce him.

"Go easy, boys," he called out to Niles, Smylie, and

Klinger. "Let them come to you. I figger there's only one able-bodied man facing our boys on the other bank. So, jus' go slow an' watch your butts, 'cause we'll soon have four more guns on our side."

"He's not so dumb, dat *cochon*," Big Nose Vachon conceded in a whisper to Soaring Hawk. "*Alors*, den we got to go after 'im, Indian-style. Right, my friend?"

The Pawnee looked into the huge trapper's eyes and slowly nodded his head. Vachon pointed to the south with one hand and indicated himself with the thumb of the other. Then, pointing north, he indicated Soaring Hawk. The two men parted noiselessly, and disappeared among the trees like spirits of the woodland.

Moving Indian-style himself, in the manner he had learned from Soaring Hawk, Davy Watson had traveled down and to the south of the spot where Jack Poole's body lay. And no sooner than he had gained the cover of a cluster of rocks, he spied a man inching his way through a stand of pines almost directly below him. The man was not aware of his presence, and consequently did not realize that he was being lined up in Davy's gunsights. And the instant after the man had halted and begun to take a look around, the loud report of Davy's Henry rifle broke the heavy silence that had fallen over Hells Canyon.

Frank Logan grunted once as the slug tore into his chest and smacked him back against a pine tree. Then his eyes rolled up in their sockets and he slid down to a sitting position at the base of the tree.

Davy Watson surveyed his handiwork for several seconds before sending another shell into the chamber of his rifle. A sudden, rustling sound behind him caused Davy to whirl around, and level his Henry as he did.

There in a stand of trees thirty feet away, the short man known as Phil Nelan was down on one knee, his Winchester already aimed at Davy Watson. And by the time that the young Kansan had got off a single shot, Nelan had fired three times. Then Nelan lowered his rifle, nodding with satisfaction as he watched Davy's body roll down the steep slope that led to the west bank of the Snake . . . .

Harry Armstrong was a big man, and it took two slugs from Soaring Hawk's Sharps to bring him down from a distance. And a moment after that, it was the Pawnee's ill luck to have both Benjamin Klinger and Ace Landry converge upon him at the same time.

Seeing Klinger before he had a chance to reload his Sharps, Soaring Hawk dropped the rifle and whipped out the knife at his belt with lightning speed. Klinger panicked when he saw this, and fired off several wild shots in rapid succession. His finger was still on the trigger when the Pawnee's knife tore into his guts.

By the time that Klinger had begun rolling down the steep incline that led to the Snake, Ace Landry jumped out from behind a boulder and fired twice at Soaring Hawk's back. The Indian threw up his hands and shot forward, skidding to a face-down halt on the rocky ground.

Landry ducked back behind the boulder and looked around in all directions, fully aware that another extremely dangerous adversary lurked in the vicinity. Then he stared at Soaring Hawk's motionless body for a long time, listening to the sounds around him, until he was convinced that the man he had just shot no longer posed a threat to him.

Emile Vachon crept up behind Robert Smylie and cut his throat from ear to ear just before he saw Davy Watson's body roll down into the cruel waters of the Snake. And by the time that Davy had rolled over the bank and hit the water with a loud smack, Vachon had reloaded his sevenshooter and was after Ed Niles. Under cover of the sounds of Ben Klinger's wild shots, the mountain man scrambled over an outcropping of rock to crouch twenty feet above the unsuspecting Niles. The man's cream-colored Stetson made an ideal target, and so Vachon put two bullets into its crown.

A sudden, strafing fire swept the outcropping, forcing Vachon to jump to safety, and landing him smack on the dead body of Ed Niles. He had been fired upon by Orrin Tweed, Phil Nelan and Marcus Lavallee, who had joined forces and were now urging their horses across the turbulent Snake.

Several seconds later, Vachon emerged from the rocks some fifty feet distant from the spot where he had lain for Niles. Steadying his pistol with both hands, the mountain man emptied it at the three desperadoes who were just emerging from the river.

Blamblamblam! Blam! Blam!

Vachon's five shots resounded like thunder in the canyon. Orrin Tweed was ripped out of his saddle and plunged into the swift, icy waters. Lavallee's horse fell down dead, thrusting the bearded giant over its neck. He fell flat on his head and shoulders with a thud when he hit the unyielding soil of the riverbank. Phil Nelan's horse got nicked in the flank, and the beast panicked and took off upriver, with Nelan swearing loudly and holding on for all he was worth.

By that time, Ace Landry was standing less than twenty-five feet behind Big Nose Vachon, smiling his cruel, wintry smile as he leveled his Smith and Wesson at the mountain man's back. And at that very instant, as though some sixth sense had made him aware of the desperado's presence, Vachon spun around, balancing himself with difficulty as he stood on his rocky perch.

Ace Landry's smile tightened at the exact instant that his finger tightened on the trigger of his big gun. Two shots rang out, to be echoed and re-echoed through Hells Canyon. The huge man in buckskins was whipped off his perch like a rag doll in a gale. The first bullet had done that, Landry reflected; he wasn't even sure if the second had found its mark. But that wasn't important; the first shot had done the trick.

He ran over to the rock ledge, hoping to watch Vachon's body hit the water, but he was just in time to see it disappear into the shadows of a thick stand of pine trees, from which it did not emerge. Then the outlaw looked down to the riverbank, and was amused by what he saw.

The Watson kid had somehow made it across the Snake, and was on his hands and knees beside the recumbent form of Marcus Lavallee, whose pistol he was in the act of prying out of its holster. Apparently, Landry speculated, the giant had broken his neck when his horse threw him.

As Ace Landry ducked back behind the outcropping of rock, pausing to reload his Smith and Wesson, Phil Nelan, in control of his mount once more, galloped around a bend in the river. He was headed straight for the spot where Davy Watson knelt gun-in-hand beside the corpse of Marcus Lavallee.

Both men were stunned by the sudden sight of each other. Firing his pistol at the same time that he attempted to rein in his galloping horse, Nelan rode low in the saddle. Davy Watson fell across Lavallee's body and steadied his gun with his left hand, propping his elbows and forearms up on the dead giant's broad chest.

Nelan fired four times, while Davy Watson fired twice. At that point, the young Kansan looked down and began to swear frantically, when he realized that Lavallee's pistol was empty. But his anxiety was of little consequence, for his second shot had smacked into Nelan's skull, just above the right eye, pitching the last of Ace Landry's bully-boys into the black maw of death.

Dazed and weak from loss of blood, Davy swayed like a drunkard as he struggled to rise to his feet. But he slipped and fell back down onto his hands and knees. Muttering to himself, he tried vainly to clear his head and stand up.

A sudden jingling sound made him look up, and he suddenly recognized that sound from the first time he'd heard it. It was the jingling of Ace Landry's spurs. He was face to face with the man who had gunned down his father.

Ten feet away, Ace Landry looked down at Davy Watson and smiled like the heart of winter.

"You're a spunky kid," he told him in a soft voice. "I'll give you that." He shook his head. "Who'da thought that a kid who was still wet behind the ears could ever do such a thing to Ace Landry?" There was admiration and awe in the desperado's voice.

Davy blinked his eyes and shook his head, fighting not to lose consciousness.

"I dunno where you picked up those other two hombres," Landry went on in that soft, cold voice of his, "the fella we pegged up there, an' that wild French bastard. They was both pretty good men, as was the Pawnee brave. I'll admit that, boy."

Groaning with pain, Davy got to his knees and straightened up. His mouth hung open and he held his hand to the wound in his side, vainly trying to stanch the flow of blood from it.

"You're more of a man than any of my bunch," Ace Landry told Davy Watson solemnly. "And as worthy an opponent as I ever come up against. My hat's off to your old man, kid. For he done raised you up right good."

Davy tried desperately to get to his feet, to charge Landry and fall with hand and foot, with tooth and nail upon the man he hated. But he could not. It took all the strength that remained in his body merely to stay up on his knees and keep from blacking out.

"But the game's over now," Ace Landry whispered with chilling finality as he cocked back the hammer of his Cavalry Smith and Wesson. "An' I'm callin' your hand."

Davy waited for the outlaw to pull the trigger, his final act of defiance consisting of little more than being able to look his enemy right in the eye.

"I'm not afraid of you, Ace Landry," he muttered as his strength momentarily returned. "An' I never was," he told the killer, swaying back and forth and waiting to be gunned down. Then he was suddenly comforted by the thought that John Jacob Watson would surely be proud of his eldest son.

"So long, kid," Ace Landry said in a voice as cold and bleak as the valley of the shadow of death. "You'll never get in my way again."

Davy fought with all his strength to remain conscious, as his life's blood continued to seep out of the wound in his side. He fought to look the man who would kill him straight in the eye. He blinked his eyes, and felt very weary. His head wobbled on his neck, and he saw dark spots before his eyes. *Why didn't Landry get it over with*?

Then he heard a rock tumble down, to his left. He looked up and saw Landry wheel around, his Smith and Wesson pointed in the direction of the sound. But no one was there.

It had been a ruse. Landry turned further around, his back now to Davy. And as he did, a sleek, silver object gleamed as it sped through the air. Suddenly the desperado gave a shrill, gurgling cry as he staggered backward, his huge pistol clattering onto the rocky ground.

Landry clutched and tore at his throat, just above the breastbone; blood spurted from his mouth, and there was a look of sheer terror in his eyes. A long knife had pierced his throat at the jugular vein, and was imbedded up to its hilt in his flesh.

Fifteen feet across from him, leaning unsteadily against a boulder, his face pale and his eyes dull, Big Nose Vachon smiled exultantly.

"Dat from my wife, Lan'ry," the dying trapper whispered, marshalling his strength and staggering over to his enemy. "She like for me to give you dat."

Still clawing at the knife in his throat, the desperado had fallen to his knees beside the roaring waters of the Snake. Davy Watson slid to the ground, and shook his head as he watched Emile Vachon advance on Ace Landry.

Landry ripped the knife out of his flesh just as Vachon was upon him. Then he coughed explosively, spattering the mountain man's broad chest with blood. Just as Vachon began to lift him to his feet, Ace Landry drove the blade into the trapper's stomach.

Vachon grunted in pain and began to double up. At that same instant Landry, clutching his bloody throat with both hands now, rose to his feet. But then the mountain man hooked his fingers into the desperado's sheepskin coat, and leaned upon his enemy with the full weight of his massive body.

Davy Watson caught his breath as he watched both Landry and Vachon tumble into the raging Snake. Ace Landry surfaced thrashing, and gave out with one gurgling scream of pure terror before the huge Vachon dragged him under the cold, swirling water. And that was the last that the young Kansan saw of either man. His eyes closed, his head went down to the ground, and Davy Watson surrendered at last to the enveloping blackness . . . .

When he opened his eyes again, it was not God and His angels, or John Jacob Watson, that Davy saw, but his blood brother, Soaring Hawk. The Indian sat across a campfire from Davy; it was dark, and the stars shone overhead. Though badly wounded himself, the Pawnee had managed to reach Davy and staunch the flow of blood from his wound by cauterizing it. Davy had then gone into shock and been unconscious for more than a day.

Soaring Hawk smiled when Davy told him of the death of Ace Landry. "It is well," he said. "Our journey is ended. Tonight I will pray for the spirits of Jack Poole and Big Nose Vachon, two mighty warriors."

"And good friends," Davy added, a note of sadness in his voice. But then his thoughts raced back to Kansas, back to his loved ones—and back to Deanna MacPartland, who was waiting for him in the town of Hawkins Fork.

Davy shook his head. "I've had enough of revenge to last me a lifetime," he said to his blood brother across the campfire. "It's time we went on home an' did us some livin'."

THE KANSAN

ACROSS THE HIGH SIERRA

This book is dedicated to my dear friends,
Evelyn Roth, John Sander and Marie F. Dockery.

Chapter One

Davy Watson was still alive. He had journeyed across the American West to avenge the ruthless murder of his father, and had faced hardship and peril sufficient for any man. In the course of his quest for vengeance, Davy had made three fast friends among the free and resourceful souls who ranged the plains west of the Missouri.

Soaring Hawk, Jack Poole and Big Nose Vachon: three of the best men he'd ever met. And now, two of them were dead; two of them would nevermore roam the free, open spaces of the West. Jack Poole, the government scout, and Emile Vachon, the mountain man: they were men who knew the frontier country like the back of their hands. Davy wondered uneasily whether their spirits were truly at rest, for he was willing to bet they would find heaven a mite too tame for their tastes.

Of his three former companions, only Soaring Hawk remained. It was on the young Pawnee brave's account that Davy had intervened in the Red Dog Saloon in Hawkins Fork, Kansas, well over a year ago. And as a result of the brawl that followed, the young Kansan's own beloved father was gunned down by Ace Landry, one of the most vicious and cold-blooded killers ever to plague the frontier.

Having become blood brothers, Davy Watson and Soaring Hawk set out after Ace Landry, on a trail that led through Kansas into the Colorado Territory, where they met Jack Poole and became embroiled in that most heroic stand against an overwhelmingly greater force of hostile Indians, the Battle of Beecher's Island.

Joined by Poole (who also had a score to settle with Ace Landry), the blood brothers traveled west, into the Utah Territory, where they narrowly missed catching up to the desperado at Corinne, where the Union Pacific Railroad had set up camp. But Landry had moved on; he and his gang (at that time, fifteen men in all) made their way over to the wild country known as the Idaho Territory.

Landry and his bully-boys plundered the gold fields of the Boise Basin, and then headed north to do more of the same. Davy and his companions increased their number to four when they met the huge, bearded trapper, Big Nose Vachon. It turned out that the mountain man had his own reasons for wanting to catch up with Landry: his Indian wife had been violated by the gang, and subsequently took her own life out of shame.

Led by Vachon, the companions closed in on the outlaws as the latter were traveling along the banks of the turbulent Snake River, deep in Hells Canyon, one of the wildest places on the face of the North American continent.

The showdown, wherein Davy and his companions were outnumbered by four-to-one, was characterized by clever tactics on the part of the stalkers and fierce fighting on the part of all concerned. When it was over,

Ace Landry and all his bunch had perished; Davy and Soaring Hawk were grievously wounded; and the mountain man and the gallant scout were both dead. The showdown in Hells Canyon had terminated Davy Watson's travels along the vengeance trail.

It was all over now, and the young Kansan was finally free to return to his loved ones, free to resume the normal course of his life. And the very first thing that David Lee Watson vowed to do when he returned to his native Anderson County in Kansas was to ride into the town of Hawkins Fork and stop at the bawdy house of Mrs. Lucretia Eaton, where he would claim the lovely young Deanna MacPartland, and take her back to live with him on the Watson farm by Pottawatomie Creek.

Deanna had been the first woman that Davy had ever slept with, and the most desirable, as well. She had promised to wait for him, and that promise had sustained Davy throughout his long and dangerous quest. But that quest had ended. He was free to return to his prairie rose, to his angel of passion. . . .

"Oh, Davy, it's been so long. I missed you so much," murmured Deanna MacPartland in a voice whose tone was an admixture of passion and relief.

The young man to whom she addressed this intense declaration was so moved that he found himself unable to speak. All he could do was to enfold her loveliness in his arms and cover her face and neck with hungry kisses, while the words of a song ran through his head. It was a song that he had heard in a honkytonk after his first meeting with Deanna, but it expressed his feelings at that moment as well as anything he himself could have said.

7

I'm ridin' out on the windswept plain,
Where only the buffalo goes,
And men will never see me again
'Til I find my prairie rose. . . .

Bright and fine as spun gold, her hair brushed his chest as they embraced; and when he kissed her cheeks, he tasted the salt tang of her tears. His arms fit around her trim, quivering body as if they had been created expressly for that purpose; their groins were pressed together and they seemed to breathe in unison, as if animated by a single heart and mind.

The moment that Davy had entered the upstairs room and stood in the dim, flickering light of the kerosene lamp, he was witness to a vision of beauty. Once he had gazed into Deanna MacPartland's eyes, those eyes blue as prairie flowers, he was bewitched. And when she undressed before him without a word, unveiling her naked beauty, the enchantment grew.

Davy understood what he felt, having read of its counterpart in his Uncle Ethan's books. It had been like this in ancient times, when goddesses revealed themselves in all their glory to the sons of men, and then took them as their lovers. And to David Lee Watson of Anderson County, Kansas, Deanna MacPartland was fully as beautiful and bewitching as Aphrodite of the Greeks or Venus of the Romans.

As Deanna undressed, mesmerizing him with her youthful beauty, her hair glowed in the lamplight with all the richness of burnished gold. Her supple body was white as ivory, save for the subtle wash of rose in her cheeks. Her strong, even teeth gleamed white as well, accentuated as they were by the carmine of her lip rouge.

8

Davy's heart was beating like a tom-tom at a Sioux war dance as Deanna removed her red velvet gown. His palms grew cold, and the breath caught in his throat as the blonde goddess proceeded to undo the ribbons that bound together her lacy, white undergarments. A moment later he groaned under the full weight of his anticipation, as she stood before him in the gentle and flickering light, clothed only in her beauty.

His glance dropped to the floor, and Davy began to take in the spectacle of Deanna MacPartland's beauty in slow stages, not yet trusting himself with the entire vision. First he would assemble the components of that vision, knowing full well that the effect of the whole was breathtakingly greater than the sum of its parts.

Her feet were small and high-arched, and as delicately carved as those of a marble statue. Slender ankles led up to calves whose singing lines beckoned the eye up to trim thighs, the hollows of which Davy remembered with his senses as basins of salt and ivory.

Catching his breath once again, Davy ran his eyes over the girl's lovely form. His ardent glance traveled over the gentle, womanly swell of her hips, the graceful alder tree waist, over the beautiful hands with their long, tapering fingers, and further up, over the firm arms and delicately rounded shoulders. She suddenly turned her head away, and he watched the ivory column of her neck disappear behind a cascade of gold.

When she turned to face him again, he studied the exquisite oval of her face, within which he saw the full, pouting lips, a pert, slightly aquiline nose, and eyes of penetrating blue, which seemed to promise deep intimacy and delight.

Then he looked down, casting his eye over the lissome, glowing body. Looking past the delicate hollow of her neck, he beheld the beauty of her high, firm breasts and felt a desire to run his tongue down the gentle cleft between them, and then over the erect nipples and areolae pink as ocean coral.

Below the dip of her ribcage, where her waist sloped down and then ran out in a gentle swell, Davy saw Deanna's navel, with its slight accent of shadow, and her belly, which was fetchingly adorned with a glinting, golden down. And slightly below that, the golden down became a thatch of darker blonde hair that covered the fleshy cupola of her mound of Venus and ran down the gently pouting lips of Deanna's sex, whose vibrant inner pink echoed with an amplified intensity the delicate tint of her cheeks.

"Davy, it's been so long," she whispered in a husky voice, stepping forward to undo the buttons on his shirt front.

"I reckon so," he whispered back, nodding his head, as he unbuckled his gunbelt. "But I'm here now. . . . I'm back."

A few moments later, he was naked. Boots, shirt, trousers, union suit, gunbelt and holster: all lay on the chair beside the big brass bed, in the room on the second story of Mrs. Lucretia Eaton's bawdy house. As Davy stared at Deanna, her own glance traveled hungrily over the young Kansan's hard-muscled body.

She gave a little cry and reached out a tentative hand to the scar on his right side, the wound that Soaring Hawk had cauterized with his scalping knife. Suddenly, Deanna startled Davy by kneeling down before him and gently touching the wound with her lips.

Shuddering with suppressed excitement, Davy reached down and stroked her fine, golden hair with both hands. He emitted a deep groan as her lips traveled

10

down over his body, blazing a trail through the thicket of his pubic hair and coming to rest at the base of his erect and throbbing maleness.

Davy groaned again as Deanna's full, red lips browsed the length of his shaft. Then he gasped as her lips parted and she took him into the encircling warmth of her mouth. Looking down, he saw her head bob in long, even motions as she stroked his sex in that intimate oral caress.

"Oh, Sweet Jesus," he moaned as the drawing warmth spread over the head and neck of his cock. Somewhere in the back of his brain a light flashed, reminding him of the fire arrows at Arikaree Creek, and he felt the first throb in the pit of his groin, the first herald of the surging torrent that would flow, wild as the Snake River in Hells Canyon, at the culmination of his pleasure.

But Deanna was only beginning, and she drew back her head and released him, rising to stand on tiptoe and kiss him, cupping and gently squeezing his balls all the while.

With the swiftness of a salamander darting into a cave, her long, pink tongue darted into Davy's mouth. An instant later, his own tongue engaged hers and pursued it back into her mouth. The passionate kisses went on, as they communicated their ardent desires in this fashion, tongues darting and teasing in a salamandrine courting dance.

His arms went around her body and traveled down the small of Deanna's back, until his big hands closed over her firm buttocks. She ground his rod between her sleek thighs, hooking back and forth over the length of his shaft, rubbing her groin against his with slow, even strokes.

11

There was a fire in Davy Watson's blood, and it blazed hotter than a Pawnee bonfire as his passion fed it. There she was, at last; there she was, naked and ardent in his arms: the woman whose memory—whose feel and scent and taste—he had carried with him throughout his travels over the wild, open country.

Deanna came away from Davy once more, leaving him hotter than a branding iron in a fire. He took her in his arms. They turned toward the big brass bed, graceful as a couple dancing the waltz; and then he dipped, taking her down beneath him. "Ooooh, Davy," was all that she could say. And he could say nothing at all.

Hungrily, his fingers explored her quivering body, as if it were a blind man's love letter. She murmured deliriously while he kissed and nuzzled her neck, fondling and gently squeezing her breasts at the same time. And it seemed to Davy Watson that the light of his life began to speak in tongues when his kisses reached her sensitive breasts and his hands stroked and grazed her thighs and the swollen, moist lips between them.

"Come inside me, Davy," Deanna urged in a voice like the rushing prairie wind. "Oh, I want you inside me now!"

Mindless now in the overwhelming grip of passion, Davy heard her voice as if over a great distance, as if she were calling to him from the far side of the funnel of a Kansas twister. And he was caught in the heart of that tornado which was his passion; so he did as he was told, moving up on her body, hovering over her with all the sureness and certainty of an eagle descending upon its aerie.

Deanna reached down one of her hands; they were delicate hands, with a tracery of blue veins beneath their marble surface and long tapering fingers: the hands of an artist. And the fingers of those hands encircled the shaft of his engorged organ and guided it into her wet and welcoming circle of delight.

He slid into her sheath, feeling the sudden warmth of that snug barrel, as well as the drawing squeeze of her sphincter muscles. And at that instant, Davy experienced an intense sensation, a feeling of completeness such as he had rarely experienced before.

"Now, don't you move, David Lee,' she whispered in his ear. "Just lie there and be close to me. And let me do this for you."

He looked into her prairie flower-blue eyes and smiled, nodding his head as he did. Then, laying his head down on the pillow beside Deanna's, and breathing deeply of the fragrance of her hair and the musk of her sweet pussy, Davy gave himself over completely to his lover's passionate ministration.

"Oh, I feel you so deep inside me," she whispered in a voice like the sweeping prairie wind, inflaming him incredibly. "Oh, you're filling me up."

Davy lay still on top of her, cushioning his weight with his elbows, his sex thrust deep within Deanna's, lost in the funnel of the whirlwind of his emotions and desires.

Deanna lay beneath him, with her eyes closed and small beads of sweat gleaming on her hairline like a band of diamonds, whispering passionate and incoherent endearments in her lover's ear. And even though her body was still, to all outward appearances, her vaginal sphincter encircled the base of Davy's shaft and communicated her longing and desire in a warm and gripping telegraphy of passion.

Contract. Expand. Contract. Dit-dah-dit. Dah-dit-dah. Deanna worked the muscles of her pussy in the

13

same inspired manner that Samuel F.B. Morse first worked the telegraph key on that earthshaking day when he changed the nature of man's communications forever.

What hath God wrought! was the first telegraphic message, and its phrasing applied equally to the sense of awe and wonder felt by Davy Watson, as he received and responded to the signals of passion transmitted by Deanna MacPartland.

Dit-dah-dit. Dah-dit-dah.

Davy's answer was non-verbal: the sum total of all his feeling and desire for the lissome blonde beauty who lay moaning in his arms. And a telegraphy of light, traveling in bursts behind his eyes, transmitted the encoded message of his combined delight, joy and release into the field of his senses. And he came with a deep, wrenching groan, with a sound that issued forth from the deepest recesses of his being. And then he awoke. . . .

Davy Watson blinked his eyes several times and looked up at the ceiling of his room with glassy, uncomprehending eyes. Then, as the cold light of reality made itself felt within his consciousness, he realized that Deanna had only been with him through the strength of his intense longing. It had all been a dream.

"Judas Priest," he muttered disconsolately, wriggling uncomfortably as he felt a numbing, but not unpleasant, sensation in his groin, suddenly realizing that he had just fired off a load of jism into his union suit. His glorious reunion with Deanna had not been the meeting he desired above all things; no, it had merely been the product of his desire. . .a wet dream.

Where was he, then?

Confused, Davy shook his head. Loss of blood and

14

the rush of recent events—as ferocious as the rush of the churning waters that swirled through Hells Canyon—had confused the mind of the young Kansan. The grim business of vengeance and killing had taken their toll of his strength and energies; his quest for revenge had come perilously near to costing Davy his life. But it was all over, now; Ace Landry would never trouble another soul again. Not in this life.

What had happened?

Davy lay his head back down on the pillow and began to recollect the events that transpired after the death of Ace Landry.

At the end of the bloody showdown, after he saw Big Nose Vachon drag the screaming desperado down beneath the icy, rushing waters of the Snake River, Davy Watson had lost consciousness. His gunshot wound was a serious one, and he surely would have died from loss of blood had it not been for the quick thinking of his Pawnee blood brother.

Although severely wounded himself, having been shot in the back earlier by Ace Landry, Soaring Hawk managed to summon up the strength and presence of mind to save Davy Watson's life. Seeing that his blood brother was bleeding to death, the young Pawnee built a makeshift fire, heated his scalping knife in it, took it from the flames, and then cauterized the young Kansan's wound.

After Davy had regained consciousness a day later, he reciprocated Soaring Hawk's act of kindness by digging Landry's slug out of the Pawnee's back. There was no anesthetic available, but the Plains Indian endured the agonizing surgery with the stoic courage of his people.

Slowly, painfully, leading the surviving pack mules that still carried the gold plundered by Ace Landry and

15

his gang, the two men made their way out of Hells Canyon. Following the Snake River south, and then east, as they left its banks to head back to the crude, frontier settlement of Boise town, the companions inched their way to sanctuary.

Hailed as heroes when they had recounted the story of the feared and detested outlaw band's end and subsequently returned a good deal of the gold dust that had been taken from the miners of the Boise Basin, Davy and Soaring Hawk were welcomed with open arms and given the best medical care that the young town could provide.

After having their wounds tended to properly, the blood brothers were taken to the boarding house of one Mrs. Carmela Mudree, where they would be put up at the expense of the grateful goldminers until they had recovered their health. And there the two remained.

Davy rolled over to one side, favoring his wound and wincing as he pulled himself up to a sitting position. It was his intention to climb out of his gummy long johns and hobble over to the washstand at the far side of the room, where he would then give himself a sponge bath.

With much exertion and a certain amount of difficulty, he wobbled over to the stand, leaning against the wall for support. It was the first time he had been on his feet in many days. Weaving back and forth, dizzy from the unaccustomed physical activity, he fought his way out of his union suit.

Once his strength began to come back, Davy left the security of the wall and hobbled over to the enameled wash basin, poured water into it from a marble pitcher, and began to sponge his naked body. Suddenly the door to the room creaked, causing him to wheel around in response to the prompting of his frontier-conditioned senses. Soaring Hawk had taught him to stalk like a Pawnee and use a knife like an assassin, so Davy's heightened senses alerted him with hair-trigger speed.

He spun around to face the door. An instant later it opened, revealing a young woman standing just beyond the threshold, her mouth open as it formed an "O" of surprise, her eyes never leaving his naked body. No, quite the contrary: they traveled hungrily over his hard-muscled form, narrowing as they came to his sex.

"Uh, afternoon, Miss Mudree," Davy mumbled, going red in the face and covering his crotch with both hands as he recognized the unexpected visitor as one of Carmela Mudree's three unmarried daughters.

"You may call me Hope, David," the young woman told him quietly, averting her eyes with great reluctance. "I didn't think you'd be able to get up by yourself."

"Oh, I'm doin' jus' fine, thank you," Davy replied, blushing as he stood there with his hands over his crotch, feeling like a damned fool.

"I brought you some clean towels," the young woman told him, entering the room and closing the door behind her.

"Yep," Davy replied lamely as she crossed the room and came toward him, her eyes on the floor and a strange, sly smile on her lips. "I'll, uh, give you these here old ones, Miss Hope." He reached over to the washstand and picked up two soiled towels.

As Davy took the towels from the stand, Hope Mudree advanced on him, her eyes still on the floor and her right arm outstretched. Like her two sisters, Hope was a short and full-figured young woman with handsome features and dark, gypsy eyes and hair.

All three Mudree girls had gone out of their way to be nice to Davy Watson, and each had grown bolder by the

17

day. And he, of course, was flattered by the attentions of such nubile young lovelies; his erotic interest in the enviable and developing situation increased as his health returned.

Hope Mudree stood before him now, while he faced her from behind the towels that he held out before his body like a matador's cape. Her sly smile broadened until she finally opened her mouth and said, "I'll take those," and reached out to grab the towels.

Davy Watson gulped, and his eyes went wide as the young woman's hand, covered now by the two towels, caressed his genitals.

The smile on her lips was now triumphant. Hope's eyes met his boldly, as she caressed his man-root through the towels. Then, after giving his balls a gentle, but assertive, squeeze, she spoke to him in a breathy whisper.

"Leave your door open tonight, David Lee," she told him, taking the soiled towels at last and then handing him their replacements.

Davy cleared his throat several times before he answered her. "Tonight?" he croaked.

"Tonight," she repeated, looking him right in the eye and smiling a hot, gypsy smile. "I have something I want to give you."

"You have?" he said after clearing his throat once more. "What?"

"Me," she whispered, bold as brass now as she reached down and took hold of his erect maleness. An instant later, she leaned over and kissed him on the lips. After that, leaving him gasping and panting and blowing, she turned abruptly and flounced out of the room without so much as a "by your leave."

Hope Mudree had scarcely departed when Davy had

another visitor. Soaring Hawk, his companion and blood brother, entered the room as noiselessly as a bobcat stalking deer.

"If you not put pants over that," the Pawnee deadpanned, pointing to Davy's blatant erection, "go outside and hang flag on him."

"Aw, shoot," Davy mumbled, turning back to the washstand and pouring more water into the basin.

"All Mudree sister got your scent," Soaring Hawk observed. "Act like catamount at mating time. All rub up against you, and want you inside 'em."

"Well," replied Davy, splashing water over his face and chest, "they ain't such a bad-lookin' covey of quail, y'know. All three of 'em's downright han'some little women."

"Which one you like?" the Pawnee asked, getting to the heart of the matter with his accustomed directness.

Davy picked up a fresh towel, unfolded it, and began to dry himself. "Gosh, I don't know," he told the Pawnee. "Guess I sorta fancies each one of 'em."

Soaring Hawk shook his head. "Too much fuck no good," he said with conviction. "Make man weak. Then he die." With this grim observation, the young brave sat down on Davy's bed.

"Well, if that applied to whackin' off," Davy retorted over his shoulder, "I'd've never lived to see fourteen."

"Tomorrow night full moon," the Indian said, abruptly changing the subject. "I go in woods and dance for spirits of Jack Poole and Big Nose Vachon."

Davy turned to Soaring Hawk, a wistful smile on his face as he thought about his fallen companions. The Pawnee would dance the dance of the departed warriors for Poole and Vachon, Davy realized. He had honored the young Kansan's father in this fashion, after John Jacob Watson's death at the hand of Ace Landry. But all three deaths had been avenged now, and in a few days the two companions would be hitting the trail for home.

"I'll go with you tomorrow night," Davy told his friend.

"How you feel?" the Pawnee asked.

"Not so bad," was the reply. "A little wobbly in the pins, mebbe. But I'm feelin' a heap stronger. How's your back?"

Soaring Hawk nodded, a stoic expression on his face. "Not so much pain. . .if I sleep on belly like dog. No like that so much."

"Hell, that ain't so bad," Davy told him. "Dog's a good animal. White man calls him his best friend."

The Pawnee shot Davy a wry glance. "That prove dog loyal, mebbe, but not smart."

"You're gettin' to be quite the cynic, ain't ya?" Davy observed.

"What is cynic?"

"It's a tribe of folks who knows the price of everything. . .and the value of nothing."

"That not Indian tribe. Sound like white man."

"Hey, tonight I'll be headin' downstairs for dinner," Davy told his friend suddenly. "What's the company like at table?"

"White men who live in Boise, and white men who go up north for gold. Big talk 'bout money. All time, heap big bullshit."

"Why, bullshit makes the world go round," Davy told his blood brother. "Before somethin' gets done, you got to warm things up a mite with hot air."

20

"White man make enough hot air to melt snow on prairie."

"Seems to me," reflected Davy, "that you ain't in one of your most cheerful moods today, my brother."

The Pawnee made a sour face. "Eat too much white man food. You hurry up, get better. Then we hunt deer or buffalo, and eat real food again."

Davy had to smile as he recollected the Indian's reaction to such diverse dishes as mashed potatoes with gravy, hominy grits, flapjacks and apple cobbler.

"Well, let's mosey downstairs," he said, buttoning up his flannel shirt, "an' hope that you're a-gonna have better luck tonight. . . ."

Sourdough biscuits, pot roast and gravy, potato pancakes with apple sauce, corn on the cob and string beans constituted the fare for Davy Watson's first meal at the table of Carmela Mudree. The young Kansan ate with gusto after his convalescent's diet of broth, oatmeal and soups, constantly reminding himself to take his time and chew his food properly; it had been more than ten days since he'd had his last full meal.

The meal also met with Soaring Hawk's approval, and he devoured everything but the potato pancakes, which he later privately referred to as "pig food."

"Would you like some more applesauce, David Lee?" Hope Mudree asked, meriting a brace of anxious looks from her sisters, Faith and Charity.

"Land sakes, girl," growled her mother, "it's his first solid meal in days. You can't stuff a man like a pillow." Carmela Mudree was a big, raw-boned woman with a shock of steel-gray hair that looked to Davy to be

21

as thick and wiry as the coils used to fence off a cattle-man's spread.

"Oh, Mama," Hope Mudree muttered, lowering her eyes and the bowl of apple sauce at the same time, while Faith and Charity nudged one another and giggled.

"I trust that you've had sufficient to eat, and that it sits well with you, Mr. Watson," said the widow Mudree, who was extremely solicitous in her gruff way.

"Yes'm," Davy replied. "I feel like I jus' done had me a banquet in the mansion of the governor of the sovereign state of Kansas, hisself. Them was right fine vittles, Miz Mudree."

The huge woman nodded and smiled contentedly.

After dinner, Mrs. Mudree's boarders, who all happened to be male, retired to the parlor of the big two-story house for coffee, brandy and cigars. Soaring Hawk, who was on record as preferring the aroma of buffalo chips burning in a campfire to the reek of cheroots, went for a stroll in the grove of larches behind the house.

Davy sank down into the embrace of an overstuffed armchair, a brandy snifter in one hand, a cup of steaming coffee in the other, and a big cigar in his mouth. There were eight other men in the parlor with him: three of them worked and lived in Boise, one was a prospector on his way to the gold fields in the north of the territory, and the remaining four were hard-looking men who had mentioned nothing more of their purpose beyond stating that they were just passing through the Boise Basin.

"Well, son," said Mr. Ketchum, a white-bearded old gentleman with a twinkle in his eye, "it 'pears to me that little Hope Mudree would like to be handin' you somewhat more than apple sauce, if you catch my meanin'."

He winked at the young Kansan.

Davy smiled amiably and shrugged his shoulders as he puffed on his cheroot.

"Yup," affirmed Mr. Beasley, a short, tubby man who was an officer of the Bank of Boise. "It appears to me that all of the Mudree sisters have taken a fancy to Mr. Wasson."

"Watson," Davy corrected, still puffing on his stogie.

"Well, I'll say this much," boomed huge and bearded Harvey Yancey, the mean-looking man who appeared to be leader of the band of mysterious strangers, "they're a passel of hot-lookin' little heifers. An' I'll wager any one of 'em could fuck yer leg off."

Davy took the cigar out of his mouth and underwent a fit of coughing. He didn't have a good feeling about the four men in general, but Harvey Yancey positively aroused a strong and persistent dislike in the young Kansan. There was something cruel and contemptuous about the man, Davy realized, some wild and defiant spirit that delighted in trampling delicate things underfoot, that needed denial and destruction for its gratification.

"Which one's to your likin', Harv?" asked Sugrue, a tall, saturnine individual who possessed the charm of an undertaker and the warmth of a hangman.

"Don't matter none to me," Yancey rumbled in his bass voice, leering at the other men in the room. "Hell, you turn 'em upside down an' they's all the same, anyways."

Yancey's cronies began to snicker.

"That's all they's good for," Yancey went on, encouraged by his toadying companions. "That an' cleanin' up after a man, an' makin' damn sure that he gits his three squares a day."

"Don't you never *talk* to no ladies, Harv?" asked a thickset, bucktoothed man named McAllister.

"Shit," Yancey replied with a frown. "I'd git more sense out of a hound dog. Man don't need to waste his time talkin' to women, 'cept for to tell 'em what to do."

"By your remarks, sir, I take it that you would have no use for the ladies who are raising such a ruckus in Mr. Watson's home state?" asked old Mr. Ketchum, offended by Yancey's coarseness.

"You mean that Susan B. Anthony an' that Cady Stanton woman? Them what'chamacall'ems—*suffer-a-gettes*? Them females who's runnin' around down there like chickens without heads, statin' that they's the equals of menfolk—that who you mean?"

"Precisely, Mr. Yancey," the old gentleman replied stiffly.

Harvey Yancey sneered. "Ain't nothin' wrong with them ol' gals that a good stiff dick couldn't set to rights," the giant rumbled in his bass voice. "They's jus' a bunch of agitated ol' maids, all a-fussin' an' a-cluckin' 'bout women's rights—whatever the hell that is. But I'll lay you ten-to-one that each of 'em would give it up for a hard ride on a stiff pecker."

"You said it, Harv!" exclaimed the remaining member of Yancey's little band, a wiry, sandy-haired man named Morison.

"I'd like to git my hands on that there Susan B. Anthony," Harvey Yancey growled. "I'd teach her a thing or two 'bout women's rights an' a woman's place in this world."

"Y'mean you'd like to slip it to 'er?" McAllister asked lewdly.

"*Her?*" Yancey said, rearing back in his seat as if

24

stung by a bee. "That dried-up prune? Why, shit, no! I'd jus' like to take that little lady aside, an' beat the piss out of her. That's all."

Old Ketchum looked indignant. "Is *that* your way of dealing with the woman question, sir?" he asked.

"Mr. Ketchum," the giant replied with a smile, "that there's my way of dealin' with everything. Anything gits in my way, I jus' slap it down."

"An' he ain't jus' a-whistlin' Dixie," affirmed Morison. "'Tain't healthy fer a body to mess with Harvey Yancey."

"All that Anthony woman needs is a good fuck," Yancey declared, suddenly beginning to grin. "But not from this buckaroo. Why, John," he said, pointing a pork sausage finger at Morison, "I wouldn't even fuck her with your dick."

His three toadies began to laugh uproariously. Old Ketchum scowled and looked scandalized, and the other two Boise men stared at Yancey disapprovingly. The prospector had fallen asleep. And Davy Watson's ears burnt as he stared into the depths of his brandy snifter.

"An' as fer them Mudree gals," Yancey rumbled on, once the laughter of his cronies had subsided, "I'll tell ya what a body could do with them." He paused to insert a thick forefinger into his left nostril.

After probing the inside of his nose for several seconds, Yancey resumed. "You could round up them plump little heifers an' herd 'em down to Virginia City, in Nevada, where any of the brothel keepers there'd lay out a heap of money for those lasses. Do you fellas realize how much money a set like them three sisters could bring a man?"

His cronies snickered at this.

He paused to leer around the room, after which he

relit his cigar. "Well, an' what d'ya think a man would pay to have them gals do a little 'round-the-world on him—all at the same time, huh?"

"Hoo-wee!" exclaimed the bucktoothed McAllister, slapping his thigh with his left hand.

Davy stared at Yancey through narrowed eyes as the latter slurped his coffee with all the grace of a hog at a trough. He was disgusted by the big, bearded man's attitude toward women, which was, he realized, merely a reflection of Harvey Yancey's attitude to life itself. No, he did not like the man at all.

"What might even be better," Yancey went on, having slurped down the last of his coffee, "would be to bring them little girls to San Francisco, where you could really turn a dollar on 'em."

"You mean sell 'em to the owner of some bawdy house there?" asked Sugrue.

Yancey shook his head. "Nope. That ain't what I mean a-tall. They's a heap of money in sellin' 'em on the Barbary Coast there. . .where they'd git themselves the benefit of a little ocean cruise." He smiled and nodded emphatically.

His smile made Davy think of a scalping knife.

"Are you referring to the practice of white slavery, sir?" old John Ketchum asked indignantly.

Yancey shot the man a look of mock-innocence. "I don't know nothin' 'bout white slavery, Mr. Ketchum," the bearded giant said coyly.

"I should hope not, sir," the old gentleman shot back, "for it is among the most reprehensible of all man's misdeeds."

"Aw, Harv was just joshin'," the man called Sugrue told the old man, his shifty glance darting around the room as he did.

"That is far from a fit subject for humor, young man," Mr. Ketchum replied briskly.

"Where are you an' your friends headin' to, Mr. Yancey?" Davy Watson asked, straining for sociability in the face of his intense dislike for the man who sat across the room from him.

Yancey gave him a cold and suspicious look. A sudden, heavy silence fell over the parlor.

Davy bit down on his cigar and stared into the cold, dead eyes of Harvey Yancey.

"We're, uh, workin' our way west," Yancey rumbled, finally breaking the uncomfortable silence. "Thought we'd strike it rich in California. How about you. . . *Mr.* Watson?" he asked contemptuously.

"I'm due to head back Kansas way," Davy replied. "Where my people is."

As he continued to stare into Harvey Yancey's eyes, the big man sneered.

"Y'know somethin', Mr. Watson?" he rumbled. "I hear tell that Kansas is known as the asshole of the West."

For an instant, Davy's body tensed. Then he relaxed again. "Do tell," he replied amiably, reaching almost imperceptibly over the arm of his chair to the brandy bottle that stood on the carpet. "I must confess I never heard it referred to that way before." He paused to wrap his fingers around the neck of the bottle. "Onliest time I ever did hear that there expression used was yesterday. . .when someone used it to refer to you, Mr. Yancey."

As he tightened his grip on the neck of the bottle, Davy watched the big man's jaw drop and his eyes go wide under the impact of the remark. Yancey's big hands went white as they gripped the arms of his chair.

He leaned forward, preparing to spring at Davy.

The young Kansan smiled coldly at Harvey Yancey, seeing at that moment the sneering visage of Ace Landry, the man who had gunned down his father. He planted his feet on the carpet, leaned forward in his seat, and hefted the half-filled brandy bottle with a hardly noticeable movement of his wrist.

"You wise-ass little shit!" Harvey Yancey roared with the voice of a bull, as he shot out of his seat and hurled himself at Davy Watson.

The young Kansan was still wobbly as a result of his gunshot wound, but his hair-trigger reflexes had not deserted him. Davy came out of his seat swinging the brandy bottle in an overhand arc as he rose to his feet, calculating with curious mental detachment the weight of the onrushing Yancey as near to two-hundred-eighty pounds of beef on the hoof.

Crash! The sound of shattering glass rang out in the parlor, followed by a bass grunt, which was itself followed in turn by a thunderous bump: Harvey Yancey's leap had been cut short in mid-air as the brandy bottle smashed to pieces against the side of his head; his huge body hit the carpeted floor with all the force of a dropped anvil.

"Holy smoke," muttered the bucktoothed man, reflecting the astonishment felt by Yancey's cronies. Each of them sat stupified in his seat, goggle-eyed and uncomprehending, as if he were at ringside after seeing David drop Goliath.

Still clutching the jagged end of the brandy bottle, his eyes on Yancey's three companions, Davy Watson stepped back from the body of the fallen giant. A moment later, the three men exchanged glances, nodded to each other, and then got to their feet, starting menacingly toward the man who had knocked out Harvey Yancey.

"That'll be all, gentlemen," Mr. Ketchum ordered curtly, causing the bully-boys to turn in his direction.

The old gentleman was out of his seat, and held a brace of derringer pistols in his hands. An instant later the other two Boise men were standing beside him, backing up his play with drawn revolvers of their own. Somehow, incredibly, the old prospector had missed all the action and was still asleep on the sofa at the far end of the room, punctuating the silence that followed Mr. Ketchum's order with stertorous bursts of snoring.

Suddenly the parlor door swung open, and in walked Carmela Mudree.

"Land sakes!" she exclaimed, going wide-eyed at the sight of the huge form that lay stretched out upon her red carpet. "What-all's been goin' on in here?"

"These here gentlemen was just about to settle up with you, Miz Mudree," Mr. Ketchum informed the widow, motioning at the three men with his derringers.

Realizing that they had outstayed their welcome, Yancey's bully-boys took out their wallets and paid Carmela Mudree what they owed her for room and board. Then, without a word, they dragged the still-unconscious Yancey out of the parlor.

"You fellas go see that their bags gets packed," Mr. Ketchum told the two Boise men, who then followed Yancey's cronies out of the parlor. "It's all right, Carmela," he went on. "Just a slight difference of opinion."

"My thanks to you, sir," Davy said, after the widow Mudree had left the parlor.

"That was well done, my boy," Mr. Ketchum said, holstering his miniature pistols inside his suitcoat. "And exactly what the swine deserved." The old man smiled. "Just consider that you struck a blow for women's rights."

Chapter Two

Later in the evening, after the two men from Boise had escorted Harvey Yancey and his ruffians out of the boarding house at gunpoint, old Mr. Ketchum proposed a little celebration. He broke out several bottles of rye whiskey and Kentucky sour mash bourbon, and a little victory celebration ensued in Carmela Mudree's parlor.

The four men were joined by the widow, who brought several bottles of wine, as well as her daughters. And when the Mudree girls heard about Davy's exploit and his defense of womanhood, they lavished praise and attention upon him, flirting furiously as they did.

Soaring Hawk had returned to the boarding house by this time, but he had little enthusiasm for the white man's carousals, and even less tolerance of his enthusiasms and verbal excesses. But, to be honest, he was not missed by his white brother: the three attractive daughters of Carmela Mudree had Davy surrounded, and he luxuriated in their passionate attentions and their competition for his favor.

"Yessiree," Mr. Ketchum said, nodding so vigorously that his long white beard waggled over the front of his suit like a pennant flying from a rampart. "That's one pack of blackguards that'll think twice afore comin' back to Boise town."

"Ain't that the truth," agreed Mr. Beasley, the bank official. "This here young fella showed 'em he warn't about to stand fer no foolishness."

The third Boise man, a balding fellow with a wispy brown beard, nodded in agreement as he spoke. "That there Yancey fella was a bad 'un. Make no mistake about that."

Mrs. Mudree gave the man a shocked look.

"That's the gospel truth Mr. Bacock is tellin' you, Miz Mudree," Mr. Ketchum assured the widow. "Yancey was talkin' 'bout stuff that were downright unfit fer a lady's ears."

"Such as what, John?" Carmela Mudree asked Mr. Ketchum pointblank.

Davy looked up with interest, and he noticed that the Mudree sisters were watching the exchange with obvious interest as well.

"Oh, shoot," the old man mumbled in his beard, whose white hairs contrasted starkly with his rapidly reddening face. "I cain't tell a lady such things."

"Well, I respect you for bein' a gentleman of the old school, John," Carmela Mudree told Mr. Ketchum, "but I'm a modern woman. I earn my own livin' by the sweat of my brow, an' I ain't beholden to nobody. I'm a growed woman, as is my girls here, an' I want you to talk frank with me."

The old man's face was burning now, and somehow its bright red color, in combination with the snowy white of his beard, made Davy Watson think of Santa Claus. Mr. Ketchum flapped his hands against his thighs in a gesture of helplessness, and shifted uncomfortably in his seat.

"How 'bout you, Will?" the Widow Mudree asked, turning suddenly to Mr. Beasley.

"Gee Willikers, Carmela," Beasley muttered. "It was right wicked stuff, y'see."

"Such as what?" the big-boned woman persisted.

Mr. Beasley gulped and wrung his hands, his glance now directed at the tips of his boots.

"Oh, pshaw!" exclaimed Mr. Babcock, waving his hands impatiently in the air, an expression of disgust on his face. "We's all adults here, far as I can see," he told them gruffly. "What that Yancey fella was talkin' 'bout was sellin' gals to brothel keepers in Virginia City."

Here Babcock paused for emphasis, his beady little eyes running over the faces of the women in the room. Davy watched the Mudree women with interest.

"Or to white slavers," Babcock went on, "on the Barbary Coast of Yerba Buena."

"It's called San Francisco these days, Todd," Mr. Beasley corrected.

"It may be San Francisco to you, Will," Babcock replied testily, "but it'll always be Yerba Buena to me."

"Oh, sweet Jesus and all the angels in heaven!" exclaimed a shocked Carmela Mudree, once the enormity of Harvey Yancey's depraved imaginings had made itself felt. "What a sinner and lost soul that man is!"

Faith, Hope and Charity Mudree gasped audibly, after which they consoled themselves with a number of large swigs from their wine glasses.

"Oh, he is the very devil incarnate!" the widow went on indignantly. "And I am truly grateful to you gentlemen for riddin' my house of such a viper." She shook her head, shivering from head to toe. "Thank the Lord we are rid of such a fiend."

"Well," said Mr. Ketchum, having finally regained his composure, "the credit really goes to our young friend here." At this, he pointed to Davy. "For he defended the honor of your fair sex with promptitude, and dispatched the despicable villain."

As the three sisters loosed a volley of *oohs* and *aahs* at Davy Watson, Carmela Mudree turned to him.

"And what did this gentleman do to defend the honor of our sex?" the widow asked, beaming at the young Kansan.

"By God, I'll tell you what he did," Mr. Babcock cried out in his high-pitched voice, unable to contain his excitement. "He broke a bottle of brandy across't the top of that sum-bitch's head—that's what he did!"

"Land sakes!" puffed Carmela Mudree, somewhat taken aback by Mr. Babcock's sudden effusion.

Faith, Hope and Charity all made cooing sounds deep in their throats, sounds which resembled the mating call of pigeons, as they stared with wide and admiring eyes at their protector.

"Indeed," continued little Mr. Babcock, still fired with enthusiasm, "let us drink a toast to the hero of the hour."

Davy sat open-mouthed as everyone in the room proceeded to stand up and raise their glasses aloft.

"I give you Mr. David Lee Wasson," Mr. Babcock proposed, raising his glass with a hand that trembled in response to the promptings of his intense emotional state.

"Watson," Davy corrected gently, as he stood up to acknowledge the tribute.

"Hear, hear," seconded Mr. Beasley.

They all drank to Davy's health, and he to theirs. Whiskey and wine were flowing freely now, and the more they toasted, the more they drank.

"To Mr. Ketchum," proposed Davy, "a man who

backs up his words with action.''

"Hear, hear!" the others called out.

"To Will Beasley and Todd Babcock," the old gentleman proposed in turn, "hale fellows and trusty companions."

"Hear, hear!" the others cried rousingly.

"To Carmela Mudree," Mr. Beasley cried suddenly, preventing them all from returning to their seats, "the pearl of the Idaho Territory, and a prime example of the flower of American womanhood."

"Hear, hear!" bellowed the men.

"Hear, hear!" fluted the women.

Glasses were continually emptied and refilled in rapid succession.

"To John Ketchum, Will Beasley, Todd Babcock and David Lee Watson," the widow proposed, pausing to stifle a belch and wipe the sweat from her brow, "the grandest boarders ever to bless a poor widow's house."

"Hear, hear!"

Clink went the glasses; *slurp* went the lips of the drinkers, followed by smackings of those lips and *umms* of delight. The celebrants were off and running now, toasting each other at the slightest provocation.

"To the loveliest girls a mother could have."

"Hear, hear!"

Davy experienced the feeling of holding a tiger by the tail as the round of toasts, out of control now, continued on its promiscuous way.

"To my beloved mother, who labored and sacrificed continually to bring my sisters and me up proper."

"Hear, hear!"

"To the prosperity and health of the Idaho Territory —to her eventual statehood."

"Hear, hear!"

"To President Ulysses Simpson Grant. May his administration be purged of corruption and incompetence."

"Hear, hear!"

"To the reconstruction of the South."

"Hear, hear!"

And so it went, until none of the men and women in the parlor drew a sober breath. The men knocked back their bourbon and rye manfully, and the women sipped their wine with heroic persistence.

"I thing I'll lee' you peeble," mumbled old Mr. Ketchum, groping his way around Carmela Mudree's horsehair sofa.

"Wake up, Will," Mr. Babcock called out suddenly, "for it's time we were abed."

"Land sakes," muttered the Widow Mudree, closing one eye in order to achieve single vision, "I've got a heap of chores to do tomorrow. So I'll just leave you young people to set a spell longer. Mind you, don't tarry down here too long, girls."

"No, Mama," Faith, Hope and Charity all told Carmela Mudree through boozy, Cheshire cat grins. And then, the moment that the widow and the three Boise men had shuffled, staggered and groped their way out of the parlor, the three sisters wheeled around to face Davy Watson and turn their hot, gypsy eyes upon him.

All three were full-bodied little wenches, pleasant enough to look upon, and each a good armful. Hope had the sweetest face and the biggest hips. Faith had trim ankles and full, sensual lips. Charity had a handsome aquiline nose and a marvel of a bosom. All three possessed a head of long hair black as the heart of night, and a languid temperament that predisposed them to voluptuousness. The Mudree girls may have been unmarried, but they were no virgins.

Davy Watson found himself suddenly alone with the three highly aroused sisters, who now surrounded him, purring like cats as they rubbed themselves up against his body.

To say that he found this exciting would be an understatement. Two of the feline sisters flanked him on the sofa, and the third stood behind him, stroking his hair and rubbing her bosom against the back of his head whenever she leaned over to whisper in his ear.

The suggestiveness and proximity of the Mudree girls set the young Kansan's blood to simmering, and the natural physical expression of this process was an erection. Embarassed by this sudden manifestation of Eros, Davy crossed his legs and leaned forward in his seat.

"It's so nice to have you up at last," Faith—who sat on his left—murmured, brushing the bulge in his pants with her right hand as she accompanied her words with a sweeping gesture.

"And we've got you all to ourselves," Charity whispered in his ear, leaning across his chest and upper arm with the full weight and warmth of her impressive bosom.

"It's really wonderful to have you here, David Lee," Hope whispered in his other ear from behind, punctuating her sentence by darting her pink tongue into his ear.

"Well, uh. . .I'm, I'm. . ." he fumbled, not knowing which way to turn as the ardent sisters closed in on him.

None of the young women were particularly sober, and consequently their inhibitions had been dissolved by the persistent application of alcohol. They crowded around Davy, moaning, rolling their eyes, and rubbing themselves up against him.

Davy Watson's libido bobbed like a ship at sea in the midst of this typhoon of unleashed female sexuality. His face was as red as a pirate's sash, and his cock as stiff as a mainmast. He was intoxicated equally by the sour mash he had drunk and the erotic presence of the three squirming young women. His keen nose caught the musky scent of feminine arousal, counterpointed by the lighter odors of soap and perfume, and he broke out in goose pimples.

"You were *so brave*," Faith gushed, snuggling up to Davy, "to tackle that big, awful Mr. Yancey."

"And *so strong*," cooed Charity, squeezing his bicep with a hand whose touch lingered, "to get the better of that huge brute."

"Oh, I don't know," Davy muttered modestly.

"And *so clever*, not to have hurt yourself in the process," warbled Hope, "not to have got so much as a scratch on your body." She stroked his neck and back, causing him to lean even farther forward.

A moment later, Hope Mudree tip-toed away from the sofa and proceeded to extinguish all the lamps in the parlor. Darkness fell, and with it fell the last vestiges of decorum and propriety. It was as if the darkness had brought with it the sanction of anonymity; and suddenly the occupants of the sofa felt free to act in response to the prompting of their desires.

It was absolutely the strangest thing that Davy had ever felt, the simultaneous contact of his flesh with those six groping hands and three hungry mouths. The sheer multiplicity of touch, and its attendant intensity of sensation, caused the young Kansan to imagine himself in the dark embrace of some spidery embodiment of passion, whose manifold kisses and caresses were directed by a single, ardent intelligence.

Firmly enmeshed in the web of desire, Davy Watson resigned himself to his fate and gave himself up as a willing sacrifice to the spider of passion. Just then, someone unbuttoned his fly.

The hands and fingers of the three excited and suddenly uninhibited sisters traveled all over his body, exploring it with a feather-light touch. Davy felt their flesh touch his, as those inquisitive hands found their way inside his shirt and down into his trousers.

"Mother said we shouldn't tarry too long down here," Hope said in a breathy whisper, causing her aroused sisters to giggle in response.

Davy caught her drift, and got up from the couch. Clinging as closely as barnacles to the hull of a sailing vessel, the Mudree girls accompanied him up the stairs, stroking his half-undressed body all the while.

"Oooh, you're *so hard*," murmured Hope, as her hand grazed the front of his trousers.

"And *so big*," whispered Charity, a credit to her name.

"And *so lovely*," muttered Faith, clutching Davy's buttocks with all the fervor of a communicant gripping an altar rail.

By the time that wave of ardent, squirming flesh rolled into Davy's room and broke over the big wood-frame bed there, the young Kansan was already undressed.

Thrilling with desire each time his hands made contact with the hot young flesh, he came to the assistance of Faith, Hope and Charity, helping each to undress. And after that, Davy sank down onto the bed with a sigh of pleasure and anticipation.

The bedroom was dark, and no light came in from the hall, but moonlight streamed in through two windows on one side of the bed, silvering the bodies of the hovering Boise nymphs, coating their shoulders, flanks and buttocks with its argent glow.

Davy moaned and squirmed under the ministrations of the Mudree sisters, almost losing his wits as he inhaled the intoxicating scents of their arousal. And as they swarmed across him like bees in the midst of cross-pollination, he sampled their respective sweetnesses, feeling as happy as a bear cub who had unexpectedly stumbled upon a honeycomb.

Groping now, his hands drawn to the firm young flesh like ten-penny nails to a horseshoe magnet, Davy explored the naked topography of Faith, Hope and Charity. Firm, taut-nippled breasts, warm to the touch; full flanks and gloriously rounded buttocks; quivering goblet-bellies, whose wine was the sweat of ardor and excitement; lushly forested mounds of Venus, below which lay the secret, fragrant grottoes of love, wherein Davy probed with his long, thick fingers and felt the running streams of passion.

The small, hot hands of the Mudrees were fluttering all over his recumbent form now, like birds settling onto the eaves of a farmhouse. One of the sisters was stroking his throbbing rod, alternating the brisk, tingling touch of her fingers, as hand followed hand, traveling the length of his sex. Another had her face between his loins, and was teasing his perineum and testicles with a butterfly tongue. The remaining sister straddled his waist, rubbing her fluffy muff against his belly as she leaned over to kiss him and dart her tongue into his mouth.

"Judas Priest," Davy Watson moaned when the

Mudree sister (he wasn't sure which one) finally took her mouth from his. The young women were by now freed from all restraints, and worked him over with a primal thoroughness, an intensity that must have arisen from the very wellsprings of their deepest sexual instincts.

The sister on his waist inched her way up his hard-muscled body and leaned over him once more, offering him her firm, large breasts. Davy sighed when his mouth encountered the vibrant warmth of her flesh, and he ran his tongue over a thick, stiff nipple. There were a number of fine, dark hairs at the edge of the young woman's areola, and Davy was so erotically sensitized at that moment that he swore he could count each and every one of them with the tip of his tongue.

Suddenly, without exchanging a word, as if in response to the urging of some instinct to migrate, the three sisters changed positions on Davy Watson's body, relocating the focus of their desire. The one at his balls slid down to his feet, where she began to run her tongue along his instep and suck on his toes. The one who had been stroking his cock crawled up beside him and then straddled his neck and shoulders. The remaining sister went backwards, down from his waist, until she hovered over his jutting cock.

"Judas Priest," Davy moaned once more, realizing that he had almost come to the end of the trail. His ears burnt like a slow, sputtering fuse, and he felt like a Fourth of July rocket about to go off.

The southernmost sister sucked lovingly on his toes, caressing his ankles and big feet all the while. He caught his breath as the second sister's fingers encircled the shaft of his cock and guided it into the juicy snuggery of her pussy; the sudden, gripping feeling and the intense

41

rise in temperature almost caused the young Kansan to black out from sheer delight. And to top things off, the remaining Mudree sister (whoever she was), the one who had straddled his shoulders and neck, moved slowly forward, sliding her thick, sopping muff up to his mouth. Davy's nostrils flared at the sharp and rousing scent, while his lips twitched and puckered and his tongue flicked in and out of his mouth, actively registering his desire.

Passion. The dark, musky fragrance of pussy. The pouting lips of the Mudree sister's sex pressing against the lips of Davy Watson's mouth in a heartfelt, welcoming kiss. The salt tang of her juices in his mouth, the attentions of his lips and tongue causing them to flow like water into a sluice.

"Oh, Davy. Oh, Davy," the unknown sister murmured passionately, squirming upon his face, jerking her pelvis forward in the oldest of all known dance movements. "Land sakes," she whispered breathlessly, reminding Davy for one awful instant of her mother. "I feel as if I'm like to explode. *Oh, Davee-e-e-eee. . .*"

Like to explode was not an inapt phrase to characterize the way that Davy felt at that particular moment. The genital kiss, as well as the lubricious sucking of his toes and the snug, sphincter-grip of the pussy that stroked the length of his rock-hard cock, was taking its toll of his ability to control the focus of his consciousness. At that moment, he made a decision to surrender himself to the warm and enveloping instinctual darkness and the fireworks on the far side of his brain.

"*Ooooh, Davy-Davy-Davy-Davee-e-e-eee!*" howled the Mudree who rose up and down on his cock, one small finger delicately circling her pink and pulsating clitoris.

"Umm, Umm," grunted the sister on Davy's toes, running her index finger along the inside of her thick, congested nether lips.

"Woo-o-oooo, woo-o-o-ooo," wailed the little woman who sat on his face.

Hoo-wee! was the last thing that Davy Watson thought before his body was wracked by an oceanic orgasm that nearly sent the devastated convalescent into relapse. . . .

Chapter Three

After his amazing and exhausting sexual encounter with the Mudree sisters, Davy Watson later sank beneath the choppy waves of a troubled slumber. The orgy had been extremely gratifying, but the young Kansan was to experience a deep unrest, one that came as the result of his encounter with the fearsome and sinister Harvey Yancey.

Davy had done what had to be done; he had no qualms on that score: the viper had deserved his come-uppance. But what accounted for Davy's basic sense of uneasiness was his deep-seated conviction that a man like Harvey Yancey, humiliated before his own bully-boys, would seek to avenge himself upon those who had been responsible for that humiliation.

Perhaps he was wrong, Davy had thought as the tittering Mudree sisters lurched out of his room and wove their way down the hall of their mother's boarding house: a goodly number of bullies and ruffians were cowards and backshooters, men who would take few risks when it came to confrontations with decent, clear-eyed men. Perhaps Yancey was one of that ilk; perhaps he had quit Boise that very night, slinking out like a dog with its tail between its legs. Perhaps that was what happened. . .but Davy doubted it.

The way he saw it, Yancey was much more likely to hold a grudge, and was probably a man who would go to great lengths for revenge. There was a brooding, ominous quality about the man, something downright evil, Davy thought.

So, as he lay down to sleep, Davy Watson laid his Walker Colt beside him on the bed. His door and windows were locked, and if ever Yancey and his boys did come back for a little moonlight visit, Davy would be ready for them. The Colt's trigger was filed down, and all that the young Kansan had to do was to open his eyes and reach beneath his pillow. Anyone who had a mind to bother Davy Watson that night would be a likely candidate for a case of terminal lead poisoning.

Just as he was about to doze off, Davy had a thought that caused him to open his eyes and sit up in bed. A moment later, he was tip-toeing down the hall, to stop and tap on the door of his blood brother's room.

"Who is it?" a voice whispered in Pawnee.

"Hammer Hand," Davy whispered back in the same tongue, using the Pawnee name that Soaring Hawk had given him.

The door opened and the Indian bade him enter. The brave was naked, except for a breech cloth that was held by a rawhide thong that went around his waist.

"What you want?" he asked in English, as Davy entered the room.

"I want you to be on your guard, my brother," Davy warned. Then he proceeded to recount the incident involving Harvey Yancey and his bully-boys.

The Pawnee nodded solemnly as he sat on the edge of his bed. His foot rested on the barrel of his Sharps rifle, and a horse pistol lay beside it. Then, smiling a grim smile, Soaring Hawk lifted his pillow off the bed. Beneath it, gleaming coldly in the moonlight, lay his scalping knife, a knife whose blade was so sharp that it could cut a single hair. . .lengthwise.

The Indian sniffed several times and made a sour face at his blood brother. "You get shit-faced tonight, huh?" he asked.

Davy swayed back and forth as he nodded his head and grinned from ear to ear.

"That ain't all I got tonight," he told Soaring Hawk.

"Ah." The Pawnee nodded, sniffing again. "You get to fuck Mudree sister."

"Tha's right, ol' buddy," Davy replied after a belch.

"Which one?"

"All three of 'em."

"Goddamn!" exclaimed the Pawnee. "No wonder you look wore out."

"Keepin' three women happy's heap big work," Davy boasted. "But nice work."

Soaring Hawk shook his head. "Too much fuck no good. Make man lose strength."

"You might be right, there," Davy said with a tired smile, surprising the Indian by his ready agreement. "I'm gonna haul ass off to bed. Just be careful tonight."

Soaring Hawk nodded as he let Davy out of the room.

Once he was back in his own room, Davy Watson locked the door and returned to his bed. An instant after his head had hit the pillow, the young Kansan was asleep. But his sleep was troubled.

Water roared and churned wildly as it coursed downstream, and flocks of black birds cried out in shrill, accusing voices as they wheeled overhead. And those shrill cries echoed and re-echoed off the sides of the walls that towered above the rushing river, walls of stone that loomed above Davy, as he rode along the stony riverbank.

When he looked up at those steep and forbidding walls, Davy Watson groaned. The walls of the canyon appeared to stretch upward for thousands of feet. . . *and they were covered with blood!* And as he suddenly looked down, Davy saw that blood flowed beneath his horse's hooves and ran into the river. . .*which had turned to blood as well.*

A hoarse, bass laughter ran out obscenely through the awful canyon, growing louder with each succeeding echo until it broke upon Davy's ears like thunder out of hell. Suddenly, a roaring noise above him caused the young Kansan to look up.

There above his head, rumbling as it rolled down the ensanguined walls, was a huge and bloodstained boulder, growing ever larger as it descended—heading straight for Davy!

He leapt out of his saddle, and grunted as he hit the rocky soil of the riverbank. Just as Davy looked up again, he saw the blood-red boulder hit his mount with a bone-crushing smack and sweep it into the crimson tide.

The bass, obscene voice rang out again, and a chill travelled the length of Davy Watson's spine as he recognized Harvey Yancey's corrupt laughter.

He was about to roll over and get to his feet when something caught hold of his foot. When he turned to see what it was, he broke out into a cold sweat as he gaped at the vision of horror before him.

Some *thing*, some awful shape of corruption and putrefaction had emerged from the bloody waters of the river, and now held his booted foot in a death-grip between its bony fingers.

Davy fought to kick loose, but the thing could not be shaken off. It was a skeleton clothed in black rags, whose flesh had not entirely corrupted or been devoured

47

by the fishes. It resembled, he realized with sudden horror, the man who had perished in the vendetta at Hells Canyon. It was Ace Landry—the man who had shot his father to death; and he was slowly and inexorably dragging Davy Watson with him into the wild, bloody waters.

He lashed out frantically with his other foot, sending his boot smashing into the thing's face, its impact dislodging bits of rotten flesh from the creature's brow. But it held on like grim death itself, and Davy shuddered as he realized that he was unable to break free.

Down into the swirling, blood-red waters the thing went, and Davy Watson, scrabbling desperately for a handhold in the soil of the riverbank, went down with it. Down past his knees he went, past his hips, the small of his back, his chest. . . .

"No! No! Let me go!" he cried out, tossing from side to side in his frenzied efforts to escape from the horrible thing that was dragging him down to his death.

Once again the obscene laughter boomed throughout the canyon; once again Davy Watson heard the raw, jeering voice of Harvey Yancey.

"No, by God—no!" he cried out in terror, fighting to break free with all the strength the remained to him.

Davy awoke when he hit the floor of the bedroom. "Praise the Lord," he muttered, dragging himself to his feet and shuddering as he crawled back into his bed in Carmela Mudree's boarding house.

The next day was a busy one for Davy Watson and Soaring Hawk. After breakfast at the Mudree boarding house—where the three sisters smiled knowing, conspiratorial smiles—the young Kansan and his blood brother put in an appearance at the Boise circuit court, and gave depositions relative to their respective parts in the showdown with the members of the Landry gang.

Next on their agenda, following lunch with Judge Morris P. Crutchley, was an appearance at Arthur Dill's Last Chance Saloon. There they were met by a delegation of grateful goldminers; the blood brothers had been voted a reward for returning the greater part of the gold that Ace Landry and his bully-boys had plundered.

After that, it was supper in Benjamin Lagerstrom's emporium, where the miners stood them to all the beefsteak and venison they could eat. Over coffee and apple pie, Davy told Soaring Hawk about his nightmare.

"Spirits not at rest," the Pawnee informed him.

"What d'ya mean?" Davy asked.

"Spirits of men we kill wander about. Make your dreams bad."

"Well, I don't know about that," Davy replied, raising his big hands as he shrugged his shoulders.

"*I know,*" Soaring Hawk told him emphatically. "You white man, you not understand. Spirits still free to wander. Poison dreams. Tonight we fix."

"What d'ya mean, 'tonight we fix'?" Davy asked his blood brother.

"You see tonight," the laconic Pawnee replied, terminating the conversation as he turned back to the table.

Several hours later, Davy and Soaring Hawk were in the woods north of Boise, seated beneath the moon in a clearing in a grove of spruce trees.

Davy felt like a fool, sitting cross-legged on the ground and pounding a tom-tom like a savage. But he was a Pawnee now, and he did what his blood brother told him to do.

Soaring Hawk was up on his feet in front of Davy, yipping and moaning and dancing a series of hopping, shuffling steps while the young Kansan kept time on the tom-tom.

"*Hey-ya-eee-ya-a-a-aaa. Hey-ya-eee-ya-a-a-aaa,*" chanted Soaring Hawk, shuffling around in a circle, his mocassins causing pebbles to skitter over the ground as he went by.

The Pawnee was performing a spirit dance, one danced by warriors after battle. It was a dance of propitiation, done with the intention of putting the spirits of one's slain adversaries to rest. Soaring Hawk held the conviction that Davy Watson's nightmare arose from the fact that the spirits of Ace Landry and his gang had not yet been propitiated.

Spirit dances are fairly drawn-out affairs, and so Davy thumped his tom-tom for a long while, as Soaring Hawk danced into the small hours of the morning. And the fact that this act of propitiation consumed as much time as it did probably saved their lives.

At the same time that the blood brothers were in the grove of blue spruces to the north of Boise, four masked horsemen rode up to Carmela Mudree's boarding house, dismounted, and then stormed inside with pistols drawn.

The man at their head was a huge, bearded fellow, and he issued orders to his companions in a deep, rasping voice. Having reached the carpeted staircase beyond the parlor, the four masked men headed upstairs. It was just past eleven o'clock.

Eleven o'clock in Boise was considered a late hour, so the widow and her daughters were already asleep—the latter only because Davy Watson was absent at the time.

50

Todd Babcock and Will Beasley were out playing poker at the house of a friend named Wallace Futterman. Only old Ketchum was up at the time, and he met the intruders at the head of the stairs, having been roused earlier by the sound of horses' hooves outside his window.

"Keep yer distance," the old gentleman called out, standing above the masked man, clad in pajamas and dressing gown, and pointing a gnarled, trembling finger at them.

Standing at the foot of the stairs, the huge, bearded man who led the raiders shook his head and began to laugh an obscene, jeering laugh. This brought the white-bearded old gentleman up sharp, causing him to quiver from head to toe at the masked man's effrontery.

"Get out of here at once," John Ketchum said in a quavering, angry voice. "There's no money to be had here."

"'Tain't money I'm here after, you knock-kneed old goat," the leader of the masked band rumbled in his bass voice.

Old John Ketchum was still fuming. "Then what in thunderation *do* you want?" he asked.

"Satisfaction," the huge man answered, leveling his pistol at the old man's chest.

Ba-boom! A tongue of almost invisible flame darted forth from the barrel of the big gun, accompanied by a thunderous roar.

"Huk!" was all that John Ketchum said as the heavy-caliber slug smacked him back against the outer wall of his bedroom.

A moment later the house resounded to the thud of boots, as the four masked men dashed up the stairs.

"That way," the huge, bearded man ordered two of

his followers, waving them over to the landing on the left side of the staircase. "Come with me," he told the remaining man.

"Right," the intruder grunted, following his chief down the right side of the landing. The huge man stopped and turned to face the door to Davy Watson's bedroom. Then, after hefting his six-shooter in his hand, he raised his big, booted foot and smashed the door open with one kick.

Lunging across the threshold, the masked man went into a crouch as he trained his pistol on the bed at the far side of the room. The man behind him entered as well, ducking down and holding his gun out at arm's length with a trembling hand.

Frozen into immobility, the huge masked man stood like a marble statue in the moonlight and silence of Davy Watson's empty room. The only sounds to be heard were those of the stertorous breathing of the two intruders.

"Goddamn his eyes," the man swore in a whisper. "Sum'bitch ain't here." He straightened up and wheeled his bulk around with surprising agility. "Okay," he said to the other man. "Le's find out who-all's here."

The man nodded, and then turned to leave the room.

By this time, Carmela Mudree was awake; she had come out onto the landing just in time to see the raiders emerge from Davy's room. She looked at the huge form, blinking her eyes as she attempted to adjust them to the light from the lamp on the wall.

The huge man had come down the landing during this time, approaching with long strides, his pistol still in his hand. And as he stood before her, the widow continued to stare at him, causing the man to self-consciously finger the blue bandana he wore over his face.

"What on earth are you doing, Mr. Yancey?" Carmela Mudree asked, causing the masked man to recoil in surprise at her easy identification. But his surprise was only momentary, and a second later he brought the butt of his pistol down upon the widow's skull, dropping her in her tracks.

"Reckon you got to work some on yer disguise, Harv," the masked man behind Yancey remarked dryly, as Carmela Mudree's great bulk hit the carpeting.

Just then the two remaining intruders emerged from a room on the other side of the landing. Both shook their heads and gestured with their gun hands, this pantomime informing their chief that the object of their attention was nowhere to be found.

Harvey Yancey gestured back impatiently, waving the men on to adjoining rooms. A moment later, a series of shrill cries brought Yancey and his masked companion running to the room which his two bully-boys had just entered.

"It's jus the ol' bat's three daughters," one of the men in the room told Harvey Yancey, as the giant lumbered into the bedroom. "Ain't no other men on the premises, far as I can see," the masked man went on. "These here fillies is the onliest people we done found."

Yancey nodded his head slowly and narrowed his cold, dead eyes as he stared at the three Mudree sisters, who sat huddled together in a big bed across the room.

"Le's shag ass, Harv," one of the masked men whispered nervously in Yancey's ear. "Ain't no sense hangin' 'round here no longer."

The huge man nodded again, never taking his eyes off Faith, Hope and Charity Mudree. "Yeah, we might as well high-tail it out of here," he said in his bass rumble, pointing to the anxious young women with the long barrel of his weapon. "Take them l'il gals with you."

"But you jus' shot ol' man Ketchum," one of the masked men objected. "We ain't got no time fer pleasurin' ourselves."

"I know that," Yancey growled back. "We're takin' 'em with us when we ride out of Boise. Sugrue—saddle up three extra horses."

"Fer them?" asked the gaunt man who stood in the doorway.

"Yeah, fer them," Yancey called out, his voice shot through with tones of exasperation. "An' git a move on it, numbnuts!"

"Harvey, I jus' don't understan'," whispered the thickset masked man who stood just beyond the giant's reach. "What's the point in takin' these here heifers with us if we ain't gonna pleasure ourselves?"

Yancey was still staring at the three Mudree girls, despite his increasing irritation, and they were sitting bolt-upright and stock-still in bed, their eyes on him now.

"I didn't get what I come for," he growled. "But I don't intend to leave here empty-handed, neither."

"So you're takin' the gals?" the thickset man asked, not fully comprehending the meaning of his chief's words.

"I am indeed," Harvey Yancey told the man, advancing upon the terrified Mudree sisters as he did. "I may not've plugged that wise-ass Watson kid, but he's sure gonna be in for a li'l surprise when he comes back an' finds his gal-friends is gone."

"But what we gonna do with 'em, Harv?" the thickset man whined.

"We gonna find some suitable employment fer these

54

here l'il ladies," the huge man said as his shadow fell over the three terrified sisters. "An' while we're at it, we're gonna turn a smart profit."

By the time he stood towering over the huddled young women in the bed, Harvey Yancey was leering behind his blue bandana.

Boom-boom-boom-boom. *Boom*-boom-boom-boom. Davy Watson's big, callused hand beat time on the piece of deerskin that was stretched taut across the head of Soaring Hawk's tom-tom.

The tom-tom itself was rather small, as Indian drums go, but this feature enabled the Pawnee brave to carry it with him, wrapped up in his blanket roll, wherever he went. Soaring Hawk, in common with many of his race, was a man with a deeply spiritual orientation. An animist in his beliefs, the young warrior conceived of the visible world as inhabited by a host of spirits and vital forces, whose wills and energies animated all nature and gave direction to the play of creation.

"There are more things in heaven and earth, Horatio, than are dreamt of in your philosophy," said Prince Hamlet, and Soaring Hawk would have been the first to agree with the melancholy Dane.

Davy's dream concerning Ace Landry and their dead companion, Big Nose Vachon, was to the Indian a confirmation of his belief that the spirits of the departed must be laid to rest as well as their bodies. Whenever those spirits were afoot, it meant that the living either needed their counsel or owed them a debt.

In this instance the explanation was simple: the two men had died in battle; their blood had been spilt, and now they must be honored and propitiated, in order that their restless spirits might find peace.

Since the matter at hand was a grave and portentous one, the Pawnee danced for the spirits of the departed warriors for a very long time. Soaring Hawk danced and chanted, chanted and danced, for several hours under the pale autumn moon, deep in the forest that lay to the northwest of Boise town. It was his intention to work big medicine, and such an accomplishment was not the work of a few moments.

The process was somewhat expedited by the presence of Davy Watson, for as the Pawnee's blood brother he had learned a great deal of the tribe's lore in the course of their joint pursuit of the late and unlamented Ace Landry. Soaring Hawk had taught Davy the essentials of the spirit dance, and the young Kansan was therefore able to assist him in the ceremony.

Boom-boom-boom-boom. *Boom*-boom-boom-boom. Davy's arm arched as he continued to maintain the intense rhythm required for the ceremony. And his heart ached as well, when he realized that two men whom he had come to admire and respect were gone from his life forever: Jack Poole, the scout who had befriended Davy and Soaring Hawk when they first hit the vengeance trail; and Emile Vachon, the mountain man and trapper whose savvy and fighting skills had enabled the companions to completely wipe out Ace Landry and his entire gang in Hells Canyon.

They were gone, Davy Watson thought sadly; but here he was, sitting cross-legged in the moonlight, surrounded by blue spruce and birch, beating a Pawnee tom-tom, giving his departed buddies a send-off that would have tickled the shit out of both of them, old hands at Indian lore that they had been.

Davy grinned when he remembered Jack Poole's

56

anxiety over the bullet holes in his Stetson, put there during the course of the near-massacre that had come to be known as the Battle of Beecher's Island. But then his grin faded as he recalled the awful sight of Big Nose Vachon's beloved Nez Percé wife, Natona, hanging by the neck from the branch of a tree behind the trapper's cabin.

Both men had known the Indian intimately, and both had respected and admired his way of life. And Davy knew that they would have been greatly honored by the Pawnee ceremony on their behalf.

When it was over, a glance at the moon told Davy that the hour was past midnight. He shook his tired right arm and went to pick up Soaring Hawk's tom-tom, as the two blood brothers prepared to mount their horses and leave the depths of the forest.

Sure was a heap more active than a Christian funeral service, Davy told himself, smiling wryly as he compared the two rituals. But in further contrast to the custom of the whites, Indians often disposed of the bodies of the dead prior to the ceremony, either burying them beneath the earth or under cairns of stone, or leaving them in the branches of trees or in high wooden frames, so that wolves would not disturb the dead bodies, in order for the elements to freely work upon those mortal envelopes and gradually reabsorb them into the seamless fabric of eternity.

They had buried Jack Poole beneath the floor of the great forest that lay just beyond the eastern bluffs of Hells Canyon. Their efforts were not required in behalf of Emile Vachon, who went down to a watery grave in the depths of the icy, rushing Snake River. The two men had their resting places in different elements, but yet both had been interred within the living heart of nature.

Both men had spent their lives ranging the vast, open spaces of the American frontier, and it was fitting that their bones should lie within those spaces as well.

The dead have been laid to rest, Davy Watson told himself as he climbed onto his saddle. Now it was the turn of the living.

He and Soaring Hawk rode in silence for a long while, their thoughts far from the Idaho Territory, as the horses threaded their way through the dense, silvery forest of pine, spruce and cedar. An owl hooted in the distance with the accusing voice of a restless spirit, and the occasional crunch of pine cones and snap of twigs beneath the hooves of the horses sounded sharply in the heavy silence that mantled the northern forest.

"I will think of Jack Poole and Big Nose Vachon many times before I go to home of Great Spirit," Soaring Hawk told Davy, suddenly breaking the lugubrious stillness of the frosty autumn night.

Davy Watson turned to glance at his blood brother. It was a rare thing for the Pawnee to make an open declaration of his feelings. A comparable state in a white man would be best described by the words, "moved to tears."

"They were heap brave men, with heap big honor," Soaring Hawk went on. "Mighty warriors. Men who walked straight path. Men whose word could be all time trusted." He shook his head. "Not like most white man."

Davy realized with awe that this was a positive paroxysm of emotion for the stoic brave. His words were a great and heartfelt tribute to the integrity and valor of his fallen companions.

"Yep. I reckon so," Davy replied solemnly, nodding his head as he did. The Pawnee spoke for him, as well;

and it was probably the first time since they had made each other's acquaintance that Soaring Hawk had used more words to express himself than did his white brother.

They rode on in silence once more, neither of them speaking until they had ridden well into the town of Boise. But their silence was broken when they entered Carmela Mudree's boarding house and caught sight of the dead body of old John Ketchum.

"What in the Sam Hill happened here, Miz Mudree?" Davy asked in a hushed voice.

The widow sniffled and wiped her eyes with a linen handkerchief. She sat on the steps that led to the second floor of her house, gingerly fingering the blood-stained cotton bandage on her head. On the landing above her, still lying where it had fallen after being hit by the slug from Harvey Yancey's pistol, was the body of old John Ketchum.

Carmela Mudree dabbed at her eyes before speaking. "That terrible Mr. Yancey," she whispered hoarsely, pausing to blow her reddened nose. "He busted in here with those other men. They all wore masks, but I. . ." She began to sob uncontrollably.

Davy sat down beside the widow and put his arm around her. He knew well enough why Yancey had come back, and only regretted that he had not been there to give the villain a proper welcome.

"Now, you jus' take it easy, Miz Mudree," Davy said in a gently, soothing voice. "An' when you feel up to it, tell me what-all happened while Soaring Hawk an' me was gone."

The Pawnee caught Davy's eye, nodded curtly, and left the room, silent as a passing shadow.

"Where's Mr. Beasley an' Mr. Babcock?" Davy

asked, suddenly realizing that he had not seen Mr. Ketchum's two friends.

The widow pointed up at the landing. "In Mr. Beasley's room," she told him, mastering herself only with great difficulty. "They ran into Mr. Yancey and his friends outside. Mr. Beasley got shot in the shoulder, and Mr. Babcock was hit in both legs."

"Oh, Lord," Davy muttered as the widow blew her nose once more.

"We need a doctor," Carmela Mudree went on. "Would you please ride over to Doc Bailey's place an' fetch him here, Mr. Watson?" she asked in a whisper.

"Well, sure, Miz Mudree," Davy told her, patting the widow on the shoulder as he rose to his feet. "How's your girls doin'?" he asked, realizing with a flutter of apprehension that he had not seen any of the three sisters.

"Oh, Mr. Watson," the widow moaned, looking suddenly stricken as she made a face sadder than a bloodhound's, "my poor girls is gone!" Saying this, she broke down completely. It was several minutes before she could regain her composure and tell Davy exactly what had happened.

"Judas Priest!" the young Kansan exclaimed when he finally learned that the three Mudree sisters had been spirited off by the sinister and obscene Harvey Yancey. And as he recalled the man's talk on the night of their fight, his hand moved instinctively to the Walker Colt in his holster.

Soaring Hawk had reentered the room as noiselessly as he had departed from it, and Davy started back in surprise when the Pawnee touched his arm.

"You see any tracks?" Davy asked.

The brave nodded. "Seven horses. Plenty tracks."

"Which way was they headin'?"

"South. Mebbe little bit west."

"South an' a l'il bit west, huh?" Davy reflected. "Let's see. . .that'd be in the gen'ral direction of Nevada, wouldn't it?"

The Indian stared back at him impassively, not having the slightest idea of what lay southwest of the Boise Basin.

"Yep, that's Nevada all right," Davy said, confirming his own speculation. "Now, where would Yancey be headin' if he was to ride into the state of Nevada?" he asked rhetorically.

Soaring Hawk continued to stare at his blood brother, his features devoid of any trace of emotion.

Suddenly, Davy grimaced as he thought of Faith, Hope and Charity Mudree once more. . .and then recalled Harvey Yancey's words about selling young women to brothel keepers in Virginia City.

"Oh, sweet Jesus," he muttered, starting toward the door. "We gotta find them girls."

Soaring Hawk laid a restraining hand upon the young Kansan's shoulder. "Wait for morning. Yancey leave tracks easy to follow. Think we go 'way before him. Get doctor now, then sleep. We ride out when sun come up."

Davy stared at the big, raw-boned woman who sat on the staircase, sobbing as she cradled her bandaged head in her hands. He nodded in agreement with the Pawnee's advice.

"Jee-hosaphat!" he exclaimed, turning to leave the boarding house and ride over to Doc Bailey's. "Here we go again."

61

Chapter Four

Harvey Yancey's obscene laughter rang out boldly in the air as his party crossed the Snake River at a point just below Swan Falls. The giant was in high spirits this morning, having resigned himself to the fact that he was to be denied, for the present, the great pleasure of wringing Davy Watson's neck as if he were a chicken on a Sunday morning.

He consoled himself by realizing that there were other compensations: the Mudree girls would surely fetch a good price in woman-starved Virginia City; and when he arrived in that place, safely beyond the reach of any posse that might have formed in the Idaho Territory, he would have ample time to instruct the three handsome sisters in the proper performance of their future duties.

The sun shone brightly overhead, and the sky was blue and clear. Yancey's band had a huge lead over any potential pursuers, and the giant knew that he would shortly find both sexual and financial gratification. He felt so good at that particular moment that he raised his rich, raw bass voice in song.

> *"Last night I slept in a hollow log,*
> *With the birds and bees beside me.*
> *Tonight I sleep in a feather bed,*
> *With the one I love beside me."*

Hearing this, the Mudree sisters exchanged anxious looks.

"She jumped in bed an' covered up her head,
An' said I couldn't find her.
But I found my sweet beneath the sheets,
An' then set out to grind her."

The expressions of alarm and anxiety on the faces of Faith, Hope and Charity Mudree changed abruptly to those of fear and loathing.

Looking around and observing this, Harvey Yancey sullied the air with his coarse and obscene laughter.

Taking their cue from him, as always, his bully-boys began to laugh.

"I think you're shockin' the little gals with that song of your'n, Harv," the man called Sugrue told his chief as he rode up beside him.

"Oh, I don't think them little heifers is exactly strangers to a man's bed," Yancey told his follower.

"Well, even if they ain't, Harv," Sugrue replied toadyingly, "I'll bet you could still teach 'em a thing or two."

Yancey nodded at that, a smug and arrogant expression on his face. "You ain't jus' whistlin' *Dixie*, friend," he told Sugrue, leering back over his shoulder at the Mudree sisters. "Soon, I'm gonna teach 'em what it's like to be bedded down with a real man."

The young women averted their eyes and wrinkled up their noses at this, registering their distaste for Yancey's proposal.

"I can tell you now that it's gonna be a mite different than beddin' down with that li'l ol' sissy-boy, Watson," the huge, bearded man gloated. "'Cause I'm gonna

63

mount each one of you like a buck ram mounts a ewe,"
he flashed them a filthy smile, "like a bull covers a
cow."

The sisters grew pale upon hearing this boast.

"I'm gonna rough you three little heifers up some,"
Harvey Yancey rumbled in amorous anticipation.
"'Cause that's what women wants down deep—each
an' every blessed one of 'em. Yup. Even that Susan B.
Anthony."

"You are a thoroughly foul and detestable creature,"
Hope Mudree, the boldest of the three sisters, told the
gigantic ruffian.

"*Haw, haw, haw!*" bellowed Harvey Yancey. "You
done earned yourself the right to get it first, you spirited
little hunk of womanflesh," he informed her.

"If you so much as lay a hand upon my sister, I will
kill you," Charity Mudree informed the bearded giant
in a voice that rang with steely tones.

"And should she fail," Faith Mudree added, staring
at the bearded giant with cold, angry eyes, "I will kill
you. . .or lose my own life in the attempt."

"*Haw, haw, haw!*" was Harvey Yancey's only reply,
as he shifted in his saddle, obviously aroused by the
avowed resistance of the Mudree sisters.

Shaken by his ominous and obscene laughter, the
three young women reined in their horses until they rode
side by side, and then reached out to comfort each
other.

"You sweet little gals has jus' made my day," Yancey
announced in his bass rumble. "On second thought, I
think I'm a-goin' to take you all to bed at the same
time."

"You'd best strip an' search the li'l minxes afore you
do," reflected the crony known as McAllister. "'Cause

64

you know them li'l tootsies'd like nothin' better'n to slice off your balls an' hang 'em on the end of your nose.''

Yancey pondered this for a moment, while McAllister looked around and winked conspiratorially at Sugrue and the other man, Morison. The Mudree sisters sent a trio of angry looks at them.

"Y'know something, McAllister?'' Yancey asked rhetorically. "I think you got a point there, ol' son. Tell ya what I'm gonna do. . .''

McAllister leaned forward in his saddle while the huge, bearded man paused for dramatic effect.

"I'm gonna do you boys a big favor,'' Yancey went on, "an' let you watch while I break in these here little fillies.''

"That's all well an' good, Harv,'' Sugrue remarked dryly. "But do we get dibs on 'em after you's through?''

Yancey's coarse, contemptuous laughter rang out once again, causing all the horses to twitch their ears as it did.

"Why, after I get through with 'em,'' he told Sugrue, "ain't none of them l'il heifers gonna have the strength left to spread her legs.''

"You are a low and degenerate beast,'' Hope Mudree cried out suddenly. "May God have mercy on your soul.''

"*Haw, haw, haw!*'' was Harvey Yancey's sole reply. And when he had finally stopped laughing, the ruffian resumed his song.

"When she opened up her legs, I drove in my peg,
And started in to grind her.
Oh, the white of an egg rolled down her leg,

But the rest stayed in inside her.''

"Haw, haw, haw!''

Riding out at sunrise, saddlebags packed with necessaries and foodstuffs, weapons oiled and loaded for bear, Davy Watson and Soaring Hawk left the young town of Boise in search of Harvey Yancey and his bully-boys, the abductors of the Mudree sisters.

After having fetched Doc Bailey to tend to the wounds of Messers Babcock and Beasley, covered the corpse of John Ketchum, and consoled the frazzled Widow Mudree, the blood brothers went to rest themselves for the morning's pursuit. They were up at the crack of dawn and, after a hurried breakfast, packed their gear and loaded their pistols and rifles; then, once their horses had been fed and watered, the two men rode out on the trail once more.

Leaving Boise town they rode south, with the red, glowing sun coming up on their left hand, heading across the Ada River. And farther south the companions rode, fording the Snake at Swan Falls, and following with little difficulty the trail of the seven horses that carried Harvey Yancey and his party.

Beyond the Snake, they rode through the town of Oreana, skirted the easternmost flank of the Owyhee Mountains, and below that, crossed the Owyhee River at a point less than twenty miles north of the Nevada border. There, on the Owyhee's south bank, they camped for the night.

"Hammer Hand," Soaring Hawk called across the campfire, using the name he had given Davy after seeing the latter unload his Sunday punch.

Davy looked up, smiling at the Pawnee words, still somewhat embarrassed by the heroic-sounding appellation, one that came about (so he considered) as the result of a lucky punch. But the Indian had been much impressed, and had made his white brother instruct him in the art of fisticuffs.

"What is it, my brother?" Davy said, feeding the fire with an armful of sagebrush.

"You think Yancey go to Virginia City for sure?" the Pawnee asked.

"Well," said Davy, tilting back his hat and scratching his forehead, "he's got the Mudree gals with 'im. An' he was sure talkin' about it the night we tangled."

"Why sell girl in Virginia City?"

"Because they's struck all kinds of silver there—a huge vein of it called the Comstock Lode. The place is jus' crawlin' with wildcat speculators an' free spenders runnin' about with fistfuls of money. An' they's miners galore. These is almost all men, y'see. There jus' ain't one hell of a lot of women there."

The Pawnee nodded. "So white man pay to fuck woman, huh?"

"That's right, my brother. In a sit-chee-ayshun like that 'un, menfolks'll pay plenty to get their ashes hauled."

"Woman carry ashes, too?"

Davy laughed. "No, no," he told Soaring Hawk. "That's jus' another way of sayin' a man has a woman."

"No make sense."

"Well, it ain't literal-like."

"Then why say?"

Davy sighed. "It's like. . .a poetic way of makin' a comparison. I think they call it a simile."

Soaring Hawk shook his head. "Sound like more white man bullshit."

It was Davy's turn to shake his head. "Not quite, ol' buddy. I wish't I had some of my Uncle Ethan's books here, so's I could read you some of that there poetry. Then you'd sorta understand what I mean."

The Pawnee made a sour face. "Buffalo is buffalo. Indian no say buffalo herd like great dark cloud that roll over prairie."

"Goddamn, *that's poetry*!" Davy exclaimed.

Soaring Hawk paused to consider this. "Hmm. Buffalo *look* like black stormcloud from far away," he conceded.

"You did it," Davy told him. "You jus' made you some poetry."

"What use poetry for?"

"To say special an' beautiful things," Davy told the Pawnee. "To make you look at the world different-like."

"Like words for spirit dance," Soaring Hawk said.

Davy's eyes widened. "Y'know, that's right," he told his blood brother in a hushed voice. "I reckon everybody done got some poetry inside 'em somewhere."

"What happen Yancey fella sell Mudree sister in Virginia City?" the Pawnee asked, returning to their present involvement. "We take 'em back an' go 'way, or go on an' kill Yancey first?"

Davy sighed once more. "Y'know, after the mess we was in at Hells Canyon, I'd jus' as soon settle for pickin' up the girls."

"Not be that easy, I think."

"Yep. I spose you're right, ol' buddy."

"Not so bad. Only four men to kill this time." The Pawnee shrugged. "Easy."

"Get's easier all the time, don't it?" Davy asked with a sad smile.

"What happen you get Mudree sister back? You marry one?"

Davy sat up suddenly, coming off the rock he had been leaning against. "Hell, no!" he said vehemently. "Judas Priest, Soaring Hawk—you know dad-blamed well I'm a-headin' back to Hawkins Fork, Kansas, to git Deanna MacPartland out'n Miz Lucretia Eaton's bawdy house an' take her home with me. Gol-darn it, you know that!"

Fighting to suppress a smile, the brave turned away. "Soaring Hawk make joke," he told Davy.

"Land sakes," Davy replied, shaking his head. "I guess I still ain't used to the Injun sense of humor."

"White man think Indian no have sense of humor. Not true. Indian make heap many joke."

Davy grimaced as he remembered the time, at the camp of Soaring Hawk's tribe, when he shook hands with one of Colonel Frank North's Pawnee scouts. . . and came away holding the severed hand of a dead Cheyenne.

"Y'know," Davy said slowly, "some of them Injun jokes is a mite strange, according to the tastes of white folks."

Soaring Hawk nodded. "Different jokes for different folks," he told his blood brother.

Through Duck Valley they rode, to the west of the Bruneau River, entering the new state of Nevada and crossing the Owyhee River once more at its South Fork. Then south-by-southwest the two companions rode, following Harvey Yancey's trail to the boundary of Nevada's Great Basin.

Until as recently as 1864, a scant four years ago,

Nevada was a territory, with a status similar to that of its neighbors, Utah and Idaho. But considering their territorial status a form of second-class citizenship, the residents of the Nevada Territory, the "state of Washoe," as they called it, clamored for statehood even before territorial organization had been completed. But the Congress of the United States had been unwilling to grant an enabling act in 1862.

The territory proved to be a veritable treasure trove of mineral wealth, gold and silver having already been discovered in several places, and this exerted great influence upon Congressional opinion as the Union entered the third year of the costly and bloody struggle with the Confederacy. And although a movement was afoot at the time to grant statehood to the territories of Nebraska, Colorado and Montana, as well as Nevada, the latter was the only territory to receive it. . .and this in spite of the fact that Nevada had less than a sixth of the population required for a single representative in Congress.

The admission of Nevada to the Union was proclaimed on October 31, 1864. By this move, President Lincoln had accomplished several ends. First, he added Nevada to the roster of Republican states, and its vote was crucial to the passing of the Congressional amendment that formally abolished slavery within the boundaries of the United States. And further, Nevada's silver and gold became part of the war levies of the government at Washington. In the great and unseemly haste to admit Nevada to the Union, the new state's entire constitution was actually telegraphed to Washington—at a cost of $3,416.77.

The historic moment was celebrated in verse by the

Territorial Enterprise, Virginia City's liveliest and most prestigious journal:

> "Rejoice, ye mountains!
> Send word to the sea,
> The people have spoken—
> Nevada is free!"

Having skirted the Bull Run Mountains upon their entry into the Great Basin, Davy and Soaring Hawk rode through the semi-arid wilderness of mountains, valleys, and dry river beds that had become salt basins —the varied and harsh environments within a state whose range went from desert to wet meadow, and whose yearly extremes of temperature covered a span of over fifty degrees in a twenty-four hour period.

Going from northeast to west in the state, the blood brothers rode through forests of pinyon and juniper trees, through drab, shallow valleys, and over mountains whose treeless lower reaches of sagebrush gave way in the ascent to stands of white fir and pine, alpine fir and Engelmann's spruce at higher elevations. And as they traveled through these various levels, the two companions stopped to refresh themselves at cold, clear mountain streams bordered by a profusion of trees: water birch, willow and alder, aspen, chokecherry and cottonwood.

Mule deer ranged in great numbers, and Soaring Hawk made sure that they were well supplied with venison. Mink, muskrat, beaver, red fox and bager were seen by the travelers, as well as raccoon, porcupine, skunk, squirrel and chipmunk.

Game birds were also found to be in abundance, with

quail and grouse of many kinds predominating. Running them a close second were great numbers of chukar partridge and ring-necked pheasant.

This made for an endlessly varied and constantly delightful menu. Rainbow trout provided yet another entree, pleasing Soaring Hawk no end, and causing Davy Watson to realize that he was in the midst of a sportsman's paradise, a place whose abundance rivaled, after its own fashion, the teeming forests of the late Big Nose Vachon's beloved west-central Idaho Territory.

As the blood brothers threaded their way through the southwest foothills of the Trinity Range, Soaring Hawk drew his pony up beside Davy's horse and casually informed him that they were no longer alone.

"Where?" Davy whispered, fiddling with his hat as he strove to assume an air of insouciance.

"Trees to west," the Pawnee told him in a low voice. "Mebbe come up behind us, too."

"Think it's Yancey an' his boys. . .set to bushwhack us?"

Soaring Hawk shook his head almost imperceptibly. "Stalk like Indian."

"Judas Priest," muttered Davy. "I plumb forgot about Injuns. I wonder what kind they got hereabouts?"

Neither man knew, and knowing the name of their stalkers would have made no difference whatsoever. Having no knowledge of the tribes of Nevada, Davy and Soaring Hawk were deprived of all foreknowledge, as it were. But their ace-in-the-hole would be the Pawnee's judgment, his ability to come up with countermoves based upon predictions of the behavior of his race in general.

It so happened that the Indians who were stalking

Davy and Soaring Hawk were a hunting party of Paiutes. Indians throughout the state had been threatened for years by the incursions of farmers and miners, who had intruded upon their lands and disrupted the flow of Indian life by their actions. And in 1859, when the fabulous Comstock Lode was discovered, thousands of whites flocked into the area of Virginia City and its environs; the local tribes—the Paiute and Bannock—had determined to resist this latest and most flagrant of all encroachments.

Tempers flared on both sides, and the result was the Pyramid Lake War of 1860. Winnemucca, a young Paiute war chief, and his followers ambushed a combined force of whites from Virginia City and Carson Valley, killing 76 men and wounding at least 15 or 20 more.

News of the defeat panicked the residents of the Comstock settlements, but good sense ultimately prevailed. Colonel Jack Hayes sallied forth at the head of a volunteer force of 549 men, and they were reinforced by 207 regular army men sent from the state of California.

A battle was joined at the big band of the Truckee River, wherein the Indians were decisively defeated by the superior firepower of the enemy. One hundred sixty Paiutes and Bannocks were killed in the encounter, whereas only two whites lost their lives.

This victory broke the back of organized Indian resistance, although raids continued to the present day, aimed primarily at Pony Express and stagecoach stations.

There were four braves in the hunting party that stalked Davy Watson and Soaring Hawk. Two of the Paiutes glided noiselessly among the forestation of the

Trinity's lower reaches, while the remaining two brought up the rear, always keeping a hill or valley between themselves and the intruders. One Paiute in each group carried a breechloading rifle; the other two were armed with bows and arrows.

"Get ready, Hammer Hand," Soaring Hawk told his blood brother. "Indian in trees start to line us up in sights of rifle."

"Where?" whispered Davy.

"Tree just in front of two big rocks. On right," the Pawnee whispered back.

"I see white feathers," Davy told him.

"Yup. That him. You see other—'bout ten feet to left? With bow and arrow?"

"Where?. . .Uh-huh," Davy whispered excitedly. "I see that sum'bitch now." His palms began to sweat as he watched the Paiute brave notch an arrow to his bow-string.

"Not have much time," Soaring Hawk told him in a low, even voice. "I shoot brave with rifle. You shoot one with bow."

"Gotcha," Davy whispered hoarsely, his right hand moving imperceptibly down to his holstered pistol.

"Count to four in head. . .then shoot," the Pawnee whispered.

"Amen to that, ol' son," Davy answered in a low, tense voice.

One, he counted, taking a deep breath and exhaling slowly to steady himself.

Two. . .Davy began to inch the Walker Colt out of its holster.

Three. . .He swallowed and then surrendered his will, in an effort to relax and trust to his reflexes, to listen to the inner voice that always guided his actions.

Four.

Blamblam! Blamblam!

Davy whipped out his Walker Colt, steadied it with his left hand, and fired off four shots in rapid succession. Behind him, acting with the speed of a set of reflexes that the young Kansan always found to be uncanny, Soaring Hawk brought his big, breechloading Sharps rifle up to his shoulder and fired at the Paiute rifleman.

Boom! The Sharps detonated with a thunderous burst, blowing apart a chest-high section of the pine tree that had partially concealed the Paiute, the impact of its slug sending the man backward, his arms flailing wildly as he fought to regain his balance. By the time he did, Soaring Hawk had already reloaded. The second booming shot blew the Paiute off his feet, and rolled his broken body into a clump of shrubbery.

Davy's four shots had been well placed, and one of them blew the top off of the bowman's skull. The instant that he saw the Paiute go down, he wheeled his horse around and leveled his Colt once more, sighting on the top of the rise that had been twenty feet behind him.

"Take left," was all that Soaring Hawk told him, in the instant before the two remaining braves came into sight.

Davy did as he was told, and fired the last two shots that remained in his Colt at the Indian who suddenly bounded over the rise.

He saw the man stagger back and drop down on one knee, just as a blast from Soaring Hawk's heavy-caliber Sharps rifle blew the last Paiute back over the rise. Davy had holstered his pistol, and was drawing his Henry rifle out of its boot when he felt the Pawnee's restraining hand on his arm.

"Let man go," the Indian told his blood brother. "He no bother us. Got shot-up arm."

As he replaced the Henry, Davy Watson nodded. Then he closed his eyes and took a deep breath, in an attempt to cool the fire in his blood.

"I reckon you're right, my brother," he told the Pawnee, whose dignity and humanity he respected at all times.

Onward they rode, through that eerie and open geography of valleys and mountains that ran from north to south, whose overlaps frequently interrupted their progress. Farther westward they proceeded, crossing the Humboldt River, skirting the Sonoma Range after visiting the town of Winnemucca. Then they followed the course of the Humboldt, between the Trinity and Humboldt Ranges, where it flowed past Woolsey and Lovelock.

Down from the mountains they came as their journey continued, through levels of pine—whitebark, red fir and lodgepole, down to the Jeffery, ponderosa and sugar pines, finally descending to the level ground at a point south of Pyramid Lake.

Working their way over to Nixon, a town situated near the dry center of what was once the huge, many-fingered complex known as Lake Lahontan, now just below the southernmost end of Pyramid Lake, Davy and Soaring Hawk made their way down to the Truckee River. Riding down from the mountains, through the whitebark timberline, down to the red fir and white pine, they came at last to the banks of the river whose course would lead them to fabled Virginia City.

The final leg of their long journey took them through the most populous and civilized area of that great, wild state. Following the winding course of the Truckee, the two riders went parallel to its south fork a few miles east of the town of Reno, and then descended through Huffakers and Steamboat Springs, until their destination was in sight, its bright lights twinkling in the dusk as night began to fall upon the wide expanse of the Sierra Nevada.

Davy Watson shifted in his saddle and peered into the dusk at the myriad points of light which were the visible and distant emanations of Virginia City's nocturnal energies. And when he thought of the imminent prospect of another encounter with the huge and brutal man known as Harvey Yancey, the young Kansan reflexively loosened his Walker Colt in its weathered leather holster.

Chapter Five

Ophir. . .Pleasant Hill. . .Mount Pleasant Point: these were some of Virginia City's early names, when the boom town was still nothing more than an undistinguished mining camp, in the days before the discovery of the great Comstock silver lode.

Described as a sleepy, "Pi-ute sort of town," Virginia City in its earliest days was referred to by the American humorist J. Ross Browne as "a mud hole; climate, hurricanes and snow; water, a distillation of arsenic, plumbago and copperas; wood, none at all except sagebrush; no title to property, and no property worth having." But the Comstock Lode had changed all that. And by late 1868, after a decade of boom and bonanza, Virginia City had become a sprawling wildcat of a town, and one of the wonders of the American West.

Celebrated as the "Queen of the Comstock," the town was on the overland route to San Francisco, and had been visited by many of the era's great names, as they traveled to or from the young California metropolis. A legion of the most colorful and controversial players on the stage of American life visited Virginia City, as well as the nation's most eminent stage or theatrical troupes.

Three presidents had been there: Benjamin Harrison, Rutherford B. | Hayes and the ' newly-elected

Ulysses Simpson Grant. Politicians and generals came as well: James G. Blaine and Schuyler Colfax, William Tecumseh Sherman and "Little Phil" Sheridan. Baron de Rothschild, the European financier, looked the town over, as did young Tom Edison, the fellow who could fix everything. The preacher Henry Ward Beecher came to Virginia City, as did the famed agnostic, Robert Ingersoll.

There were more, many more: humorists Artemus Ward and Mark Twain (who first speculated in silver-mine shares, and later worked as a reporter); Mrs. Maggie Van Cott, the first woman licensed by the Methodist Church to preach in the United States; the great advocate of women's rights, Susan B. Anthony, and one of the leading females advocates of free love, Tennessee Claflin. The great figures of the age were drawn to Virginia City as iron filings were drawn to a magnet, all anxious to see and experience the wealth, energy and romance of the town that silver had made.

In the beginning, Virginia City was somewhat less impressive, as J. Ross Browne well knew: "On a slope of a mountain speckled with snow, sagebrushes, and mounds of upturned earth, without any apparent beginning or end, congruity or regard for the eternal fitness of things, lay outspread the wondrous city of Virginia. Fame shanties, pitched together as if by accident; tents of canvas, or blankets, of brush, of potato-sacks and old shirts with empty whiskey barrels for chimneys; smoky hovels of mud and stone; coyote holes in the mountain side, forcibly seized and held by men; pits and shafts with smoke issuing from every crevice; piles of goods and rubbish on craggy points, in the hollows, on the rocks, on the snow, everywhere, scattered broadcast in pell-mell confusion, as if the clouds had suddenly burst overhead and rained down the dregs of all the flimsy, rickety, filthy little hovels and rubbish of merchandise that had ever undergone the process of evaporation since the days of Noah.''

Miners and speculators, drunkards and ruffians; seekers and slickers, wild-eyed dreamers and cold-eyed sharpers; these were among the more colorful types who had flocked to populate the young boom town, where gambling, drinking and prostitution flourished openly in that raucous, desperate carnival atmosphere.

The town's other face was that of its solid citizens —married couples, churchmen, businessmen, merchants and civil servants, people who lent the place a daytime normality much akin to other towns its size throughout the United States.

Virginia City was a microcosm, a mixture of personalities that seemed a veritable condensation of the American experience. English, French and Canadians, Germans, Scots, Welsh and Italians were there, as well as American Indians, Chinese, Mexicans, Irish and Negroes.

There was a German *Turnverein* society and three Irish military companies, the Emmet, Sweeney, and Scofield Guards. The Scots clans gathered under the auspices of the Caledonian Society, and there were numerous picnics and balls sponsored by the Italian Benevolent Society. The Mexicans paraded annually on their Independence Day, as did the Chinese on their New Year. The blacks had established their own organizations as well, including the African Methodist Episcopal Church and a Freemasons' Lodge. Virginia City, although barely ten years old, was unusually cosmopolitan.

It was her chaotic, carnival aspect that the Queen of

the Comstock presented to Davy and Soaring Hawk, on the night the two rode into town. Drunkenness was rampant, and the streets of the honkytonk district were crowded to overflowing with the worshipers of Bacchus: reeling drunks, staggering drunks, drunks puking their guts out and drunks with the "dry heaves," drunks passed out on the boards of sidewalks and drunks lying face-down in the muck of the streets.

It seemed to Davy that practically everyone he saw was drunk. That impression was not far from wrong. Boozing was the town's number one pastime, and the hard-working miners and the nervous, obsessed mining speculators, as well as the men who made their living off both types, all soothed their frazzled nerves under the aegis of John Barleycorn. In fact, so much drinking went on in Virginia City that the man who refused a "friendly drink" was almost universally regarded with suspicion.

"Not look like men, look like pig," Soaring Hawk remarked, frowning in disgust as he reined in just in time to prevent his horse from stepping on the bald and shiny skull of a fallen drunk.

Davy sighed. "It ain't a pretty sight, I'll give you that. I never did see such a rowdy collection of toss-pots."

"Watch there," the Pawnee told him.

"Oops!" Davy exclaimed, guiding his mount sharply to the right, in order to prevent its being splattered by a man who was weaving back and forth in the street while he puked his guts out.

"Pig not so dirty as drunk," Soaring Hawk commented, amending his earlier statement.

The companions were riding along D street, Virginia City's bustling honkytonk and red-light district. None of the streets were parallel to each other, nor were they of the same width, and it was extremely difficult to make one's way across them because they were so rarely interconnected.

To the left of D was C Street, the local equivalent of San Francisco's Montgomery Street. To the right of D was Chinatown. Expensive houses on the slope of nearby Mount Davidson, and in Six-Mile Canyon to the east, constituted the town's suburbs.

Beyond Gold Hill, at the head of Devil's Canyon, there could be seen the lights and fitful fires of the many quartz mills and ore dumps bordered by tunnel tracks, of mining and milling companies with names like Ophir, Gould & Curry, United States Central, Sierra Nevada, Potosi and LaCrosse. And smouldering in the night was the Burning Moscow mine, its ominous appearance causing Davy Watson to liken it to hell's back door.

"That's where all the silver's bein' dug up," he told Soaring Hawk, sweeping his arm from the diggings on Gold Hill to those that bordered on Virginia City itself.

"Make white men crazy," was the Indian's only comment.

"Sure does," agreed Davy, stiffening in the saddle as he heard gunshots in the distance. It was not the last time he would hear them, either; for gunfights and shooting sprees were not uncommon occurrences in that wild frontier town, where men were killed with an alarming frequency.

"Well," said Davy, pointing to a place whose sign and gold-lettered front window proclaimed it to be Piper's Saloon, "I 'spose that's as good a place to start as any."

Having remembered the essentials of Harvey Yancey's conversation on the night prior to the abduction of the Mudree sisters, Davy had resolved to scour the bawdy houses of Virginia City. With a little luck, he would find Faith, Hope and Charity, and rescue them before they had been exposed overmuch to the shocking and reckless behavior of men on the frontier, where lawlessness was rampant.

Should his path happen to cross that of the huge Harvey Yancey, Davy Watson was prepared to bring the scoundrel to justice. And if that particular task required gunplay. . .well, a man did what he had to do, the young Kansan reflected.

"Believe me, if all those endearing young charms
That I gaze on so fondly today
Were to change by tomorrow, and flee from my arms
Like fairy gifts fading away. . . ."

As the two men hitched their horses to one of the posts that stood before Piper's Saloon, they heard a tenor voice raised in song, ringing clear and true above the jangly, lumbering sounds of a barrel organ.

". . .Thou would still be adored,
as this moment thou art,
Let thy loveliness fade as it will,
And around the dear ruin, each wish of my heart
Would entwine itself verdantly still."

A great hush fell over the saloon as the tenor, a young red-bearded man, finished his song. The beauty of his voice and the impact of the sentimental lyric had combined to still the voices of the otherwise rowdy denizens of Piper's. Hardened miners sniffed as they bent over their whiskies, and grizzled prospectors let their tears drop into the amber depths of their beer schooners. Sharpers and conniving lawyers—who were known locally as the "Devil's own"—remembered sweethearts long gone, and pimps and tinhorns felt a lump in their throats as they thought of their distant or departed mothers.

Silence mantled the saloon as Davy and Soaring Hawk bellied up to the bar. The young Kansan experienced a fleeting sensation, which he likened to a solemn moment at an Irish wake.

"Sing *Rose of Tralee,* would ye now, Dennis?" an old man with a crooked nose and red face called out from the far end of the bar.

"Damnation!" exclaimed the man at Davy Watson's left hand. "If you do that, they'll float the spitoons out of here on a river of tears. Sing us something jolly, for the love of God!"

"Sing *Bonnie Annie Laurie,*" a pimply-faced blond man called out.

"No, no!" insisted the man on Davy's left in a loud voice. "That's about as jolly as dinner with a High Church bishop. How about *The Wild Colonial Boy*, Dennis?"

"Sure, an' what's in it fer meself, if I do?" the red-bearded tenor called back to the man.

"Two fingers of the finest Irish whiskey in the house," was the prompt reply.

The tenor nodded. "Wet me whistle, an' I'll have the entire population of Virginia City purrin' like the cats of Kilkenny."

"Arthur!" the man called out, flagging down the nearest of the three bartenders behind the packed bar. "A wee dram for yon Gaelic minstrel."

Just as the bartender nodded and began to turn to the shelves of bottles behind him, Davy heard the sound of a barrel organ. An instant later, the Irish tenor began to sing.

"There was a wild colonial boy,
Jack Duggan was his name. . . ."

"Now, that's more like it," the man on his left told Davy. "Anything's better than seeing this aggregation of mugs, ruffians and cutthroats bawl like babies cutting their milk-teeth."

Davy gandered the speaker and saw that he was a spare, curly-haired man of middle height, whose oval face was distinguished by a pumphandle nose and eyes that glittered with mischief and the workings of a perfervid imagination.

"You wouldn't believe," the man went on, "just how sentimental hardened types like these can get." He smiled wryly and shook his head. "They'd crack your skull like an egg at the slightest provocation, and think nothing of blowing out the brains of the casual stranger who might have the misfortune to rub 'em wrong. And yet, when they hear a sentimental ditty, they snivel and caterwaul like a covey of grandmas seeing *East Lynne* for the first time."

Davy extended his hand. "I'm Davy Watson, of Anderson County, Kansas," he told the man. "An' this here gent is my friend an' blood brother, Soaring Hawk, of the Pawnee Nation."

The man shook his hand and pumped it enthusiastically. "Mr. Watson. Mr. Hawk," he said, wincing as the brave gave his hand a bone-popping squeeze. "I'm Marcus P. Haverstraw, local for the *Territorial*

Enterprise."

"Local?" Davy asked, immediately following that question with "Schooner of beer and a sarsparilla, please," as the bartender came up.

"Local items reporter, city news," Haverstraw told Davy, raising his schooner as he did. "I tell everyone what they've been doing, as well as make up events. . . just to liven things up." He smiled mischievously. "To the truth of the imagination," he toasted.

"I'll drink to that," Davy said with a wistful smile, remembering the tall tales of his late companion, Jack Poole.

"Judging from the dust that flies whenever each of you takes a deep breath," said Marcus Haverstraw, "I'll wager that you've just come off the trail."

Davy and Soaring Hawk both nodded.

Suddenly, Davy realized that the affable and garrulous newspaperman would be the perfect ally in his search to discover the whereabouts of the Mudree sisters.

"You fellas hungry?" the reporter asked.

"We could eat some," Davy conceded. "But first, I'd like to ask you some questions about Virginia City, if'n I might, Mr. Haverstraw."

"That would be my pleasure, Mr. Watson," the reporter answered cordially. "But let us, as has long been my established custom, combine business with pleasure."

He flagged down the barkeep. "Arthur, I'd like three platters, if you please."

The bartender nodded and walked off.

Davy ordered another round of drinks for the three of them. And moments after they had cordially toasted each other, the platters ordered by Marcus Haverstraw arrived.

"This one's on me, gentlemen," the reporter told Davy and Soaring Hawk, plunking six bits down on the damp, mahogany surface of the bar.

Eyes wide and mouth watering, Davy beheld a big platter heaped with Limburger cheese, radishes, mustard and caraway seed bread. He inhaled the sharp aroma of the cheese as if it were perfume to his nostrils. Soaring Hawk, who had no tolerance for the white man's aromatic cheeses, made a sour face as he popped a radish into his mouth.

Marcus Haverstraw insisted that the two companions eat their fill before commencing the interrogation. He passed the time by regaling them with anecdotes about the staff of the *Territorial Enterprise*, that virile, colorful and influential paper edited by Joseph T. Goodman.

Samuel Clemens had been on the staff of the *Enterprise* in the early '60's, and his doings there were already legendary. Haverstraw claimed that the author's pen name had arisen from his custom of charging drinks at the local brewery, wherein he would order a lager beer for himself and an associate, and tell the bartender to chalk up the brace of drinks on a slate used to run a talley in such instances. Sam Clemens would raise his hand, hold up two fingers and call out to the bartender, telling him to "mark twain."

Then, as Davy and Soaring Hawk continued to eat, Haverstraw further regaled them with stories of Mark Twain's lively reporting, including his fondness for hoaxes, and his devastating theatre criticism, such as the following piece he had written for the *San Francisco Call*:

On Tuesday evening that sickest of all sentimental dramas, "East Lynne," will be turned loose upon us at the Opera House. It used to afford me much solid comfort to see those San Franciscans whine and shuffle and slobber all over themselves at Maguire's theatre, when the consumptive "William" was in the act of "handing in his checks," as it were, according to the regular program of "East Lynne"—and now I am to enjoy a season of happiness again, I suppose. If the tears flow as freely here as I count upon, the water privileges will be cheap in Virginia next week. However, Miss Julia Dean Hayne "don't take on" in the piece like Miss Sophia Edwin; therefore she fails to pump an audience dry, like the latter.

"But old Mark left under a cloud," Marcus P. Haverstraw concluded. "He got himself embroiled in a ridiculous controversy involving a flour sack and the use of the loaded word, 'miscegenation.' Having challenged a man to a duel, he left Nevada one step ahead of a grand jury citation, not wishing to be jailed for violating the state's anti-duelling law.

"But Mark Twain had the last word," Haverstraw told Davy with a smile, as he quoted the American humorist one last time:

I was young and foolish when I challenged that gentleman, and I thought it was very fine and very grand to be a duellist and stand upon the "field of honor." But I am older and more experienced now, and am inflexibly opposed to the dreadful custom.

If a man were to challenge me now—now that I can fully appreciate the iniquity of that practice—I would go to that man, and take him by the hand and lead him to a quiet room—and kill him!

Davy laughed at this, splattering the head of his latest beer all over Soaring Hawk's arm and back. "This Mark Twain's one hell of a fella," he agreed, nodding at Marcus Haverstraw as the Pawnee reached for the bar rag and shot him a look of annoyance.

"He was indeed," the reporter agreed. "Things were never dull when old Sam Clemens wrote for the *Enterprise*."

"Now, gettin' down to business, Mr. Haverstraw," Davy began.

"Call me Marcus," the newspaperman told him, motioning for the bartender to set up another round of drinks.

"Well, Marcus," Davy went on, "what me'n Soaring Hawk is here for is to rescue three young ladies—the uh, Mudree sisters, who been abducted by a disreputable character name of Harvey Yancey."

"Do tell," murmured the reporter, an interested look on his face as he leaned forward to pick up his schooner of beer from the bar.

"*I dre-eamt I dwe-elt in mar-r-rble halls,*" the voice of the Irish tenor rang out over the rackety jangle of the barrel organ.

"We been followin' Yancey's trail all the way down from Boise town," Davy continued. "It's been easy, 'cause there's seven horses, an' Yancey don't reckon nobody come into Nevada after 'im."

"Seven horses," was all that Haverstraw said.

"Yup. There's Yancey, the Mudree sisters, an' his three pals."

"Why has this Yancey gent abducted the Mudree sisters?" the reporter asked.

"Well, me an' him had a run in," Davy told Haverstraw. "An' he come back for revenge, but I wasn't there. He killed some ol' gentleman name of Ketchum, an' then took off with the Mudree sisters."

"He in love with one of 'em?" the reporter asked hopefully.

Davy shook his head. "He's a real brute, this Yancey is. I'm not sure that bein' able to love is in his nature." He sighed. "The night before it happened, he was already talkin' 'bout sellin' them gals to a Virginia City brothel keeper, or a white slaver on the Barbary Coast."

"By Godfrey!" exclaimed Marcus Haverstraw. "This has the makings of a great story."

"I was hopin' you'd see it that way, Marcus, because I'd like to make a little deal with you."

"Do tell," the reporter murmured just before he drank, staring at Davy over his beer schooner.

"What I've got to do, I reckon," Davy told him, "is to inspect all the bawdy houses in Virginia City."

"That could take a little time," the newspaperman told him as he wiped the suds from his mouth with the back of his hand.

"Well," sighed Davy, "that's what I've got to do. . . in order to locate the Mudree sisters."

"Uh-huh," grunted Marcus Haverstraw. "And where do I fit into the picture, Mr. Watson?"

"Call me Davy, Marcus."

"With pleasure, Davy."

The two men smiled and shook hands. Davy finished

his beer and ordered another round. Soaring Hawk sat on his barstool, an impassive expression on his face, and studied the crowd at the bar of John Piper's Saloon.

Marcus Haverstraw's smile was a knowing one. "So, you'd like me to take you boys on a guided tour of Virginia City's cat-houses, eh?"

As Davy nodded in agreement with this observation, a Chinaman on the reporter's left turned to the three men.

"Woman who put husband in dog house," the man told them, "soon find him in cat-house."

Davy and Haverstraw broke out into a volley of guffaws. Soaring Hawk merely stared at the Chinaman.

"That's right edifyin', Mr. Chin," Haverstraw told the man, who nodded and smiled at him. "Did you think that up?"

Still grinning, the Oriental shook his head. "No," he told them. "Come from other Chinese."

"Who might that be?" Haverstraw asked.

"Confucius," the man replied, just before turning back to the bar.

"Well, back to business," the reporter said, shaking his head and grinning.

"So, if you was to be our guide, so to speak," Davy resumed, "it jus' might turn out to be a whale of an interestin' story for you."

"You don't run across kidnapping and white slavery every day," admitted Haverstraw, a look of gleeful anticipation on his face. "When do we start, my friends?"

"Right after Soaring Hawk an' me finds us a place to bed down."

"Why, that's no problem at all, Davy. You fellas are welcome to stay at my diggings. My roommate and

91

fellow reporter, Henry Twitchell, is presently taking the water at Steamboat Springs. There's room enough to accommodate you both, if one of you doesn't mind sleeping on the sofa.''

"That ain't no problem a-tall," Davy assured him, jerking a thumb in the Pawnee's direction. "Ol' Soaring Hawk, he don't sleep on nothin' else but the floor when he's indoors.''

After finishing their platters of food, Davy and Soaring Hawk accompanied Marcus Haverstraw to the rooms the latter shared with Henry Twitchell, city editor of the *Enterprise*.

Haverstraw's rooms were located on A Street, and it took them some time to get there, owing to the particular arrangement of Virginia City's streets. Since the town had been thrown up in an extremely haphazard fashion, one had always to walk great distances out of the way before crossing from one street to another.

Leaving their horses at a nearby livery stable, the two companions carried their saddles, saddlebags and blanket rolls up to Marcus P. Haverstraw's rooms. Then, heating water on the reporter's gas stove (one of Virginia City's municipal wonders, along with the lighted streets, municipal water and sewerage, as well as rail and stage terminals, four daily and four weekly newspapers), Davy and Soaring Hawk availed themselves of the bathtub that stood on four ornate, cast-iron legs and washed the dust of the trail from their bodies.

At approximately ten-fifteen p.m., the blood brothers, fed, washed and groomed, led by their guide and ally, sallied forth into the rambunctious night of the West's premier mining town, on their way to the bowers of the "fallen angels" of D Street.

While there were very few "proper girls" in the rugged male frontier town (the 1860 census put the man-woman ratio at seventeen-to-one), there was a goodly supply of the other kind: prostitutes in the honkytonks and brothels, taxi dancers in the hurdy-gurdy cellars, and female dealers at the faro tables of the gambling houses.

The narrow streets, where drivers earlier cursed as their six-mule teams wended their way through the dusty congestion of four-footed traffic, were now crowded with people in search of excitement and a respite from their daily cares. Befitting a sprawling town that grew from a population of mere hundreds to almost 20,000 in ten years, Virginia City's daytime aspect was fairly frantic. Most worthy of the stranger's notice were the chronic traffic jams, and the many sidewalk auctions, where merchandise of an incredible diversity was offered up for sale: mine stock (sold for non-payment of assessments) and items as different from each other as horses, haberdashery and brass watches.

Omnibuses made round trips to Gold Hill and Silver City sixteen times daily, and stage coaches arrived frequently, bearing in addition to their human freight wooden boxes containing machine parts, blanket rolls, dressed pork carcasses and ungainly bales of hoopskirts. A million dollars of bullion a month was transported by Wells Fargo, and jaded expressmen casually handled fortunes in silver bricks daily.

At night, the Queen of the Comstock grew seductive, luring men into the streets with the music of barrel organs and pianofortes, with the promise of whiskey, gambling and ready sex. She was a wicked and fickle enchantress, but men readily forgave her and came back for more, still intoxicated by the heady wine of her promises.

Men of all kinds, in all conditions, strolled along Virginia City's bright nocturnal streets: leather-chapped Mexican vacqueros and gowned Chinese; tattered miners and neat Germans puffing on long, clay pipes; staid gray clerks and felt-hatted, fashionable gents from the monied suburb of Silver Terrace. D Street, in particular, was a rowdy, raucous place where the babble of voices and the jangle of honkytonk music was interrupted from time to time by the sounds attendant upon knifings or gunfights.

The first place that Davy, Soaring Hawk and Marcus P. Haverstraw entered was called Scobey's, not the fanciest of Virginia City's honkytonks, but the closest to Marcus' apartments. They looked around, had a drink, and Davy saw that the reporter was on good terms indeed with many of the boom town's less reputable-looking citizens. . .including William J. Scobey, the owner of the place.

"You haven't taken on any new girls lately, have you, Will?" Marcus P. Haverstraw asked the man.

"Can't say as I have," Scobey replied, picking his teeth with a silver toothpick.

Satisfied that nothing was to be learned there, the trio finished their drinks and left Scobey's. Six more honkytonks and bordellos were visited, with drinks tossed down in each and every one of them. Continuing their progress down D Street, they next entered a bawdy house owned and run by one Etta Captree, formerly of Baltimore.

"Madam," Haverstraw said suavely, just before he kissed Etta Captree's hand, once they had entered the bawdy house. "And I mean that literally. How are you, my dear?"

The madam in question, a short and stocky dyed blonde with a gold front tooth, smiled warmly at the engaging young reporter.

"Where've *you* been, dearie?" she asked Marcus. "The girls have been asking for you. They done figgered you musta got shot or pizened by bad likker."

Marcus Haverstraw smiled back at her. "No, Etta," he sighed. "Nothing quite so romantic. Y'see, all play and no work makes Marc a poor boy. I had to put my nose to the grindstone once again."

"That ain't where he puts it when he's here," the procuress said, winking at Davy and Soaring Hawk.

She offered them drinks, including ginger beer or sarsaparilla for the Pawnee. Accepting, they accompanied Etta Captree into the parlor of the bawdy house, where Marcus Haverstraw received a warm welcome from the eight painted women who were lounging there.

"That *all* you come for?" the procuress asked in disappointment, after she had learned of the purpose of the trio's visit.

"Don't look at me, Etta," Haverstraw told her with a crooked smile. "I'm merely the guide, just playing Virgil to Davy Watson's Dante."

"Perhaps Mr. Watson would care to seek his Beatrice here?" the tubby little madam suggested, herself acquainted with Dante.

Haverstraw took a brass watch from one of the pockets of his tattersall vest. "Y'know, it is pretty late," he told Davy, snapping shut the cover of the watch and lowering it back into the pocket by its gold chain. "Why don't we, ah, rest ourselves a spell? Then we can get a fresh—and early—start tomorrow night.

"What d'ya think?" Davy asked his blood brother

95

through a yawn.

The Pawnee nodded, his dark eyes lingering on the bodies of the painted women in the bawdy house parlor. "Do enough today. Get rest now. Mebbe get laid."

Davy's eyes widened. Heretofore, he'd only known the brave to have sex with Indian women.

"Well said, Mr. Hawk," endorsed Marcus P. Haverstraw, clapping the Pawnee on the back. "I couldn't have put it better, myself."

"Ol' Soaring Hawk, he got a way of gettin' right to the heart of things," Davy told him.

"You're an example to us all," the reporter told the brave. "And now, Etta," he went on, turning to the madam, "why don't you introduce us to your lovely staff?"

And so she did. Another round of drinks was had by the guests, Soaring Hawk still imbibing sarsaparilla, after which each of the young men made his way upstairs behind the woman of his choice.

Haverstraw chose as the object of his desire a tall, bosomy young woman with chestnut-brown hair, who went by the name of Martha. Davy fancied a dark, willowy Mexican called Evalina. And Soaring Hawk went to the room of a young redhead known as Desiree.

"I nevuh done it with a Injun before," the pert girl informed the Pawnee, as she removed her outer garments in a seductive and langourous sequence.

Soaring Hawk nodded slowly, watching Desiree undress with considerable interest. "Soaring Hawk never do it with white woman before."

"Ooooh," moaned the redhead, aroused by the thought that this interracial liaison would be the first of its kind for both of them. "This is goin' to be hahly excitin'," she said in the syrupy accent of her native

Mississippi.

Soaring Hawk's eyes began to narrow as she started to wriggle out of her lacy white underthings. Several moments later Desiree stood naked before him, her beautiful apple breasts surmounted by areolae and nipples whose tint was as delicate as coral from an ocean that the Plains Indian had never seen.

Desiree smiled at the brave and sauntered over to him. "I'm right pleased to see y'all show so much interest, Mistuh Hawk," she whispered reaching out to stroke the bulge in the front of the Indian's buckskin breeches.

Soaring Hawk permitted himself a brief smile as he put out a hand and let his fingers lightly graze the fleshy cupola of Desiree's mound of Venus, gently browsing through the thick matting of auburn hair that covered it.

"Red hair down there, too," the Pawnee observed, his fingers running over the warm lips of her pussy.

"That proves I'm a nat'chul redhead, Mistuh Hawk," Desiree whispered in a husky voice. "Ooooh," she moaned, her eyes widening, as Soaring Hawk's middle finger slid between her outer lips, just below the base of her clitoris.

Desiree threw her head back and gasped with delight as the brave's finger ran a deft course over the sensitive membranes of her inner parts.

"Do you folks kiss, Mistuh Hawk?" she whispered in the young brave's ear.

"Not kiss," he told her as he finished undressing. "But do this," he told Desiree, picking her up in his arms and carrying her over to the bed.

So saying, he deposited her warm nakedness upon the bed. Then Soaring Hawk lay down beside her, and began to sniff at her body, running his nose over her soft young flesh in what is known to anthropologists and scholars of erotica as the "olfactory kiss," a form of nasal osculation practiced by a number of non-white peoples.

"Ooooh, that sholy is diff'unt," Desiree gasped, excited by this strange and earthy form of foreplay.

"*Ooh, ooh, ooh,*" Desiree murmured, squirming as the Pawnee's nose traveled southward, through the little pubic grove and then down over the slope of her nether lips.

The musky fragrance of Desiree's arousal made the brave think of the strong, rich scents of the possum and the otter. The contrasting perfume that also emanated from her skin reminded Soaring Hawk of the wind that sweeps across the prairie, carrying the bright fragrances of flowers in bloom.

Having covered the writhing southern belle's hot body from head to toe with ardent olfactory kisses, Soaring Hawk embarked upon a return trip, finally coming to rest with his dark aquiline nose in the pale hollow of Desiree's neck.

"Heavens above," the aroused redhead gasped as the brave rolled over and lay down beside her. "That sholy was excitin'. Now, I'll try to do somethin' agreeable to y'all, Mistuh Hawk."

"Ugh," the Pawnee grunted, as Desiree ran her bright, pink tongue down over his chest and belly with all the dexterity of a Gila monster flicking a sand fly off a rock.

"You have such lean, mus-cu-lah thahs, Mistuh Hawk," Desiree commented admiringly as her small, warm fingers encircled the base of the warrior's lance. With her other hand she gently and persistently squeezed his scrotum, alternating the sequence of pressure and release with all the insistence of a tom-tom beater at a war dance.

While continuing to squeeze his balls, Desiree began to stroke Soaring Hawk's cock, running her fingers in light *pizzicati* up its shaft, from base to glans, with all the virtuosity of the first violinist in the orchestra at the Virginia City Civic Opera House.

A few minutes of this intense and loving musicianship made their effects felt upon the constitution of the stoic Indian. His eyes had narrowed to mere slits, and his face looked as if it had been carved out of wood; but he was breathing with the sound of a Virginia and Truckee Railroad engine laboring up a steep mountain grade.

"Here's another form of kissin', Mistuh Hawk," Desiree said in a husky voice, flashing the trembling brave a hot, hungry smile. "I don' know if yo' folks does this, but it sholy is one of the ree-finements of mah profession."

Grasping the base of his cock with her right hand, and running her left over his lean belly and thighs, Desiree leaned over, parted her moist, red lips, and proceeded to take the brave into her mouth.

"*U-u-u-u-uuugh*," moaned Soaring Hawk, feeling the smouldering glow in the pit of his groin suddenly flare into a raging bonfire as he felt the wet, elastic grip of Desiree's mouth sliding up and down over the head of his sex. At the same time, the redhead moaned and writhed as she hovered over the brave, rubbing her hot, wet pussy against his left leg.

Soaring Hawk's blood pulsed wildly through his veins, beating against his eardrums with the sound of a buffalo herd thundering over the Kansas plains. He raised his fingers to his nostrils and breathed deeply of the scent of Desiree's excitement. Her mouth stroked and sucked, reminding the Indian of the goatsucker—the bird that drank at the udders of she-goats; and her nimble, skipping tongue brought him visions of shadows, mossy rocks and darting salamanders.

Stroke. Suck. Dart. Lick. Tickle. Desiree increased the tempo of her virtuoso performance, causing the Pawnee to groan in surprise as his body stiffened and his pelvis hooked in sharp, involuntary movements.

"*Ugh! Ugh!*" the Indian grunted, closing his eyes and offering his soul up to the Great Spirit, who spoke in strange and wondrous ways, who spoke to the Pawnee in this instance through the wondrous mouth of the Mississippi redhead known to Soaring Hawk only as Desiree.

Chapter Six

"Cripes, Marcus," Davy Watson groaned over his platter of ham, eggs and home-fried potatoes, "when we go a-visitin' them bawdy houses tonight, I think I'll pass up the social drinks." He closed his eyes as he gingerly touched his head.

The three companions had not arrived back at Haverstraw's rooms until well after three in the morning. It was almost noon when they were served their breakfasts in Redmond's Eatery, on C Street. To their left, a party of Germans smoked their long pipes and drank steins of beer, and two Highland Scots conversed in Gaelic on their right.

"I notice that neither of you gentlemen has placed any restrictions on getting your ashes hauled in the line of duty," the newspaperman said with a sly smile. "I trust that you both received satisfaction?"

"Lord, yes," Davy told him. "That ol' Evalina was plenty attentive to my needs."

"And you, Mr. Hawk?" Marcus P. Haverstraw asked.

The Pawnee looked up at him and nodded slowly, the faintest hint of a smile upon his lips. "Woman have red hair down there, too," he said, pointing to his crotch.

"Ain't nature grand," Haverstraw said blithely.

"Tonight, we got to stick to business," Davy told his

companions. "We got to find the Mudree sisters soon as we can."

"Of course," Haverstraw replied, slicing through the inch-thick slab of hamsteak on his plate. "When we've finished lunch—er, breakfast, we'll amble over to the *Enterprise*, and I'll canvas all the low-lifes on staff. And there certainly are a goodly number of such unregenerate types working for a newspaper, as you will soon see for yourselves," he told them with a wink.

"Never see woman with red hair on pussy before," Soaring Hawk observed, apropos of nothing. "Much hair, thick like pelt of beaver. Not like Indian woman. Indian woman have straight black hair on pussy, not full like beaver pelt. More like otter, when come out of water."

Davy Watson smiled at the mention of Indian women, and recalled the excitement of his lovemaking with the young Pawnee, Bright Water.

"In Araby, far across the great water," Marcus Haverstraw told Soaring Hawk, "the womenfolk shave all the hair off that sweet part of their bodies."

Soaring Hawk thought about this for a moment. "When shave," he said at last, "pussy no more look like pelt of beaver."

"Kinda looks like a clam, I imagine," added the newspaperman.

"Why do they shave themselves there, Marcus?" Davy asked.

The reporter shrugged. "I don't rightly know. It's just the custom thereabouts. But, as a product of the western world, I say give me beaver—or otter—every time."

"Jus' remember," Davy admonished, "we ain't got us no time fer trappin' beaver tonight. We got to find the Mudree gals.''

The reporter's expression grew solemn. "Indeed we do," he agreed.

The *Territorial Enterprise* had its beginning in Genoa, which was then in western Utah, and was the oldest paper in the Nevada Territory. Having moved to Virginia City, the journal retained its name, even after statehood had been granted in 1864. Virile, high-spirited and humorous, the paper did well, and was extremely influential in the West; in fact, even the faraway *New York Herald* subscribed to it.

The crowded and chaotic office of the *Enterprise* was located on the corner of A Street and Sutton Avenue, in a decrepit wood-frame building. The staff reporters worked at a long table, fed there as well by a Chinese cook called Old Joe, while the printing presses screeched and clattered beside them.

Joseph T. Goodman, a fighter as outspoken as his individualistic staff, was a newspaperman and a poet. Not a man to hedge his bets when he defended a cause, he did it wholeheartedly, with passion and vigor. A classic instance of this was his defense of the celebrated and controversial actress, Adah Isaacs Menken.

Intense and fearless, volatile and uninhibited, Adah Mencken scandalized the prudes and bluenoses of the day. She was constantly being accused of conducting promiscuous liaisons with the great men of the age— Charles Dickens, Alexandre Dumas, Algernon Swinburne, Theophile Gautier, Dante Gabriel Rossetti and others. But she constantly denied these allegations. For instance, she is reported to have said: "I never lived with Houston; it was General Jackson and Methusaleh and other big men."

The theatrical piece responsible for much of her fame and notoriety was *Mazeppa*, a dramatization of Lord Byron's poem of the same name. At the climax of this rousing piece, Miss Mencken was stripped, and then strapped to the back of a live horse, which carried her offstage. The undressing created a controversy, even though the actress' simulated nudity consisted of flesh-colored tights that covered her from wrist to ankle.

The critis of the *Virginia Union*, however, was scandalized, and he wrote: ". . .what we say is that an exhibition without restraint and without shame, of the most lascivious nature that lewd imagination can invent, ought to meet with the public reprehension."

Joe Goodman leapt into the breech, telling the critic of the *Union* to "blush that he is made in the image of his God—if, indeed, he is. He should rail against painting and sculpture, and the other arts which have developed their most beautiful and divine conceptions in ideal likenesses of the human form."

The next day, he administered the *coup de grâce* by labeling the *Union* critic's reaction "a venomous hate which stings because despised—a reptile revenge, which knowing how it is loathed and hated, would trail its slimy form over all that is good and lovely in this beautiful creation."

From the first minute he met the man, Davy had liked Joe Goodman. And he had laughed heartily, reading that gentleman's characterization of Mark Twain, when that young worthy had reigned by "the Grace of Cheek" as the *Enterprise*'s local items reporter.

The extravagant Goodman had described Twain as the "Monarch of Mining Items, Detailer of Events, Prince of Platitudes, Chief of Biographers, Expounder of Unwritten Laws, Puffer of Wildcat, Profaner of Divinity, Detractor of Merit, Flatterer of Power, Recorder of Stage Arrivals, Pack Trains, Hay Wagons and Things in General.''

Goodman, this genial, lively man, made Davy Watson and Soaring Hawk welcome to the *Territorial Enterprise*. Arriving at the same time that Marcus P. Haverstraw led his companions into the office of the newspaper, was Mr. Battersby, the Episcopalian rector.

The reporter introduced the companions to the churchman, who was tall and stooped, had thinning brown hair and a kindly smile. Then Haverstraw excused himself and left the office, in order to make inquiries of his co-workers as to the whereabouts of the three Mudree sisters.

The rector displayed a sincere interest in the affairs of the state of Kansas and the habits of the Pawnee Indians, so Davy and Soaring Hawk became involved in a conversation with the man.

All of a sudden, a bloodcurdling and furious outburst of profanity, issuing from the room outside, stopped things cold. The rector's mouth hung open, and even Davy, who'd heard muleskinners, turned an inquiring eye to Joe Goodman.

''Oh, Lord,'' said the editor, a wry grin on his face, ''the printers must have hid Marcus' lampshade again. They do that from time to time just to get him riled up.'' He gestured helplessly. ''Sorry about that, Mr. Battersby.''

The Episcopalian rector, walking with the tread of a sleepwalker, a look of intermingled horror and fascination upon his face, approached the door, on whose other side the lurid and seething stream of foul and abusive language continued.

Joe Goodman turned to Soaring Hawk and Davy with a "this ought to be good" expression on his face. The blood brothers turned to the door.

When it was opened by the reverend gentleman, Davy saw Marcus P. Haverstraw slowly walking around the staff office, working himself up to a fever pitch of profanity as he railed against the printers and lavished wave upon wave of malediction upon the culprit or culprits who had spirited away his lampshade.

"You bow-legged, knock-kneed, ricket-ridden pack of ornery miscreants," Marcus Haverstraw told the chuckling printers in a voice that rang out in the big room like the crack of doom.

"You bat-brained, big-bottomed, swag-bellied band of idlers and illiterates," he went on. "You side-winding, shit-faced, piss-imbibing, butt-sucking, rapacious crowd of sneaking cocksuckers and toadies!"

The printers turned to each other, hiding their smiles behind ink-stained hands, shoulders heaving as they fought to suppress their laughter.

"You pig-licking, dung-dropping, ink-drinking, boot-licking brow-beaten assembly of assholes! Which one of you has purloined my lampshade—God-fucking-dammit!" the reporter roared, his face going red as a sugar beet.

"You boy-buggering, pig-fucking, sheep-sucking, passel of piss-faced incompetents! You half-witted, shit-stinking, pud-pulling bags of manure! You lip-smacking, nit-witted, hog-sloppy sons of bitches! *You-u-u.* . ."

Haverstraw's tirade as cut short unexpectedly, when the newspaperman's next circuit of the big room brought him to the doorway, where he suddenly found himself face to face with the mesmerized and flabber gasted man of the cloth.

The rector just stood in the doorway and gaped at the profane reporter, who gaped back at him in turn, looking as if he had just seen a ghost. The young man was goggle-eyed with surprise, and his face was even redder than before, a thing which Davy would not have believed possible.

"Oh, my stars," Marcus P. Haverstraw croaked in a tiny voice, when he was finally able to speak again. Looking guilty and totally abashed, the young reporter wrung his hands and began to apologize to the rector.

"I know you're shocked to hear me, Mr. Battersby," Haverstraw said. "It stands to reason you are. I know this ain't language fit for a Christian man to utter nor for a Christian man to hear, but if I could get my hands on the spavined, rat-fucking, pecker-headed whoreson who stole my shade, I'd show you what I'd do to him, for the benefit of printers to all time!"

As Marcus P. Haverstraw raised his eyes to heaven and proceeded to shake his fists in the air, the rector gulped and then began to clear his throat furiously.

"You don't know printers, Mr. Battersby," the newspaperman went on. "You don't know them. A Christian man like you can't come in contact with them, but I give you my word they're the sneakiest, orneriest, most incestuous pack of numb-nuts that a body ever had anything to do with!"

Saying this, Marcus Haverstraw reached out, grabbed hold of the doorknob, and then proceeded to close the door on the stupefied rector. An instant after the door had shut, the reporter renewed his ear-blistering tirade.

At that very moment, in Joe Goodman's office, Davy Watson and the editor of the *Territorial Enterprise* both burst into maniacal laughter and bolted through the door that led to the street. Even Soaring Hawk, that most impassive of men, was shaking with barely contained laughter.

"As God is my witness," the rector stammered to no one in particular, "I have never in my life heard such a display of blasphemous pyrotechnics. That man is truly a wonder."

"What the poor man doesn't know," Joe Goodman whispered into Davy Watson's ear as they peeked into the office at Mr. Battersby, "is that most newspapermen tend to talk like that when they get riled up. . . although I'll grant you that Marcus Haverstraw ranks among the masters of the black art of malediction."

Shortly thereafter, by means of Joe Goodman's intervention, Marcus Haverstraw regained his shade. Then, once the reporter had filed his copy, he proceeded to interrogate his compeers. The results of that interrogation proved most interesting.

One of the reporters, a man named Van Zandt, had word of Harvey Yancey and the Mudree sisters. The ruffian had shown up, it turned out, two nights earlier at the Pearl of the West, a sporting house run by an Alabaman named Malcolm Shove. Van Zandt, having a drink at an adjoining table, and being a reporter by profession, made it his business to overhear Shove's conversation with the huge and extremely noticeable Yancey.

Yancey, it turned out, had offered to sell Shove the "three heifers" he had brought to Nevada from the Idaho Territory. Were they professionals? Shove had asked, warming to the offer when he discovered that the young women in question were sisters.

No, they were not, Yancey told Shove emphatically. They were maidens fresh and virtually unused; Va

Zandt told Davy and the others that the giant had offered the Alabamian procurer the rare opportunity of breaking them in himself.

That *could* mean, Davy hoped against hope, that—for one reason or another—Harvey Yancey had chosen not to violate Faith, Hope or Charity. But he doubted it, and suffered whenever he thought of the sisters' plight, of those fair, sleek bodies crushed beneath the gross and obscene bulk of the gigantic ruffian.

Davy winced and took a deep breath. All he could do, in view of the circumstances, was to hope for the best. It was out of his hands for the present.

But, concluded Van Zandt, Malcolm Shove considered Harvey Yancey's price exorbitant, and was unwilling to meet it. Yancey then left the Pearl of the West in a huff.

In the evening, as the sun went down behind the Sierra Nevada, Marcus Haverstraw and his two companions had their dinner on D Street, at the Pearl of the West.

After their meal, the reporter led them to an office at the rear of the second floor. Haverstraw knocked on the door.

"Come in," a man called out in a whiskey tenor.

"Hello, Mal," Haverstraw said cheerfully as he opened the door. "Mind if we come in?"

When they entered the office, Davy looked across the room, and saw a fat, blond man seated behind a big mahogany desk.

"Please do," the man replied affably.

"These are my good friends," the reporter said, indicating his companions with a wave of his hand. "Mr. David Watson of Kansas, and Mr. Soaring Hawk, of the Pawnee Nation."

Malcolm Shove looked at the blood brothers with mild interest. "What can I do for you, Marcus, or for these gentlemen?" the proprietor of the Pearl of the West asked softly.

"We'd like to ask you a few questions," Haverstraw told him with a smile.

"I'll do my best to give you a straight answer," Malcolm Shove told them reassuringly.

"Do you happen to recollect speaking with a man recently, a man called Harvey Yancey?" Haverstraw asked. "He's pretty easy to remember, Mal: a massive, bearded man who speaks in a *basso profundo*."

Malcolm Shove's fair, jowly face assumed a thoughtful expression. Then, after a long, contemplative silence, he spoke, looking each of his three visitors in the eye before he did.

"Can's say that I have," he told them in that soft, yet rough, voice of his. "I certainly would have remembered anyone who answered that description, Marcus."

Davy and Soaring Hawk exchanged looks.

"What if I were to say," Haverstraw said in a pained, tired voice, "that Harvey Yancey offered to sell you three sisters?"

"I'm afraid I don't recollect anything of the sort, Marcus," Malcolm Shove said quietly, with a wry grin and a shake of his head.

"What if I also told you that I have a source for this information, Mal?" the reporter persisted, his eyes narrowing as he studied the face of the man at the desk. "An acquaintance of mine overheard your entire conversation with Harvey Yancey."

Malcolm Shove continued to smile, but his smile had

begun to harden like plaster setting on a cast.

"That's absolutely ridiculous, Marcus," the fat blond man told the newspaperman quietly, a dangerous look coming into his eyes. "Your acquaintance must have been drunk. I tell you categorically that I have no knowledge whatever of this man."

Davy was exasperated by now, and could no longer contain his anger. "What if I was to say that you're a lowdown, lyin' polecat, Mr. Shove?" he asked in a low, even voice, feeling his ears burn as he did. Shove's eyes suddenly met his, and Davy saw a glint of anger in them that matched his own.

"My only reply to that, Mr. Watson," the proprietor of the Pearl of the West said in a voice that shook with suppressed emotion, "is to request that you stay in town another day, so that I may demand satisfaction of you."

"Well, I'm lookin' for some of the same from you," Davy shot back in frustration, not fully getting the drift of the fat man's words.

Marcus Haverstraw cleared his throat. "I think we'd better be leaving now," he told his friends.

"I want satisfaction for this affront, Marcus," Malcolm Shove told him in steely tones.

The reporter sighed. "Is it really worth it, Mal?" he asked tensely.

"I'm not in the habit of letting myself be insulted by rubes and country bumpkins, Marcus," the Alabamian replied coldly. "And I intend to teach this lout a lesson he'll never forget."

"You know you're in the wrong, Mal," Marcus Haverstraw said, shaking his head as he opened the door to the office.

"Just have your friend at your place later," Shove

told him, "in order to receive my second."

The reporter sighed again as he followed Davy and Soaring Hawk out of the office.

"Jus' what the hell was that bold-faced liar talkin' 'bout, anyway?" the young Kansan asked when they were out of the Pearl of the West. "I don't know what-all he meant with that there high-falutin' lingo of his."

Marcus Haverstraw took out his linen handkerchief and began to mop his brow. "The man just challenged you to a duel," he told Davy Watson.

"Harvey, did you hear the latest word 'round town?" the somber, cadaverous man called Sugrue asked Harvey Yancey, as the latter came downstairs in the gambling and bawdy house owned by Edwin Huskey, at the southeastern end of D Street.

Sugrue's excitement caused the bearded giant to regard him with narrowed eyes and a suspicious look on his face.

"What d'ya mean?" he asked in his harsh, deep voice.

"That Watson kid—he's come here, a-lookin' fer the Mudree gals."

Yancey smiled an obscene smile. "Well," he rumbled, "Now I can have my cake an' eat it, too. I get to sell the heifers, an' blow that l'il weasel's head off at the same time."

"No need for that, Harv," Sugrue told his chief. "He done got hisself on the wrong side of Malcolm Shove. The fat man done challenged Watson to a duel."

"A duel?" Yancey said incredulously.

"Yup. They does a heap of pistol duelling here-abouts, as if they was southern gentlemen. This here town's chockfull of tetchy gents. It's one of their favorite pastimes. An' ol' Mal Shove, why he done shot him seven or eight men already.''

"Hmm," the giant rumbled thoughtfully. "I 'spose it *is* satisfyin' enough to know the l'il bastard's gonna get plugged. But I'd sure like to tear that squirt apart with my bare hands.''

"Well, Malcolm Shove is 'bout to save you the trouble.''

"Wouldn't be no trouble a-tall. I'd just love to break that boy's back. Well, I guess we could still show up at the duel." Yancey began to chuckle. "Now, that wouldn't do the kid's nerves any good, would it? Imagine Watson seein' us in the crowd, an' knowin' that even if a miracle happened, an' he downed Mal Shove, we'd still be waitin' for him.''

"I don't reckon we-all can do that, Harv.''

"Why the hell not, Sugrue?''

The grim man sighed as he looked into Harvey Yancey's cold, dead man's eyes. "Marshal Fred Klingebiel's in Virginia City. He got wind of your bein' here, an' is makin' the rounds right now, lookin' fer you. An' they's two dep'ties a-ridin' with him.''

The giant's face darkened as he scowled. "Fred Klingebiel, huh?" he grunted angrily. "Why, that sum'bitch done hounded me out'n Nevada in '66. By God, I ought to put two bullets up his nose—that's what I ought to do!''

"We's hampered by the gals, Harv," Sugrue said patiently. "Whyn't we sell 'em an' jus' light out of here? You know it ain't nothin' but trouble gunnin' down a federal marshal.''

Yancey spat on the floor.

"By the way," Sugrue continued, hoping to change

113

the subject, "did Edwin Huskey meet your price?"

The huge man's face grew even darker than before. "They's a heap of big talkin' done hereabouts—what with all this speculatin' an' horseshit 'bout the Comstock Lode, but when it comes to plunkin' down cash on the barrelhead, ain't nobody up to puttin' their money where their mouth is."

"They ain't met your price," Sugrue said in a mournful voice, this time as a statement of fact rather than a question. "D'ya think, mebbe, that your askin' price might jus' be a leetle steep, Harv?" he asked timorously.

"Shit, no!" Yancey roared. "I'm offerin' these sum'bitches a real bargain—on somethin' that's right rare! Them's all sisters, remember—an' young, hot-blooded little wenches, to boot. How many times you ever get three queens in your hand, man?"

"So what you gon' do?"

"Well," Harvey Yancey rumbled in his earthquake bass, "Malcolm Shove done gimme the address of this here fancy dude in 'Frisco—man name of Bertram Brown, who'll see to it that we get us top dollar for them gals on the Barbary Coast."

"That was right kind of Mr. Shove. How come he did that fer ya, Harv?"

The giant smirked knowingly. "Me 'n ol' Mal's pretty tight. I done brought him a number of wenches for his brothels in the past. We takes care of each other." He scratched his full beard. "How's the li'l heifers doin'?"

Sugrue shook his head and grinned. "Feisty as ever. But don't nothin'—not sorrow nor loss nor anger— interfere with their appetites, God bless 'em! Them gals eats like trail hands at the end of a round-up."

Yancey smiled his menacing, obscene smile. "Too bad I been so busy negotiatin' an' a-partyin' that I ain't had time to tend to those plump little heifers. I'm lookin' forward to teachin' 'em what it's like to be swived by a real man.'' He shook his head. "But I reckon I'll have to wait 'til we get to 'Frisco."

"When we leavin', Harv?"

"Well, since that tin-starred sum'bitch, Fred Klingebiel is lookin' fer me, we're gonna skeedaddle in the middle of the night. So draw on your longjohns, Sugrue, for we'll soon be ridin' across't the High Sierra."

"The ghosts of a hundred men surround us," the *Virginia Union* declared in November, 1863, "whose murderers walk the streets today in contempt of the law through whose fingers they have slipped; our pavements are slippery with the blood of men shot down in open day, and the genius of assassination walks riotant through our crowded thoroughfares."

Honor was an obsession among the men who lived on the edge in Virginia City, and the duel was their prime means of satisfying it. Although the duelling code was often ridiculed by more sober citizens, even newspaper editors such as Joe Goodman and his rival, Tom Fitch of the *Union*, were arrested for attempting to settle their differences of opinion upon the field of honor. But the two persisted, and Goodman ultimately brought Fitch down with a bullet in the right leg.

Many of Virginia City's coarser inhabitants ignored the niceties of chivalric observance, and had it out right in the middle of the boom town's busy streets—blasting away at each other like maniacs, in broad daylight, totally oblivious to passersby.

Nevada had a strong anti-duelling law which regarded sending a challenge, as well as taking part in a duel, as a felony. And if, within a year's time, one of the parties to a duel died as a result of it, the person responsible for his death was charged with murder.

Duellists usually played it safe, even though the law was not strictly enforced locally; they tended to aim for each other's legs. But this was not the way that Malcolm Shove dealt with affronts to *his* honor. The Alabamian was well-connected in the town, and was very secretive about just where and when he would duel. And his effectiveness, once he stood upon the field of honor, was attested to by the fact that he had shot some seven men, killing four of them.

The normal procedure called for the exchange of subtly insulting letters rather than glove-in-the-face challenges. This ritual often went on for days, until the person challenged agreed to a time and place for the duel. The rulebook for this piece of romantic folly was John Lyde Wilson's *The Code of Honor; or Rules for the Government of Principals and Seconds in Duelling*, a manual originally published in the year 1848, in Charleston, South Carolina.

Protocol was always observed: each principal was allotted two seconds and a surgeon. The standard firing distance varied from between ten and twenty paces. Pistols were loaded in the presence of the seconds, a bullet being put in only one chamber of the five-shooters used for this purpose. The weapons were then presented to the principals, who grasped them by the barrel with their non-shooting hands. Such was the elaborate ritual of the duel.

When Malcolm Shove arrived at his palatial home in the exclusive suburb of Silver Terrace late that night, the Alabaman was surprised to find Davy Watson waiting in the hall for him.

The portly blond man raised his eyebrows before

116

nodding courteously to his visitor. "This is a surprise, Mr. Watson," he said amiably. "But you are welcome in my home, sir."

"Well, here's the point, Mr. Shove," Davy began abruptly, with absolutely no regard for the social amenities. "I got your challengin' letter a little while ago at Marcus' place. But y'see, I ain't got much time to spare" (at this Malcolm Shove gave Davy a thin, cold smile), "for this sort of rigamarole."

The fat man gestured for Davy to accompany him into the drawing room. "Brandy, Mr. Watson?" he asked once they were in the room, heading for an ornate wooden cabinet.

"No thank you, sir," Davy told him. "I'm here on business." He held up his hands and shook his head. "What I mean to say is I ain't got time for all this duellin' foofaraw."

Shove sipped his brandy and looked Davy right in the eye. "I trust this does not mean that you are backing out of our duel, sir?" he asked in a soft, cold voice.

Davy shook his head again. "Nothin' of the sort, Mr. Shove. I consider I was in the right when I said what I did, an' I fully intend to meet you on the duellin' field."

"That is most gratifying, sir," Shove replied. "Most gratifying."

"But I want to settle our differences first thing in the mornin', Mr. Shove. For I intend to be movin' on right afterwards."

"That's incredibly optimistic of you, Mr. Watson," the fat man said, obviously enjoying Davy's candor. "Because I fully intend to shoot you dead."

Davy grinned as he looked Malcolm Shove in the eye. "That's as may be, sir. You got your plans, an' I got me mine. But only the good Lord knows which one of us'll be a-standin' upright after the shots have been fired. So I go ahead an' make my plans, even though I believe in livin' one day at a time. An' tonight I come here to make you a little offer.''

Shove's eyes widened as his smile began to fade. ''And what might that be, sir?'' he asked.

''Well,'' said Davy, ''I'm carryin' a heap of gold I got as a reward from the miners of the Boise Basin. And what I'll do is wager my half of it against somethin' I want from you, Mr. Shove. I'm bettin' this gold that I'm a-gonna drop you.''

Malcolm Shove finished his brandy. ''You are a most amusing young man, Mr. Watson,'' he told Davy, obviously intrigued by the Kansan's offer. ''What do I have that you want?''

''The knowledge of where Harvey Yancey an' them three gals is,'' Davy told him in a level voice. ''Or where they's a-headin'.''

Malcolm Shove was smiling. ''But if you shoot me dead, sir, how on earth will I be able to impart this information to you?''

''Why, you will hopefully impart it to me tonight, Mr. Shove,'' was Davy Watson's reply. ''On the condition that I will not act on it until after our duel.'' He paused, his eyes searching on the Alabaman's florid face. ''I give you my word as a gentleman on that.''

''The more I know of you, sir,'' Shove told Davy warmly, ''the more I admire you. I'm almost sorry to have to kill you. But your word as a gentleman is more than sufficient for me. I accept your wager, and its terms. . .Now will you take a glass of brandy with me, sir?''

Davy smiled back at his adversary. ''I reckon I will, Mr. Shove.''

"Gentlemen, prepare to receive the word," the starter instructed in a loud voice. *"Are you ready? Fire—one, two, three—halt! Nor fire after the word, 'halt!'"*

As they stood upon the slope of Mount Davidson, in the first bleak light of dawn, as the sun began to peep over the rim of the Sierra Nevada, Davy Watson and Malcolm Shove both nodded their heads, indicating that they had understood the starter's instructions. As the principals and their seconds exhaled, their breath left their mouths in a wispy vapor that rose up to disappear in the chill November air. Each of the principals held at his side a big Navy Colt loaded with one shot. A high wind rose from the west, one that was sure to affect the accuracy of the duellists' marksmanship.

Davy had earlier explained the entire procedure to Soaring Hawk, culminating with instructions to give Malcolm Shove his share of the Boise gold if the Alabamian were to vanquish him. The Pawnee was fascinated by the concept of the duel, and having an Indian's pride, heartily approved of this form of ritual combat.

If Davy were to be killed, it was understood that the brave would be free to return to his people on the prairies of Kansas and eastern Colorado. But the Indian had not forgotten that Davy Watson had once risked his own safety for his honor; and therefore, Soaring Hawk pledged himself to continue the search for the Mudree sisters.

"That means a lot to me, my brother," Davy told the Pawnee, blinking his eyes.

The Indian smiled gently. "We are blood brothers," Soaring Hawk told him with simple dignity. "In life and in death."

Now, as he readied himself to turn and take the twenty paces away from the starter, Davy felt a twinge

119

of fear as he allowed himself, for the very first time, to contemplate Malcolm Shove's impressive record as a duellist.

The man was obviously a good shot with a pistol, Davy realized, taking several deep breaths in order to calm his nerves. But the high, rising wind would work in his own favor, the young Kansan told himself, making it harder for Shove to aim and gauge the trajectory of his bullet.

"Aim low," Soaring Hawk counseled, clapping his blood brother on the shoulder. "Wind come up fast. Aim for fat belly. Not miss that way."

"Good luck, ol' son," Marcus Haverstraw said between clenched teeth as he came up and shook his friend's hand. "When this is over, the drinks are on me," he told Davy, not daring to look him in the eye.

Davy nodded and was about to speak when the starter's voice rang out in the air.

"Gentlemen, take your positions!"

Davy took one last look at Malcolm Shove before turning. The fat man smiled thinly and bowed to him.

"Gentlemen, turn!"

For an instant, Davy recalled the shooting of his beloved father at the hand of Ace Landry.

"Gentlemen, count off!" barked the starter. *"One. Two. Three. . . ."*

Davy took a deep breath and strode forward, fighting to master his fear.

"Four. Five. Six. Seven. . . ."

He thought of the thousand miles he had traveled since that fateful day in the autumn of 1868 when he turned his face toward the path of vengeance. Then he thought of the Watson farm by Pottawatomie Creek and of his mother, his sister Amy, and his brother

Lucius Erasmus. . . .

"Eight. Nine. Ten. Eleven. . . ."

The ground was rocky and uneven beneath his feet, and Davy wondered whether a dead man would roll down the slope of Mount Davidson like a keg of nails, to end up somewhere in the heart of Virginia City.

"Twelve. Thirteen. Fourteen. . . ."

Davy was nervous. Davy was afraid. But Davy told himself that there was no way in hell he was going to be killed. Deanna MacPartland was waiting for him at the end of the trail: he had too much to live for.

"Fifteen. Sixteen. . . ."

Davy recalled that the Alabamian had killed his men by shooting them in the head. He was cheered by two thoughts, one relevant to the encounter, and the other less so. First, he thanked Almighty God for the high, whistling wind that swept the slope of Mount Davidson. Then he smiled for a brief moment, when he realized that his head was much smaller than Malcolm Shove's.

"Seventeen. Eighteen. . . ."

He told himself that his task was to keep a cool head and shoot straight. The way he saw it, worrying about dying was Malcolm Shove's lookout.

"Nineteen. Twenty."

Davy's bootheels crunched on the rocky soil of Mount Davidson as he ground to an abrupt halt, hefting the Navy pistol in his right hand. Time to do some fancy shootin', he told himself.

"Gentlemen, turn and take aim!"

As Malcolm Shove turned and raised his pistol, holding it out at arm's length, Davy saw that he wore the same thin smile as before. Suddenly his breath caught in his throat as he realized for the first time that the day marked his nineteenth birthday!

"Are you ready?"

Davy nodded once, and then sighted along the barrel of the Navy Colt. Malcolm Shove did the same.

"Fire—one, two, three. . . ."

Blam! Blam! Two pistol shots rang out in close succession in the frosty air, suddenly echoing and re-echoing as they traveled down the slope to disturb the dreams of Virginia City.

"Halt!" the starter cried out, his voice going suddenly hoarse.

For an instant the air was filled with the sound of flapping wings, as all the birds on the mountainside scattered at the exchange of shots, taking to the air with high-pitched cries of protest and *rawks* of alarm.

Soaring Hawk's face registered no emotion as the Pawnee watched Malcolm Shove stagger backward, his left hand clutched to his chest, and then fall down clumsily on his back. But the brave's eyes narrowed as he turned to see his blood brother spin around sharply, fling his pistol into the air, clutch at the left side of his head, and then pitch face-forward to the ground.

Both men had scored hits, the Indian noted ruefully as he ran over to Davy's side, followed by an anxious Marcus Haverstraw and the attending surgeon, Dr. Horace Plunkett.

To Soaring Hawk's great relief, Davy Watson was sitting up before any of his seconds had reached him.

"Oh, God A'mighty!" Davy swore, taking his hand away from the side of his head and staring at it.

The hand was covered with blood, causing the young Kansan to wince at the sight. But once Dr. Plunkett had knelt by his side and begun to examine Davy, it was evident that the duellist had not sustained a grave head wound.

"Well, Mr. Watson," said the doctor, dabbing at Davy's ear with an alcohol-soaked handkerchief, "I'm afraid you'll have to do without your left earlobe hereafter, but I'm pleased to inform you that it's nothing more serious."

"That's—*Ouch!*—right good news, Doc," Davy replied, grimacing as he felt the bite of the disinfectant. "What about Mr. Shove?" he asked, once he had become accustomed to the pain of his wound.

"You bring him down like buffalo," Soaring Hawk gleefully told his blood brother.

Marcus Haverstraw shook his head. "From what I can see, Davy," he said in a quiet voice, "your shot was somewhat more telling than Mal Shove's."

It was indeed, Davy Watson determined, once he had risen to his feet. The fat man lay on his back, his body stiff and still, looking somehow forlorn and helpless to the young Kansan, reminding him of a lithograph he had once seen depicting a whale beached and dying on the shore of Nantucket Island. The slug had plowed through the fat and meat of Malcolm Shove's chest, to burst open there and tear apart the Alabamian's heart. The southern gentleman had fought his last duel.

"Well, my friends," Marcus P. Haverstraw cheerfully informed Davy and Soaring Hawk, as Doctor Plunkett bandaged the surviving duellist's head, "now we're free to recover the Mudree girls."

"You make it sound plumb easy, Marcus," Davy said, grinning wryly at the newspaperman.

"Oh, it will be," Haverstraw replied blithely. "Providing we don't run into that monster Harvey Yancey."

Less than two hours after the duel, having stopped only to arm themselves, drink a quick toast to Davy Watson's health on his birthday, and then eat a hearty

123

breakfast at the Jenny Lind Saloon, Davy, Soaring Hawk and Marcus P. Haverstraw stormed into Edwin Huskey's sporting establishment on D Street, with guns drawn and pencil and pad at the ready.

After Davy had kicked open the door, the three men burst into the big, two-storied frame house and looked around warily. The only party to be found on the ground floor was a tortoise shell cat, so the three seekers trouped upstairs.

Women began to squeal and curse as the intruders burst into the rooms of the prostitutes who worked and lived at Edwin Huskey's establishment, causing a stir that reminded Davy of the sounds made by hens whenever a fox had gained entry into the chicken coop.

"Jesus God!" one woman shrieked in terror as she laid eyes on Soaring Hawk, as he stood in her doorway, silhouetted against the light of the kerosene lamp in the hall behind him. "Injuns!" she screeched. "We's under attack by Injuns!"

This caused the woman who slept beside her to come awake suddenly, gibbering with fright. Screams began to go up from the adjoining rooms.

"Sorry, ma'am," a red-faced Davy Watson mumbled, as he ducked out of a room full of naked, screaming women.

"Marcus Haverstraw!" a big brunette with pendulous breasts called out, suddenly ceasing to rummage in the drawer of her night table in search of the tiny Smith and Wesson .22 that was secreted somewhere within it. "What in the Sam Hill are you doin here at this hour?" she asked huskily, in a near-baritone voice.

"Oh, it's nothing to worry your pretty little head about, my darling," the newspaperman whispered smiling reassuringly as he backed out of the room and closed the door. "I'm just here on business."

The second story of the building was in a total uproar by the time that a groggy Edwin Huskey staggered out of his corner room, groping behind his back to find the belt to his dressing gown as he did.

What wakened the procurer abruptly, as he looked up, was the cold barrel of Davy Watson's Walker Colt. . .resting on the tip of his nose.

"Now hold on, son," Huskey whispered tensely.

"I want some straight talk, mister," Davy told him, an ominous look on his face. "For this here Colt is primed to go off 'twixt your eyes at the first sound of bullshit."

"By Gad, that's a great phrase!" Marcus Haverstraw called out behind Davy, his pencil scratching furiously as it sped over the white surface of his pad.

"I ain't in no position to bullshit nobody, son," Edwin Huskey whispered, blinking as a droplet of sweat ran down into his right eye. "What can I do for you?"

"Where's them three girls Harvey Yancey done brung with him?" Davy asked, peering over the barrel of the Colt to stare into the procurer's eyes.

"Oh, them," Huskey sighed in relief. "They're all gone, son. I didn't meet Yancey's price, so he took them along with him when he left."

Davy lowered his pistol, holstering it an instant later. "Got any idee where Yancey's a-headin', Mr. Huskey?" he asked in a voice turned suddenly conversational.

"Californee," was the procurer's relieved reply. "That's all I done heerd him say."

"That's good enough," Davy Watson told him. "When'd he vamoose?"

"Sometime after midnight, as I recollect," Huskey informed Davy and his companions.

"Well, it's off to Californee we go," the young Kansan said. "You comin' with us, Marcus?"

"Hell, yes!" the reporter said emphatically. "I've been praying for a honey of a story for some time. And now I've got it."

Davy turned and began to walk toward the staircase, ready to set out in hot pursuit of Harvey Yancey. But all at once he stopped dead in his tracks, his jaw dropping as he looked down to the foot of the stairs.

"Judas Priest," the young Kansan muttered weakly as he stared down into the black, gaping maws of the huge pistols that were aimed straight at him by the group of hard-faced men who stood below. . . .

Chapter Seven

The man who peered squint-eyed at Davy Watson over the barrel of a huge Smith and Wesson .44 had a lined, weatherbeaten face and a thick handlebar mustache whose color was a shade darker than his light brown hair. Behind him stood two more men, their stances replicating the first man's ominous posture as they, too, pointed their weapons up at Davy and his startled companions.

"Judas Priest," the young Kansan muttered again, his throat going suddenly dry as he raised his hands into the air. Peering down at the gun-wielding trio, Davy realized that he did not recognize them, and was at once visited by the hope that, perhaps, the gunmen were not connected with the desperado, Harvey Yancey.

What convinced him of this was the glint of metal that shone from the first man's chest, as the latter moved to one side, still holding his .44 trained on Davy. The object that had reflected the light of an overhead lamp was, Davy saw, a five-pointed star. His eyes immediately darted to the chests of the other two men below, and he breathed a sigh of relief when he saw that they wore badges, as well.

"Keep your hands high," the mustachioed man told him in a low, even voice. "An' start walkin' down them stairs—one at a time."

127

"Yessir," Davy Watson answered respectfully as he made for the steps.

"Is there any more of 'em upstairs, Edwin?" the lawman asked. "Any in the rooms?"

Edwin Huskey leaned over the railing of the landing and shook his balding head. "Nope," he replied. "Just these three is all. How'd you get wind of this anyway, Fred?"

"Me 'n the boys,"—here the mustachioed man indicated the two men standing behind him—"was jus' moseyin' on into town, an' we happened to be ridin' past this place, when we seed one of your wenches climb out'n her window an' begin to slide down the drainpipe."

Here the leather-skinned man grinned behind his bushy mustache. "Well, when we-all got a gander of her a-comin' down that pipe, with the purtiest li'l ol' butt you ever did see a-stickin' out'n the back of her nightie, well, we jus' sorta drew up to a halt."

Behind the three lawmen, Davy saw that a young woman stood in the doorway to Edwin Huskey's establishment and peered in expectantly.

"Well, sir," the man with the badge and the Smith and Wesson .44 went on, "after a bit I recognized that li'l ol' gal as Doris, who I'm like to visit in your place from time to time when I'm in these parts. So I leans over as she walks up and says to her, 'Honey, don't you know that it's a heap easier comin' downstairs if you use the steps?'

"An' then she looks up at me with them ol' Kansas sunflower eyes of hers an' says, 'O marshal Fred,' "—here Davy noticed the twinkle in the man's eyes—' "come quick! They's three bad-asses come a-bustin' into the house, an' done waked us all up at gunpoint. An' one of 'em's a wicked-lookin' Injun!'"

The marshal paused to sniffle and then wipe his nose with the back of his hand. "So natcherly we decided to come in an' have us a look-see."

"Glad you did, Fred," Edwin Huskey told him warmly.

" 'Pears these is the ruffians," mused the mustachioed marshal. "But they don't look so wicked to me. 'Cept'n mebbe that shifty-lookin' skinny marink behind you, Edwin," he said with a sly smile, indicating Marcus Haverstraw with the barrel of his gun.

"Damn it all, Fred," the reporter whined peevishly, coming out of the shadows and stepping forward to the railing, his hands still above his head. "You know goddamn well it's me."

"Why, howdy, Marcus," the man replied in mock-innocence, grinning from ear to ear now. "Who's yer friends?"

"Mr. David Lee Watson and Mr. Soaring Hawk, both natives of the noble state of Kansas," Haverstraw replied, letting his hands down slowly. "They're friends of mine, and are endeavoring to rescue three kidnapped young sisters from a pervert and murderer."

The marshal beamed up at him.

"And there's a helluva story in it," Marcus added as an afterthought, as Davy and Soaring Hawk began to lower their hands.

"I'm right pleased to meet you fellas," the lawman said cheerfully, startling Davy as he twirled his huge pistol and then holstered it with a showy gesture.

"I'm Marshal Fred Klingebiel," the lawman told the blood brothers. "An' these here fellas," he indicated the two men standing behind him, "is my dep'ties." He pointed to the one facing Davy on the left. "E.J.

Karioth," the marshal said, causing the red-faced man to whom he referred to grunt something by way of reply. "And Bradford N. Swett," he continued, pointing to a short man with blond hair and a wispy mustache who nodded solemnly at the mention of his name, the expression on his poker face never changing for an instant.

"The girls were abducted by a desperado who sells young ladies into prostitution and white slavery, it would appear," Haverstraw told Klingebiel.

"An' who might that be?" the amiable marshal asked as the men behind him holstered their weapons.

"His name is Harvey Yancey," Davy Watson called down to him.

"Harvey Yancey," Fred Klingebiel repeated, his face going dark as a thundercloud.

Davy watched intently as the pleasant expression on the jovial man's face hardened into a mask of anger and determination.

"That wicked, lawless bastard," Klingebiel growled. "That low-down, ornery, back-shootin' sidewinder. I'm after that sum'bitch, and I'm gonna bring him to justice, if'n it's the last thing I ever do."

"He's gone, Fred," Edwin Huskey informed the peace officer. "Done took hisself off to Californee."

"When did he light out?"

"'Bout six hours ago."

"He take them girls with him?"

"Reckon so."

"Then I'll have the sum'bitch!" Fred Klingebiel cried out in fierce exultation. "By Gad, I'll ride that rattlesnake down once an' fer all!"

"He lit out west," Huskey told him, "toward the Sierra Nevada."

"That don't make no never mind," Klingebiel shot back, shaking his head emphatically. "Ol' Bradford 'n E.J.'s two of the finest trackers in these parts. Why, we'll cut that lead of his to nothin' in no time a-tall."

"But you'll be in Californee," objected Huskey.

"That don't change things neither," Klingebiel told him. "I'm a federal marshal, an' I can catch holt of that sum'bitch's tail jus' as long as he's in the U-nited States."

"Sierra's rough country this time of year, Fred," warned the marshal. "An' Yancey done picked hisself up three or four local rowdies. I reckon you got to go up against seven or eight bad hombres if'n you take after him."

"Shoot, Edwin," the marshal replied, "that's all in a day's work. I ain't no Sunday school teacher, myself. That's what me 'n my boys gets paid for."

E.J. Karioth and Bradford N. Swett both nodded their heads in agreement with this statement.

"Why, Harvey Yancey's 'bout the rottenest sum'bitch I ever did run across," Fred Klingebiel continued vehemently. "Puttin' that viper out of cir-cu-lay-shun is one of the importantest things I could ever do."

"My friends and I would be obliged if you'd let us accompany you, Fred," Marcus Haverstraw told Klingebiel.

"You-all's welcome," the marshal replied, "if'n you think you can keep up with us, for we're goin' to burn leather."

Haverstraw winced and then looked to Davy Watson and Soaring Hawk, who both nodded back at him.

"I think we can handle it," he told the marshal.

"I shorely hope so," Fred Klingebiel said, his spurs

clanking as he turned and began to walk out of the house, taking long, purposeful strides as he did. "'Cause it ain't gonna be no picnic."

The big, hook-encrusted cones of the Digger Pine crunched forlornly beneath the horses' hooves, filling the late autumn air with their brittle sounds as Harvey Yancey's band made its way from the bare foothills of the northeastern Sierra Nevada up to the lush forest belt of that majestic range.

Autumn in the lower passes of the Sierra Nevada was a time of beauty and wonder. Golden aspen trees, common throughout the range, stretched out like a rolling sea golden with the glow of sunset. Birches and maples grew in colorful stands upon the canyon walls. And the floors of those canyons were carpeted with the leaves of the great oaks, while the smaller live oaks which adorned the ledges of the canyon walls contributed their share of leaves as well.

The ouzel flew behind the screens of waterfalls, penetrating the rapids like a feathered dart. Its song, joyous and exquisite, rang out in the crisp mountain air. Higher up in the range, the raucous, cawing bird known as the Clark nutcracker pursued its solitary course in the high timber. And the rosy finch cast its shadows over the frost fields above, chirping tunelessly in the intervals between its reconnaissances for dead insects.

Tamarac pine grew at the higher altitudes, and the whitebark pine flourished at the timberline, affording an ideal camping site, thanks to its closely knit branches and beds of soft needles. On the eastern wall of the great range that stretches for about two hundred and fifty miles from north to south, and whose breadth is between forty to eighty miles, there is found the pinyon tree, whose compact cone yields up the small delicacy known as the pinyon nut.

Prominent in the forest belt were the white and red firs, while above on the rocky slopes and plateaus, the stocky-trunked juniper displayed its dark green masses of foliage, dotted at intervals with clusters of turquoise berries. Douglas fir, western white pine, incense cedar and mountain hemlock: all graced the Sierra Nevada, as well as the Bennett tree, one of the oldest living trees on earth.

Of all the trees in that great range, the crowning glory was the sequoia. This tree, in the form of *sequoia gigantea*, exists solely within the confines of the Sierra Nevada; a close relative, *sequoia sempervivens*, grows near the ocean, by the northern California coast. Legendary among the "Big Trees" of the Sierra Nevada was the now-fallen "Father of the Forest," which had a circumference that measured a full 116 feet, and which formerly rose to a height of somewhere between 400 and 450 feet.

The rugged, rolling landscape of the Sierra Nevada was a sea of beauty, the snows of its upper reaches crowning the range as foam crowns a whitecap. But Harvey Yancey was too preoccupied to enjoy the breathtaking surroundings, as were his captives, the three daughters of Carmela Mudree.

Martin Spiller, Calvin Lytel, John B. Kerrigan, and Owen Mason were the names of the bully-boys who had thrown in with the bearded giant in Virginia City. Spiller was a thickset man with freckles, pale blue eyes and auburn hair. Lytel was tall, lean, and sported a Vandyke and wore a patch over his left eye. Kerrigan was a fair-skinned fellow with hair as black as the underside of a raven's wing. And Mason was short and fat, with long, greasy brown hair.

These men, along with Sugrue, Morison and McAllister had ridden out of Virginia City with Harvey Yancey. For it was a giant's plan to learn the ropes of the white slave trade on the Barbary Coast and then, once he had mastered it, carve out a niche therein for himself.

Having departed from the boom town under cover of darkness, in order to escape the notice of his nemesis, Marshal Fred Klingebiel, Harvey Yancey rode west, toward the eastern wall of the High Sierra.

Going along the northern slope of Mount Davidson at first, Yancey led his band through Washoe City, along the Climber Flume, and thence into the Sierra foothills, until they came to the banks of the Truckee River. After traveling on the banks of the river for a while, the riders left the Truckee at the point where it forked south, and then rode westward, to the approach to the Donner Pass.

It was at this point, following the path that the Southern Pacific Railroad had recently created, riding up to the northwest beside the snow-capped tracks, heading up from Donner Lake to Donner Pass, that Harvey Yancey discovered he was being followed.

"'Pears to me we got us some unexpected company, Harv," the gaunt, dour Sugrue told his chief as he shielded his eyes from the glare of sunlight on the snows that lined the entrance to the pass. The two men fell silent as they squinted at the riders in the distance below.

"You reckon it's ol' Fred Klingebiel, Sugrue?" Yancey asked in a concerned rumble. "The sum'bitch usually rides with jus' two dep'ties."

"That's as may be, Harv," Sugrue told the giant as he scratched the stubble on his chin. "But you know a federal marshal can whip him up a posse faster'n bluetail flies gets wind of a lump of horseshit."

"I see. . .six figgers on horseback," Yancey muttered, blinking his eyes as he strained to see.

"That's right," agreed the sharp-eyed Sugrue. "An' one of 'em 'pears to be a Injun."

"Oh, ho," the huge bearded man said. "I believe I know just who that Injun might be. That means the Watson kid must be with him. Come fer the little heifers, I reckon."

"We are saved!" Hope Mudree cried rapturously. "O we are saved!"

"Praise the Lord," Charity Mudree intoned piously.

"O I knew we would not be forsaken and left to the mercies of this brute!" was Faith's contribution.

"You jus' shet your damn mouths," Harvey Yancey growled, wheeling around in his saddle to glare at the Mudrees. "The next one to start gabblin' is gonna get her teeth knocked out an' her jaw busted."

He turned back to Sugrue. "Can you make out who they's with?"

The cadaverous-looking man nodded. "Yup. I can tell Fred Klingebiel by the way he sits a horse. An' judgin' by that big gray Stetson behind him, I'd say he's got ol' Bradford Swett with him." He paused to lean over the side of his horse, holding his fingers to his nostrils as he blew his nose.

"Cain't figger out who them other two gents is," he told Yancey after he had wiped his nose on his sleeve. "But one of 'em can't ride fer shit."

"Oh, shit. Oh, dear," Yancey rumbled thoughtfully he continued to stare at the distant figures of Fred

Klingebiel, Davy Watson and the others. "Them crazy sum'bitches is out after me, follyin' me to Californee. Ain't that the shits?"

"They's movin' at a good clip, Harv," Sugrue told Yancey. "What we gon' do?"

Harvey Yancey straightened up in his saddle, drawing himself up to his full and imposing height. He looked around then, his eyes making brief contact with those of each of the cutthroats in his band. He smiled a menacing, wolfish smile as he did, and his teeth looked like tombstones.

"What're we gonna do?" he asked rhetorically, his deep voice rumbling through his graveyard smile. "What're we gonna do?"

Then Yancey paused for effect, his hangman's eyes darting over the eager visages of his bully-boys and the strained countenances of the three Mudree sisters.

"Why, we're gonna blow the livin' shit out'n them sum'bitches. *That's* what we're gonna do," was his reply.

"Oh, God!" Marcus Haverstraw exclaimed through clenched teeth as the band of pursuers reined in and stared up at the imposing spectacle of the Donner Pass. "I think I've pulverized my innards!" he told Davy. "I'll never be able to sit down comfortably again—never!"

"You got to get the hang of postin' in the saddle, Marcus," Davy told his friend. "You hang on well enough, but you're gonna beat your brains out that way. You got to rise up some. Like this."

Davy pantomimed the essentials of posting for his companion.

136

"Someday," the suffering reporter prophesied, "some great man's gonna come up with an alternative to the horse, some machine that'll take a body around in a dignified manner."

"You got the railroad," Davy told him.

"I know that, Davy. But what I'm talking about is a machine, a gizmo that will hold one or more passengers and go all over, not relying on tracks."

"Shoot, Marcus," scoffed Davy. "Next you'll be tellin' me you want to fly."

"Why the hell not?" Haverstraw replied testily. "If men can float all over the place in balloons, I don't see why they can't rig up flying machines."

"If Great Spirit mean for man to fly," interjected Soaring Hawk, "would give wings."

"Why isn't it possible?" Haverstraw asked.

The Pawnee made a sour face. "Bird weigh three pound. Man weigh hundred-fifty. Never happen."

Their discussion was interrupted by the federal marshal. "That there lump of horseshit ahead is still steamin'," Fred Klingebiel observed. "That means ol' Harvey Yancey an' his bunch can't be but a short ways beyond."

"Way I figger it," Deputy Marshal Bradford N. Swett told the marshal, "we ought to step on Yancey's tail jus' when he's a-comin' down the far side of the pass."

E.J. Karioth nodded in agreement with this. "That way, when they've swung west again, they'll all have the sun in their eyes, an' ain't none of 'em gonna be able to hit the broad side of a barn door. An' we'll be a-settin' above 'em, up top the pass. It'll be like shootin' fish in a barrel, less'n they surrender."

Klingebiel pushed back his hat and began to scratch

137

his head. "Yup," he said, grinning behind his handlebar mustache. "That seems like a right smart way to go." He looked up at the sky, at the white flurries of snow that had begun to fall with ever-increasing intensity, blown about by the strong wind that came from the Donner Pass.

"Aw, shoot," the marshal growled. "It's snowin' up there."

"Been snowin' afore, too," Bradford N. Swett told Klingebiel from under his huge gray hat. "Lookee there." He pointed past the long draw before them.

"I'll be hornswoggled," Marshal Klingebiel said, a note of dismay in his voice. "The gol-durned pass is full of snow."

"Isn't it sorta early for snow?" Marcus Haverstraw asked querulously.

"Not hereabouts," E.J. Karioth told him.

"An' even if it was a tad early," Bradford N. Swett told Marcus with a shrug, "here it is."

"What does that mean to us?" Davy Watson asked, looking up to the snow-covered Donner Pass that now seemed to loom above him with an air of cold, granitic menace.

"That means we-all'd better git our butts through that there pass while we still can," Fred Klingebiel told the young Kansan.

"Damn! This is colder than a landlord's heart," groused Marcus Haverstraw, adjusting the huge woolen scarf he wore around his face and neck.

"You ain't jus' whistlin' *Dixie*," Davy Watson agreed, drawing the collar of his sheepskin coat up around his ears. "That wind comin' down the pass feels 'bout to slice through me like a Bowie knife.''

"Gets worse as you go up," commented the taciturn Bradford N. Swett.

Soaring Hawk, even more laconic than the deputy, said, "This not good place."

The snow was falling heavily now, adding to the previous snows, which were themselves already banked heavily on the many granite ledges that towered on both sides of the little band of horsemen.

Onward they rode, up into the forbidding reaches of the Donner Pass. It was a hard, brooding place, Davy realized, suddenly feeling a chill that had nothing to do with the cutting wind. They were passing through the hard heart of the granitic mountain, and it was a place of desolation and despair. But the one consolation afforded to Davy during the grim ascent was the realization that Harvey Yancey and the Mudree sisters were just on the far side of the Donner Pass.

"What d'you think?" Davy said, leading his horse closer to Soaring Hawk's pony.

"This bad place,," the Pawnee told his blood brother, looking around at the jagged, snow-topped rocks above and the snowbound path ahead.

"Goin's gettin' rough," Davy agreed. "That there stretch of pass up ahead's plumb full of snow," he said, pointing in the direction of the distant Donner Peak, which was framed on both sides by the brooding, rock-ribbed walls that towered above them, dwarfing the riders by the cruel majesty of their sheer and almost perpendicular ascent.

"You fellas ever hear of the Donner party?" Marcus Haverstraw spoke up, reining in his mount beside Davy's.

"Donner party?" Davy repeated, speaking louder in

the face of the wind that now came howling down from the summit of the Donner Pass.

"That's right," Haverstraw called back to Davy and Soaring Hawk. "The pass got its name from George Donner, the leader of a band of emigrants from Illinois. The old name for this place was the Truckee Pass."

The snow now fell in blinding sheets. Davy looked ahead, and was just barely able to make out Fred Klingebiel hunch forward in his saddle as he conferred with his deputies.

"Well," continued Marcus, "Donner's party had made a number of serious tactical mistakes crossing Utah and Nevada, and by the time they reached the meadows along the Truckee River, they were totally exhausted."

He paused to use his long scarf to tie his hat down, as the screaming wind threatened to tear it off his head. "In their camp by Alder Creek and Donner Lake," the reporter went on in a loud voice, "the party were snowed in. Their cattle had managed to wander off, and were buried in snowdrifts.

"One group tried to find a way out, but wound up in dire straits, snowbound and huddled over their pitiful campfire. After the storm had subsided, four men were dead. . . . The survivors ate their bodies."

Davy shivered, from horror as well as the slashing wind.

"Later, another man was eaten," Haverstraw said, continuing the grim narrative. "And then, after eating their moccasins, the strings of their snowshoes, and a pair of old boots, the survivors of that unfortunate group killed and ate their two Indian guides."

Soaring Hawk frowned at Marcus Haverstraw.

"Thirty-two days after they had left the base camp,

140

the survivors—five women and two men—came to an Indian village. Then, with help, they made their way to the Johnson Ranch at Wheatland." The newspaperman caught Davy's eye. "They crossed those last miles barefoot, leaving a trail of bloody footprints in the snow."

"Judas Priest!" exclaimed Davy.

"Oh, that's not all," Marcus added, with an emphatic shake of his head.

Davy shook his own head then, and frowned behind the upturned collar of his sheepskin coat. "Lord, you're 'bout as cheerful as a hangman at an eleventh-hour reprieve."

"Well, you want to hear the whole story, don't you?" the newspaperman asked incredulously.

Davy shrugged his shoulders as he and the Pawnee exchanged "here-we-go-again" looks.

"Right," Marcus continued, taking this for a sign of assent. "When rescue parties from the Sacramento Valley got to Donner Lake—now, this is months later, remember—most of the people they found there were dead, or in a torpor. They came back with mainly children, but another blizzard came up and trapped *them*, freezing the hands and feet of many, and eventually killing them. Their bodies were eaten by the survivors."

"Gol-lee," Davy murmured.

"Five started back, but Tamsen Donner left and made her way back to Alder Lake, where her husband lay dying. When the rescuers finally arrived there, her body had vanished, and only one man remained alive there, living in a pitiful state. . .surrounded by the bones of his former companions."

Soaring Hawk shook his head and hunched forward as the keening wind blew the snow about in a furious gale.

"Eighty-one had pitched camp at Alder Lake in November," Marcus Haverstraw concluded, "but only forty-five lived to make it across the mountains."

"That's a horrible damn story, Marcus," Davy called out over the wind that howled down through the Donner Pass.

Marcus P. Haverstraw nodded. "It is indeed," he yelled back, his words barely reaching Davy Watson's ears. "Truth is more horrible than fiction."

Bradford N. Swett had dropped back from the head of the band, and now reined in his horse alongside those of Davy, Soaring Hawk and Marcus Haverstraw.

"Ol' Fred, he sent me back here to tell you boys to get a move on," the deputy tersely informed the three companions. "He says we're gonna be lucky to clear the pass as things stand now, so you better keep up with us."

The others nodded and began to urge their mounts on as the deputy rode ahead, heading them into the heart of the raging blizzard, up to the summit of Donner Pass.

By this time, the wind was howling with a maniacal fury, its sound growing angrier as the party fought its way to the summit. Horse and rider alike were buffeted by that cruel wind, and at times Davy Watson had to fight to keep from being ripped from his saddle by the icy blasts. The blizzard was deadly and numbing, and held within its white, swirling mantle the seductive promise of oblivion.

As the cold numbed him to the very marrow of his bones, and caused his eyes to close, his consciousness faded, to return only when he caught himself, about to pitch out of the saddle, startled to see the snowy floor of the pass so close to his face. But once he was settled back in his saddle, Davy Watson listened once more to the siren-song of oblivion crooned by the wind, and felt the almost irresistible allure of its white music.

To drift forever, needing absolutely nothing, rocked as if by the cradle of the sea, surrounded always by glowing warmth and pure whiteness, by a sweet forgetfulness that held no threats or secrets, no promises or expectations. To live eternally in that white, silent womb, free from care and the bondage of self, from love and longing, from thought and feeling. . .from the pain of humanity and the burden of mortality. For the first time in his life, Davey understood the longing for oblivion. . .the longing for death.

But Davy Watson had not quite let go of life yet—not by a long shot. "Hell, no! Shit, no!" he roared, scrambling back onto his saddle and shaking his head long and vigorously. He was not ready for the cold embrace of death yet.

"No way!" he bellowed, startling Soaring Hawk and Marcus Haverstraw, who were enmeshed in their own flirtations with oblivion.

The young Kansan spurred his horse on, making his way through the blizzard with great difficulty, until he came up beside Marshal Fred Klingebiel and his deputies.

"Ain't this a pisser!" Davy cried out, leaning over until he was at the marshal's ear.

Klingebiel nodded. "Mite more'n I expected," he admitted in a hoarse roar. "But we's nigh to the top of the pass, son. An' once't we done shunted the hump, we'll have us some easy goin' on the downward side."

"That's if we can get through the pass," E.J. Karioth added tartly, shouting over the insane wind. "It's plumb full of snow up thataways."

"Don't reckon we got a whole lot of choice at this

here point," the marshal told the deputy with a shake of his head. "Jus' keep goin'."

Davy nodded stoically and wheeled his horse around, heading back to ride beside Soaring Hawk and Marcus Haverstraw. The bitter, killing wind was howling so loudly that Davy barely heard the volley of gunshots that rang out behind him, coming from the summit of the Donner Pass.

He waved frantically to Soaring Hawk and Haverstraw, catching their attention and then signaling for them to get low in the saddle and make for the cover of the granite ledges that jutted out from the cliff walls, all but hidden by the tones of snow that they bore.

Bwapf! Something ripped through the thick leather of the shoulder of Davy's sheepskin coat, its impact nearly wrenching him out of the saddle. Then he felt a sudden, stinging pain and a warmth that suffused his shoulder. He reached reflexively inside his coat, and then withdrew a hand lightly smeared with blood. Davy was convinced by his probing and the sight of so little blood that his wound was a superficial one.

As he dug his spurs into the flanks of his mount, having wheeled it around, he looked ahead in the instant before he shot forward toward the safety of the ledge. He was dismayed to see Fred Klingebiel and Bradford N. Swett pitch out of their saddles, almost at the same time. Swett landed on his back, and even at the distance that separated him from Davy, and the intermittent sheets of snow which continually threatened to obscure all vision, the young Kansan could see the man clutch at his chest as he thrashed about on the ground. Fred Klingebiel had pitched headfirst off of his horse, and the federal marshal lay face-down in the snow, not moving a muscle.

E.J. Karioth spurred his horse over to one of the low-hanging ledges at the far wall of the pass, bullets flying all around him, sending sprays of snow into the air as they plowed into the drifts. More snow flew, as the deputy's mount kicked up its heels and raced toward the relative safety of the overhanging ledges.

By this time, Soaring Hawk was off his horse and crouching by the wall of the pass, his heavy-caliber Sharps rifle at his shoulder. Then, just as Davy saw Marcus Haverstraw's horse rear and throw the reporter backward into a snowdrift, he heard the roar of the Pawnee's weapon.

As he reined his horse in under the same ledge where the Pawnee had taken shelter, Davy looked in the direction in which the Indian's rifle was pointing. And there, on a high shelf near the summit, a body jackknifed through the air, hurtling down to disappear into the heart of the swirling white blizzard that mantled the pass.

It became almost impossible to see through the shifting latticework of the snowstorm for more than a moment at a time, and the ambushers above lost their initial advantage. Their remaining pursuers had gained shelter, and the combat was now almost on equal terms.

Pistols cracked and rifles roared, cutting through the screen of the howling wind, their repeated echoes shivering the walls of the Donner Pass, and causing the great masses of snow on the ledges to rumble ominously.

"By Gad," said Marcus Haverstraw, looking like a hastily-made snowman as he scuttled into the shadow thrown by the ledge overhead. "Do you hear that?"

As if to underscore the reporter's words, E.J. Karioth fired off a volley of rifle shots from the wall opposite the companions, causing the snows above to rumble and come down in a sweeping slide, not far from the ledge that protected the deputy.

"Avalanche," the newspaperman told Davy and Soaring Hawk. "If that keeps up we'll all be buried alive beneath the snows."

Further consideration of this morbid topic was cut short as the companions saw another man tumble down the side of the pass. The deputy had got his man.

"Tell you what we got to do," Davy Watson informed his companions, dismounting and then pulling his Henry rifle out of the saddle boot that held it. "Them fellas is shootin' at us from both sides, up ahead. We can't get past 'em."

"Hell, we can't even see 'em," complained Marcus Haverstraw.

"Yup," Davy agreed. "But they can't see us no more, neither."

A volley of gunshots rang out, and bullets ricocheted randomly off the rock shelf above them as the ambushers began to fire again.

Across the pass from him, Davy saw E.J. Karioth take aim with his Winchester and fire once. An instant later, he heard a faint, shrill cry up ahead, by the summit.

"Boy, that E.J.'s got an eye like a hawk," Davy marveled.

"See far and clear," Soaring Hawk murmured admiringly.

"Well, as I was sayin'," Davy resumed as the summit was once more obscured from view by a screen of white turbulence, "we gotta do somethin' different now, 'cause Harvey Yancey an' his bunch's got us pinned down. We're hog-tied as it stands, and Lord knows they got time on their side."

"What can we do?" asked Marcus Haverstraw, reloading the huge Navy Colt that he had borrowed from the sheriff of Virginia City before the pursuers had ridden out after Harvey Yancey.

"See them ledges up there?" Davy asked, pointing to the high walls at the summit. "Up above them bushwhackers? On both sides of the pass?"

"Yes, I see," Marcus grunted as Soaring Hawk nodded, his face devoid of all expression.

"Well, it's that there avalanche you was jus' talkin' 'bout, Marcus," Davy told the reporter eagerly. "If'n we can concentrate enough of our fire on them ledges, mebbe the noise an' the slugs'll jar loose a heap of snow, an' send it down on their heads."

"What about the Mudree girls?" Marcus asked.

Davy sighed. "Well, we ain't spotted 'em up there, so I reckon it's safe to figger that Yancey got 'em tucked away somewhere on t'other side of this here pass."

"No see Yancey," Soaring Hawk added.

"Well, with a little luck," Davy told him with a fierce smile, "mebbe he jus' took him a bullet right 'twixt the eyes."

It was Marcus Haverstraw's turn to sigh. "That's too much to hope for," he told his companions in a wistful voice.

"Avalanche good idea," Soaring Hawk told his blood brother, clapping him on the back.

"Can't think of nothin' else to do," Davy said. "Can you?"

The Pawnee and the reporter both shook their heads.

Implementing his plan, Davy took advantage of the next lull in the blizzard to engage in an energetic pantomime, as he communicated his idea across the width of the pass to E. J. Karioth.

Several moments later, the deputy marshal took off his brown Stetson and waved it over his head.

"He's got it," Haverstraw cried out exultantly.

"Now he signal you," Soaring Hawk informed Davy as Karioth began a pantomime of his own. "He want us to shoot one ledge, he shoot other," explained the Pawnee. "Both at same time."

"Good idea," Davy told him, waving his Henry rifle in the air as a signal of his agreement.

The ambushers fired several random and ineffectual shots at their pursuers just before the blizzard intensified in its fury. It was a long time before the white tempest abated. But when it did, Davy Watson and his companions went into action.

Blam! Blam! Bambambam! Boom!

On Davy's signal, he and his companions began firing for all they were worth, each blazing away until his guns were emptied.

A sudden and ominous rumbling sound rose above the cracking echoes of the gunshots, and the very ground beneath Davy's feet seemed to shudder and heave.

"Get back!" he cried, catching sight of the great white waves that had begun to spill over the ledges on the heights of the Donner Pass.

An instant later, the shrill, panicked screams of men and horses reached his ears, only to be drowned out a moment afterward by the bass roar of the oncoming avalanche. The pass shook to the power of that river of unleashed energy, and the roaring sounded in Davy

148

Watson's ears like the voice of the earth crying out in angry protest.

"Oh, Lord," Marcus Haverstraw whispered in a quavering voice, once the avalanche was over. "Will you look at that?"

"Well," Davy sighed, looking at the huge bank of snow at the head of the pass. "I 'spose we got us a heap of diggin' to do afore we get to the other side. But we stopped them sum'bitches from shootin' at us, didn't we?"

"Certainly looks that way," the reporter answered. "I just hope to heaven we didn't go and bury the Mudree sisters as well."

It took them nearly a day and a half to dig their way out of the Donner Pass, and hours more to discover who had been buried in the avalanche. To Davy Watson's relief, the bodies of the Mudree sisters were not to be found. Nor, to his chagrin, was that of Harvey Yancey. Deputy Karioth identified several of the latest additions to Yancey's bunch. As it turned out, six of the giant's men had either been shot or buried beneath the snow. Only Yancey and the man called Sugrue remained. Soaring Hawk returned from his reconnaissance, and informed the others that he had picked up the tracks of five horses.

Before they left the pass, the four men dug into the snow and earth once more; but this time it was to bury Marshal Fred Klingebiel and his deputy, Bradford N. Swett. E.J. Karioth, the remaining deputy, chose to return to Nevada, to his base at Elko, where he would duly report the deaths of his fellow lawmen.

"Yancey's bound for Californee, with the Mudrees

on his knee," Marcus P. Haverstraw informed his companions, singing to the tune of *O Susannah*.

"Well, I reckon we're off to the Barbary Coast," Davy Watson told his friends as they watched the surviving deputy ride back through the Donner Pass.

Marcus Haverstraw squinted into the distance, looking westward at the mountains that rose up in a long and mighty chain.

"That may well be," he replied. "But first, we've got to cross the High Sierra."

Contrary to Marcus' pessimistic expectations, the crossing of the Sierra Nevada proved to be relatively uneventful. None of the other passes were snowbound, and therefore the unpleasant and perilous experience of the Donner Pass was not repeated. The riders made consistently good time, and crossed the range with little difficulty.

Heading down the westernmost slopes of the Sierra Nevada, leaving the majesty of Sequoias and the grandeur of snow-capped peaks behind them, Davy Watson, Soaring Hawk and Marcus Haverstraw rode down to the California plain.

Following the course of the American River, after restocking their supplies in the town of Emigrant, the companions rode south, passing Nevada City Gap and Grass Valley, Placerville and Folsom, stopping for the night in Sacramento, capital of the state.

The next day they rode southwest, entering San Joaquin County, riding east of Lodi and Stockton heading west as they came to Contra Costa County Then the horsemen went south once more, passing close by Oakland, San Leandro and Fremont, as they skirted the Great San Francisco Bay.

To the north of San Jose, the riders started up the

peninsula that ended in the wild and extravagant city that had begun as a small Spanish settlement at Yerba Buena Cove. Once they had ridden past Palo Alto, San Carlos, San Mateo and Daly City, they would come to the bright city that stood on the shore of the vast Pacific Ocean.

They were embarked upon the final leg of their journey; the next time they dismounted, it would be in San Francisco, that wild city founded upon golden dreams, that young metropolis seething with wealth and poverty, virtue and corruption, untrammeled optimism and black despair.

In San Francisco, Davy Watson hoped he would find Faith, Hope and Charity Mudree at last. And in that wicked, glittering city by the shore, the young Kansan was certain that he would also run smack into the violent and obscene Harvey Yancey.

Chapter Eight

By the time that the year 1869 drew near, the city of San Francisco had developed from the raw mining town of the late '40's into the premier metropolis of America's western shore. And while millionaires nested contentedly amidst the beauty of the hills overlooking the Pacific, vice, degradation and murder flourished in the slums by the broad ocean.

Formerly called old Sydney Town, the territory of the Australian convicts known as the Sydney Ducks, who were extirpated by the equally notorious Committee of Vigilance, the Barbary Coast was a wild, exotic and sinister place when Davy Watson and his companion set foot within its precincts.

Bounded by East Street, Commercial and Clay Streets, Chinatown and Grant Street, parts of North Beach and Telegraph Hill, the Barbary Coast was drab, stinking slum in the daylight hours, and phantasmagoria of corruption, license and violence during the night.

Grog shops, brothels, dance halls; pawnshops, opium parlors and saloons; cafes, sailors' boarding houses and crimping establishments—joints that specialized drugging and shanghaiing sailors; shops that specialize in the sale of stolen loot, gaming houses of every sort and seamy places that offered the pleasure seeker every conceivable form of vice: such was the landscape of San Francisco's notorious Barbary Coast. The place was wide open, and its motto was "Anything goes!" It was said that if a form of vice or gambling was not found there, then it was not practiced anywhere.

The companions scoured the district, starting from Pacific Avenue and Davis Street, where the sailors put in. From there, they made their way over to Kearney Street, which was studded with cellar joints, dance halls, melodeons (filthy holes named after the lugubrious reed organs which supplied their music), and deadalls (cheap wine and beer houses). Obscene acts and bawdy songs passed for entertainment in these establishments, and the Kansan and the Plains Indian were shocked when they discovered the brutal nature of life beyond their portals.

"Judas Priest, it's a hellacious way to live," Davy remarked to Soaring Hawk and Marcus Haverstraw.

The newspaperman shook his head in dismay. "It appears that while men often seek higher things, there is a part of the human spirit that also courts destruction."

"Have to be sick in head," Soaring Hawk told them, tapping a finger against his temple, "to live like this."

"Well, it don't seem like they're wantin' for business," Davy replied as they walked past the Mexican fandango joints that stood directly across from the city jail. Guitar music and the smell of chili filled the air.

"I've read somewhere that there's an average of one murder and a dozen robberies and assaults a night here on the Barbary Coast," Haverstraw told his friends, stepping over the body of a fallen Mexican wino as he did.

"That ain't my idea of a good time," was Davy's reply.

They continued their rounds, stopping at dives and establishments whose names were the Louisiana, Cock o' the Walk, Canterbury Hall, Big Dive, Opera Comique, Brooks' Melodeon and Montana. At Pacific Avenue and Kearney Street, in a hell-hole called the Billy Goat, a stable of a place run by a ferocious Irishwoman known as Pigeon-toed Sal, the trio got their first information as to the whereabouts of Harvey Yancey and the Mudree sisters.

The giant had passed through recently, asking for Bertram Brown, a garrulous, besotted newspaperman of Haverstraw's acquaintance told them.

Following this lead, the man having passed out before he could tell them where Bertram Brown was to be found, the companions next stopped at the Hell's Kitchen Dance Hall, the roughest, toughest joint in all the Barbary Coast. There they learned from the place's colorful owner, Bull Run Allen (a man who powdered his bulbous red nose with flour), that Bertram Brown now owned an establishment on Jackson and Kearney Streets called the Covent Garden.

Another thing the trio learned before they left the place—to the extreme delight of Marcus P. Haverstraw —was the origin of the word "hooker." Apparently, prostitutes owed their name to Joe Hooker, the Civil War general. He was reputed to have spent a great deal of time during the War Between the States in Washington's red-light district. As a result of his prestigious patronage, that neighborhood soon acquired the name of Hooker Division, and the women who plied their trade in it came to be known as hookers.

Covent Garden was a huge, three-storied establishment on the corner of Jackson and Kearney that specialized in the Barbary Coast's most notorious obscene shows and acts. These performances were popular with the rich of Nob Hill, who patronized the place when they were out "slumming." Standing directly across the street from the Opera Comique (at a place known as Murder Corner), the Covent Garden featured Spanish and French waitresses and entertainers, most of whom doubled as prostitutes. Bars and dance floors occupied the cellars and the ground floor; the hookers had their stalls and beds on the building's upper stories.

Bertram Brown was a tall, slender man with curled brown hair, handsome features, mutton-chop whiskers and a pencil mustache. He wore skintight trousers and a silk vest; his white ruffled shirt was set off by a bow tie, and over it he wore an elegantly-cut frock coat, of the type known as "claw hammer tail." This fashionable man was a gambler of great nerve and renown, as well as one of the shrewdest business men in all San Francisco.

He had many legitimate business interests outside of the Barbary Coast, and was even reputed to be a stockholder in several of the city's larger banks. In addition to his many illicit investments, Bertram Brown was the major supplier of young women for the lucrative, but highly illegal, white slave trade.

White women, young and fair, were greatly prized in the harems of the East, and sheikhs and other potentates would pay exorbitant sums to obtain them. These young women, often from quiet neighborhoods in the larger cities of the United States, were waylaid and kidnapped in the course of an innocent visit to the more exotic districts of these major urban centers.

A goodly number of these unfortunate victims wound up in the hidden rooms in the basement of Bertram Brown's establishment. Once they had arrived, the owner of the Covent Garden notified a network of underground contacts, and shortly thereafter, bids from prospective buyers began to pour in. Then, once the highest bidders had plunked down cash on the barrel-head, Brown saw to it that the newly-made slave girls were swiftly shipped out to their respective owners in North Africa, Arabia or Asia.

Bertram Brown was a mover and a shaker; he was not a man to cross—as many men had discovered, often learning that hard lesson at the cost of their lives or fortunes. And it was to this man that Malcolm Shove had sent Harvey Yancey, certain that Brown would come to terms with the giant regarding the sale of the Mudree sisters.

While the handsome gambler loved no one but himself, he was much loved by women; Bertram Brown was one of those cold and dangerous men to whom a goodly number of females are always irresistibly drawn.

His current mistress was a black woman named Della Casson, who was possessed of both great beauty and an intensely passionate nature. The gambler often behaved like a scoundrel toward her, but her great love for the man blinded her to his faults. Brown had often exploited her devotion, using her beautiful body as a lure to those men he would dominate or use.

Bertram Brown was not visible when Davy Watson, Soaring Hawk and Marcus Haverstraw entered his crowded, boisterous establishment. He was at that very moment concluding his negotiations for the purchase of Faith, Hope and Charity Mudree, skillfully calculating just how much additional money would be required to induce Harvey Yancey to part with the girls. Brown was prepared to settle a handsome sum on the bearded giant, for he knew that the sheikhs of North Africa would surely triple, or even quadruple, that amount. . . .

> *"The miners came in forty-nine,*
> *The whores in fifty-one;*
> *And when they got together,*
> *They produced the Native Son."*

A laugh went up from the crowd gathered around the Covent Garden's pianoforte, as the man at the keyboard launched into the bawdy and disrespectful song about the San Francisco elite.

It was a raw, chilly night, one whose dampness penetrated to the very marrow of a man's bones, so Marcus Haverstraw ordered a hot buttered rum and cider for himself and Davy, and a mulled cider for Soaring Hawk.

By the time he'd taken his second swig of the potent drink, the irrepressible Marcus was off and running, telling Davy and the Pawnee all about the lurid and extravagant history of San Francisco. He was deep into a description of the totalitarian and lynch-happy vigilantes of the 1850's, who cleaned out the notorious Sydney Ducks and wound up with an army 8,000 strong, defying even the government of the United States of America before they finally consented to disband.

"But lynching seems to have gone out of style in 'Frisco these days," Haverstraw informed his companions. "Here's a definition for you; it's by a fellow-newspaperman. '*Gallows:* A stage for the performance of miracle plays, in which the leading actor is translated to heaven. In this country the gallows is chiefly remarkable for the number of persons who escape it.'"

Marcus Haverstraw paused to spit into the silver gaboon at his feet. "The fella who said that was a born literary hell-raiser—half catamount, half alligator, just like good ol' Mark Twain," he said fondly. "He watches the San Franciscans like a hawk."

"Funny fella," Davy agreed, ordering them a second round of drinks.

"He had definitions for just about anything you could think of," Marcus told Davy as Soaring Hawk yawned and looked around the bar through half-lidded eyes.

"What else'd he say, Marcus?"

"There was this one. *'Pray:* To ask that the laws of the universe be annulled in behalf of a single petitioner confessedly unworthy.'"

Davy began to laugh.

"And this," Haverstraw went on, once the young Kansan had quieted down. " *'Christian:* One who believes that the New Testament is a divinely inspired book admirably suited to the spiritual needs of his neighbor. One who follows the teachings insofar as they are not inconsistent with a life of sin.'"

"He's a hot one, by Gad!" Davy exclaimed, after laughing loudly.

Suddenly the crowd roared with delight, as the man at the pianoforte played the introduction to another favorite song.

"In eighteen hundred and fifty-eight,
I learned to take my whiskey straight.
It's an elegant drink and can't be beat

For working on the railway.
Fili-me oori-oori-aay. . . ."

"Lively damn town, ain't it?" Davy said with a smile, succumbing to the seductive charm of the vital and optimistic city of San Francisco, whose panoply of wealth, color and violence was dangerous and appealing at the same time. It was a heady and energizing place, and the young man from Pottawatomie Creek, Kansas, had never seen the like.

"Say, old fella," Marcus Haverstraw said expansively as he tossed a silver dollar across the bar to a waiting barkeep, "where might ol' Bertram Brown be keeping himself this evening?"

Bertram Brown shook his head and frowned when he heard Harvey Yancey explain what Davy Watson, Soaring Hawk and Marcus P. Haverstraw were after.

Yancey had been prompted to tell his story after a barkeep had come into Brown's office and informed his employer that the trio were seeking him. The giant then began to apologize profusely, and explained that he had not thought it possible for those men to have traced his steps to the Covent Garden.

"That means they know what we're up to, Mr. Yancey," Brown told the bearded giant in a matter-of-fact tone of voice.

"Sweet Jesus!" Yancey exclaimed disconsolately. "That fuckin' kid must've shot Malcolm Shove. I don't believe it," he rumbled. "I jus' don't believe it."

"And evidently Mal told him about your ultimate destination," Bertram Brown concluded, a thoughtful expression on his handsome face.

"I jus' don't believe it," Harvey Yancey repeated, a dismal expression on his own face.

"You realize, of course, that they can't leave the Barbary Coast alive," Brown told the stupefied giant. "They know too much."

"Sure, sure," Yancey agreed, nodding his head vigorously. "I'll fetch my buddy, Sugrue, an' we'll lay for 'em outside."

Bertram Brown shook his head. "That's far too messy, Mr. Yancey. And totally unnecessary. I'll take care of it."

Yancey stared at the gambler, a disappointed expression on his face. "But I got me a score to settle with that Watson kid, Mr. Brown. So I'll jus'. . ."

The gambler interrupted him by holding up a hand. "Don't worry about it, Mr. Yancey," he told the giant softly. "I'll take care of it. This is my part of town, remember?"

"What're you gonna do?" Harvey Yancey asked in a small bass voice.

"I'm going to let the Watson kid and his friends meet a nice lady," Bertram Brown said, flashing Yancey a sinister smile, "before I have them killed."

Della Casson was a handsome woman with a lithe elegant body and flawless, glowing skin the color of bittersweet chocolate dusted with cinnamon. She had long, graceful hands, with tapered fingers, and nails as red as the tips of conspirators' daggers; and she wore a single ruby ring on the third finger of her left hand, as a token that she considered herself married to Bertram Brown in spirit.

160

She was long-legged and full-bodied, with a hand-span waist that took a man's breath away when he compared it to the broad hips below and the swelling breasts above. Her eyes were dark, and as beautiful as a gazelle's; her nose was *retroussé*; and when her red lips parted, it was to reveal a smile that one of the local poets had described as "incandescent as the noonday sun."

Her high cheekbones and long, oval face were framed by a full head of elaborate and oiled corkscrew curls, done in the style of the women of the ancient world. And in fact, men who were acquainted with the works of antiquity swore up and down that the famed enchantress, Cleopatra, could not have looked any more bewitching than Della Casson.

She had been born twenty-eight years ago, to slave parents on a plantation in the Louisiana parish of Saint Tammany. At the age of fourteen, with the aid of a band of abolitionists, Della went north via the "underground railway."

The next four years of her life were spent at an abolitionist school in Concord, Massachusetts. In her last year at school, while shopping with friends in Boston, Della made the acquaintance of one Martin St. John, a gay young blade who was the scion of one of the city's wealthier families.

Immediately, the young rakehell and the black beauty became infatuated with each other, and conspired to run off together. They they promptly did, with St. John taking Della Casson to London. Despite his youth, he was a man of the world, and it was in his arms that she first learned the arts of love. The Bostonian became her first lover, but he was far from her last.

It was at this time that Della began to move in

London society, as the protégé of the well-connected St John. But after six months of intense passion, the two had a falling out, and Della left London for Paris.

Having the advantage of her great beauty, animal sensuality, and the French she had spoken as her first language on the Louisiana plantation where she had been born, Della soon had the men of Paris at her feet. She remained in the City of Light for more than three years, taking many lovers and thereby becoming an adept at the skills of the boudoir. But she grew homesick in the end, and returned to her native land.

By the time that she returned to the United States, Della was almost twenty-four years old. In New York City she became the mistress of, first, a Wall Street financier, and then an up-and-coming Democratic politician. But this last lover grew intensely jealous, and had her followed day and night; so Della packed her bags and quietly slipped out of the metropolis.

Returning briefly to Saint Tammany Parish, Della went to visit her family, after an absence of almost twelve years. Her father had died during this period, but she was reunited with her mother and her two brothers, who had all been freed from slavery at the end of the Civil War. After remaining with them for several months, Della Casson decided to go to New Orleans.

It was in that city, in the *Vieux Carré*, the French Quarter, that she first met the love of her life, Bertram Brown. The two met at a grand ball given by her then lover, one Gaston Thibaudeaux, a wealthy shipping magnate who had survived the Civil War with the greater part of his assets intact, thanks to his extensive connections in the north.

Della fell in love with the gambler immediately. After having spent the night with the black Venus, Brown sug gested that she accompany him to San Francisco, where (so he told her) they would share a bright future. That same evening, the two were on board a ship that would take them around the Horn, bound for the new California metropolis.

As it turned out, the future was somewhat less bright than it had been promised, with the gambler often treating his beautiful mistress disgracefully. . .but Della Casson was content merely to be in Bertram Brown's presence.

Now, as she prowled the Covent Garden's main floor, with men ogling and paying court to her as she glided by, sleek and beautiful as a black leopard, Bertram Brown's dark lady fell victim to the depredations of an uneasy conscience.

It was not the first time that Brown had used her as a lure for other men; Della accepted that as something she had to do in order to earn the few meager scraps of affection that her ambitious lover threw her from time to time. She had been required to sleep with a number of men in the course of her duties, and Brown had always required her to describe their lovemaking in the minutest detail. That had made her extremely uneasy, even as it stoked the fires of the gambler's ardor. Normally, she accepted that; but this time Della had heard more than she wanted to hear.

On her way to Brown's office, Della Casson had paused at the door, transfixed by the harsh, eerie sound of Harvey Yancey's dismayed *basso profundo*. And as she stood outside that door, she heard Bertram Brown explain to the man inside that he was going to use Della to lure Davy Watson and his companions to their deaths. This was more than she had wanted to hear. . . much more. But the beautiful and passionate woman

163

loved Bertram Brown, even though he treated her like a dog. . . .

"Oh, my stars," muttered Marcus Haverstraw, when he looked up and saw the dark vision of beauty that was coming his way. Hearing the newspaperman, Davy looked up from his drink. And as he did, his breath caught in his throat when he saw the gorgeous young black woman. Then he suddenly realized that she was smiling at him—and no one else!

"Buy me a drink, cowboy," she murmured in a rich, musical voice, drawing near to Davy, and thereby causing Marcus Haverstraw's eyes to goggle and his jaw to drop.

Davy cleared his throat and returned the woman's smile. "Uh, anything you like, ma'am," he muttered, shifting uneasily from foot to foot.

"Ask the man for a Blue Blazer," she told him in a breathy voice.

"Blue Blazer," he repeated lamely, turning from her with great reluctance. "Blue Blazer," he said once more, loudly and emphatically this time, as he gave the bartender the order.

The Blue Blazer was a drink native to San Francisco, and it consisted of a tablespoon of honey in a silver mug half-filled with hot water, placed side by side with another mug containing an equal volume of scotch. The bartender ignited the whiskey, and then poured the flaming liquid into the mug containing the hot water and honey. This mixture was then poured from one mug to the other, until the flames were extinguished.

There was an awed silence at the bar, as the three companions watched the flashy performance of the red-vested bartender who mixed Della Casson's Blue Blazer.

"That's one of the sights of San Francisco," the

lovely black woman whispered in Davy Watson's ear as she moved still closer to him.

"Here y'are, Miss Della," the bartender said cheerfully, placing the drink on the bar before Bertram Brown's mistress.

"I'll take care of that," Davy told the bartender, attempting to rise to the occasion and impress the gorgeous young woman who stood so close to him that he could feel the warmth of her body.

"An' set up another round for me 'n my buddies here," he added magnanimously. Then Davy reached out, picked up the Blue Blazer, and with a graceful sweep of his arm, handed the glass to the dusky belle at his side.

"My name is Davy Watson, ma'am," he told her, his confidence growing as he looked into her dark eyes.

She nodded and smiled at this, her eyes never leaving his.

"An' I'd consider myself honored," Davy went on, his sudden smoothness causing Marcus Haverstraw to gape at him, "if'n you'd give me the great pleasure of hearin' you say your name. . .'cause the beauty of your person is matched only by the beauty of your voice."

"Well, I'll be damned," Haverstraw muttered under his breath.

"My name is Della, sugah," the black Venus told Davy, laying a graceful hand on his arm, and thereby stopping his heart. "I think you're very sweet," she murmured in her musical voice.

Davy flushed and cleared his throat as the bartender set the fresh drinks down on the sopping bar. Then, picking up his drink, he raised his glass high in the air.

"Gents, I propose a toast to Della, the black pearl of San Francisco—its most beautiful sight."

Marcus gave Davy a "not bad" look and an approving nod as he and Soaring Hawk raised their glasses. Davy could see, by the way that the Pawnee was eyeing Della Casson, that his blood brother was much taken with the beauty of the tall black woman.

"To the ravishing Della," Marcus toasted.

"Della," was all that the Pawnee said before he downed his ginger beer.

"Thank you, gentlemen," the object of their admiration replied, with a smile that could have served as a beacon in San Francisco's thickest fog. Then she turned to Davy Watson, an expectant look on her Cleopatra-face.

"I'd, uh, like to set down an' palaver with ya for a spell, Miss Della," he said awkwardly, feeling his ears burn. "But I got important business with Bertram Brown—business that can't wait."

"I think it will *have* to wait," she told him in a voice that was a honeyed purr. "Bert's out in San Jose, on business. And I'm afraid he's not due back until tomorrow morning."

Davy's reaction to this was an expression that reflected equal measures of disappointment and eager expectation.

"So, if you've got nothing better to do. . .Davy," the handsome woman went on, "why don't we sit down and get to know each other better?"

"I'd. . .I'd really like that, Della," he replied hoarsely.

"And I'll have some of the girls come over for your friends," she told him. "How does that sound?"

"Sounds fine to me," Marcus told her affably.

"Soaring Hawk like to talk with that one," the Pawnee told Della Casson, pointing to a big redhead a he near end of the bar.

"That can be arranged," she told the brave.

Marcus Haverstraw cleared his throat. "And perhaps might chat with that little blonde by the faro table?" e asked hopefully.

"You got it, sugah," Bertram Brown's mistress urred.

"Another drink, Mr. Yancey?" Bertram Brown inquired cordially of the bearded giant who sat on a lush sofa across the room from him, in his private ffice on the Covent Garden's first floor.

"Umm," the huge man rumbled in his subterranean ass. "Don't mind if I do, Mr. Brown."

"Just help yourself," the gambler told his guest.

Yancey reached over to the table on his left, and roceeded to freshen his bourbon and branch water. When you gonna do it?" he asked suddenly, referring Brown's promise to deal with Davy Watson and his riends.

Bertram Brown took a gold watch out of his vest ocket, opened its cover, and then squinted down at its ace. In delicate, tinkling tones, a mechanism inside the atch played *I Dream of Jeannie*.

"Oh, not for some time yet," the gambler told Iarvey Yancey, snapping shut the cover of his watch nd cutting off the music within. "Della needs a little me to soften those boys up for me."

Yancey leaned forward and regarded Bertram Brown ispiciously. "You mean you ain't worried 'bout that olored gal of your'n?" he asked slowly, frowning as he ooke the words.

"She's mine forever, friend," Brown told him with a

cold smile. "Why should I be worried?"

Open-mouthed by this time, Yancey took a deep breath before speaking. "Ain't you worried that li'l punk might jus' wind up in the sack with your dolly?"

"Della does what's required of her," Brown replied, his cold eyes glinting in the lamplight as he raised his head proudly. "And in her own way."

The giant stared at Bertram Brown in disbelief. "But what if he fucks her—for the love of God?" he asked in a whisper.

"That's the name of the game right now, Mr. Yancey," the gambler told him. "I *want* all them boys to whoop it up, to drink like fish and fuck their heads off."

As Harvey Yancey sat open-mouthed and slowly began to shake his head, Bertram Brown smiled like a shark.

"And after they have," the gambler went on, "then I'll move in for the kill."

Chapter Nine

"You take the high road, an' I'll take the low
    road,
An' I'll get to Scotland afore ye,
Where me an' my true love will never meet again,
On the bonny, bonny banks of Loch
    Lomond. . . ."

The pianoforte player had the drunks in tears now,
howling like a banshee, as he poured out his heart into
the words and music of the sad song.

Big Terry and Angel were the names of the redhead
and the blonde who drank champagne and sat beside
Soaring Hawk and Marcus P. Haverstraw on plush
sofas in a suite of rooms on the third floor on the
building that housed Covent Garden, Bertram Brown's
huge, elegant and dangerous establishment on the
Barbary Coast.

Beside Davy Watson sat the striking and feline Della
Basson. The wine and liquor had been flowing steadily
for several hours, and the party was in full swing. And
in the full and grim knowledge that she would soon
hand Davy, Soaring Hawk and Marcus over to the
executioner—her lover, Bertram Brown, the Louisiana
beauty had begun to drink as heavily as her intended
victims.

"Gee, I wonder if Joe Goodman'll let me write this off as a business expense," mused Marcus Haverstraw, puffing on a foot-long Corona-Corona and squeezing the breast of the blonde beside him.

"Hell, no," Davy called out from across the room. "This one's on the miners of the Boise Basin." He gestured expansively with his free hand. "Don' you worry 'bout nothin', ol' pal."

Soaring Hawk looked bored as he listened to this exchange. Suddenly his eyes flashed, and he leaned over and began to whisper into the ear of the big redhead next to him.

Big Terry laughed a loud, brassy laugh and turned to the Pawnee. "You want to *what?*"

The Indian's stone face crumbled as he began to grin from ear to ear. "No tell," he whispered in the hooker's ear. "Come inside, I show. You like."

"Well, if that ain't the damnedest thing," the redhead said as she rose from the sofa and began to follow Soaring Hawk into one of the rooms that adjoined the one they presently occupied. "Sounds like it could be fun, though," Big Terry admitted with a grin.

"What's he gonna do, Terry?" Angel asked anxiously. "What's he gonna do?"

"I'll let you know after he does it," the big redhead shot back over her shoulder. "Then I'll be in a better position to explain it to you."

"Oh, but I don't want to miss out on anything," the petite blonde said in a small, disappointed voice.

"Well, I don't think you'll have to worry about that, my little yellow rose," Marcus Haverstraw told her, punctuating this remark with an affectionate squeeze of her breasts. "I have a few tricks up my own sleeve y'know," he whispered. "Come on into that other room with me, and I'll give you a little demonstration."

"But what was the Injun goin' to do to Big Terry?" the persistent little hooker asked.

"Come inside, my little partridge," Marcus P. Haverstraw cooed, a sly smile upon his lips, "and I'll show you."

"You know what he's gonna do?" Angel asked incredulously.

"Of course, I do," the newspaperman said reassuringly as he got up and began to lead the little blonde off to an adjoining room opposite the one occupied by Soaring Hawk and Big Terry. "We're blood brothers," he told her solemnly. "Mr. Hawk has no secrets from me."

"Well, what is it?" Angel asked in a voice colored by anxiety and expectation.

"I, ah, have to show you, my sweet," was Marcus Haverstraw's reply, as he led her into the bedroom and closed the door behind him.

Davy and Della were alone now. Bertram Brown's dutiful mistress knocked back her bourbon and branch water, and then put the tumbler down with a thud on the table beside the couch.

She was feeling extremely guilty at the moment. Davy had taken to her immediately, as had she to him, and the young Kansan confided his deepest wishes and longings to the dusky beauty. He told her of his father's murder and his subsequent quest for vengeance, his life on the trail with Soaring Hawk and his departed friends, and of his first, magic meeting with his beloved Deanna MacPartland.

There were small tears shimmering in the corner of Della Casson's dark eyes when Davy Watson had

171

finished his moving recitation. And by the time they were alone in the big, expensively furnished central room of the suite, she was all but overwhelmed by her tender feelings toward the young man at her side. He had willingly shared his innermost thoughts and feelings with her, thereby freely offering the Louisiana enchantress something that Bertram Brown would never give her: himself.

She felt a great, welling tenderness toward him, there was no question of that. And on top of this tenderness, the floodgates that had for so long contained her turbulent and dammed-up emotions were opened by this sudden access of feeling. . .as well as by the considerable amount of bourbon she had consumed. Further, Della Casson experienced an intense physical attraction to the blond and handsome young man beside her on the couch. The only thing she could do, enmeshed as she was in a web of guilt, confusion, longing and passionate desire, was to live in the present: to live for the moment, and the moment alone.

"C'm'ere, sugah," she murmured, as Davy felt her hand on the back of his neck. And as she drew him close to her bosom, his lips came into contact with the firm, cool flesh that swelled above the low neckline of her red satin gown. Her smooth, dark skin gleamed with brilliant points of light, highlighted by the lamp overhead.

When he raised his head, they kissed, long and passionately. Davy found her full, red lips soft as eiderdown, her tongue long and nimble, and her mouth sweet and inviting. He cupped her breast in his hand and began to caress it, feeling her nipple erect beneath the fabric of her dress and underthings.

Della unbuttoned the top buttons on Davy's flann

shirt, hooked a finger over the neck of his union suit and pulled down on it. Then she leaned forward and kissed his hairy chest just below the breastbone, after which she darted her long pink tongue down the alley between his pectorals.

"Oo-wee," Davy murmured, suddenly rising from the plush sofa. "Let's get on over there," he said, pointing to the huge, canopied bed at the opposite side of the room, "where we'll have a little space." So saying, he bent over, picked up Della Casson, and wove his way over to the regal bed, now intoxicated by the charms of the lovely woman he held in his arms, her beauty and radiated animal sensuality affecting him more than all the booze he had imbibed that evening.

Losing his balance as he put her down upon the blue satin counterpane, Davy sprawled onto the bed with Della. Giggling mischievously, she sat up right away, grabbed hold of his shoulders, and sprang to her feet.

"What the hell?" he muttered, standing up and turning around to face her.

"Now, you just hush up," she told him, laying a long, tapered finger across his lips. Davy saw that Della was smiling a mischievous, excited smile as she began to undress him.

She undressed him deftly, occasionally pausing to caress him in various places or to lean over and brush his flesh with her lips, which somehow caused him to think of butterflies lighting upon prairie flowers.

He shivered with delight as, still fully gowned, Della went down on her knees to help him out of his last remaining garment, his longjohns. His cock jutted out aggressively from the matted curls on his groin, standing stiff as a Pawnee lodgepole.

Della's long, slender fingers encircled his pole at its

base, and began stroking it with slow and even motions. And then, as those motions grew faster in tempo, before Davy realized what was happening, the black beauty inclined her head toward him, parted her full, glistening lips, and took the head of his cock into her mouth.

"*Ju-u-u-u-das Priest!*" Davy moaned, almost overwhelmed by the combination of Della's cupping, sucking lips, the intimate warmth of her mouth and the sweet deviltry of her agile tongue. He looked down and saw her head bob in time to the strokes of her wet, gripping mouth on his pulsing sex.

Before long he came, shaking like a man with St. Vitus' Dance, and moaning as if he were about to meet his Maker. The fingers of her left hand digging into his muscular buttock while those of the right continued to stroke the shaft of his sex, Della kept him in her mouth, hungrily swallowing down his juices.

After she got to her feet, Della wiped her mouth, and led Davy over to the side of the bed where, without a word, she gave him a drink and then let him undress her.

The sight of her sleek and gorgeous black body roused Davy Watson again, and his pole stood once more in tribute to the beauty and sensuality of the Louisiana courtesan.

She stood before him, naked and graceful as a panther, while he sat on the edge of the bed and stared at her in open-mouthed admiration. As he reached out and ran his fingers up through the thick and tight-curled black fleece on her pubic mound, cupping them to continue up over the gentle slope of her trim belly, Della Casson shivered and sighed with delight.

Her breasts were full and round above her tiny waist with full, elliptical black areolae and high, thick nipples

When Davy put his hands on those beautiful breasts, Bertram Brown's mistress groaned loudly. He squeezed their warm, incredible firmness, moving up after that to circle her areolae with his fingertips, and then to graze her erect, jutting nipples and rub them between his thumb, index and middle fingers.

When he put his mouth to her breasts, at the same time running his fingers down along the prominent outer lips of Della's pussy, the black Venus groaned even more loudly than before. His hand continued its downward course, and Davy penetrated the lips of her vulva with one of his fingers. She gasped as his thick middle finger entered her sheath with an audible squish.

When the young Kansan withdrew his finger from Della Casson's honeypot, it was dripping with the black beauty's fluids. The scent of arousal wafted up to his nostrils, thrilling Davy to the marrow of his bones. His cock stood even stiffer as he recognized the pungent fragrance of female arousal.

Della's body began to twitch, and she cried out as she grabbed hold of Davy's shoulders, fighting to stay on her feet as a sudden and violent orgasm threatened to obliterate her consciousness and overwhelm her.

She bucked and heaved in his arms, while Davy kept up his attentions to her inner lips and the area surrounding and including the base of her long and erect clitoris. From time to time, he would dip his finger back inside her, in order to lubricate the outer parts that he stroked and rubbed. And after the final spasm of a multiple orgasm of amazing duration, Della Casson went limp in Davy Watson's arms.

He drew open the curtain that screened the elegant bed and laid her down gently. Davy studied her beautiful face, noting the planes of her high cheekbones, the gentle rise of her forehead, the beads of sweat gleaming like gems at her hairline, the full lips and open mouth, the eyes rolled up in their sockets, as in death or ecstasy. After a long time had passed, her eyes blinked as she focused them and Della turned to Davey with a tender smile.

"Child, you move me," she whispered fervently as he leaned over and took her in his arms once more.

Davy covered her face with kisses, tenderly brushing her eyes, nose, lips and chin. As he reached her neck, his kisses grew more intense. And that intensity grew as his mouth traveled downward, kissing and sucking as it went. He was drunk with the fragrance of her garden body, and the heady aroma of their sweat and commingled juices.

Down over her full, stiff-nippled breasts his kisses ran, over the glossy skin below her ribs, over the little, inverted goblet of her belly. Then he detoured in his line of march for several minutes, as his tongue and lips flirted with her long thighs and the perfumed basins where they joined her groin. But finally, as she cooed and moaned with pleasure, his lips came to rest within the musky grove below her groin.

At this point, Della was highly aroused, but Davy purposely left off French-kissing her lower lips and began to move up on the lithe, dark body as he made to penetrate her. Positioning himself over Della, he suddenly felt her fingers grasp his taut rod, and then insert it into the sweet socket of desire between her quivering, sweat-glossed thighs.

As Davy's cock entered the wet, welcoming embrace of Della Casson's musky, sopping pussy, he thought, for some unaccountable reason, of the proud ships of the *Iliad*, as they glided down their slipways and were launched into the warm and wine-dark waters of the Aegean Sea. He entered her as smoothly as a galley parted the waters, and continued his glide into that dark and friendly sea until their pelvises made contact.

"Oh, God, sugah!" she cried out, writhing beneath him, sightless now in the instinctual night of her passion. "Do it to me, sugah," she moaned in that rich, dark voice of hers. "Oh, do it! Do it!"

Her groin bucked as it worked toward his in a synchronization of their separate ardors. The woman's pussy was one of the snuggest he had ever been in, and it felt to Davy as if it were grasping and sucking his cock like a hungry mouth.

Whenever, after a number of slow, shallow strokes, he withdrew to the boundary of her vaginal vestibule, just barely keeping his glans penis with the tight grasp of her sphincter, he would suddenly lunge forward and plunge his sword to the hilt in her snug and juicy sheath, Davy would hear a wet, slurping sound that arose as the vaginal accompaniment to the vocal music of their passion.

She wrapped her long legs around his lower back, crooning in her rich contralto a wordless song of desire consummated, a song of the wonders and joys and beauties of the flesh—a cantata wherein she was joined to her bedmate, for the duet of their joint orgasms, as well as by the bucking, writhing coupling of their ardent flesh.

When it was over, and Davy Watson's flaccid member had finally slid out of the relaxed embrace of Della Casson's dilated sheath, the young Kansan rolled off the dark beauty, tenderly kissed her face and neck, and then fell into a sound and dreamless sleep.

Della Casson raised herself up on her elbow and

stared thoughtfully down at the fair young man who slept beside her. There was a faint smile on her full, red lips, and two pearl-like tears were forming in the corners of her dark and lovely eyes.

It was after two o'clock in the morning, when Bertram Brown took out his gold watch once more. But this time, as the cover sprang open on its hinge, the delicate mechanical rendition of *I Dream of Jeannie* was drowned out by the din in Covent Garden, for the activity in that establishment had begun to reach its peak. Life was topsy-turvy in the Barbary Coast: people there tended to sleep when the sun was out; the small hours of the morning constituted the shank of the night for the denizens of that wild and wide-open district.

The music of the pianoforte was bold and strident now, and the roars, laughter and hubbub of the crowd often drowned out its sound. Jeers and curses cut through the general cacophony, punctuated by the roar of a crowd smelling blood as a fight broke out or an occasional gunshot sounded in the lurid and sinister night outside.

"Yeah, I think it's about time I paid a visit to the Watson kid and his friends," Brown said, snapping shut the cover of his watch and returning it to his vest pocket. Then he pulled out the top drawer of his desk, reached into it, and came out a moment later holding a derringer.

"You gonna do it yourself?" Harvey Yancey rumbled in surprise.

"Mr. Yancey," the gambler replied coolly, "if Watson and his friends ever use their knowledge of my, ah, transactions with the potentates of the East, they could blow this entire operation to hell—all of it!—and have me put behind bars for a long, long time. Remember, one of their number is a journalist."

Impressed by this reasoning, Yancey nodded solemnly.

"So," Brown continued, "I deem this a matter of sufficient import to merit my personal attention."

Yancey smirked. "You gonna shoot someone with that pop-gun, Mr. Brown?" he asked as the gambler put the small, two-shot pistol into one of his frock coat's inside pockets.

"It has several advantages, Mr. Yancey," Brown replied. "First, it doesn't make much noise—it'll never be heard above the noise of that crowd out there. And second, it's accurate and lethal at close range." The gambler smiled his shark's smile. "I've had occasion to demonstrate that several times."

The huge bearded man was impressed. "Now, I get it," he said slowly. "An' if anyone catches wise, you shot that li'l bastard 'cause you found him in bed with your gal."

"The woman I love," Brown told him, his smile shifting from the cold-blooded to the cynical.

"An' you're gonna do it yourself," Yancey rumbled, much taken with Brown's course of action.

"If you want anything done right," Brown replied, "do it yourself. Besides, the police in this district are in my pocket. It costs me a pretty penny, but it's well worth it."

"You're nobody's fool, Mr. Brown," the giant said admiringly.

"Care to join me?" the gambler asked, still smiling.

Harvey Yancey's hangman's eye lit up, and he began to smile. "Yessir, I would," he told the gambler.

"'Cause even if I don't get to wring the Watson kid's neck, I can still settle that dad-blamed redskin's hash."

"You're the perfect man for the job," Brown told him softly. "And you won't need to use your gun, will you, Mr. Yancey?"

"Hell, no," the giant replied. "Why, I'll stretch that red dog across't my knee as if I was stringin' a bow, an' snap his back like 'twas a matchstick."

Brown stood up. "Time we went about our business," he told Harvey Yancey.

"What about that reporter fella?" the giant asked.

"I was going to bring along one of my associates, a good man with a shiv, to take care of him."

"Ain't no need to trouble yourself, Mr. Brown," the huge bearded man told the gambler, a look of eager anticipation on his face. "I'll be more'n glad to take care of him for you, right after I settle with the Injun. Won't take but a moment."

Brown nodded, and they smiled at each other, hangman to shark. "You're a man after my own heart, Mr. Yancey," he told the giant, opening the door of his office and stepping out into the smoky din of Covent Garden, where men roared, swore and jeered, and by some eerie coincidence, the pianoforte player, in a mood of drunken perversity, played the same sweet and melancholy tune that issued forth whenever Bertram Brown opened his solid gold pocket watch.

When the door to the suite's central room swung open noiselessly, and his executioner's shadow fell over him, Davy Watson was fast asleep, with a blissful, angelic expression upon his face and the traces of Della Casson's lip rouge on his mouth.

Bertram Brown's eyes narrowed, and his grim, predatory smile hardened into a frown of displeasure, as he beheld his lovely black mistress, clad only in a filmy yellow chemise, sitting up in the bed beside the recumbent Davy Watson, her dark eyes a-light with concern as she hovered over him, looking like an ebony guardian angel.

The gambler waved her away, gesturing impatiently with the Derringer he held in his right hand. But Della Casson's only response was to turn her wide, accusing eyes on him and slowly shake her head.

No, Bert, she mouthed silently, appealing to her lover with all her heart. *Don't do it. Please.*

Again Brown waved her away, his mouth now set in a tight, grim line.

And again Della Casson shook her head. *Please, Bert,* she mouthed in silent anguish, as Davy Watson slept in the shadow of the gunman. *Please. For the love of God. . .*

At the same time that Bertram Brown's shadow had fallen over the sleeping form of Davy Watson, Harvey Yancey, his massive bulk flattened against the wall of the third-story landing, tip-toed to the front door of the room adjoining the one where Della Casson and the gambler staged their silent confrontation. The giant flexed his huge, bone-crushing hands, in expectation of the moment when they would encircle the neck of Soaring Hawk.

He grabbed the doorknob, and it looked like a marble in his palm, just before his fingers closed over it. Holding his breath, he swung the door open slowly. . . silently. . .and peered into the Pawnee's room, as the light from the landing outside spread through the darkness within as the door swung open on its hinges.

Inhaling deeply of the sharp, salt air that came in through the wide-open windows, and shivering momentarily from its chill, Harvey Yancey nodded with satisfaction as he noted the lone figure curled up beneath the covers of the brass bed.

His hangman's eyes gleamed as they reflected the cold moonlight that shone through the windows opposite the doorway. The giant shook himself all over, like a mastiff getting to its feet, and then flexed his huge, dangerous hands once again, as he moved in for the kill. . . .

"Get out of the bed!" Bertram Brown ordered sharply, in a harsh whisper that caused Davy Watson to stir in his sleep.

"No, Bert!" Della Casson whispered back in calm defiance. "Let him go. He's innocent. You can't kill him."

As he raised the derringer and pointed it at the canopied bed, Brown shot his mistress a flashing, angry glance. "Don't be stupid," he hissed. "Get out of that bed—or else!"

This time Della replied with a smile of contempt, shaking her head as she realized what a fool she had been to ever fall in love with a man as low and unregenerate as Bertram Brown.

"*You* get out. Get out of this room," she told the gambler, just as he stepped across the threshold and began to peer along the length of his outstretched arm, sighting his pistol on the young Kansan.

At that moment, Davy Watson awakened. Blinking his eyes, he looked past Della Casson, his breath catching in his throat with an audible gasp as he saw Bertram Brown's derringer pointed at his chest.

"Bert—don't!" Della cried out, leaning over suddenly to interpose her body between Davy and his would-be assassin.

Just then, as Davy struggled to sit up and push Della Casson to one side, Bertram Brown swore and fired his pistol.

The Louisiana beauty screamed as the gambler's bullet entered her body. She fell to one side, just as Davy Watson managed to sit upright in the canopied bed. Having shot his mistress, Brown turned his attention to Davy Watson, and fired his second shot straight at him. . . .

Silhouetted by the light coming into the room from the landing behind him, Harvey Yancey resembled an ogre out of *Grimm's Tales*, some horror born of the combined effects of darkness and fear upon the human imagination, more than he resembled a human being at that particular moment.

Just as the giant stood poised at the end of the bed, like some horrible, vampiric apparition, Bertram Brown's pistol cracked in the adjoining room. Spurred to action by this, anxious to retain the advantage of surprise, Harvey Yancey leapt into the air and dove at the figure huddled beneath the covers in the big brass bed.

While Yancey launched himself through the air, Bertram Brown's pistol cracked a second time. And by the time that the giant's huge body hit the bed and shuddered its springs with the full impact of its great weight, Soaring Hawk was wide awake.

Harvey Yancey grunted as his huge, aggressive bulk hit the mattress. And as he began to rip away the covers that separated him from his prey, a woman screamed in terror. At that very same moment, the Pawnee brave rolled out from underneath the brass bed, having slept on the hard surface of the wooden floor, as was his custom whenever he spent the night indoors—drunk or sober.

"*Hu-u-u-uuh!*" wheezed the flabbergasted giant, when he realized that the party whose throat he squeezed between his big, deadly hands was not Soaring Hawk.

By the time he let go of her, Big Terry's face was livid and her eyes had rolled up in their sockets. She fell back onto the pillow with a ghastly sigh, while the giant scrambled clumsily to his feet.

Driven by the fear that his intended victim would escape, Yancey acted with great singularity of purpose, and threw himself at the door which opened onto the landing. Then, after slamming it shut so hard that the walls shook for the entire length of the landing, the huge bearded man turned to the Pawnee with a leer of triumph on his face.

And there before him, not ten feet away, naked but for a loincloth, a look of grim determination on his face, stood Davy Watson's blood brother.

"*Haw! Haw! Haw!*" Harvey Yancey laughed derisively, in the instant before he lowered his head and charged at the naked Indian. . . .

"Oh, shit!" Davy Watson grunted as he rolled out of the canopied bed and threw himself onto the floor, Bertram Brown's second shot having creased his short ribs on the left side. The young Kansan rolled over on the floor, naked and unarmed; but as he scrambled to his feet he was filled with relief, being fully aware that his would-be killer had just fired the last shot in his derringer. And he became suddenly energized when he recalled Della Casson's last words, and realized that the man who faced him was none other than Bertram Brown—the man who was now in possession of the Mudree sisters.

Aware that his last shot had not achieved the desire

effect, Bertram Brown coolly surveyed the room as the man he had just attempted to kill got to his feet. Then, as Davy Watson started toward him, the gambler hurled the empty derringer at his face.

"*Ow!*" Davy Watson hollered as the pistol glanced off his shielding forearm. Then he shook his arm and, an instant later, launched himself at Bertram Brown.

The gambler stood his ground, waiting for Davy to come to him, holding in his right hand the sharp and jagged upper half of the champagne bottle he had just smashed against the table where several of its companions stood. . . .

"Oh, my stars!" muttered a confused Marcus Haverstraw, as he scrambled out of bed. The reporter began to hop about on the floor, cursing like a mule driver as he tried to get into his pants.

"What is it? What is it?" Angel called out, her shrill, anxious voice cutting through the darkness like a Bowie knife slicing through velvet.

"Stay where you are," Marcus told the hooker, grunting as he stubbed his toe on the pistol he had left lying on the floor by the bed. A moment later, he bent over and picked up the gun. Then he straightened up and blundered over to the door that led to the adjoining room.

The first thing that Marcus saw when he opened the door was the glare of the lamp on the landing that shone through the open door of the central room. He shielded his eyes, and stepped back as if stung by a blow. Blinking his eyes and shaking his head, he peered back over the threshold, forcing himself to look into the room once more.

What he saw there made him cry out in alarm: Davy Watson, holding up a bloodied forearm in front of his face, off-balance and lurching backwards, as a man in a claw hammer tail frock coat slashed away at him with all the fury of a madman.

Marcus wanted to cry out, to order the man to stop, but his voice would not come forth from his throat. He was mute. Suddenly, as Davy Watson, still holding his red and dripping forearm before his face, slammed into the room's far wall, and the man moved in for the kill, Marcus P. Haverstraw raised the big pistol he had borrowed from the sheriff of Virginia City.

Boom! Boom! Boom!

The shots rang out thunderously in the room, their roar cutting through the din below and silencing even the raucous, rowdy patrons of the Covent Garden.

Marcus was a newspaperman, and not a gunman; and his first two shots went high and wide, blasting great chunks out of the wall opposite him. But they were sufficient to save Davy Watson from further injury, by stopping Bertram Brown in his tracks. And then, as the gambler spun around in the direction of the deafening blasts, Marcus' third shot caught him just below the breastbone and flung Brown back against the wall with great force.

As Bertram Brown slid down the wall, he began to cough. And he coughed for several moments, until a veritable cascade of blood suddenly streamed forth from his mouth and nostrils at the same time. The floor around the gambler, as well as the front of his body, soon became covered with blood. Then, with a series of gurgling sounds, he rolled over and fell face-down upon the carpet.

"Goddamn, Marcus," Davy whispered hoarsely. "You done saved my life."

"Ah, yeah," Marcus replied in a faint, quavering

voice, as he looked with awe upon the body of the first man he had ever shot.

Davy stared at Brown, and realized that it was only a matter of seconds before the man would be dead. There was nothing to be done for him, he realized, turning to rush to Della Casson's side.

The ebony beauty lay face down on the bed in a pool of her own blood, her left arm hanging down to the floor.

"Della!" Davy cried. "Della—are you all right?" He rolled her over gently, just as Marcus Haverstraw reached his side.

"Is she—?" the newspaperman asked haltingly.

"No, thank God," Davy told him, after having torn away the bloody section of chemise that covered her wound. The bullet went in her shoulder. She'll be all right."

"Thank heaven," Marcus said quietly.

"Bert," Della moaned, trying to sit up.

"Now, you jus' lie there, Della," Davy told her firmly. "You ain't in no shape to get up."

"But Bert," she said again, falling back onto her pillow, her teeth clenched in pain.

Davy looked down at her grimly and shook his head. When she understood what he was telling her, Della Casson closed her eyes and began to cry.

"You saved my life, Della," he whispered, taking her hand in his as he knelt by her side.

She looked up at him, suddenly smiling through her tears and her pain. "No, sugah," she whispered. "You saved mine."

Davy leaned over and tenderly kissed her forehead. Marcus patted him on the shoulder supportively.

"Judas Priest!" Davy exclaimed, springing to his feet abruptly. "I plumb forgot about Soaring Hawk!"

"Oh, yeah," Marcus agreed. "Where is he?"

"Lemme have that," Davy said, snatching the big pistol out of the reporter's hand and then turning to the door that led to the Pawnee's room. And as he bolted toward it, Davy broke out in a cold sweat, thinking about Soaring Hawk. . .and Harvey Yancey.

The first thing that Davy Watson saw when he opened the door to Soaring Hawk's room was Harvey Yancey! He ducked back instinctively—not even having time to raise the pistol he held—as the bearded giant screamed and burst through the room, cradling something in his arms at the level of his waist.

Davy spun around and trained the pistol on the giant's broad back. But even as he did, Harvey Yancey emitted a strange, bleating cry and fell to his knees before the door that opened onto the landing.

Both Davy and Marcus were gaping as they turned and looked across the room to each other. A great pool of blood was forming on the carpet where Harvey Yancey swayed back and forth unsteadily on his knees. Suddenly the two men watched his broad back heave, and they heard him emit a long bass sigh. Then he pitched to one side, and rolled over on his back.

Marcus Haverstraw was the first to reach him. "He's dead," the newspaperman told Davy Watson. "And will you look at that," he went on in a whisper, pointing to the giant's bloody midsection.

"Ooooh," groaned Davy Watson, when he saw what Harvey Yancey had been holding in his hands. And what he saw reminded the young Kansan of a hog-butchering at the Watson farm on Pottawatomie Creek. The reeking, bloody bundle that the giant still held in his two great hands, steaming now in the chill air of the room, consisted of ten or fifteen feet of his intestines.

The man had been gutted, Davy realized, and about as neatly as any hog he'd ever seen butchered.

He turned back to the door to Soaring Hawk's room and was suddenly spooked as he saw the Pawnee in the doorway, naked but for a loincloth, and the bloody scalping knife he held at his side.

"Gol-lee," Davy whispered, after reassuring himself that his blood-brother was all right. "What happened?"

Soaring Hawk looked from Davy Watson to the huge corpse lying in the pool of its own blood, and smiled a grim smile. "If I tell," he said, "you never go sleep in bed again."

"'All's well that ends well,'" Marcus Haverstraw said, cheerfully quoting the Bard of Avon as he toasted Davy Watson and Soaring Hawk. The reporter was celebrating the outcome of the day they had spent in a San Francisco courthouse, participating in the inquest that had cleared them all of any wrongdoing in the grisly affair at the Covent Garden.

The three companions had located the Mudree sisters in the cellars of the late Bertram Brown's establishment and freed them. On their way out of the building, they were all arrested by a squad of San Francisco police. Thereafter, they spent several days in custody while things were being sorted out. But when Della Casson had sufficiently recovered from her wound, she testified in behalf of Davy and his friends. And this, as well as the moving testimony of the kidnapped and sold daughters of Carmela Mudree, was more than ample evidence to exonerate Davy Watson, Soaring Hawk and Marcus P. Haverstraw.

The reporter was in especially high spirits, for he had

managed to bribe his police guard (not the most difficult thing to do in San Francisco) and was able to scoop all the native reporters in the town, selling the exclusive rights to the thrilling story of violence, kidnapping and white slavery to the *San Francisco Chronicle*. And to add the icing to the cake, when he telegraphed the story to Joe Goodman in Virginia City, Marcus' beloved *Territorial Enterprise* scooped its rival, the *Virginia Union*, thus assuring him a hero's welcome when he returned to his paper. The proceeds from these sales, when realized, Marcus declared, were to be divided equally among Davy, Soaring Hawk and the three Mudree sisters.

That night, after a long and hearty dinner, when the sisters had excused themselves and left for the night, Davy, Soaring Hawk and Marcus found themselves alone in the bar of the hotel in which they were spending their last night in San Francisco. The blood brothers, along with the newspaperman, would begin their journey eastward, taking their leave of Faith, Hope and Charity, who would take a stagecoach northward to Oregon and from there back to Boise town.

"Well, I reckon you got your story, Marcus," Davy said as he and his companions made to leave for their respective rooms.

"That and more," the reporter told Davy with a broad grin. "I became part of the story. And just imagine: white slavery, kidnapping, a shootout, *and* Della Casson. Oh, my stars!"

He grew serious. "Y'know," Marcus told Davy confidentially, "if she had asked *me* to stay, I'm not so sure that I'd be heading back tomorrow."

Davy smiled back at his friend. "You would if Deanna MacPartland was a-waitin' for ya at the end of the trail." He began to walk off. "G'night, gents," he

190

called out over his shoulder.

By the time that he was walking down the carpeted hall that led to his room, Davy began to wonder about the surprise that the Mudree sisters had promised to leave for him that evening. It was to be a sincere expression of their gratitude. As Davy turned his key in the lock and let himself into the room, he found himself growing more curious by the moment.

After shutting the door and turning up the gaslight, Davy Watson turned and suddenly discovered the unique nature of his surprise.

"Now that we're alone, we can thank you properly, David Lee," said Hope Mudree, the boldest of the three sisters.

"You just come over here and set for a spell," Charity whispered breathlessly, as Davy smiled and turned down the lamp.

"We've got something for you, Davy," Faith Mudree whispered shyly as he proceeded to unbutton his shirt.

At that moment, he realized that the three sisters who lay side by side in his bed were totally naked beneath the linen sheet that covered their shapely bodies.

"We'll take care of that," Hope told him, reaching out and beginning to open his shirt.

As Davy sat down on the edge of the big bed, the three sisters watched him with hot, gypsy eyes. His senses became inflamed as his mind was suddenly flooded with the voluptuous image of three eager mouths and six artful hands.

"I got to hand it to you gals," the young Kansan told Faith, Hope and Charity, as they sat up in bed, allowing the sheet to slide down over their upper bodies, exposing their full and stiff-nippled breasts. "This is one helluva way to say thank you."

SPEND YOUR LEISURE MOMENTS WITH US.

Hundreds of exciting titles to choose from—something for everyone's taste in fine books: breathtaking historical romance, chilling horror, spine-tingling suspense, taut medical thrillers, involving mysteries, action-packed men's adventure and wild Westerns.

SEND FOR A FREE CATALOGUE TODAY!

Leisure Books
Attn: Customer Service Department
276 5th Avenue, New York, NY 10001